This was the woman who hated his books?

Soldier moved a little closer, preparing to swoop in for the kill, when she raised her face to look up at him.

Betsy Tremaine's driver's license probably stated her eye color as hazel. But hazel didn't begin to cover it. Her eyes were like shards of colored glass, green and gold and aquamarine. Those intelligent eyes were large and fringed with dark lashes. Something he couldn't name shone from those eyes, and Soldier felt his heart poised to dive into their depths and drown there.

Delicate brows arched in expectation. Her soft lips parted as if she were about to speak. Or be kissed.

Soldier gave himself a mental shake. "I neglected to introduce myself earlier, didn't I?"

Taking her hand in his, he said, "My name is McKennitt. Jackson. Soldier. McKennitt. Most people call me Soldier."

A look of sheer panic crossed her face. She squeaked and tried to pull her hand away, but he held on tightly, incarcerating her fingers between his palms . . .

MARIANNE STILLINGS

The Damsel in This Dress

AVON BOOKS

An Imprint of HarperCollinsPublishers

This is a work of fiction. Names, characters, places, and incidents are products of the author's imagination or are used fictitiously and are not to be construed as real. Any resemblance to actual events, locales, organizations, or persons, living or dead, is entirely coincidental.

AVON BOOKS
An Imprint of HarperCollins*Publishers*
10 East 53rd Street
New York, New York 10022-5299

Copyright © 2004 by Marianne Stillings
ISBN: 0-06-057533-6
www.avonromance.com

First Avon Books paperback printing: August 2004

Avon Trademark Reg. U.S. Pat. Off. and in Other Countries, Marca Registrada, Hecho en U.S.A.
HarperCollins® is a registered trademark of HarperCollins Publishers Inc.

Printed in the U.S.A.

10 9 8 7 6 5 4 3 2 1

For Michael. You were my first reader, my first champion. When I cried into my pile of rejection slips, you reassured me, then urged me back to my computer. I could not have succeeded without your emotional and practical support. You're my husband, my partner, my hero. Thank you for helping make my dreams come true.

Chapter 1

September
Seattle, Washington

Hold on while I get out my thesaurus; this review is going to require more words than my paltry vocabulary contains. Ah, here we go: junk, dross, rubbish, detritus (oh, that's a good one), baloney, claptrap, drivel . . .

To continue would require more space than this column allows, so let me simply conclude by saying that Strike Three for Death, *J. Soldier McKennitt's latest so-called crime drama, is a waste of time and money. The plot is ludicrous, the characters stereotypical, the writing amateurish. What less could you ask for? This is the third installment in the* Crimes of the Northwest *series and while each entry has defied common sense and literary style,* Strike Three for Death *is the worst to date . . .*

* * *

"There's more. Wanna hear it?"

Soldier McKennitt sprawled on his brother's tan-striped couch, his long legs crossed at the ankles. Pinching his eyes closed, he rhythmically thumped his skull against the wall behind him. With each bump, the watercolor hanging above his head bounced.

Finally letting his head rest against the white plaster, he opened his eyes and stared at the ceiling. "I think I've suffered enough," he sighed. "Besides, something tells me it doesn't get any better."

Soldier sent his brother a pleading look. "What in the hell does this woman have against me, Taylor? Six weeks on the *New York Times* best-seller list, but this, *this* broad hates everything I write!"

Taylor McKennitt grinned as he handed Soldier the bottle of beer he'd just popped open. "Where have you been, sonny? '*Broad*' is politically incorrect when referring to the female gender."

Taking a long swig of beer, Soldier swallowed, then offered, "Okay then, how about 'bitch'?"

"Bitch works. Have you ever met Ms. Whatsername?"

"Tremaine. Elizabeth Carlisle Tremaine, and no, I've never had the pleasure."

Taylor tossed the Sunday paper onto the coffee table. "You live in north Seattle. What are you doing subscribing to the *Port Henry Ledger*? It's way the hell up on the peninsula."

"I don't subscribe. The lovely Ms. Tremaine sends me an edition whenever she trashes one of my books.

She calls them reviews. I call them literary castration."

Taylor dropped down on the couch next to Soldier. Grabbing a note pad and colored pencils from his desk, he flipped to a clean page.

"Okay, Detective McKennitt. Let's do a little artist's rendering here. Describe this flower of womanhood to me."

Soldier sat back and relaxed, closing his eyes again. As he took another pull of beer, he formed a wicked smile on his lips.

"Okay. She has a long, thin face. Rather bony."

Taylor dutifully began sketching.

"She's really old, maybe sixty—"

"Hey, *Mom's* sixty."

"Okay, sixty-one. And she's got carrot-orange hair that sticks out all over like she shoved her finger in a light socket. Her eyes are evil and black and too close together, and she has only one eyebrow, sort of shaped like a big M across her heavily wrinkled forehead."

"That's good. What else?"

Soldier sucked on the bottle for a second. "Her nose is long and thin with a bulb on the end. Oh, and don't forget the wart," he said, gesturing toward the paper with his beer bottle.

"Does the wart have hair on it?"

"It wouldn't be wart-worthy if it didn't."

"Right. Hair on the wart." Taylor's pencil scratched the paper in broad strokes.

Soldier contemplated his nemesis once more. "She has a blunt chin and a thin, cruel mouth. All tight and puckered like she just licked the bottom of somebody's shoe." He grinned. "And she's never had sex."

Taylor arched a dark brow. "Not even when she was young and wartless?"

"Nah. I don't see Ms. Tremaine letting a man near her," Soldier said through a vicious grin. Swallowing another gulp of beer, he mumbled, "But I'll bet she owns stock in Eveready batteries, if you get my drift."

Leaning over the sketch pad, he examined what Taylor had created. Gesturing with his index finger, he said, "You've got her tah-tahs too big. They should be more like prunes."

Taylor smirked. "She's beginning to look like my ex-wife."

"I never saw your ex-wife's prunes."

"Well, God knows every other man in town did."

Turning once again to the dour effigy Taylor had created, Soldier tapped his finger on the paper. With the beer bottle poised at his lips, he said, "Chin needs to be more mannish. And don't forget the scar . . ."

Betsy Tremaine rubbed her chin. It felt odd, as though somebody were tickling it. She wished. The stanza of an old song ran through her head: *Another Saturday night and I ain't got nobody* . . . Except it was Sunday, but that didn't really matter, not when you were alone *every* night of the week.

Twenty-eight years old, and the only male in her life was Piddle, her mother's five-hundred-year-old Chihuahua. Even now, the ancient creature lay hairless and trembling at her feet beneath the kitchen table. She was careful to move slowly around him, for the slightest noise would shatter his tenuous control and he'd live up to his name all over her floor.

Scooping the last bite of chocolate mint chip ice cream into her mouth, Betsy tossed the empty container in the trash and her spoon into the sink. Gently lifting Piddle from the floor, she rose and padded toward the living room.

The house had been built in the Victorian style over a hundred years ago. For a structure of its era, the rooms were large, and what had once been the parlor was now used as the living room. The front of the house faced west, allowing the setting sun to filter through the long lace curtains. Everything in the room—from her grandmother's antique porcelain vase, to the mahogany coffee table, to the tatted doilies that decorated the back of the couch—was tinted amber by the fading light of day.

A flagstone fireplace dominated the center of the interior wall, its wide mantel displaying photographs of Loretta and Douglas Tremaine, laughing, their arms wound around each other, as well as photos of Betsy as a little girl, in what she had come to refer to as "the Before Time," when her mother and father had loved each other and they had been a family.

Nestled in the corner to the right of the fireplace sat Betsy's work area. She shuffled over to the roll-top desk, an antediluvian piece of furniture that had once belonged to her great-grandfather. Now, it was piled high with books and papers, pencils, pens, more family photographs, and the latest *National Geographic*. An extra set of car keys peeked out of a cubbyhole, while a roll of stamps, paper clips, staples, and an assortment of office supplies lay strewn about in disorganized order.

Betsy had anticipated a cool evening, so she'd built

a little fire in the fireplace, its woodsy fragrance and warmth cheering her a bit. Glancing out the window, she noted the heavy clouds rolling in from the sea. Night would come early, she thought, along with lots and lots of rain.

Another rainy night, she mused. In a couple of hours, while the raindrops tapped along the eaves, she'd be all snuggled down in her warm bed. Alone.

She sighed. She needed to snap out of it. Sure, she lived by herself, but she was seldom truly lonely. It was just that . . . well, lately, she'd been feeling restless, expectant somehow, yet each new day was no different than the previous one. That was a little depressing, and depression made her introspective, and introspection always led to the fact that she was alone, and that always made her feel . . . well, lonely, dammit.

Setting the dog on the Oriental carpet at her feet, she eased into the desk chair and punched the button to turn on her computer.

"Okay, let's see what's happening in Cyberland," she said to Piddle. The dog shivered but gave no response. Circling slowly, he finally settled between her feet, where he gave an exhausted sigh, then lowered his long lashes.

Checking out the letter icon on the desktop, Betsy grinned. "Oh, lookie here, Pids. *We've got mail.* Maybe your mommy is coming home and you can go back to *her* house and ruin *her* rugs and stink up *her* kitchen. . . ."

Piddle's response was a congested wheeze as he drifted off to doggy dreamland.

There were two e-mails from people whose names

Betsy recognized. The one from her mother, vacationing for two months in Paris was just a quick hello. But the other one was from J. Soldier McKennitt. Her review of his latest book had hit the paper last week. Considering how much she had hated it, and had said so, he probably wasn't writing to thank her.

Dear Ms. Tremaine:

I'm sorry you didn't like my book. Since I have received a fairly good response from other critics around the country and have a somewhat faithful readership, I am curious as to what you found so objectionable about *Strike Three for Death* (not to mention *One Gun* and *Murder for Two*)?

Any enlightenment you can give would be most appreciated.

Yours,
JSMc

Betsy nudged the zoned-out dog with her toe. "Can you believe this, Pids? The nerve of that old geezer."

Her chair squeaked as she settled more deeply into the peony-and-rose-print chintz cushion. What should she say to this guy that hadn't already been said in her review? It wasn't as though anything she wrote in the *Port Henry Ledger* would make a difference in the sale of his books. Hers was a small town newspaper with a limited circulation, while he was published nationally. How on earth had he even seen a copy of the damn thing?

In her job as editor of the *Port Henry Ledger*, she

occasionally wrote book reviews just to give her something else to do. She enjoyed it and considered it a sort of public service, letting readers know which of the latest books were worth shelling out twenty-five bucks for and which to avoid.

According to the back cover blurb of *Strike Three for Death*, J. Soldier McKennitt was a Seattle detective who fancied himself a writer and had taken to fictionalizing some of what he considered his more interesting cases. There was only a brief bio and no photo, which Betsy thought unusual. But maybe that was to prevent any problems with undercover work. Or maybe he was just plain old ugly.

Betsy glanced down at Piddle. Speaking of ugly. Well, she had to come up with some kind of answer to Detective McKennitt's note. Her heart squeezed in protest. She didn't like confrontation, not even when it was only electronic.

"Pids? Do you need to go out?" Stirring from his slumber, Piddle opened his luminous brown eyes, his long lashes fluttering as he gazed up at her. He gave one final shudder, then closed them again and went back to sleep.

So much for creative avoidance, she thought. Taking a deep breath, Betsy began to type.

Dear Detective McKennitt:

Everything I had to say, I said in my review. Please keep in mind that mine is only one opinion. I'm glad you have such a large following and wish you continued success in your writing career.

Betsy Tremaine

There. Short, sweet, and to the point. Was she gracious or what. Not argumentative, not defensive, but definitely not an invitation for further discourse. End of story.

Allowing herself a hearty yawn, she glanced at the clock on the mantel. It was almost seven. Okay, she'd get ready for bed, then read for a while before going to sleep. Tomorrow was Monday and she needed to get in early to prepare for the weekly staff meeting. Ryan Finlay, her boss, always ran the meeting, but she prepared the agenda. Her assistant Carla Denato would be in early too, to make coffee and set up the conference room.

Bending, Betsy picked up a woozy Piddle and carried him through the kitchen to the back door. "Time to do your duty, Pids."

Opening the door, she set the dog on the porch. Cool, damp air drifted around her body, making her shiver. Stepping back inside, she closed the door against a whirl of dry leaves.

She'd give him ten minutes. It would take him five just to move that ancient carcass to the middle of the yard and find a good spot, then five to stagger back. By that time she'd be ready for bed.

As she jogged up the stairs to her room, she thought about her mother. Why on earth had she decided to go to Paris *now* of all times? And for two whole *months*.

Betsy had planned to attend the four-day-long Northwest Crime and Punishment Writer's Conference starting on Thursday in Seattle. She'd have to take the Pidster with her since she couldn't afford to hire a dog-sitter for that amount of time, and a kennel was out of the question. God knew she needed the time away from work. With or without her mother's dog in tow, Betsy intended to shove her job firmly into the recesses of her brain for four lovely days.

She loved her job, adored it, but lately things seemed strained, and she couldn't quite put her finger on why. People were talking about *something*, but they hushed up whenever she got within earshot. Since she'd never done anything out of the ordinary or weird in her life, her coworkers couldn't possibly be whispering about her. Still, it gave her an uncomfortable feeling, and she was looking forward to a little breather.

Quickly stripping off her clothes, Betsy tossed her lightweight flannel gown over her head then went into the bathroom to wash her face and brush her teeth.

She turned on the faucet then quickly turned it off. Was that a noise? She waited. Nothing. She twisted the faucet a second time, then quickly turned it off again. Yes, there had been a noise, but what was it and where had it come from?

Wiping her hands on a towel, she padded down the stairs. Throughout the house, her drapes were pulled. Nobody could see in. Reaching the kitchen, she snapped off the light, then stood in the gloom and silence, listening. . . .

There! A high-pitched yelp and then nothing. *Piddle?*

The kitchen door screeched on its hinges as Betsy flung it open and snapped on the back porch light. She wrapped her arms around her waist against the chill and searched the landscape with narrowed eyes.

Beyond the meager reach of the porch light, her quest was useless. Night fell quickly and completely this time of year, turning the lovely yard into unknown territory filled with shifting black shapes and foreboding shadows.

Though she couldn't see much at the moment, Betsy knew the yard itself was deep and wide, graced here and there with trees. An ancient willow filled the back corner, its long leaves turned yellow by an early frost. A few tall firs, dark and pungent, stood sentry around the perimeter. Several rhodies marched in a line against the back fence, and old roses—pink, cream, gold, their blooms fading as they succumbed to the change of seasons—hugged the back of the house near where she stood.

Now, the atrium lay in shadows. All was still. Not so much as a leaf fluttered, and yet Betsy had the distinct feeling she could hear, or feel, the pulse of movement. Breathing.

She sensed that eyes were fixed on her, but from where, she couldn't tell.

A mournful whine rose from the area of her feet, and she gasped and instinctively took a step back.

Piddle? What the—

The Chihuahua lay on his side on the porch, all four

legs thrust stiffly away from his body. His chest heaved with labored breaths and his huge eyes stared helplessly into hers. He looked like a large paralyzed rat with a red collar.

Betsy quickly stooped and picked him up, then slammed and locked the back door.

Snapping the kitchen light back on, she examined every inch of him. He appeared unhurt, but something was definitely wrong. He seemed more shaky than usual. If she didn't know better, she'd say he'd been traumatized.

Whimpering, he thrust his face under her arm and tried to burrow as far in as he could get, a featherless, bonsai ostrich hiding his head in the sand.

It was then she saw what was bothering him.

She reached out and warily touched the piece of paper tucked tightly under his collar. Pulling it out, she absently set Piddle on the floor and unfolded the paper.

> HEY DIDDLE-DIDDLE,
> I COULD HAVE NAILED PIDDLE
> BUT I DIDN'T DO SUCH
> 'CAUSE I LOVE YOU SO MUCH
> OR DO I?

Betsy's heart skipped a beat while her breath caught in her throat. She lay the paper on the kitchen counter, and fumbling for a chair, sat down and stared at the scrap.

Her gaze moved warily to the back door. Should she open it to see who was out there?

Immediately her common sense shouted, *Hell no! What a stupid idea!*

The more she stared at the paper, the faster her heart raced. A lonely woman in a lonely house living a lonely life should be thrilled that somebody loved her. Except it was plain he didn't love her.

Quite the contrary.

Officer Sam Winslow looked like a million bucks: tall, an all-American type with brown eyes, dark blond hair, a cleft in his chin, the works. Betsy held Piddle close to her chest as Officer Winslow completed his paperwork.

He grinned. Straight, white, perfect teeth. Inwardly, Betsy sighed with longing. It was a pleasure just to look at the man.

"Now, Ms. Tremaine—" he began.

"That's *Miss*," she corrected, trying not to appear too obvious.

"Ah, yes, then *Miss Tremaine*. You're certain, ma'am, that you have no idea who could have written this note?" The note in question now resided in a small plastic evidence bag he held in his large clean hand.

Betsy shook her head. "No, sir."

Winslow grinned again. "You don't have to call me sir."

"You called me ma'am."

"Yes," he said through a sheepish grin. How charming. "We're supposed to do that. As a courtesy. Ma'am." He grinned again as he tossed the evidence bag into his leather case. Betsy slid a glance to his left hand as he snapped the lock shut.

No wedding ring. Should she tell him now that she wanted to have his baby, or should she wait until she knew him better?

She wiped the silly grin off her face before he turned back to her. All he would see now was a serious young woman of medium height, with a plain face but rather good complexion, hazel eyes, short, chunky-cut blond hair, shoulders that were too square, a bust just a tad too full, a slim waist, and her grandmother's thighs.

Like a mental ticker tape, her mother's sad-but-true appraisal of her deficiencies ran yet again through her head.

You've got an hourglass figure, dear. Men hate hourglass figures. Look at movies and TV if you don't believe me. Sleek and toned, lots of muscle, small breasts, long legs, trim hips. You do have good teeth, though.

Good teeth? Who did her mother think she was, Trigger?

Officer Winslow stood. Betsy rose, too, subtly pulling her pink sweater down over her hips. She'd changed back into her jeans and a top after phoning the police, and now wished she'd stayed in her nightgown. At least it covered her body, including those damned hips, from neck to toe.

"It looks like our guys have finished in your backyard," he said. "I'll get in touch with you if anything turns up on the note. I doubt we'll find any prints on it besides yours, but you never know."

"You never know. Right." Betsy smiled. She absently wound a short curl around her finger then let it go and shoved her hand into her pocket when she realized she had come very close to being coy. "Do you think I'm in danger, Officer Winslow?"

The lawman stopped in the doorway. His shoulders were so broad, she couldn't see past him to the street. He looked . . . heroic. Or was it just that she was . . . desperate.

"Read the literature I left for you. It'll give you some tips on keeping yourself safe. Also," he said, granting her another perfect smile, "we'll increase the neighborhood patrols for a while. Oftentimes, a visible police presence is enough of a deterrent, but, well, we'll see. I don't want to scare you, but I do want you to be aware."

He reached down to pat Piddle on the nose, but the dog took offense and growled. Officer Winslow's smile stayed frozen in place. "Uh, nice dog."

"No he isn't."

Piddle sneezed.

As one of Port Henry's finest walked back to his patrol car, Betsy couldn't help but notice the man's empyrean body.

Empyrean! What a stupid word. It meant ideal, sublime. She knew because she'd been forced to look it up. J. Soldier McKennitt had used it to refer to somebody in his book, and now she couldn't get the damn word out of her head.

Empyrean. Well, if it meant perfect, Winslow surely was that all right. He slid behind the wheel, gave Betsy a smile and wave, then drove down her quiet, tree-lined street and out of sight.

"He works out," she confided to Piddle. "He wouldn't want a woman who doesn't work out, I'll bet." With a man like Winslow, hourglass figures wouldn't do. He was buff; he would want buff.

Against the now late evening chill, Betsy closed and locked her front door. In the Olden Days, she thought as she meandered toward the kitchen, men courted women for their ability to cook a good meal, keep a clean house, raise healthy kids, plow a straight furrow, milk a cow single-handed. Nowadays, you could cure cancer on Monday, climb Everest on Tuesday, solve world hunger on Wednesday, but unless you had a perfect body, a sexy guy like Sam Winslow would never give you a second glance.

The hunky cop had instructed her to keep her doors and windows bolted, her drapes closed, and her eyes and ears open. Whether he found her interesting or not was the least of her problems.

She was being stalked. Maybe. She wanted to go deeply into denial, but that wouldn't make the situation go away. As much as she hated the very idea, she was going to have to behave like a crime victim, because the simple fact of the matter was, she *was* a crime victim. Well, maybe.

In the blink of an eye her orderly life had changed, and she had to respond accordingly. To ignore the warnings could mean her life. Or not. Only if she really *was* being stalked.

The urge to dismiss the whole thing was overwhelming. Gosh, she thought, maybe she was just turning this little molehill into a mountain. Perhaps the note was intended for Mrs. Banes next door. Sure, Mrs. Banes was an eighty-five-year-old widow, but you never knew who had the hots for whom. Maybe some old gent at the Port Henry Senior Activity Center had designs on her.

Besty nibbled on her lip. She didn't know who, she didn't know why. But someone had come secretly into her backyard and terrorized her dog. By mistake? Well, the note he'd left her was now being analyzed at the county crime lab.

She shuddered when she recalled pulling the back door open without turning on a light or even checking to see if someone was out there. As a woman living alone, she should have known better than that.

Betsy looked down at Piddle. "As my Canine in Shining Armor, I trust you will protect me if and when the time comes?"

The dog's luminous eyes stared into hers. He looked guilty. But then, he always looked guilty. His long lashes fluttered nervously, his wet nose twitched.

"I'll take that as a yes."

Betsy went into the kitchen and opened the pantry door. The brass knob felt cool and smooth in her fingers.

"Hm," she said, leaning down to pick up the dog. "Just like Old Mother Hubbard who went to her cupboard to fetch her poor dog a bone . . . although why she kept bones in the cupboard, we have no way of knowing." Piddle burrowed deep under Betsy's armpit and began quaking hard enough to register on the Richter scale.

"A little something to settle the nerves, I think," she mumbled as she pulled a dust-covered bottle of Jack Daniel's from the depths of her spice shelf. "My nerves, not yours."

It took concentration to keep her fingers from trembling as she unscrewed the cap with one hand, but she managed it.

For a moment she considered calling her best friend just to hear a reassuring voice, but after checking the time, Betsy realized Claire would still be at the hospital. And, after all, what was happening to her wasn't exactly an emergency, so interrupting her doctor friend's rounds would be a selfish thing to do.

Splashing an ounce or two or three into a tumbler, she added Coke and a few ice cubes.

"It's probably not a good idea to drink too much of this stuff on an empty stomach," she said to her companion, "but I'm too freaked out to stay totally sober."

Fortifying herself with a gulp from her glass, she went through the house to her desk once again and plopped into the vintage chair. Setting Piddle on the floor, she straightened and took another swallow of the fizzy drink.

Who had written her the note? And for God's sake, *why?*

Visions of some sicko with gnarled, hairy knuckles scratching out those horrible words made a chill creep up Betsy's spine. She had to leave in four days for the conference. Would her house be okay while she was gone? Perhaps she could get Carla or Dave from work to keep an eye on the place for her over the long weekend?

Did *he* know her routine? Would *he* follow her into Seattle? Maybe she should buy a gun.

Right. Like she knew how to use a gun. She'd end up shooting herself or Piddle . . . hmm. Piddle. Naw. Her mother would never forgive her.

After a few minutes Betsy realized her vision was getting a little hazy. A decidedly warm feeling infused her entire body. She felt relaxed. More than relaxed. She grinned to herself and twirled the chair around a couple of times, holding her drink in the air as though toasting some unseen visitor. Downing another large gulp, she giggled into the tumbler.

This is cool, she thought ten minutes later as she held the empty glass in her hand. Nothing like getting shit-faced when you were being stalked and could be murdered at any moment.

The trill of musical notes caught her attention. She glanced at the computer. Uh-oh. Another note from J. Soldier. Taking a steadying breath, Betsy absently wondered what the J stood for and why the old guy preferred to go by his middle name. She wasn't sure she cared enough at the moment to find out.

Ms. Betsy:

Granted, yours is only one opinion, but because it is so divergent from the sentiments expressed by others, my curiosity is piqued and I thought I'd give it another try.

What is it about my books you don't like, exactly? I'm an adult and a professional. I can handle criticism.

If you'd take a moment to enlighten me, I'd appreciate it.

Thanks,
JSMc

So he couldn't let it rest, huh? Betsy thought as her eyes tried to focus on the screen. So he can handle criticism, can he? Well, be careful what you wish for, Detective Mr. J. Something McKennitt. You just might *get* it.

Her fingers lightly tickled the keyboard as she considered her reply.

She sucked on her lower lip. Then she sucked on her upper lip, which was not nearly as easy to do. Finally, she giggled and blew her bangs out of her eyes, then got down to business.

"Okay, Detective Mr. J. Soldier McKennitt Person," she mumbled to the computer screen. "You want enlightenment? You got it."

Detective JSMc, sir (I learned that from the police today):

Pfffft! That's right. Pfffft! That's my reply. Why don't I like your books? Pfffft!

Not to put too fine a point on it, the writing is about as polished as my kitchen floor (which really isn't very polished, thus the comparison, but you'd have to see my kitchen floor to understand what I mean). Your plots are about as believable as Santa Claus, which whom I used to believe in him but life is nothing if not occasionally disappointing. So sue me.

Your characters are bland. Bland, bland, bland. No life. The dead ones have more life than the live ones have who have no life. And they're stupid. The live ones. They act irrationally.

I've read my share of mystery novels and crime thingies, and, given the facts you give, your conclusions are faulty. I find I do not buy them, sir! I would characterize your style, such as it is, as cold, impersonal, vulgar, and graph-ick!

My sincerest apologies if I have in any way hurt your feelings. I'm really a very nice person, but I've had a rough day. Somebody says they love me except they don't and I'm frightened.

And then I got your message and I just feel it's important to tell the truth. I've always been that way. People don't always want to hear the truth and sometimes it serves no one, but I don't know any other way. My father taught me that honesty is the best policy, but he's been out of my reach for years now, so he won't ever say that to me again, even though I can still hear his lovely voice in my heart.

Continued success on your writing career. I meant to tell you what a jerk I think you are for accosting me with your e-mail and demands for explanations, but now that I think about it, I just can't do it. I mean, I do think you're a jerk, but I'm just not going to say it.

Empyreanly yours,
Betsy Tremaine

Soldier looked up from the screen and blinked at his brother, who was laughing so hard he was drooling.

When Soldier spoke, his voice was low and solemn, filled with awe at what he had just read.

"Drunk," he said. "She must be blitzed on her butt." He shook his head. "I've read letters from Kazakhstani crack addicts that made more sense than this."

Taylor laughed harder as he read the e-mail again. "I think you should frame it," he howled. "Hang it right next to the picture we drew of her." He wiped the tears from his eyes. "God, this is a classic, Jackson. Maybe you can blackmail her with it."

Soldier shrugged. "Hell, I don't know whether to put out a hit on her or give her a hug. The woman is in worse shape than I thought."

Taylor pulled up a chair. "Go for the hit. I'll do it if you want."

"Very funny."

"You gonna respond?"

Soldier widened his eyes. "What in God's name would I say? 'I'm sorry you're a lunatic? Perhaps a little therapy would be in order here?' "

Pressing the print key, Soldier watched as the laser jet rolled out a copy of the e-mail. He picked up the paper and folded it together with the picture Taylor had drawn. Shoving them in his pocket, he sighed. "Well, my life may be crap, but I'm a lot better off than Betsy Tremaine. Not only is she ugly," he smirked, thinking of his brother's artistic rendition, "but she's nuttier than a Snicker's bar."

However, even as he said the words, he felt uneasy. He sure didn't agree with her reviews, but they had at least been well-written and coherent. Her e-mail had been okay, too. Something must be wrong. Perhaps she was just getting up there in years. Undoubtedly, she was a spinster and lived alone. Probably had a dozen cats, or some yappy little dog. The fact that she'd mentioned the police and that she was frightened bothered him, even if she'd been drunk or crazy at the time.

Soldier didn't know the woman, yet he felt a sense of connection with her. She didn't like his books and had said so. No crime in that, except it had pissed him off. He knew the male ego had the tensile strength of a wet Kleenex, but he'd always thought he possessed a stronger sense of self than to let some little old lady from Nowheresville upset his apple cart.

Abruptly, the thought that had been subtly nagging at Soldier for weeks pushed itself to the forefront. Shoving his hands into his pockets, he rested a hip on the kitchen doorjamb.

"What do you think, Taylor. Should I go back to work full-time?"

In the meaningful silence that followed, Soldier stepped away from the threshold and sauntered over to where his brother was constructing a towering sandwich. "Make me one of those, will you?"

Crunching on a dill pickle, Taylor nodded and pulled out a second plate. "Why are you asking my opinion?" he said. "You never ask my opinion. You're the big brother. You know everything." He took another bite of pickle and sent Soldier a grin.

"Just because I know everything, doesn't mean I know *every*thing. So, should I go back out on the street?"

Both McKennitt sons had inherited their father's intensely blue eyes, eyes that appeared to sear directly to the bone. Taylor leveled those eyes now on Soldier.

"You've been sitting on your ass long enough," he said, working on Soldier's sandwich. "That thing with Marc sucked, but it wasn't your fault and it's time you got over it. You're a cop. So, get it together and go be one."

"I failed Marc," Soldier all but growled. "I made an error in judgment that cost him his life. Now his widow and kids are paying for my blunder."

He felt his stomach knot. Marc's death had been a horrible blow. They'd been partners for four years and he'd grown to love the guy like a brother. When Soldier had realized he'd been fed false information, and that he'd sent Marc right into the trap, he'd broken every speed law on the books trying to get to his partner in time. But it had been too late.

Soldier had found Marc's torn body thrown in a trash bin. He'd pulled him out of the garbage and called for help. But by the time the paramedics had gotten there, it was over. Marc had died in his arms, his wife's name on his lips, his fingers gripped around Soldier's wrist.

Whether Marc's death grip was a demonstration of trust or hatred remained an unanswered question that haunted Soldier's dreams.

From day one, cops knew the score. You could take a hit any time. But this was different. This had been his fault. Marc had been careful, it had been he who'd screwed up, and his partner had paid the price.

Soldier had tracked and collared the killer, but it wasn't enough. It wouldn't bring his friend back, soothe his widow at night, feed his kids. Regret was a useless demon, but it had eaten away at his conscience for months, weakening his confidence, making him fear the same thing might happen to his next partner. To the next man who trusted him with his life.

And it was what kept him from looking for a wife, from making a family with some nice woman. It could all be gone so fast.

"So," Taylor interrupted Soldier's thoughts, pushing the plate and completed sandwich toward his brother. "You're thinking, how can I ever trust myself again? What if I screw up again and somebody else gets killed?"

Soldier hitched in a tight breath. "Yeah, something like that."

"Hey, I'm a cop, too. Remember?"

"Yeah, but you've never—"

"No, I've never. Not yet, anyway. But we all know the risks. All we can do is our best, Jackson." He took another bite of his sandwich and stared into Soldier's eyes.

Soldier liked being with his brother. He and Taylor had always been close, but never so much as lately, since Soldier had lost his partner and Taylor had lost his faith in women.

At thirty-three, Soldier had never been married, let alone divorced, so he didn't know how this was all supposed to work. Having watched Taylor go through hell because of that faithless slut, Soldier was glad that years ago he'd sworn he'd never get married. But he'd been there for Taylor, no matter what it took, no matter how long it took. And Taylor had been there for him when Marc was killed.

Wiping his mouth with a napkin, Taylor said,

"When are you leaving for the conference?"

Soldier looked up from his own sandwich and glanced over at the wall calendar, an obvious freebie from Joe's 24-Hour Towing Service. "Uh, Thursday. I'm not scheduled to speak until Saturday night."

"I'll lay you odds that Old Lady Tremaine will be there."

Soldier popped the last bit of his sandwich into his mouth, chucked his plate into the sink and wiped his hands on a paper towel. "Nah. Too much excitement for an old broa— I mean, a lady with such fragile sensibilities."

"*Fragile sensibilities?* You've been watching PBS again, haven't you?" Taylor accused. "It would be funny, though, don't you think," he chided, "if you met her face-to-face? Like, what if she's young and beautiful and you fall for her?"

Soldier laughed and patted his jeans pocket where he'd shoved the drawing and her obtuse e-mail message.

"Fall for *her*?" he chuckled, squinting at his brother over the top of the fresh beer he'd just opened. "Taylor, if I ever met Elizabeth Tremaine, the last thing in the world I would do is fall for her."

Chapter 2

Enchantment struck him like a doubled fist. His pulse raced, his mouth went dry. If somebody asked his name right then, his tongue would have been too thick to form the words.

Soldier knew he was staring, but he couldn't stop. There was something about her that held him in thrall, but he couldn't have put words to his feelings even if that fist was circling around for another blow.

He swallowed and stared. He fiddled with his pen and stared. He scratched his chin and stared. He felt like he had the first time he'd had sex. Real sex with a real girl, not some wet dream. He felt . . . anticipation. Sweet and strong and elemental.

Whoever she was, every inch of her was made for every inch of him.

She wasn't beautiful in the classic sense, and she wasn't exactly thin, either. And she didn't look like the kind of woman a man dated or just messed around with. She looked like the kind of woman a man married.

That should have caused an alarm bell to ring loudly in his head, and the fact that it didn't took him by surprise.

Soldier liked a woman who looked like a woman. A lady with full breasts and real hips and curves that made his hands ache and his nether parts stand up and take notice. And this lady had it all.

The Northwest Crime and Punishment Writer's Conference was always a popular event, so he'd anticipated that the Evergreen Ballroom at Seattle's Crowne Plaza Hotel would be packed like a sardine can, and had come down from his room a little early to get a good seat. He'd just relaxed into his chair when he looked across the room as *she* entered through the ballroom's double doors.

The cop in him had immediately kicked in. Female Caucasian. Between twenty-five and thirty. About five and a half feet. Blond hair. Eye color unknown: too far away to tell. No visible scars or marks. No weapon. Creamy skin, rosy cheeks, plump, kissable mouth. When she smiled, she had deep dimples in both cheeks. *Damn!*

She was dressed in a soft, kind of cashmere looking peach-colored sweater and a long floral-print skirt. The fabric of both the sweater and skirt hugged her curves, tempting a man to run his hands over her hips and down over her bottom. On her head, she wore a summery straw hat encircled by pastel satin ribbons and delicate pink flowers. She looked feminine and . . .

well, nice. She looked like a real nice woman he'd like to get to know.

And take to bed.

Just looking at her, his heart raced and he felt like that damned bunny rabbit in *Bambi*, the one that got all twitterpated.

He doubled his fist. A thirty-three-year-old Seattle detective did *not* get twitterpated. Except that he was.

As she moved between the closely set chairs, she smiled at each person she passed, flashing those dimples, making Soldier nearly overheat. Every man she left in her wake grinned after her, their eyes following the sway of her skirt. She, however, seemed completely oblivious.

He frowned at a couple of the men, but they were paying no attention to him.

The lady must have felt his stare, for at that moment she looked up. Their gazes locked. Her eyes widened and she blinked. Those plush lips formed a small O. Then her cheeks flushed and her lips became a shy grin as she modestly lowered her lashes.

Soldier was halfway out of his chair when a voice boomed over the loudspeaker.

"Good afternoon, everyone. Please take your seats, and we'll get this show on the road."

As the conference was called to order, all Soldier could do was sit down and wait. When he looked back at the woman, she was focused on the note pad in which she had begun to write. Disappointment pierced his chest.

Suddenly, the conference didn't interest him in the least, but getting near that woman did.

The first things Betsy noticed about the spacious ball-room were the elegant windows at the far end. Light spilled into the cavernous expanse, lending it a cheery quality, helped no doubt by the mauve-and-cream-striped wallpaper. Crystal chandeliers dangled like clusters of brilliant stalactites from the ceiling, creat-ing miniature rainbows that danced up and down the walls.

Around her, people were settling in. Chairs scraped against the hardwood floor. Writers from all over the country were in attendance, chatting in small groups or in couples.

Amidst the hubbub, her world collapsed into a small soundproof bubble. She was aware of only one thing, one man.

She'd caught him staring at her, and for a moment wondered if she knew him, but quickly realized that if she'd ever met this man, she would surely remember. Nobody had ever looked at her like that before. It cer-tainly couldn't be that he found her attrac—

The stalker. He could be the *stalker*. The pamphlets Officer Winslow had given her explained that over a million ordinary citizens were stalked every year, and that sometimes the stalker simply fixated on a com-plete stranger. It was possible she was being stalked by someone she had never actually met, and this man could be the one.

The back of her neck prickled and she tried to focus on something else, anything else.

It didn't work. She fought down the panic rising from her stomach. *Remain calm,* she instructed herself. If he was the one, she'd know it soon enough, but in the meantime she'd just concentrate on the conference. They were in public. What could possibly happen?

But she wanted to cry out in frustration. Even if that stranger—that man sitting innocently across the room—was not the stalker, her own thoughts, her own mind, had begun to stalk her. Until the mystery was solved or simply went away, she would wonder about every new acquaintance, every casual glance, every seemingly innocuous overture.

Of course, there was always the possibility she wasn't being stalked, she reminded herself. After all, a single note attached to a dog's collar did not a stalking victim make. Did it?

Denial. According to the literature Winslow had provided, she was in a classic state of denial. Well, until and unless something else happened to convince her she was indeed being pursued, she would be cautious but not neurotic. If she could just stop thinking about it, she might be able to relax.

She cleared her mind and turned her attention to the podium.

As the first speaker was introduced, Betsy applauded politely while sliding a clandestine glance at the man across the room. He was so good-looking, she found it difficult to direct her gaze anywhere else, but she didn't dare get caught staring. She didn't want to invite unwanted attention, especially considering her predicament.

The speaker was Dr. Stanley Durant, a former New York City coroner. He was holding everyone spellbound with his tales of unusual cases he'd recently had published. Across the room, her admirer appeared engrossed in the doctor's every word. Good. Now she could look her fill without being caught.

Even though he was seated, she knew he was tall. His shoulders were broad, filling out the black suede jacket he wore to perfection. His short-cropped hair was sable dark and held a hint of curl. His clean-shaven jaw was square, his cheeks hollow, accentuating high cheekbones. As she watched, he laughed at something the speaker said, revealing straight white teeth and a killer smile.

Still grinning, he turned his head and looked straight at her. *Busted.*

Betsy felt her face sting with heat, and she hurriedly looked away. Blinking rapidly while digging through her purse, she committed his incredible eyes to memory.

They were laser blue with thickly fringed lashes. That fierce gaze had pierced through her skull and right into her mind. Certainly he'd been able to read her thoughts. He must know that she found him incredibly attractive.

Betsy didn't dare look in his direction again for fear he'd catch her eyeing him. Even now, she could feel his perusal as though he were actually running his fingers lightly over her skin.

Her heart began to flutter. Was he attracted to her or was it something else? *Could* he be the man stalking her? Had he followed her to the conference?

Should she call hotel security, or wait and see if he tried to approach her?

Damn, she hated this! He was the sexiest man she had ever seen, but he could also be the most dangerous.

Betsy pretended to make some notes while Dr. Durant completed his remarks. The audience applauded as the master of ceremonies approached the microphone. Tapping on the metal bulb, he cleared his throat.

"Now it's time to move on to the various workshops we have planned for you. It's first come, first served, so if you want a good seat in the workshop of your choice, it would be a good idea to get going." He laughed good-naturedly and gestured toward the doors at either side of the large room. "Have fun, everyone. We'll see you all back here at noon for lunch."

With that, the crowd rose from their seats and began grabbing jackets from chair backs, adjusting skirts, referring to the crumpled programs in their fists, and packing up pens and papers in binders or briefcases. The noise of conversation mixed congenially with the shuffle of footsteps as people headed off toward the various lectures and workshops planned for that morning.

Betsy scanned her program. She wanted to sit in on the "Writing Is a Journey" workshop, so she picked up her things and moved toward the double doors to her left. A tilt of her head, and her hat brim concealed her eyes. Surreptitiously, she scanned the room looking for *him*, but he had disappeared.

Her heart constricted. She raised her chin and looked

about more carefully. He was gone, all right. Well, that was either really good or really bad. Of course, the room was crowded; he might just be mingling.

Before she could think about it further, she forced herself to head out the door, her new mantra keeping time with her footsteps. *I am not being stalked. I am not being stalked. I am not . . .*

The workshop was in the Sequoia Room, just down the long carpeted hallway and to the right. The small room was already packed when she got there, and only a few seats remained near the door.

Betsy scurried to one of the empty chairs and sat down. As she bent to set her bag on the gray and white carpet at her feet, someone took the empty chair on her right. Whomever it was sure smelled good, soapy, clean, and very masculine.

Her head came up. Her spine straightened. Her heart slammed against her rib cage in a wild jungle rhythm. Without even looking, she knew.

The heat from his big body drifted around her, snaring her, mingling with her own warmth, pulling her in like a powerful tractor beam. She was still partially turned away, but she could already feel his pyrotechnic blue gaze on her.

She tried to swallow, but her mouth had gone bone dry. Lifting her chin, she calmly faced forward. As she clasped her hands tightly in her lap, she was certain she looked to the casual observer as though she were waiting respectfully for the wisdom of the ages to be revealed.

She probably looked more like a hypnosis subject, she thought, eyes wide and unblinking, staring straight ahead, her expression a total blank. But she couldn't risk looking at *him*. He sat too close and was simply too overpowering. If she turned her head the slightest bit to the right, she'd meet his eyes, and that was just too damn close for comfort.

If he were her stalker, he couldn't possibly do anything in this room full of people, could he? But what if he was just a regular guy trying to get her attention? Then all her agonizing would have been in vain, so she might just as well relax and enjoy the rest of the conference.

I am not being stalked. I am not being stalked . . .

Whatever. She had to form a plan. When the lecture was over, she'd rise quickly and hurry out the door. She'd go straight to the front desk and demand—

". . . a pen? Excuse me. Do you have a pen I could borrow? I seem to have misplaced mine."

Betsy froze. His voice was deep, melodic, meltingly sexy. A man who was stalking her wouldn't ask for a pen, would he?

Taking a deep breath, she turned to him, but did not meet his eyes. She met his nose, which was long and thin, with a small scar across the top. Dropping her gaze a bit, she met his mouth. Oh my. Such a mouth. Wide and curved and smiling at her. Her heart skipped another beat, or two. Or three or four. She was beginning to lose count. Soon her heart would have skipped too many beats, and she would die.

Even sitting, he was much taller than she. Nodding her head and mumbling something incoherent, she dove for her bag and pulled out a bright green crayon. How in the hell did that get in there?

He surveyed the crayon and gave her an exaggerated frown. " '*Screamin' green*'?" he said. "Sorry, but I'm a '*raw sienna*' man myself."

"Oh, uh, no," she stumbled. "You see, my neighbor's grandson—"

"Leave it to kids," he interrupted. "Well, you might want to hang on to that one. We may get to color our place mats at lunch." His beautiful mouth widened into a grin.

The man simply oozed charm. If she couldn't find a pen, she'd prick her finger and he could use her blood.

With the speed of a bullet train, a feminine fist bearing a blue pen appeared out of nowhere, screeching to a halt in front of the man's surprised face.

Betsy peeked around him to see the woman sitting to his right smiling hugely. "I heard you ask for a pen," she gushed. "I'm just loaded with pens. You can certainly borrow one. I have so many more. I always come prepared to these things with tons and tons of pens. And paper. Do you need some paper? Because I have just tons and tons of paper—"

"No," he said, smiling at her. "But thanks. Actually, I think I might have one right here in my pocket." He reached inside his jacket and pulled out a pen.

The young woman was about Betsy's age, had strawberry blonde hair and pretty brown eyes. Her name tag proclaimed her to be Kristee Spangler from Lompoc, California.

Kristee Spangler smiled up at the handsome stranger so hard, Betsy thought the woman's teeth would break. He grinned politely back at her and she practically went orgasmic.

He turned to Betsy once again. "Thanks anyway. For checking for a pen," he said in a low voice. His smile was warm, and the blue of his eyes sparkled like pools of tropical rainwater.

She nearly whimpered. Was it possible she was dreaming? He looked like a movie star and he was talking to *her*? Perhaps there was a camera hidden somewhere and any minute a bald man with a microphone would humiliate her with the truth and everybody in TV-land would laugh at her naiveté. She started to turn away from him when he extended his right hand.

"I should probably introduce myself," he said. "My name's—"

"Is this on?" The workshop monitor interrupted the stranger's promising introduction by tapping on the microphone, which blasted the audience with the shrill screech of electronic feedback. Everybody covered their ears and winced.

The host smiled, shrugged, adjusted the microphone, and apologized. Finally, he called the workshop to order and presented Chester F. Bordon to the waiting crowd. The distinguished-looking, gray-haired mystery writer stepped up to the microphone and began his lecture, but Betsy knew she might as well have had cotton in her ears. Her eyes were on Bordon, but her nerves were tuned to the man sitting next to her.

Her name tag was on her left shoulder, while Mr. Dreamboat's tag was on his right. She couldn't see it without facing him, and that, she was not about to do.

Defiantly flinging all her attention to the speaker, she straightened her spine and tried hard to focus.

It was obvious that Chester Bordon was enthused about his subject as he detailed how the workshop would proceed. The first half, he would lecture on writing technique; the second half would be devoted to a simple exercise.

"I want you to choose a partner, preferably a stranger. Make a friend. Who knows," he chuckled, "the stranger sitting next to you may be your perfect soul mate. Your life's partner, the man or woman of your dreams."

Individuals in the group slid glances at the people around them and everyone smiled and tried to suppress nervous giggles. Betsy continued to stare straight ahead, until she felt a gentle jab. Her neighbor was nudging her with his elbow!

Turning her head as slightly as possible in his direction, her gaze drifted unwillingly to his mouth. *Mmmm.*

Be my partner? he asked silently. Lifting his brows in inquiry, he gave her an encouraging nod.

Betsy glanced desperately to her left just as the woman seated there sneezed, then coughed, then sneezed again. Taking out a huge handkerchief, she proceeded to blow her nose with the passion of a foghorn eliciting a small craft warning.

Bordon was still detailing the instructions. "One person will go first and write a paragraph on a topic I'll give you. Keep the paragraphs to two or three sentences. Then, the partner will compose the next paragraph based on what the first person wrote. Trade back and forth in that manner until I call time. When we're done, I'll read one of them so you can see how ideas can play off each other. You may find your story going in a direction you never dreamed possible, but which is much more interesting for the element of a second person's perspective."

A tingle of excitement skittered up Betsy's spine. She wasn't sure she'd be able to concentrate enough to actually compose an entire paragraph, let alone several. Not with her nerves and emotions in such a state.

The speaker proceeded to elaborate on the importance of accurate research in fiction, but for her, what had been a much anticipated lecture suddenly turned into a countdown to the partnership exercise.

Betsy suppressed a groan. Glaring at Chester Bordon, she wondered if the damned man couldn't talk any faster. All she could think about was that when he was done speaking, she would be partners with the totally hot guy sitting next to her.

Her mind spun and her stomach flipped. She was a nervous wreck by the time the famed mystery writer finally wound things up and asked for questions.

No questions! she wanted to yell. *Just everybody sit quietly and let's move on to the partnership exercise. Okay?*

She resisted the urge to tap her toe nervously while several people asked their questions. Bordon took his time answering them. How nice. How thorough. How very professional of him. *Next!*

In a few minutes the questions and answers came to an end. *Finally!* But just as she turned to her partner, he stood.

"I'll be right back," he assured her. "I'm going to speak to Chester for a sec. Don't go 'way . . . partner." Stepping through the crowd, he strode toward the podium.

Oh yes, he was tall. Dressed in that black suede jacket, open-collared white shirt, and faded blue jeans and boots, he looked like he'd just stepped off a men's magazine cover. And his butt! Betsy nearly swooned. Shoulders to die for and a butt to match.

Out of the corner of her eye she could see Kristee Spangler gazing at him in open admiration as his athletic body twisted this way and that through the clusters of people. Across the chasm created by his empty chair, she flattened her mouth into an angry line and sent Betsy a narrow-eyed glare. In obvious fury that she hadn't gotten to partner with the man who sat between them, she rigidly turned away from Betsy to speak to the elderly lady to her right.

Paper and pen at the ready, Betsy waited with deceptive calm while her new partner approached the renowned writer standing at the podium. The two men shook hands as though they were old friends, and chatted for a few moments. Betsy still couldn't get a clear view of his name tag. It looked like it said Something McSomething, but then his lapel flopped over it, obscuring his name from view.

With a final nod to Chester Bordon, her new partner turned back to her. He smiled as his gaze met hers. Then his focus drifted to her name tag. He stopped, blinked, glared into her eyes as though she'd just slapped him, and cut his gaze back to her name tag.

For a moment he did nothing. Then his blue, blue eyes narrowed on her. Betsy's heart beat once, twice.

She watched as a huge grin split his face and he began to laugh.

She glanced down at her name tag. Was it upside down? Had somebody written "Total Loser" on it when she wasn't looking? BETSY TREMAINE, PORT HENRY, WASHINGTON. Nothing funny about that.

Despite her partner's odd behavior, deep inside, where all her fears were kept in a tight little bundle, Betsy felt a bit of calm infuse itself into her nervous system, and the bundle eased a bit. From his genuine reaction, it was obvious he hadn't known who she was until that very moment. There was no disguising his surprise at seeing her name.

He was not the one stalking her.

I am not being stalked. I am not being stalked . . .

Well, *that* sure was good news.

Now all she could do was sit and wait while he made his way through the crowd back to her. Her fear of him having vanished, she now felt a little piqued at what so obviously was some kind of inside joke. She stiffened her spine and put on her haughtiest face.

No matter what his explanation for laughing at her, it couldn't be good enough to excuse him from being so rude.

Well, if that didn't beat all, Soldier thought. Taylor had been right. "Old Lady" Tremaine was young and pretty, and he had come very near to falling for her like a ton of bricks.

Very nearly.

Betsy Tremaine. The name fit her like a glove. *Damn*, she was cute.

He quickly shoved that thought aside as he remembered her scathing reviews of his books. All those nasty words she'd used to describe his work flashed across his memory and he felt his good humor slide right down the toilet.

So this was the uppity Ms. Tremaine, hm? Well well well. Perhaps it was time to give the lady an object lesson in humility.

As he approached her, his heart gave a glad jump and he fought down a grin. He was going to enjoy this. In the blink of an eye, the initial attraction he'd felt for her burgeoned into something else, something he liked even better: acute sexual expectation. Mm-hmm, he thought. This was going to be good.

Soldier liked smart, feisty women, and verbal sparring only added to their intrigue. Now he'd get a chance to find out what this woman was made of, how her mind worked, and just how far she was willing to go in a battle of wits.

Besides, women who were smart and feisty during verbal intercourse were usually just as smart and feisty during the other kind.

Soldier's blood was all but humming as he turned his back to her for a moment and quickly pulled off his name tag. He wasn't going to reel her in just yet; he wanted to play her for a while.

Sliding into his seat, he took her hand as if to shake it in greeting. "So," he said nodding toward her name tag. "You're E.C. Tremaine."

She eyed him suspiciously. "Yes," she said. In his palm, her hand felt small and warm and tense.

"You don't look anything like your picture." He gave her his best Cheshire cat grin.

"My p-picture?" She seemed a little disconcerted by that. Perhaps more than the situation warranted. In fact, she looked alarmed.

He set that thought aside as his mind went to the sketch Taylor had drawn. No spiky orange hair, no beady black eyes, no wart, no scar. And her tah-tahs were most definitely not shrunken prunes. Although, he didn't think he'd mind nibbling on them if he got the chance.

"I don't mean I've seen your photograph," he said, holding her hand captive. She looked relieved, but wary. "It's more that my brother is an artist of sorts, quite famous in his own way."

"An artist? Would I have heard of him?"

"Oh no. He works with the police a lot. Draws those renderings you see in the papers, you know, from witness's descriptions."

"Oh. Criminals. He draws criminals. And, you say he drew a picture of me?" She actually looked frightened. When she tried to withdraw her hand, he didn't let go.

Ms. Tremaine seemed more confused by the minute. Wide-eyed and innocent, she looked so soft and sweet. . . . *But hang on a minute*, he told himself. *This* was the woman who hated his books and wrote heinous reviews and aberrant e-mails.

He scooted a little closer, preparing to swoop in for

the kill, when she raised her face to look up at him. The sarcastic words died on his lips.

Elizabeth Tremaine's driver's license probably stated her eye color as hazel. But hazel didn't begin to cover it. Her eyes were like shards of colored glass, green and gold and aquamarine. Those intelligent eyes were large and thickly fringed with dark lashes. Something he couldn't name shone from them, and Soldier felt his heart poised to dive into their depths, and drown there.

Delicate brows arched in expectation. Her soft lips parted as though she were about to speak. Or be kissed.

"Sketch a picture of you?" Soldier gave himself a mental shake. "Uh, yes he did. He's a devout reader of the *Port Henry Ledger*. As am I."

Her brows snapped together and she blinked. Disbelief was written all over her face. She was probably lousy at poker, her every thought and emotion plain for all to see. He suddenly found himself wondering what her face would look like when she came. When her back was arched and her lips parted as she softly gasped his name . . .

"You. Read . . . the—" she stuttered. "You read the *Ledger*?" Never taking her eyes from his, she shook her head from side to side, as though in denial. When she pulled her hand away this time, he let it go. "What did you say your name was?"

Soldier smiled. The moment had arrived on a sleigh with little golden bells ringing with glee. Payback. It was going to be a pleasure.

"I neglected to introduce myself earlier, didn't I?" It

wasn't a question, and his quiet voice must have alerted her, for she gave him a guarded smile.

Taking her hand in his once again, he gave it a warm shake of greeting. "Then allow me to remedy that right now. My name is McKennitt. Jackson . . . Soldier . . . McKennitt."

A look of sheer panic crossed her face. She squeaked and tried to pull her hand away, but he held on tightly, incarcerating her fingers between his palms.

"I believe we have corresponded recently, ma'am." He grinned, and knew it was his most evil. "Most people call me Soldier, except for my brother, who calls me Jack. Of course, you could call me '*Detritus*,' but that sounds more like a cruel Roman emperor bent on vengeance, don't you think?"

Chapter 3

Oh . . . my . . . God. Save for those three words, Betsy's mind went blank.

J. Soldier McKennitt, face-to-face, here and now, and he was her partner for the writing exercise. And he was gorgeous and he was sexy and he was young and his eyes, his eyes . . .

Oh . . . my . . . God.

All she could think of was that wretched e-mail she'd sent him the night she'd had too much to drink. She'd read it over the next day through bleary and aching eyes. She'd never been a drinker, and that night had convinced her she never would be.

McKennitt must think her a complete idiot.

Taking a deep breath, she managed to tug her hand from his. He had nice hands. So warm and strong. She was simply too stupid to live. . . .

"Detective McKennitt, about that last e-mail—"

Before she could continue, he interrupted. "Yes,

about that e-mail. You know, Bessie, there are several good alcohol rehabilitation centers—"

"No! No no no! I'm not an alc—I mean, I don't normally . . . I mean, I was just having a bad—" She stopped. "My name isn't Bessie," she said calmly. "My father named his car Bessie."

He smiled, but this time it did not crinkle his eyes in the same affable manner it had when they'd first met. No, he was out for blood now. Hers.

"Never mind," he said, his tone flat. "We need to get this exercise written or this whole workshop will have been a waste of time. Don't you think?" His eyes bored into hers. "I repeat, don't you think, Bossie?"

"And my name isn't Bossie, either. Bossie is a cow—"

He lifted a brow. His earlier friendliness and interest had suddenly changed into arrogance and control. Fine. They'd do the damned exercise, then she'd spend the remainder of the conference avoiding him like the plague.

Soldier McKennitt settled back into his chair and appeared to concentrate on the instructions.

"The information sheet says we're supposed to make up a story about a man and a woman who have just met on a train." He set the paper aside. "Since it's ladies first, you write the initial paragraph. I'll write the second, and so on."

"Fine." She scribbled a couple of sentences, then handed him her paper. He scanned it, then wrote some sentences of his own. With a smug look on his face, he returned it to her.

Gazing at what he'd written, Betsy straightened her

spine then glared at him. She quickly wrote her sentences and passed the paper back to him.

She watched as his gaze moved across the lines. He shot her a look, then grimaced. In his left hand, his pen moved swiftly as he completed the next paragraph, then practically threw the paper back in her lap.

She grabbed it, read it, then gasped. With furious motions, her pen flew across the page, her writing less legible as she neared the end. Just as she dotted her last *i*, he grabbed the paper from her lap. His mouth was a thin line and his eyes were cold as he thought for a second, then began to write.

Tossing her the paper, he crossed his arms, a look of smug satisfaction tilting his mouth.

Betsy read his words, then puckered her lips as though she were sucking on a lemon. "Huh," she huffed, then began to write.

"Okay, time's up." Chester Bordon had taken the podium and stood smiling at them. "I trust you all had fun, and learned something while you were at it."

A general buzz of agreement filled the small room as people nodded and laughed.

Leaving the podium, he strolled down the aisle and stopped at Betsy's row. Smiling at her, he held out his hand. "May I, Ms.—" He leaned forward to see her name tag. "—Ms. Tremaine. May I have your paper, please?"

Betsy smashed the paper against her bosom. She shook her head violently, but before she could grind out, *Over my dead body,* Soldier McKennitt pried the paper from between her fingers. With a grin that could only be described as satanic, he handed it to Bordon.

"No need to be shy, my dear," the writer assured her. "These things are never perfect and are just in fun, after all."

Betsy turned to glare at Soldier, only to find him glaring at her, a sadistic gleam in his eye. She lowered her lashes and slid as far down into her chair as she possibly could, preparing herself for the humiliation to come.

Back at the podium, Bordon cleared his throat. "I should tell you all that we have quite a celebrity in our midst." He raised a hand and indicated Mr. Dreamboat. "Would you mind standing, Soldier?"

Soldier rose from his chair and nodded to the curious crowd.

"Let me introduce J. Soldier McKennitt, Seattle detective and author of the Crimes of the Northwest series of books."

Oohs and *ahhs* and light applause surrounded them, while Betsy could only sit there awaiting her doom. Just as she opened her eyes, Soldier grabbed her elbow and jerked her to her feet. A sea of faces turned toward her, all smiling, all curious.

Soldier put his arm around her waist and tugged her close, as though they had a relationship, as though they liked each other, as though they were lovers.

"Thanks, Chester. Allow me to introduce another celebrity, Ms. Elizabeth Tremaine, editor of the *Port Henry Ledger*, and renowned literary . . . crit-ick."

If the audience hadn't heard the sarcasm in his voice, they were all deaf, but they smiled weakly and nodded, clueless as to who she was. *Thank God for that,* was all she could think.

As they took their seats, Bordon held her and Soldier's epistle from hell in front of him. "I'd like to read this to you now. With two such exemplary members of the writing community participating in this exercise, you should get an idea of how one person can influence another and how that influence can elevate a story and send it off into unanticipated reaches, possibly making it better, fresher."

Betsy pinched her eyes closed. *Better. Fresher. Saints preserve us.*

Bordon cleared his throat and began to read.

> *"Amanda Jones hated flying, which was why she'd decided to take the train home to her high school reunion instead of booking a flight. Amanda relaxed into her seat and turned her attention to the landscape speeding by outside her window. At least this gave her some time alone to think about André and their future together."*

Bordon smiled at Betsy. "Was that your paragraph, Ms. Tremaine?" he asked.

She nodded mutely.

"Good start. And now for Detective McKennitt's responding paragraph." He returned his attention to the paper.

> *"André was a jerk. With a rap sheet a mile long, he was a bad boy from the wrong side of town. Maybe that's what attracted her to him, for in spite of the fact that he was trash, rubbish, junk,*

dross, baloney, and claptrap, she wanted him. Couldn't get enough of him. The man was sex on a stick."

Bordon paused a moment and adjusted his glasses. "My," he said, his voice too loud and too cheery. "This *is* unexpected."
Betsy sank lower into her chair.

"But sex wasn't enough for Amanda. She was a very nice woman who always treated people with fairness and respect. After all, just because a man was tall, athletic, and sexy, didn't mean anything if he was a talentless hack devoid of all taste or literary acumen.

"Suddenly, a stranger approached her. He was huge, empyrean even, and mean-looking, and it was obvious, even to a virginal dimwit like Amanda, that he was engorged with desire. His lustful gaze took in her bounteous breasts and he licked his lips in eager anticipation. The seat next to hers was empty and he was eyeing it, and her, like he was a starving man about to sit down to a hearty meal.

"Before he could make a move, however, Amanda smiled sweetly and said, 'Sorry, this seat's taken.' He nodded politely and moved on down the aisle and out the door into the next car, never to return.

"Just then, the door at the other end of the car slammed open. 'André!' Amanda squealed. 'How did you . . . when did you . . . ' Her lim-

ited vocabulary spent on those few words, Amanda simply shut up and let André approach. He grabbed her and pulled her to him. His mouth came down on hers and she gasped, thrilled by his touch. 'You're mine!' he growled. 'Don't ever try to leave me again!'

"Amanda raised her knee and slammed it into André's crotch, immobilizing him. He squeaked in pain, like the wimpy, girly mouse he was, before collapsing to the floor of the car. Reaching into her handbag, Amanda pulled out a 9mm Glock and shot the bastard right through the heart.

"The bullet missed André's heart and hit the seat behind him. Jumping to his feet, he yanked the weapon from Amanda's weak little fist and turned the gun on her. 'Pfffft I say! Your kitchen floor is unpolished, you don't believe in Santa Claus, and you are bland! Bland, bland, bland!' Squeezing the trigger, he put a bullet right between her eyes, not in the seat behind her. She was dead. Dead, dead, dead. A doctor traveling in the next car confirmed it.

"André was immediately arrested by the doctor's wife, who was an undercover policewoman. André the rat was convicted of murder in the first, and sentenced to be drawn and quartered. His lawyer appealed, saying that was cruel and unusual punishment, but there was such a public outcry at the senseless murder of the lovely and wonderful Miss Jones that the judge ordered André be strung up by his ba—"

* * *

Bordon halted. All over the room, eyes were huge, mouths were frozen mid-gape. Nobody moved.

"Well . . ." Bordon wiped the beads of sweat from his forehead. "My. Okay then. Uh, as you can see, uh, yes. Well, it's lunchtime. Class, uh, dismissed."

Oh, the horror. The humiliation. She would have to leave the conference.

Betsy sat on the edge of the queen-sized bed, her feet apart, her elbows on her knees, her face in her hands, her self-esteem about three floors down.

Oh, the shame. *He* had made certain they all knew her name before Bordon innocently read that travesty out loud. She loved mystery stories and crime novels, which was the whole reason she'd used her limited vacation time to attend the conference. It wasn't fair that one arrogant ass could spoil it all for her.

Thanks to him, for the remainder of the conference she would probably be greeted with odd looks and curious stares. Word would certainly get around, him being handsome and famous and everything. *Great*. As if she wasn't insecure enough.

But leave the conference because of him? No, she would stay.

But she was certain to run into Soldier McKennitt again, and she hadn't the foggiest idea what she'd even say to him. Just the thought of seeing him once more made her insides churn. Okay, she would leave the damn conference.

But on the other hand, there were still three days left, featuring some really important writers whose lectures she wanted to hear. There were also some good workshops coming up on journalism and editing. All right, all right, enough buts. She would *stay* at the damn conference.

Pushing her hair out of her eyes, Betsy lifted her head. "Pids?" To get her mind off her dilemma, she decided, she'd take the Mongrel across the street to the park for a little R&R. He hadn't rushed to greet her when she returned to her room ten minutes ago, but then, Piddle never rushed to do anything anymore. Betsy's mother had warned her that the dog's hearing wasn't what it used to be. He was probably asleep under the bed and hadn't heard her come in.

Lifting the lacy bed skirt, she gave a quick look. No dog. The hotel room just wasn't that big. An oak dresser and mirror faced the bed and nightstand, a TV sat atop a minifridge, and a writing desk and chair stood in the corner. The muted plaid drapes were pulled across the single window.

After a quick check in the bathroom, she was more confused than ever, and a little worried. Where in the hell was that damn dog? Had the maid left the door open? Betsy had given special instructions to the desk to take care that the dog not get out. She wondered if the geriatric Chihuahua had somehow managed to creep past the maid in an insane bid for freedom. If so, he could be anywhere. Her mother would just die if anything happened to that stupid dog.

Running to the door, Betsy yanked it open and peered down the hall, to the left, to the right, and back again. No dog, and nothing to indicate a dog had ever been there.

Okay, she thought, *now it's time to panic.* Running

for the phone, she was about to call for hotel security when she heard a short, weak yap. It sounded as though it was coming from inside the room, but there was simply nowhere for the dog to be. She'd checked the closet. In fact, she'd looked everywhere, except . . .

Dropping the phone onto the bed, Betsy rushed to the minifridge. The enormous Seattle Metro phone book had somehow fallen from the nightstand and lay against the front. Shoving the book aside, Betsy pulled the door open.

Two huge brown eyes, desperate and terrified, met hers. He was curled in as tight a ball as he could get, his golden fur damp from the cold.

"Pids! Oh my God! How did you get in the refrigerator?"

Reaching inside, she scooped him up and into her arms. He was shaking so hard, she was having a difficult time holding on to him. She grabbed the lavender knitted throw she'd brought from home and wrapped him in it, keeping his body next to hers to warm him as quickly as possible.

She thought of running some hot water in the bathroom sink and dunking him in it, but after what he'd just been through, that might give him a little doggie heart attack, so she just held him close and kept talking to him.

"Oh, Pids. I'm so sorry. It'll be all right, sweetie. Mommy's here. Mommy's right here." Well actually, Mommy was thousands of miles away, but her own insides were pained at what had happened. She felt her latent maternal instincts kick in, and even though she wasn't Piddle's biggest fan, she never would have wished something like this on the poor creature.

A man's voice interrupted her thoughts. "Knock knock. Anybody home?"

Betsy's head jerked up. A large silhouette filled the threshold, broad shoulders, long legs. He was the last man she had ever expected to see darkening her doorway.

McKennitt gave her a mock frown. "I feel it necessary to warn you, ma'am," he said in what she figured was his best law enforcement voice, "that a lady in a hotel room all by herself really should keep her door closed and locked."

Betsy narrowed her eyes. "Thanks for the tip, Officer Friendly. You can close it on your way out."

He placed both his large hands over the area of his heart. "Madam, you wound me." As he stepped into the room, he said, "May I come in?"

"I'm busy right now. Perhaps another time, like, say, July thirty-second. I'll pencil you in." She pulled the trembling throw closer to her bosom and sent Soldier a no-nonsense glare.

Soldier eyed the small coverlet in her arms and lifted a brow. "Cute. Did you bring your blankie with you all the way from Port Henry?"

"Some detective *you* are," Besty snapped. "There's a dog in here. A terrified, half-frozen *dog*." Just then, Piddle began emitting a howl that sounded like a hyperactive squeaky toy.

Soldier eyed the lavender bundle. "I guess we can rule out Labrador retriever."

He moved into the room, closing the door behind

him, then shoved his hands in his pockets. Strolling casually toward Betsy, he said, "If I can guess what kind of dog it is, do I win a prize?"

"Go away. I have enough on my mind without you showing up to gloat about the humiliation you heaped on me today."

"You humiliated me when you wrote that you hated my books."

"That's different."

"How?"

"First of all," she said, taking in the intense color of his eyes, "you weren't humiliated. You were just mad."

He thrust out his lower lip and tilted his head as though considering her words. "You're right," he said. "I was mad. And then I met you in person and I'm not mad anymore."

Betsy huffed. "Yeah? Well, you sure couldn't prove it by me, the way you acted in the workshop this morning."

Soldier pulled the writing desk chair toward him and straddled it. "Oh come on, Miss Betsy Tremaine from Port Henry, Washington. Loosen up a little. I was hoping you'd have dinner with me. We can discuss our collaboration."

Betsy's eyebrows lifted nearly to her hairline. "That wasn't a collaboration. It was an abomination, and you know it. I wouldn't be caught dead with you after what happened today. In fact, I was considering leaving the conference."

Soldier scowled. "Just because of that stupid writing exercise?"

She shook her head. "Well, at first maybe. But then I got back to my room and discovered Piddle."

His brows shot up. "Somebody peed in your room?"

Abruptly, the Chihuahua's head popped up through the folds of the blanket. He looked around and blinked a few times, his long lashes sweeping up and down. Then, like a groundhog in February, he dove back inside the blanket and shoved his head under Betsy's arm.

"*That* was Piddle," she said. "I'm doggie-sitting while my mother's in Paris."

Soldier stared at the bundle in her arms, then began to laugh. Betsy watched him with a mixture of fury and hunger. Not only did he have a great laugh, he was the perfect male specimen: tall, dark, handsome, smart, and sexy. And he wanted to take her out to dinner, the bastard.

If she was halfway truthful with herself, she would have to admit that the hunger she felt right now had nothing to do with steak and baked potatoes.

He was still laughing when she interrupted him. "I need to take him home, to the vet. Now. Today."

Soldier wiped his eyes. His dark lashes were damp and spiked from his tears of laughter. "Why? Is he sick or something?"

"No. It's just that, well, when I got back from the workshop, I found him inside the refrigerator. He was terribly cold and frightened. If I hadn't returned when I did, he might have suffocated or died from exposure."

Subtly, Soldier's demeanor changed. He glanced at the minifridge. "I have one of those in my room, too," he said. "You must have left the door open when you went out."

"No, I didn't. I haven't opened the thing at all since I've been here."

He stood and walked to the small unit, its door still sitting open. Pushing it closed, he reopened it and looked inside. Settling down on one knee, he examined the rubber rim around the door's frame.

"The unit is sitting level, so I don't understand how it could have closed on its own. And I don't see any scratches to indicate the dog somehow got it open." He ran his fingers across the inside edge of the door. "The magnet that keeps it closed isn't that strong. No matter how he got in or how the door somehow closed on him, he should have been able to push it open and get out."

Betsy sat on the bed, the blanket and the dog still bundled in her arms. She stared at Soldier for a moment, trying to remember something. Glancing around the room, she spotted the phone book. "Oh! He couldn't push it open because the phone book had fallen—"

She stopped. Now that she'd had time to think about it, she realized something about the phone book wasn't right.

Soldier's sharp eyes narrowed on her. "What?"

Betsy shook her head in denial. It must have just been an accident. The maid knocked it over, or it was on the edge and just fell. It couldn't really be that . . .

"When I left, the telephone book was on the desk, not on the nightstand." Her voice trembled. She battled for control as she spoke the horrible words out loud. "Somebody must have put Piddle in the refrigerator and stuck the phone book in front of the door to make sure he couldn't get out."

Soldier stood and walked toward Betsy, but her eyes remained glued on the phone book sitting innocently on the mauve and gray carpet. Slowly, he sat down beside her, his weight dipping the mattress, subtly easing her body toward his.

"Why would anybody put your dog in the refrigerator, Betsy? Who could have done this?"

She lifted her chin and looked up at him. His brows were knit in concern, and he seemed angry for some reason. His cool eyes searched hers as if he could find some answers there. Betsy's throat felt tight, like she had a rock lodged in her breathing passage. She swallowed around it.

True terror hit her like a bullet to the heart. "He must have followed me here," she blurted. "It's the only explanation! The *phone* calls. I didn't tell Winslow about the phone calls. They came before. I didn't think anything of them. And then there came the note that night you sent me the e-mail. And the weird stuff at work! I didn't tell him about that either. I thought it didn't really mean anything. I . . . I was hoping it didn't mean anything. I even thought it might be you, when I saw you, because you were staring at me. And you were so attractive and everything, and I didn't think that you were interested in me, you know like, just for *me*. And then you told me you had seen my picture, and I was terrified. But you didn't know who I was, not until you read my name tag, so it wasn't you after all. But—But if *he* followed me, and if *he* did this to my mother's dog—"

"Betsy," Soldier interrupted sharply. "Calm yourself. It's okay. You're okay."

She'd been babbling. The man must think her a complete moron. But the impact of what was happening to her, what was *really* happening to her, was almost more than her rational mind could bear.

Betsy pinched her eyes tightly closed and took a deep breath. After a moment she lifted her face to Soldier and let her eyes search his.

Desperately pushing down the well of anger and fear rising from the pit of her stomach, she whispered, "This can't be happening. I don't *accept* this. I don't believe this. I am not, not, *not* being stalked!"

Soldier moved closer. Gently taking her by the shoulders, he turned her body toward his. "Betsy." His voice was calm yet commanding. She looked into his face and wanted to speak, but instead closed her eyes and pressed her lips tightly together.

She felt Soldier's fingers trail from her shoulder up to cup her cheek softly in his warm palm. Through her haze of hysteria she heard his voice.

"Who is not stalking you, Betsy? What note?" She raised her lashes to see Soldier looking deeply into her eyes. "Tell me everything."

Chapter 4

Soldier hadn't meant to touch her, but she looked so vulnerable and alone that he had reached for her without thinking. And now he was thinking about how he could pull his hand away without missing the silky feel of her skin too much.

In her arms, the blanket twitched, the tiny dog still shivering and terrified from his Nordic ordeal. Every so often he would whimper or let out a muffled yelp, but so far he'd kept his head down and his body as close to Betsy's breasts as he could get.

Lucky mutt.

Soldier put his lusty thoughts aside as Betsy told him about the note stuck under the dog's collar, the police officer instructing her on taking precautions, and how she had come back to her room only to find her dog imprisoned in the refrigerator.

"I'm probably just being paranoid," she said through a half laugh. "I mean, I'm nobody special.

Why would somebody stalk me? This is all just coincidence, right?"

Her mouth formed the words, but her true feelings were plain to see in her big, beautiful hazel eyes. She didn't want to believe she was in danger, but she was smart enough to realize that denying it wouldn't make it go away.

I'm nobody special, she'd said. *Wrong,* he thought. She was more special than she could possibly know.

Reaching behind him, Soldier retrieved the phone and picked up the receiver.

"Wh-Who are you calling?"

"Hotel security," he said as he punched the O button.

"Oh. Thanks. I don't know what's the matter with me. I don't seem to be thinking straight."

He could see that she was scared, and she had every right to be. Stalking was nothing to be taken lightly, and even though she had been aware and taken precautions, the guy still managed to get near her. Too near.

Betsy Tremaine was the typical stalking victim. She was attractive and she was nice. Approachable. Attainable. Not so beautiful that a guy felt he didn't stand a chance, but pretty enough to capture someone's imagination to the point of obsession.

Obsession was one thing, but this guy had put her dog in the refrigerator. An aggressive act, one that might have ended with the dog's death. Did he mean it as a lesson to her? Had he meant to frighten her, make her feel vulnerable, as though he could get to her anytime he wanted?

Probably.

As he waited to be connected, Soldier let his gaze slide all over Betsy Tremaine. She'd removed her hat, allowing him a view of her shiny blond hair. It was thick and streaked with honey and sunshine. The shorter cut framed her face. She was still wearing the outfit from this morning, and the little diamond drops in her lobes reflected the afternoon light as she moved her head. Clutching that blanket to her breasts the way she was, she looked like a pretty young woman holding her baby, and Soldier immediately got a picture in his head that he wasn't sure he wanted.

He wasn't sure he didn't want it, either.

After a brief conversation with the Crowne Plaza's manager, Soldier hung up the phone. "They're on their way," he said, but Betsy only nodded.

A few minutes later hotel security arrived at the door in the form of one Walter Lemsky. Lemsky was a tall, thin man, a former Chicago cop. He had sharp black eyes that looked like they didn't miss much. The two men shook hands and Soldier introduced himself.

"Yeah, I reco'nize you," Lemsky said as he released Soldier's hand. His nasally voice was gruff, the flat tones pure Chicago. "You're with the Seattle PD," he continued. "Robbery and Homicide, right? Read your books." Soldier noted the man said he'd *read* his books, not that he'd *liked* them. Christ, everybody was a critic.

Lemsky was cordial and gentle with Betsy, asking her questions and taking notes. He'd apparently already requested that the day maid, Mrs. Fionorelli, be sent up, for a few minutes later the woman appeared at the door, meekly entering the room.

The maid's answers to Lemsky's questions were brief but certain. *Sì*, the dog had been in the room when she'd cleaned it. *No*, she hadn't let anybody in. *No*, she most certainly had not put the *piccolo cane* in *il frigorifero!*

The poor woman appeared genuinely appalled at what had happened to the animal, and looked at Betsy with concern in her eyes.

The computer printout listed the times the door had been keyed open. The times matched both Betsy's and Housekeeping's estimates. The lock had not been forced, and no unauthorized entries had been made.

"Mrs. Fionorelli?"

The maid gazed up at Soldier with fear and wariness in her faded brown eyes. Her white hair was pulled back and knotted at the nape. The uniform she wore was clean and she was tidy, but the job of hotel maid could not have been an easy one for a woman of her years. Soldier thought of that old song, *She works hard for her money . . .* And now she was practically being accused of trying to harm a guest's dog.

"Mrs. Fionorelli, when you clean, do you close the door while you're in the room?"

She shook her head. "No, *signore*. I leave the door open to get *puliti i tovaglioli*, eh, the clean towels, you say, from my cart. Empty the trash, *sì?* Like that? But always, I am careful of the *piccolo cane*."

"When you were in the room, where was the dog, the *piccolo cane?*"

Her eyes widened and she clasped her hands in a nervous gesture. "He runs under the bed when I come in, *signore*. He stays there and, eh, does the growl to me the whole time I am here, but he does not bite me. He just stays under the bed, yes?"

Soldier looked around the room. The proximity of the door and the closet were such that, with her back turned to make the bed, the maid wouldn't have seen anyone slipping through the door and into the closet.

"Mrs. Fionorelli, did you open the closet door while you were here?"

"No, *signore.*"

He asked her a few more questions, then dismissed her. On her way to the door, she patted Betsy's arm. *"Sono molto spiacente per le vostre difficoltà, mancanza."*

Betsy smiled. *"Grazie, signora."*

"You speak Italian?" Soldier asked.

"I saw *The Godfather* three times."

"Well, that just about makes you fluent." He gazed into her eyes, but she glanced away, then lowered her head.

Lemsky sat on the desk chair while Soldier walked to the window. The drapes were open now and he could see all the way down to Pike Place Market. Beyond the rooftops and chimneys were the cold waters of Puget Sound. The sun formed a hazy disk in the sky, quiet declaration to the day's impending decline.

"We can try to get some latents from inside the closet," Soldier said to no one in particular, "but I'm willing to bet we won't find anything we can use."

"I agree," Lemsky said. Looking around, he puffed his cheeks then let out a breath. "Okay. Perp comes in while the maid's busy. Hides in the closet until she leaves. Grabs the mutt, shoves it into the fridge. Then, when the coast is clear, he hightails it. Exits aren't keyed, so his departure don't show up on the computer."

"And the maid didn't hear him come in," Betsy said, "because Piddle was growling the whole time. Even if he had been aware of an intruder, the maid wouldn't have paid any attention since she thought he was growling at her."

As Soldier turned, his gaze was met by Betsy's worried stare.

"But the question is, why? Why on earth would someone sneak into my room and put my dog in the refrigerator? I don't get it at *all*."

Soldier moved to the bed and sat near her. He could see confusion and frustration in her eyes, but he didn't have any solutions to offer her. "It's been my experience," he said, "that stalkers have their own reasons for doing what they do, and it seldom makes sense to anyone but themselves."

"Do you think it's the same guy? The one that wrote me the note?"

"Yeah, I'm afraid I do. I'm not much on coincidences."

Soldier rose from the bed. "I'm going to call this in," he said. "Maybe they can get some useful prints, but this is a hotel room. There are probably thousands of prints all over the place."

"Detective McKennitt?" Lemsky indicated with a nod of his head he wanted to have a word out of Betsy's earshot. She had her face buried in the blanket, cooing to the mutt, so Soldier followed the security man outside.

Lemsky leaned close to Soldier in a conspiratorial manner. "I sure don't like this," he said under his breath. "I mean, this kinda gives me the creeps. She's a real nice lady. I don't like to think of what this guy might try next."

Soldier felt his entire body go rigid. He didn't like to think of what the guy might try next, either.

Lemsky tilted his head down and raised both brows. "It probably ain't none of my business, but, uh, you gotta thing for the lady?"

"What do you mean?"

Lemsky shrugged his shoulders. "Hey, pal," he whispered, "I'm a cop, too. I been attracted to my share of lady victims over the years. There was this one gal, bee-u-ti-ful. A real sweetheart. She was a witness to a murder. I was assigned—"

"We should discuss jurisdiction," Soldier interrupted. "As far as I can tell, no crime has been committed. I have no real evidence that anybody put the dog in the refrigerator, even though we both pretty much know somebody did. But with no evidence of a crime, there's no crime scene. No crime scene means no jurisdiction. My hands are tied, leaving security in the hotel's hands."

Lemsky lifted his chin. "Okay, then. But because I got the same gut feeling you got, I'm going to have to assign somebody to stick with her while she's a guest in the hotel. That's why I asked if you had a thing for the lady."

Soldier pursed his lips. He blinked, and in that flash of darkness saw Betsy's pretty face, her smooth cheek, soft mouth. He saw her glaring at him as though he were the lowest life-form on the planet, the sparkle in her eyes as she challenged him. He glimpsed the white column of her throat and his own mouth on it. And in his head, he heard her soft moans as she wrapped her naked legs around his hips.

Studying the carpet at his feet, he blew out a breath. "Whether I have a thing for the lady isn't the issue here. Her safety is." Raising his head, Soldier met Lemsky's stare. "But I'll, uh, I'll watch over her while she's here at the conference."

A knowing glint flared from Lemsky's eyes. "But it'll be official business. Nothing personal."

"No. Nothing personal. She's the potential victim of a crime, and I'm her watchdog."

The hotel detective snickered and shook his head. As he started to move away, Soldier's words stopped him.

"Tell me something, Lemsky," he said. "That murder witness in Chicago?"

Lemsky nodded.

"So, what happened to your *bee-u-ti-ful* lady victim?"

Lemsky's face split into a wide grin. "Who, Gracie?" He chuckled. "I married her. Twenty years, three kids. Life's good." He winked. "Gotta watch out for dem cute ones, pal."

By that evening, things had settled down a bit. The fingerprint guys had come and gone, Soldier had ordered Betsy some food, and her dog had thawed from pupsicle to room temperature and seemed none the worse for wear. As for Betsy herself, she had been distracted and flustered and had clung to the small animal as though he were a life buoy that would save her from going under.

Soldier had wanted to put her in another room, but because of the conference, every vacancy in the hotel was filled. He'd quietly arranged to trade his room on the fourth floor for Betsy's on the third, but she was reluctant to do so at first. The independent little wench.

It took some doing, but he was finally able to convince her that she'd be safer in his room, under his name, and nobody would know of the switch except for the two of them and Lemsky.

Now, sitting on the edge of the king-sized bed in his former room, Soldier watched Betsy unpack her suitcase with one hand while holding the mutt in the other.

Soldier raised his arms. Wiggling his fingers in a come-to-papa gesture, he addressed Betsy. "Hey. Why don't you give me the dog so you can rest? I'll take Piddle with me and go down to your room. You can get some sleep."

"No, thanks," she said. "I'll just hang onto him for a while."

"Betsy," he cajoled. "A dog that small must have a bladder the size of a Rice Krispie. It's been hours. Why don't you let me take him out?"

She stopped unpacking and nodded her head. "Oh. You're right. I wasn't thinking."

He rose from the bed and took the dog, leaving her looking lost and bereft.

"By the time I get back," he said softly, "dinner should be up. After we eat, I'd like to ask you a few questions."

"Wh-What kind of questions?"

Can I sleep with you tonight? And tomorrow night? And the night after that? "We'll talk about it later. Lock the door behind me. Don't let anybody in except me or Lemsky. I'll only be gone a few minutes."

Betsy locked the door and peered through the fish-eye to see Soldier's distorted figure disappear from view.

What in the hell was she doing? She didn't even know this man, and now she was staying in his room? In frustration, she ran her fingers through her hair as she paced the carpet. She felt like a caged animal who had once known freedom and wasn't prepared to accept her change in circumstances.

Fury curdled her blood at how she had to change her schedule, her very life, to keep herself safe from a complete *stranger.*

In frustration, she fell onto the bed on her stomach and opened her purse, digging through it until she found her notebook. She would call Paris. She *needed* to call Paris. It would be very early morning there, so hopefully her adventuress mother would be in her own bed in her own hotel room.

It took a few minutes to make the connection, but finally a sleepy female voice said, *"Oui?"*

"Loretta? Loretta, it's me, Elizabeth."

There was a moment of silence while the woman on the other end of the line obviously came a little more awake. For a moment it sounded as though she pressed her hand over the receiver and spoke in French to someone in the room. She must have removed her hand, because abruptly Loretta Tremaine's strident voice came through loud and clear.

"Elizabeth! Why are you calling? Is everything all right there? Is it my Pids? Has something happened to Piddle?"

Betsy swallowed her instant regret. Things never changed. Loretta . . . never changed. If she had expected maternal words of comfort, the joke was on her. Again.

But she had wanted, needed, to hear her mother's voice. With Daddy out of the picture, there was only her mother. It had always been a contentious relationship, but it was the only one Betsy had.

"Actually, everything's fine, Loretta. I just wanted to see if you're having a good time. Um, are you alone?"

"Oh, that was just Richard," she said in a light, dismissive tone. She did not elaborate. "Elizabeth, darling. It's four in the morning here." Her voice deepened. Betsy recognized that tone. It was Loretta's attempt at being a Concerned Mother. "If it's not Mummy's doggie, then what is it? Have you been in an accident?" She gasped. "They didn't let your father out by mistake again, did they? Dammit, don't they realize he's a danger—"

"No, no, nothing like that," Betsy said through a strained laugh. "The thing is, Loretta . . . well, it's possible I'm being stalked. I've received some odd phone calls and a note, and today, at the writer's conference, somebody broke into my room."

She didn't dare tell her mother how close her dog

had come to being a frigid fatality. "Detective McKennitt—"

"McKennitt? McKennitt . . . McKennitt. Oh, yes, now I remember. The one you wrote that deliciously scathing review about last year?"

"Yes, well, he has a new book out now, but, well, never mind. It's more that—"

"Now, Elizabeth. I rather liked his book. By his writing, he seems rather manly," she purred. "Is he a manly man, Elizabeth?"

"Yes, Loretta. Infinitely manly. But the point is—"

"Well," scoffed Loretta, "stalking. I'm speechless." That would be the day. "Are you sure you're not just imagining all this? I mean, you've always had an overactive imagination. Perhaps the stress of being rejected by so many men has finally caught up with you, poor darling. Perhaps—"

Hot tears burned the corners of Betsy's eyes. Keeping her voice as steady as possible, she said, "I'm so sorry to have disturbed you, Loretta. I've got to go now. Really, I'm fine."

"You're *not* fine. You're being stalked, or some such thing. What kind of *maman* would I be if I didn't worry so over my little chick? What's that detective's name again, the illiterate Neanderthal you despise?"

"Soldier McKennitt. But—"

"You say he's watching out for you?"

"Yes."

"But he's not the one stalking you."

"No."

There was a pregnant pause. "Is he as good-looking as he sounds?"

Betsy resisted the urge to scream. "I repeat. He's *manly,* Loretta. A manly man. Naked gladiators should be so manly. He's tall. He's dark. He's got blue eyes. He's handsome as they come. Broad shoulders, perfect teeth, long, muscular legs. Beautiful . . ."

She was going to say that Soldier had beautiful hands, but that would be too personal. She wanted to keep that part for herself. He had touched her with his beautiful hands, and it might never happen again.

Betsy recalled the gentleness of his touch, the warmth of his fingers as he caressed her cheek and talked to her when she'd been so afraid. No, she would keep his beautiful hands in her own memory and not give it away so frivolously to a woman who would neither understand nor care.

"Loretta," she sighed. "Go back to sleep."

"Well, all right. Now, you're to call me if anything juicy should happen. Don't do anything foolish, and *do* listen to your detective." Only Loretta Tremaine would give a daughter advice that involved the use of the word *juicy*.

"He's not *my* detective, Loretta," Betsy insisted. "He's not my anything." But her protests met only silence. Her mother had already hung up.

Soldier was careful not to be seen on his return trip from the small park across the street from the hotel. The dog had lived up to his name on every bush and blade of grass, and Soldier had to grudgingly give the little guy credit. He'd held it in for a long time, through his near-death experience and for hours afterward when Betsy had cradled him close. Who would have thought a dog named Piddle would have an iron bladder?

Glancing up and down the empty hallway as he slid the plastic key into the lock, he pushed the door open and quickly entered. The bathroom door was shut and he could hear water running.

Soldier grimaced. A shower might do Betsy some good, but the thought of all that hot water sluicing over her naked body didn't help reduce his lust at all. The poor woman had enough trouble without her bodyguard coming on to her.

The last thing she needed was his hands running all over her flesh, kissing her soft, plump skin.

No, she didn't need that, but he sure as hell did.

Shaking the images from his brain, he sprawled on the bed and made a grab for the phone. After three rings, Taylor answered.

"Hey, Tayo. How's it hangin'?"

"Long and low, brother, long and low. How's the conference?" He could hear Taylor munching on something that sounded like a potato chip.

Soldier let his gaze wander to the closed bathroom door. "There's been an interesting development here."

"Yeah? Don't tell me, don't tell me! You fell for the lovely Ms. Tremaine and now you're going to elope to Niagara Falls?" He snickered into the receiver.

"As a matter of fact, she is here, and I did meet her."

Taylor choked on his potato chip. "You are shitting me! That's great! Did you give her hell? Did you rough her up a little? Do you need bail money?"

"Uh, no. No bail, but—"

"So what's she look like? Is she wartless?"

"Totally."

Taylor's voice rose a notch. "She's young, isn't she? And pretty, I'll bet? And you fell for her, didn't you? Ha! Son of a freakin' bitch! I can't believe it!" He started to howl with laughter.

Soldier realized that the shower in the bathroom had stopped. She'd be out in a few minutes, so he had to make this quick. "This is serious, Taylor. Somebody tried to whack her Chihuahua."

A momentary pause. "Whack her Chihuahua? Sounds kinky. Is that what the kids are calling it these days? Hey, have *you* whacked her—"

"Shut up, you numbnuts! *Listen.* I'm certain Betsy Tremaine is being stalked. The guy has made two direct contacts. He left her a note, then broke into her room here at the conference. She's in the initial impact and denial phase, but pretty soon it's going to hit her like a freight train and she's going to implode. I'm going to try to get her to let me take her home."

Taylor's voice became solemn as the cop in him snapped to. "What do you want me to do?"

"I'm going to interview her tonight to get as much down as I can, then I'm going to send you an e-mail with all the data. I want you to get your ass up to Port Henry and run some checks."

"What? Is the Seattle PD closed for repairs or something? Why me?"

"Because you're off this weekend, and this is all still unofficial. We've got nothing."

There was silence on the other end of the line for a few seconds. "Sure, big brother. But can't the cops in Port Henry handle this?"

"No."

A moment passed. Finally, "You want to tell me about it?"

Soldier closed his eyes and thought for a moment. "It's hard to explain. She's . . . she's not what I expected."

As though timing her entrance perfectly, Betsy emerged from the bathroom in a cloud of steam. She absently toweled her hair as she smiled down at the dog nipping at her toes. Her cheeks were pink from scrubbing, her plush lips curved into a gentle smile. She wore an old-fashioned flannel nightgown that had tiny pink flowers all over it and lace at the neckline and wrists. Though it covered her from her chin to her ankles and revealed absolutely nothing, it was the sexiest nightgown Soldier had ever seen.

"Jack? Hello? Hey, you're not falling for this woman, are you? Jackson?"

Chapter 5

"I've gone twenty-eight years without being interrogated by the police. I see no reason to start now, especially over something so silly." Betsy took a sip of the steaming hot chocolate Soldier had ordered for her from room service. She was hoping it would settle her nerves, but it wasn't working.

They were seated in his hotel room at a small table near the window. Piddle lay curled in her lap, deep in doggie slumber. It was nearly eleven o'clock and she was exhausted, but the detective wanted to get some information from her to pass on to his brother, who was apparently also a cop.

Soldier looked up from his laptop computer. "Not interrogated. Interviewed. There's a difference," he stated. He looked just as tired as she felt, but where her energy levels were waning, his seemed to be revving up.

The Seattle investigators had come in and taken some fingerprints from inside the closet, the closet door, the minifridge, and a few other places. Soldier didn't seem to hold out much hope of finding any kind of match, but then, you never could tell, as the saying goes.

He'd asked her a few more questions, but since she was not a resident of Seattle and would be returning home in a few days, there wasn't much more he could do except file a report.

Across from her now, Soldier McKennitt's face was unreadable as he prepared to interview her. Every aspect of her life would be keyed into his computer. *To know the victim is to know the criminal,* he'd said.

She let the warmth from the mug she held infuse her palms as she regarded Soldier. His fingers moved over the keyboard as he entered information about her into the database.

She had decided she wouldn't answer his questions. He couldn't make her do this. There was no official investigation going on. He'd even told her that no actual crime had been committed.

While in the shower, she'd determined that she wasn't really being stalked. No way, no how. She also decided she was sorry she had dragged her mother into it. That, as usual, was a given. She'd call her mother in the morning and set things straight.

"Soldier?"

"Hmm?" He didn't look up, but kept typing.

"Soldier, I don't think . . . I mean, I don't want to do this. It's not necessary."

The rapid clicking stopped as his fingers stilled on the keyboard. He raised his gaze to meet hers. "It *is* necessary."

The words hung between them as the seconds passed. Betsy lowered her lashes, focusing on the chocolate froth at the bottom of her cup. Her stomach was tied in a thousand little knots. Her nerves were stretched from Seattle to Port Henry and beyond. Her mind was thick with uncertainty. The decision she'd made was about the only thing over which she had any kind of control.

"I just want to go home. I'm not being stalked. I . . . I just want to go home and have everything be normal again."

There, she'd said it. Calmly, rationally, concisely. She would return to Port Henry and life would go on as it had before. To think she was being stalked was ridiculous. In a few months she would look back and have a huge laugh at how silly she'd been.

Soldier had changed his clothes and was now wearing jeans and a long-sleeve black T-shirt. She tried not to stare, but looking at him made her feel good. He seemed so self-assured, comfortable in his own skin, and so nice to look at, she was having trouble concentrating. At her remarks, he'd pushed himself away from the table and crossed his arms over his chest. Betsy had never been in the presence of a man so wholly sexy that she had trouble focusing on the matter at hand. She forced herself not to sigh.

Just who was she kidding, anyway? A man like Soldier McKennitt would never give a plain little nobody like her the time of day. The thought made her feel depressed, and she suddenly felt like crying. *Uh-oh, here they came. The tears.*

Fear, intimidation, loss of control, sexual attraction, possible rejection . . . all churned together in her mind, and she knew she was very close to losing it.

Her eyes stinging, Betsy tried to look away, but Soldier had seen. He leaned forward and cupped his hands around hers, still wrapped around the mug.

"What you're feeling is normal, Betsy. It's a common human reaction to a situation like this. First, you're certain it's all a mistake. Then, you start to feel it's true. But your mind begins working overtime on it and you convince yourself you're being silly. You vacillate until the next encounter, and even then you have trouble believing it's happening. Nobody likes to believe they are the victim of a stalker."

"I'm not being stalked."

"The evidence is there, Betsy. Sure, there's no physical proof yet, but I feel you're in danger . . . and you feel it, too."

"No. A stupid note, that's all. Nothing else has happened."

"Something else did happen. Somebody put your dog in the—"

Betsy pulled her hands away. "No. I can't accept that. Piddle s-somehow got himself into the refrigerator. I've been thinking about it, and I'm sure it's just . . . it was just . . ."

Just what? She didn't have a good explanation, but she was damn sure she wasn't being stalked.

With a heavy sigh, she stood, lifting the sleeping dog into her arms. "I'm tired. I want to go to bed now. You'll have to leave." She refused to meet Soldier's eyes.

He stood and placed his hands on her shoulders.

"All right. We can do this in the morning, after you've rested." His tone seemed resigned. She knew he didn't want to let her go to sleep now; he wanted to do the damn interview. But she had another plan in mind, a plan that didn't include detectives or interviews or hotel security guards or nonexistent stalkers.

Soldier knew it just as sure as he knew his own name: she was going to bolt.

It had been a long day, and he felt dead on his feet, but as long as Betsy Tremaine had that "I'm outta here" look in her eyes, he had to stay awake and alert. Glancing at his watch, the dim hallway light revealed it was nearing three o'clock in the morning. Any minute now.

As predicted, he heard the knob turn, the hinge creak, felt the little suck of air as the door swung open.

He'd positioned himself in a chair in the hallway, his legs stretched out before him, his arms crossed over his chest. The door opened a little more, and slowly she poked her head out. She looked to the left and opened the door a bit more. She looked to the right, directly into Soldier's eyes.

The shock that registered on her face was well worth his having stayed up half the night waiting for her to make a break for it.

He'd known the minute she decided to run. He'd seen the flicker of decision and determination in her eyes, and knew she was still deeply in denial and would go to ground, thinking herself safe. But she wasn't safe. Every nerve in his body told him so.

Admittedly, there wasn't a whole hell of a lot to go

on, but the little prickles on the back of his neck warned him she was in real danger. She probably knew it, too, which was why she was fighting so hard to ignore it.

Now, she had the dog carrier in one hand and her suitcase in the other. The expression on her face told the rest of the story. Betsy Tremaine was furious.

"What are you doing here?" she snapped. "You shouldn't be here. Go away. Get out of my life. I promise I'll never review another book of yours. You're the best author I've *ever* read. Pulitzer prize material. Now go *away*."

Soldier let her babble, and watched helplessly as the hysteria began to overtake her.

She tried to move past him and into the hall, but he stood and gently guided her back into the room. Closing the door, he made sure it was locked before turning to her.

She was trembling, her eyes huge and glassy. He could see she was nearing an emotional breakdown, so he didn't say anything. Taking the dog carrier from her and grasping her suitcase, he moved past her to set the dog on the bed and the suitcase on the floor. "You need rest," he said, his back to her.

Behind him, he heard her rapid breathing. Any second now she was going to collapse.

Just as he turned, she put her face in her hands and began to cry. He moved to her and put his arms around her, pulling her close. "Shhh. It's all right, sweetheart. It's all right. You'll get through this. I promise. I won't let anyone hurt you."

Betsy's face was smashed against his shoulder, her

sobs wrenching, heartbreaking. She wrapped her arms around his waist and let herself melt into him, using him for strength and support. He didn't mind. She'd been holding her emotions in check since receiving the note last week. All through the evening, with security and police and interviews and fingerprinting, she'd stayed calm, steady, focused on the tasks at hand.

And now the time had come for her to let it all go.

Soldier rested his cheek on the top of her head. Her hair smelled like flowers and felt like silk. She was one sweet and sexy little bundle, and the feelings of protection she garnered in him were unlike anything he'd ever felt before.

After a few minutes, the sobs eased up a bit and she sniffed into his shirt. Reaching into his jeans pocket, he pulled out a clean handkerchief and shoved it under her nose. One hand came up to grab it.

Dabbing her eyes, she lifted her face to him. "I'm s-sorry," she stammered.

"Blow your nose."

Releasing her hold on him, she did as he instructed. "I didn't know men still carried cloth handkerchiefs around anymore. I'll wash this and return it to you."

He smiled down at her. "You can keep it. I have more." Betsy still stood in the circle of his arms, and he made no move to step away from her.

"I don't know what came over me," she said, her voice hoarse from crying, her nose stuffy. "I'm sorry. I got tears all over your shirt." She placed her palm over his heart, where the fabric was soaked. Her hand was warm and he could feel its heat against his skin. Anyone watching would have assumed they were in an intimate embrace. He liked that. He liked her.

Betsy's dark lashes were spiky and damp, her cheeks rosy. She kept licking her lips as she stood against him, unmoving, apparently considering what to do or say next.

"I'm afraid," she whispered. "I don't want to be, but I am. I . . . I have always been able to take care of myself, do whatever I needed to make my life work. I've never had any enemies. But this . . . this is so unexpected. And so frightening. I don't know what to think. What to do."

She paused for a moment as though searching for the right words. "Honestly, I don't know where to turn."

She blinked and looked up at him. The trust and pain he saw there made his heart lurch.

Now he was in real trouble.

"Goddammit," he ground out through clenched teeth. Her hazel eyes widened and she looked more innocent than any woman had a right to look. He pulled her closer. "Just remember I tried. I tried to keep this from happening."

"Keep what . . . ?"

He lowered his head and took her mouth. Her reflexive gasp parted her lips, and he took full advantage. Tightening his arms around her, he pulled her closer yet and kissed her deeply, his tongue sliding against hers, his mouth savoring the softness of her lips. Inside his chest, he felt his heart pound in a crazy rhythm. His breathing turned to panting.

For an instant, Soldier pulled back and looked

down into her face. Her mouth was wet and swollen, her plush lips more inviting than ever. Slowly, he bent his head again, giving her plenty of time to turn away.

But she didn't. Instead, she slipped her arms around his neck and pushed herself up on her toes, offering him her mouth once more. He took it.

These weren't the searching, tentative kisses of new lovers. He didn't go slowly to learn her mouth, but delved deeply into her sweetness as he pressed his hard body into her soft curves. Beneath her clothing, Soldier could feel her full breasts pushing against his chest, her hips, flush against his groin. His extremely rigid groin.

It was nearly four in the morning. The sun would be coming up in a few hours, lightening the room with its pink softness. In his mind's eye he saw Betsy naked on the bed. He saw himself tracing every inch of her body. As the early morning glow licked her skin, so did his tongue.

He slipped his hands down her back to grasp the firm globes of her bottom through her skirt. Pulling her hard into him, he nearly went crazy with desire. His brain shut down and all he could do was feel the heat pounding in his loins.

Abruptly, he became aware that Betsy was squirming. He broke the kiss and stood away from her.

She looked confused and terrified.

Raising his palms in a "hang on a minute" gesture, he tried to regain some measure of control. "I didn't mean for that to happen." He searched her wide eyes. "No, that's a lie. I've been wanting to do that ever since I met you, and I'm not going to apologize for it.

But I won't do it again unless you want me to. You do want me to, don't you? Because I really want to."

Betsy's look went from terrified to shocked. Slowly, her eyes narrowed on him and the hint of a smile tilted one corner of her mouth. Her pink, swollen mouth. But before she could say anything, the phone beside the bed began to ring.

She jumped like she'd just been shot. In two strides he was past her. With one hand lingering on her arm, he picked up the receiver with the other. "McKennitt."

He strained to listen, but was met with only silence. Was the caller still there or had they been disconnected? "Who's there?" he said. "Hello?"

"You can try and protect the little bitch, McKennitt, but it won't do any good. I'll win. I always win." The voice had been electronically altered. There was no telling the age or sex.

"Who is this?" Hey, it never hurt to ask.

"I know she's in your room. I know everything."

"Why are you doing this?"

The caller laughed. "You're the detective. You figure it out."

Betsy could still taste Soldier on her mouth. She could feel his hands roaming her body, and knew she wanted more. Her heart beat rapidly and her fingers curled into tense fists as she stood watching him talk on the phone.

His hand was still on her arm, his eyes locked with hers. As he spoke, he kept her frozen in place with a penetrating stare.

Soldier placed the phone back in its cradle. Tugging gently on her arm, he said, "Come sit down."

His cell phone lay on the nightstand. He picked it up and punched in some numbers.

Betsy sat on the edge of the bed, never taking her eyes off him.

"Yeah, this is McKennitt. I want a trace . . ."

He gave whomever he was talking to the information, then slapped the phone closed and replaced it on the nightstand.

As Soldier lowered his body to sit next to her, he moved his hands to cup her shoulders, turning her to face him. She already knew what he was going to say.

"It was him."

"You must think I'm pretty dim not to have figured that one out." She was proud at how calm her voice sounded. She blinked several times in rapid succession, then tried to bring her tattered emotions under control. "So," she said, a little louder than she had intended. "Wh-What did he say?"

Soldier released her shoulders but continued looking into her eyes. "Basically, he warned me that protecting you wouldn't do any good, which is a lie, by the way. He also said that he knew '*everything*,' whatever that means."

"Did you recognize the voice?"

Soldier shook his head. "No. He was using a voice transformer."

"I thought only guys in creepy movies used those things."

"Not anymore. They're cheap, easy to use. Anybody can buy one. But that's okay, he told me a lot, whether he realizes it or not. By calling, and actually speaking, he's being more aggressive. He's accelerating his plans. He's probably somebody you know, although it may only be a man you've met once. Today, at the conference, did you see anybody at all that you recognized? Anyone from Port Henry or someone you may have met casually at one time?"

"No. No one." Her head was beginning to ache like hell. Lack of sleep, not eating, stress . . . they were all beginning to take their toll. "So," she sighed, "what happens next?"

"I call my captain to let him know the UNSUB—or unknown subject—has made contact, even though the guy didn't make any outright threats and didn't do anything illegal. I've already requested a check on the phone records, but I'm pretty sure they won't find anything we can use."

"Well, as long as everything's under control. I feel so much better now."

Soldier smiled, making his dark lashes tangle together at the crinkly corners of his eyes. "That's my girl," he said. "Keep that sense of humor. You're going to need it."

She lifted her chin. "I'm not your girl."

He leaned forward, settling his elbows on his knees, and looked deeply into her eyes. She thought he was going to say something. It was there, in his eyes, then he blinked and the look disappeared.

They stared at each other as the moments ticked by. Betsy's heart kicked violently against her rib cage as she tried to keep her breathing even. He was too confident, too sure of himself, too . . . everything. And she was in no mood to fight him. And she was too stubborn to give in.

Folding her hands in her lap, she asked, "So, are you going to be assigned to my case, officially?"

"That's what I'm going to ask my captain, yes."

"Haven't you been on some kind of leave or something?"

"Yes."

"Why?"

Soldier stood and walked to the window. He drew open the curtains. The first, weak light of morning cast a soft glow on his brow and cheek, the line of his jaw, the strength of his neck.

He turned his back to her, giving Betsy a chance to admire his broad shoulders and tight, excellent buns. Sure, he'd kissed the hell out of her, but in the long run this man would never settle for plain ol' Betsy Tremaine from Port Henry, Washington. Oh, he might sleep with her, have a brief affair with her, but he'd move on.

As he looked out the window, he reached up and rubbed the back of his neck. "There isn't much to the story," he said. "My partner was killed and I was accused of arranging his murder." He placed his hand on the window, splaying his fingers against the glass. Beyond his tapered fingertips, Betsy could see the deep green of Puget Sound, the early morning fog giving the view a surrealistic quality.

"I nailed the killer," he said. "The guy had not only murdered Marc, but had tried to set me up to take the fall for it. I was really pissed off that I'd even briefly come under suspicion." He shrugged. "And then there was the fact that Marc had left behind a widow and two little kids. So, I've been riding a desk for the last few months instead of being out there on the street."

"You feel guilty, about your partner's death?"

"Yes."

"Even though it wasn't your fault?"

Silence.

"When are you going back, you know, full-time, to being a detective?"

He moved away from the window and came to stand directly in front of her. Lifting a lock of her hair, he twirled it around his finger. A moment later he let the curl go and shoved his hands in his jeans pockets.

With a shy grin and a sparkle in his eye, all he said was, "Today."

Chapter 6

Betsy had been holed up in Soldier's room since the night before, and it was now nearing noon on Friday. After another conversation with Lemsky, Soldier had sent an e-mail to his brother, ordered lunch, wolfed down that same lunch like a man who hadn't eaten for a week, then hopped into the shower.

He'd warned her that when he emerged from the bathroom, they were going to do that interview whether she liked it or not. She was not looking forward to documenting her entire life, or at least the last six months of it, for the benefit of J. Soldier McKennitt, but apparently it had to be done.

He would log the information she gave him and forward it to his brother, who was going to meet them in Port Henry. Soldier and Taylor McKennitt, also a detective and the occasional police sketch artist, would work with the Port Henry Police Department to try to put a name and a face to the voice Soldier had heard on the phone.

Soldier had assured her it was not going to be an easy task.

"Ready?"

Betsy nearly jumped out of her skin at his question. She'd been deep into her own thoughts and hadn't heard him finish up in the bathroom. "I'd rather have a root canal," she stated primly.

Standing over her, he seemed so tall and strong, as though just his mere presence would keep her from harm. His hair was damp and a little curly, his lashes wet from his shower. He'd shaved, and looked as though he just stepped out of a men's health magazine, all fit and sexy. His body was made for blue jeans and T-shirts, and Betsy tried her damnedest to keep her eyes away from his crotch. She merely glanced then looked away.

Button-fly. Mmm, pop, pop, pop.

Although she wanted to ignore them, her feelings of attraction were working triple time and, though common sense told her that he would only hurt her in the end, she couldn't help but find Soldier fascinating. He was good to look at, he was smart, and he seemed genuinely interested in keeping her safe, above and beyond his responsibilities as a cop.

He was a knight in shining armor and every girl's dream, whether she wanted to admit it or not.

"A root canal?" He grinned. "Ah, this won't be so bad."

She stood and faced him. "Whatever. I'm ready."

They sat at the table where he had his laptop booted up and ready to go.

"I have to tell you before we begin," he said. "I'm a

little worried that this stalker hasn't identified himself yet."

"Why is that? I mean, what about that worries you?"

"Well, mostly, not always, but mostly," he answered, "they *want* you to know who they are. They want your attention. They are desperate to have you notice them, love them, give them the satisfaction of being forced to deal with them. The fact that this guy is still anonymous after at least three contacts bothers me."

"Thank you for sharing that. I feel ever so much better."

He cracked that killer smile again. "To keep yourself safe," he said, "you have to be well-informed. That includes things you may not want to hear."

"I don't want to hear any of it."

His smile widened. "There's that sense of humor again."

Betsy frowned. "Who's joking? I'm *serious*."

Ignoring her last comment, he began typing. "What's your date of birth?"

"The tenth of June."

"A June bug. Cute."

"Shut up."

"Okay, then, physical traits." Though he asked her no questions, he mumbled as he typed *blond, hazel, Caucasian, female,* and a few more assorted physical details. Pausing for a moment, he gave her the once-over, then said, "How tall are you, exactly?"

"Five-foot-four."

His fingers moved. "How much do you weigh?"

"Right."

"What?"

"Like I'm going to tell you how much I weigh."

"I need to know."

Her laugh dripped with sarcasm. "No you don't."

He stopped typing. "Betsy, I don't care how much you weigh. You look great. A woman's weight is—"

"Two hundred pounds."

"No way!" he blurted. His gaze examined her from the top of her head to the tips of her toes. "I'm six-two and even I don't weigh—" His eyes narrowed on her and his mouth flattened. He crossed his arms over his chest.

"See?" she said. "It *does* matter, and you can't deny it. You reacted." She had him there, all right.

Resettling himself in his chair, he returned to typing. "How does . . ." He glanced at her again, his fingers pausing above the keys. "How does one thirty sound?"

What a comedian! "I'll take it." On a good day without any clothes on, if she shaved her head, pumped her stomach, wore no heavy makeup, and put only one foot on the scale, yeah, she could weigh 130 pounds.

"Next is occupation," he declared. "Tell me everything you've done in the last five years, beginning with your current job. I'll also need to know any special training you've had, any classes you've taken, that sort of thing."

After she'd dug out every memory she had of her professional life, he asked her to name everybody she could think of at work.

"Stalkers are commonly somebody you either work with now," he insisted, "have worked with in the past, or have some kind of working relationship with either in your own office or in an office you do business with."

Betsy shook her head and gestured at him with her hands. "That could be hundreds of people. I can't possibly name—"

"All right. For the sake of expediency, just name the people you work with the most. We'll do the others later. First of all, besides your mother, who are you closest to?"

"That would be Claire. Claire Hunter. She's a doctor. We've been friends since we were kids."

"You two getting along okay? Any problems lately? Jealousy over a guy or—"

"Absolutely not!" Betsy snapped. "Jealousy between us over a man? That'd be the day."

"Why do you say that?"

"Oh, you'd really have to see Claire. She's stunning. Men fall for her all the time. Gosh, anybody meeting the two of us, well, I gave up a long time ago and just sort of step back and let . . ."

She felt herself blush, realizing what she was about to reveal. Although she loved Claire like the sister she'd never had, Betsy had learned that when it came to men, they always preferred Claire and that was simply the way it was.

"What I mean to say is, we never compete over men. Other doctors, technicians, patients, they all fall for Claire, but she never gives any of them a tumble. She's all work and no play, which I have tried to tell her is simply no way to live, but she's a very dedicated internist and—"

"Okay," Soldier interrupted. "I get the picture. Now, what about the people you work with?"

Soldier typed as Betsy began naming her coworkers. She closed her eyes as the images of the people she worked with every day trotted through her brain, people she liked, people she cared about, people who could not possibly be stalkers.

"Ryan Finlay is my boss. He's the executive editor of the *Ledger*. I've known him for about five years. He's a good man, has a wife and three daughters."

"Has he ever made a pass at you?"

She nearly gasped at the shocking suggestion. "Oh *gosh* no. Ryan's devoted to his wife and family. Besides, he's old enough to be my father!"

Soldier's lips curled into a wry grin. "Like that ever stopped a man from hungering after a sweet young thing. Who's next?"

Sweet young thing? The way he was looking at her now, she just about believed it.

"Well, next would be Carla Denato, I guess. She's been my assistant for about five months, ever since I became managing editor. Before that, I was features editor. The paper is so small, though, that we all do a little of this and a little of that. Both Carla and I do some reporting and write special interest articles when the needs arise. But she's been primarily the editorial assistant for the last year. Carla's very quick and efficient. I certainly couldn't do my job without her."

"Who was the managing editor before you were promoted?"

Betsy pushed herself away from the table. She needed to stretch her legs. Walking toward the window, she wrapped her arms around her middle and turned to face Soldier.

"That would be Linda. Linda Mattson. She was the managing editor when I hired on five years ago. As far as her leaving, she met some guy and got married and moved away. It happens, I guess. I miss her, though. She was terrific to work with. Really smart and fun."

"Where'd she move to?"

"I don't exactly know. It was actually pretty sudden. She was about thirty-five, divorced, no kids. She went on vacation and met some guy, and the next thing we know, she sends us a letter saying she'd gotten married and was quitting."

"She didn't come in and pick up her stuff?"

"No. Her letter asked that Carla or somebody just toss her things into a box and mail it to her. She must have had someone pack her personal belongings from her apartment, because I went by there hoping to be able to tell her congratulations and say good-bye, but she'd already been moved out."

Soldier had stopped typing. Rubbing his chin with his thumb, he said, "This didn't seem suspicious to you? It was kind of fast, don't you think? And you never met the guy she married?"

"Oh, we were *all* suspicious, but what were we supposed to do about it? Her new mailing address was somewhere in Minnesota. Ryan was so worried, he was going to fly to Minnesota and check on her when we got an e-mail from her saying how happy she was, and how sudden it all was, but that sometimes things just happened. We pretty much had to accept it after that."

"When was this? About five months ago, you said?" She nodded.

They continued for the next half hour or so. After Betsy relayed her medical and dental history, she recounted her activities over the last month in as much detail as she could remember. A gnawing depression began to eat at her insides when she realized how tedious and mundane her life really was. Until she was forced to relive it, she'd allowed herself to ignore it. After this was all over, she told herself, she really *had* to get a life.

She named the rest of the staff of the *Port Henry Ledger*, thereby creating a list of possible suspects.

"It's none of them," she insisted. Soldier just looked at her and smiled. "No, really," she said. "None of the people on that list is a stalker."

Changing direction, Soldier asked her about her educational background. Betsy went over it and the people she'd known in high school and college, including the few boyfriends she'd had.

In the five years since she'd graduated, she had been so busy working, she hadn't dated much. Plus, Port Henry wasn't exactly a single woman's playground. Most of its residents were older, retired. The tourist season brought in a lot of people, but they were mostly couples or families on a weekend getaway.

While Soldier had undoubtedly had thousands of girlfriends, she had only six honest-to-God boyfriends in her entire life to boast of, if you could call it boasting.

Soldier stopped typing. Probably knowing this part might get embarrassing for her, he kept his eyes on the keyboard. "So, what about sex?"

"I'm female."

He focused his attention on his fingers. "Yes, I know. But female is a gender. I'm talking about *sex*."

"What *about* sex?"

"Do you have it?" He kept his eyes lowered, but he'd begun to take little bites out of his bottom lip.

"Is knowing that important?"

"Very." He locked gazes with her. "The stalker could be a former boyfriend, a spurned lover."

Betsy couldn't imagine any guy getting in an uproar about being spurned by her, but she was reluctant to tell Soldier about her sex life, regardless. If it just wasn't *Soldier* . . .

Apparently sensing her hesitation, and why she felt it, he said, "Betsy, I don't care how many men you've slept with. I'm not asking you as a man, but as a detective."

She lowered her eyes and focused her attention on the birthstone ring her father had given her when she'd graduated from high school. Staring at the creamy pearl, she said, "When you kissed me, was it as a man, or as a detective?"

He leaned forward, placing both palms on the table. "Listen, lady," he said, his voice soft and husky, "I kissed you because I'm so attracted to you I can hardly stand it. I want to kiss you right now. I'd rather skip this whole damned thing and just strip you naked and lick you until you whimper my name and beg me to never stop."

He sat back in his chair and folded his arms. A

scowl crossed his features, making him look dangerous, a man to be reckoned with.

"That's what I *want* to do," he continued, "but I
can't. What you're going through, well, I don't want
to add any stress to your life, so I promised myself I
wouldn't kiss you again until this whole mess gets
straightened out. Besides, my presence in your life
now is more official, and I can't cross that line even
though I knew you on a personal level before any of
this happened.

"But I need to know about your sexual history, only
because it might give me a clue to who is doing this to
you. I'm a professional. I've done this hundreds of
times. I *can* and *will* remain detached, no matter what
you reveal to me. All right?"

He had painted a mental picture that Betsy was having a difficult time expunging. She and Soldier, naked.
Him on top of her, kissing her, sliding his tongue over
her skin. His fingers rubbing her between her legs—

She felt her breasts tighten and her nipples peak and
ache. If she unbuttoned her blouse right now, he could
soothe that ache with his tongue and his hands. Little
nibbles with his teeth—

"Betsy?"

She swallowed. He thought she was completely innocent, untried, chaste. Small-town girl saving it for
marriage. Unglamorous spinster more interested in
her career than finding a man.

In the blink of an eye her lust for Soldier metamor-
phosed into anger at him. Fury at his arrogance. Re-
sentment of his assumptions.

Plus the fact that he was right. Mostly.

So he could remain detached, hmm? Her pulse quickened. She'd show him detached.

"All right," she said. He nodded, satisfied they were going to get on with it at last, certain of what he would hear. His fingers were poised over the keyboard as she began to speak.

"My first time, I was fourteen—"

"What!" he yelped. "Uh, *sorry. Sorry.* I would have thought, I mean, you don't seem very . . . fourteen?"

Har. So much for professional detachment, she mused. Betsy slowly walked back to the table. She let a dreamy look come into her eyes as she sat in the chair. Placing her elbows on the table, she cradled her chin in her hands and tilted her lips into a sweet, satisfied smile.

"Oh, it was . . . *wonder*ful. He was much older, of course."

"How much older?"

"Mr. Sumpter was my ninth grade teacher. He must have been about forty."

Soldier's typing became little staccato jabs, as though he were trying to squash a flea that kept hopping around the keyboard.

"Did the son of a bitch know what he was doing was illegal, not to mention as immoral as hell?"

"Oh, we didn't care. We were too much in love."

Soldier typed, but said nothing. Betsy noticed a flush creep onto his cheekbones that hadn't been there a minute ago.

"Things were fine until his dumb ol' wife found out." She rolled her eyes in exasperation. "She hit him a few hundred times with a flyswatter. He had little square spots on his face for the longest while."

He sighed. "Go on."

"Well, in high school, to start with, there were Jimmy Jenkins, Frankie Gordon, Stewart Pritchett, and the Archibald twins."

Soldier's fingers froze. "All at once?"

"Oh, no, silly! Well, except for the Archibald twins, of course." She giggled. Inanely.

Across from her, Soldier pounded on the keyboard, the table shaking with each furious stroke. "Okay, so what about *after* high school?"

Betsy laughed, a light, carefree laugh. "Oh, no, that was just in the tenth grade! Let's see, in the eleventh grade there was—oh gosh, I can't remember all their names. The drugs really did a number on my memory."

"Drugs! Drugs, Betsy? *Drugs?*" He stared at her open-mouthed, his fingers splayed on the keyboard. A sound emitted from the computer, warning him he was striking too many keys at once.

She smiled benignly. "Hey, like, let the good times roll. Party hearty."

He stared at her, then said flatly, "Fourteen. Sex. Drugs."

"Well, when you put it *that* way. With my father in-stitutionalized, we didn't have a lot of money."

"Mm-hmm. Your father was institutionalized."

The smile faded from Betsy's lips and she felt her throat tighten.

"Daddy was a wonderful man, but he and my mother didn't get along very well. She divorced him. The night the papers were finalized, he was so de-pressed he got really drunk. He got into a fight with some guys. They beat him up so badly, he nearly died."

She stopped for a second to gather her second wind. "He . . . he had brain damage and it changed his personality. He has what's termed mild paranoid schizophrenia. He thinks everybody's out to get him."

"Like, the Nazis or something?"

"No. The Republicans. Doctors have had him in and out of hospitals over the years. Mostly in."

Soldier didn't type that into the computer. He just sat and stared at her for a moment. "I'm sorry."

Shaking her head, she returned her mind to the task at hand.

"We didn't have a lot of money, so I traded sex for school supplies." She gave Soldier an exaggerated wink. "I had all the pens, pencils, typing paper, art supplies . . . why, I had the best oil pastels in the school."

"Oil pastels."

"Yes."

Arching a brow, he said lightly, "Who'd you sleep with to get those?"

"Mr. Gruber, the art teacher."

"Mm-hmm."

"Don't you want to hear about college?"

He looked into her eyes and smiled like a predator who had just cornered his prey. "You hungry? Thirsty?" he said casually.

"No thanks."

"Okay then. Let's move on to college. Did you ever do it with the Archibald twins again?"

"The . . . oh, the *Archibald* twins. Oh yes. Boy,

talk about double your pleasure, double your fun!"

He leaned forward, capturing her eyes with his cool stare. His gaze narrowed on her. "So, tell me, Betsy. How does it work? With twins. Who does what?"

Betsy's heart stopped. He wanted *details*? The pervert! "A lady never tells."

He leaned closer. "C'mon," he whispered, his voice husky, as though he'd just gotten out of bed. "Did they get naked first? Did they undress you . . . slowly . . . while you squirmed and teased them on the bed? Did one of them lick your nipples and pull your panties down so he could slide his fingers inside you while the other one kissed you and nibbled your body? Did they lay you down, gently push your legs apart and bite the insides of your thighs? Up, and up, and up, until one of them could slide into you with his tongue? How many times did you come, Betsy? How did—"

"I don't remember!" Her voice was both a shout and a high-pitched squeak, a hysterical mouse caught in a trap. "None of your business! How dare you . . . you . . ." Her heart was jumping all over the place and her cheeks felt hot. Her palms were sweating and her mouth had gone completely dry. "You have no business—"

Soldier leaned closer and slipped his warm hand around to the nape of her neck. Gently pulling her closer, he put his mouth to hers.

His lips were firm but his kiss was soft. So sweet. He tasted good. Betsy sighed into his mouth, and he slid his tongue in to caress hers. Oh wow. Could he ever kiss.

They rose from the table at the same time, coming together, arms locked around each other in a full body embrace. Betsy whimpered, just a little, and Soldier pulled back, his eyes half closed and dreamy with lust.

"We can't do this. I'm sorry. I shouldn't have . . ." His breath bellowed from his chest and she could feel his erection jabbing her through his jeans. Placing her palms against his chest, Betsy stepped back, out of Soldier's embrace.

She lowered her head and tried to force her breathing to return to normal, but it was difficult.

Finally, Soldier seemed to compose himself.

"How much of what you just told me is true?"

She cleared her throat. "Um, the part about my father. Except it happened much later, when I was eighteen. And, Jimmy Jenkins was . . . well . . . I did . . . I mean *we* did, but it wasn't in high school. It was in my junior year of college. I made up the rest."

"Why?"

Betsy shuffled her feet and twisted her fingers together. "Because you made me mad when you said you could remain detached. I wanted to prove that you couldn't."

She looked up at him, distress churning away at her insides. "You couldn't, could you?"

He shook his head, a bemused look crossing his face. "No," he said through a harsh laugh. "I couldn't. Congratulations, Ms. Tremaine. You've destroyed my professional objectivity."

Soldier thrust his hands in his pockets and pursed his lips. "We'll take this up later," he growled. "We're not done with this. Not by a long shot, sweetheart."

Was that a threat? Betsy wondered. Or a promise?

Chapter 7

It was nearing lunchtime, and Soldier was starving. Lemsky provided Mrs. Fionorelli as dog-sitter so Soldier could take Betsy down to eat and attend the afternoon and evening classes without worrying if somebody was going to make a second attempt on the Chihuahua's life. A couple of Lemsky's people were keeping an eye out for any suspicious behavior, but at a conference filled with mystery writers and their fans, spotting the odd bit of behavior might prove tough.

Soldier sent Taylor as much information as he could based on what Betsy had told him. Taylor was a good cop and a sharp detective, and Soldier was certain if there was anything on any of the people she had named, his brother would dig it up.

As the elevator door opened, Soldier slipped a glance at the woman on his arm. She was nervous, but refused to stay stuck in her hotel room. He figured that as long as he was near her and keeping a watchful eye, she should be okay. Stalkers usually didn't make their moves—if they were going to make one—in such a public forum.

There were always exceptions, which was why his Colt Detective Special .38 was securely in its harness, under his jacket, snug against his body.

Not for the first time, Soldier wondered why this guy was stalking Betsy. Generally, it was obsessive love or a feeling of betrayal that set stalkers on a particular woman's trail. Then, somewhere along the line, preoccupation turned into hate. Hate evolved into aggression and often physical harm.

Betsy had probably not done anything to garner such anger from this guy, but that wasn't important. It was his *perception* of betrayal that was. She could have done anything, from taking a parking space he thought was his, to buying the last orange on the cart, to not supporting him in a political campaign or dancing with somebody else at a party. Stalkers were nuts and their reasoning was nuts and their actions were nuts.

Mostly, they were just bothersome, but sometimes they could be a genuine threat. And every instinct Soldier had screamed at him that Betsy was in imminent and extreme danger. He couldn't ignore it, and the need he felt to personally shield her from harm was unlike anything he'd ever experienced.

Somehow, in the short time he'd known Betsy Tremaine, she had become important to him, important in a way he was trying hard not to think about at the moment.

As they walked into the dining room, he glanced down at her. She turned her head at that moment and gave him a shy smile. She was so defenseless, he thought, with her naive heart and friendly eyes. Every male dominant protector of females gene he had was fully armed and ready. He knew it was primitive, and if he told her about it, she'd probably bop him on the head with something.

An image of Marc's grieving young wife forced its way into Soldier's head, but he shoved it back. He wouldn't let Betsy down as he had his dead partner. Even if it killed him, he would never make that mistake again.

Studying the room, and all the people in it, he said, "You want to sit by the fountain?"

"If it's okay, I'd rather sit by the window."

"Oh. Sure. Would you like me to get you some coffee?"

"Actually, I think I'd rather have an iced tea."

Pulling out a chair at one of the large round tables, he said, "That chowder smells great." A couple of the other people at the table nodded their agreement.

"I was thinking of going for the salad," she replied.

Scooting into his own chair, he opened his white linen napkin and set it on his lap. Placing his fists on the table, he narrowed his gaze on her. He watched her for a second, then said in a challenging voice, "I like steak. Rare."

Her head came up. She eyed him suspiciously. So, it was going to be like this, was it? He could see the wheels turning in her brain.

Finally, she said breezily, "Rare, red meat is bad for you. I'll probably have the baked fish."

The other six people at the table said nothing, but

turned their faces in quiet expectation. The gauntlet had obviously been flung at his feet.

Mentally, he picked it up.

Pouring himself a glass of water from the frosty pitcher on the table, he declared, "I'm a conservative."

"Figures," she huffed, crossing her arms and meeting his steady gaze with her own. "Liberal, as my father before me." Her hazel eyes were bright with challenge. She raised her chin a notch and waited for the next volley.

He poured water into her glass. "Plastic."

The crowd shifted their attention to Betsy. Twelve eyes blinked in rapt anticipation.

She arched a brow. "Paper."

"I sleep naked."

"Flannel."

"SUV."

"VW."

He growled. "Winter vacation. Snow."

"Summer. Beach." Her eyes were ablaze with energy and he wanted to laugh out loud.

Soldier thought for a moment. "Over easy."

Oooooh, said the crowd.

"Scrambled," she replied.

Ahhhh.

"Innies."

"Outies."

"Baked."

"Mashed."

"Boxers."

"Briefs."

"Christmas Eve."

"Christmas morning."

"Red M&Ms."

"Green," she proclaimed.

He leaned close and whispered theatrically into her soft pink ear. "I like to be on top."

Everyone at the table gasped. There was a clatter of silverware as they all dropped their utensils in anticipation of her response. Gleaming with triumph, Soldier's eyes narrowed on Betsy.

His grin was one of conquest. He had her this time. If she said "Bottom," it would be the same as agreeing with him, for if he was on top, she would be under him and that would work out just fine. If she said *she* liked to be on top, it would also be agreeing with him, leaving him the clear winner, any way you stacked it.

She took a sip of her water and set the glass down. Pursing her lips, she lifted her face to his. The coup de grace was on the tip of her tongue, and he could see it. She had him.

Betsy opened her mouth to speak, but as she did so, the elderly woman on Soldier's right put her hand on his arm and patted it gently.

"So, dear," she said sweetly. "How long have you two lovebirds been married?"

After lunch, Soldier escorted Betsy to a series of classes, the last one before dinner, focusing on fingerprinting techniques. The presenter, forensics expert John Abbott, was a member of the Seattle police force, a man well-qualified in criminal science, and an old friend of Soldier's. He was also an unrepentant womanizer whose specialty was ditzy blondes.

With a single, sweeping glance, Soldier could see that the tall, sandy-haired SOB had already charmed the ladies in the class with his brilliant smile.

"Fingerprinting is successful as a tool in identifying someone," Abbott began, "because the undersides of our fingers, palms, and feet have ridges and valleys." He lifted his open hand to the audience and traced his palm with his finger. "These elements form patterns of lines, some of which are continuous or stop, others that divide, and a few that make formations that look like pockets or dots. The patterns are divided into four basic groups: arches, whorls, loops, and composites. In all the years fingerprinting has been used to identify people, and with all the millions of fingerprints on file, to date, no two have ever been found to be alike, not even in identical twins."

Sitting next to Soldier, Besty concentrated on taking notes. Her head was bent to her task, giving him a chance to simply be with her, enjoy her light, feminine scent, the shine of her hair, the straight line of her spine.

She wore blue jeans and a sage green sweater with pink rosebuds embroidered around the neckline. Her bangs were pulled back a bit and fastened with small, glittering clips, and the diamond drop earrings she wore sparkled with brilliance whenever she moved her head. Very sexy.

He felt his heart give a thump, and he wondered at how little it would take to fall in love with her.

". . . don't you agree, Detective McKennitt?"

At the sound of his name, Soldier snapped his head up to catch John Abbott's mocking smile. Everyone in class had turned to look expectantly at him. "Sorry, John," he said. "Your voice is so mesmerizing, I sort of drifted off. Did you ask me a question?"

John Abbott's grin broadened as he slid his glance to Betsy, then back to Soldier. "Yes. I asked whether you agreed that DNA testing has revolutionized criminal investigations."

"Sure, yes, of course." *Duh*. "DNA testing has recently solved some cold cases that would probably have gone unsolved otherwise. With DNA, we can literally go back hundreds—perhaps even thousands—of years to solve not only crimes, but prove ancestral connections, such as the one involving Thomas Jefferson."

Just what was John driving at by soliciting his opinion? Soldier wondered. Then he realized that of all the women in the room, John had set his sights on Besty. *Try again, dickhead*, he thought, sending this message to John with narrowed eyes and a flat mouth.

Ignoring Soldier's warning, John smiled and continued with his presentation, turning his intense gaze on Betsy at every opportunity.

This one's mine, Soldier thought. *Get your own woman, Abbott.* But it was undoubtedly because John sensed Betsy was with him that he had focused on her. John Abbott was a man who enjoyed a challenge, and charming Betsy away from him probably seemed an enticing entertainment to him.

An uneasy feeling pinched Soldier's chest. Would she go? Would she find Abbott attractive and prefer Abbott to him? It bothered him to think that she might.

Soldier had never had to work very hard to get

women; they seemed to like him well enough. He'd had a few steady girlfriends over the years, but as soon as it came time to make some kind of commitment, he'd backed out. He knew there was nothing wrong with the women—it was him. He'd decided years ago, when he became a cop, that he would never marry, and that was that.

His dad was a cop, and even though his parents had a good, solid marriage, as a boy, Soldier had seen his mother cringe and bite her lip every time the phone rang when his dad was on duty. He'd catch her staring at the phone just before she picked it up, with that look of caution on her face. *Is this the phone call?* she must have wondered. *Is this the one that says, sorry, Mrs. McKennitt, but your husband . . .*

It had never happened for the McKennitts, but it had happened to Marc Franco's wife, and Soldier had never been so glad he'd decided to stay single as on the day of his partner's funeral. The day when Marc's widow had looked over at him across the abyss of her dead husband's grave and stared at him, her weary accusation had been plain to see in her red-rimmed eyes.

Marc's death aside, Soldier had never wanted a woman in his life on a permanent basis. Then he'd met Betsy.

Now, he wasn't certain about any of that anymore.

And if John Abbott *did* lure her away? So what? Did he care?

Shooting a quick glance at the woman sitting next to him, he thought, *Yeah, dammit.* Yeah, he'd care a whole helluva lot.

For the remainder of the hour, Soldier sat there,

glum and irritated, and feeling unsure of himself for the first time in a very long time.

As the hour wound to a close, John Abbott wrapped up his lecture. "Any questions?" he said as he scanned the room. Although several hands were raised, he ignored them.

Indicating Betsy, whose hand was not raised, he said, "How about you, miss? Is there anything about fingerprint techniques that you're just dying to know?"

"Oh," Betsy softly gasped, obviously uncomfortable with being singled out. "Well, yes, I guess there are a couple of things."

Her full lips curved in a shy smile as she flipped through the pages of notes she'd taken during the lecture. Soldier couldn't help but notice her neat handwriting and how she'd taken down nearly every word John had said. He looked on with disgust as Abbott bent forward over the podium, giving her his undivided attention.

"Um," she cleared her throat. "Earlier you said that since 1972 fingerprints have been compared and retrieved via computer, and by 1989 they could be sent back and forth on-line. You also said that a computer scans and digitally encodes prints into a geometric pattern according to their ridge endings and branchings, and in less than a second the computer can compare a set of ten prints against a half million. At the end of the process, it comes up with a list of prints that closely match the questioned prints. Then the technicians make the final determination, which involves a point-by-point visual comparison. In addition to fingerprints, you said, there are also palm and footprints, and even ear and faceprints." She paused and smiled again. "My question is, what with DNA testing and advanced fingerprinting, computer analysis, blood splatter techniques, databases, and instant transfer of information, is it possible that someday crime will be a thing of the past, since nobody will be able to get away with it?"

She closed her note pad and held it to her chest as though it were some kind of shield. Her eager eyes focused intently on Abbott, who stood stock still, in obvious confusion that a woman who looked like a scatterbrain was anything but.

Soldier smiled to himself. If anything would make Abbott keep his hands to himself, it was an intelligent woman.

Abbott curled his fingers over the edge of the podium. "Miss . . . um, what is your name please?"

"Tremaine."

"Miss Tremaine, then. Uh, Soldier?" he said through his teeth. "Why don't you answer that one for the lady."

Caught off guard, which he knew was exactly what that ass Abbott wanted, Soldier gathered his thoughts. Standing and turning toward the audience, he said, "Criminals are nothing if not arrogant. Even with all the techniques we have available to determine whodunit, people still murder other people, or steal, or cheat. They always think—if they think at all—that they'll get away with it. In answer to your question, Ms. Tremaine," he said, looking deeply into her lovely eyes, "I'm sorry, but no, I don't think crime will ever become extinct. Unfortunately. As long as people envy, hate, and covet, they will kill and steal. Capture and the penalty for their crimes seem not to be deterrents. When somebody wishes someone else harm, or wants something someone else has, they find a way, regardless of whether it makes sense or not, whether their chances of getting away with it are virtually nil."

Soldier knew Betsy was thinking of the stalker. He watched as she quietly thanked him, then lowered her eyes to her hands, clutching her note pad. The little pearl ring she wore gleamed softly as she tightened her grip.

Although the question and answer period went on for another ten minutes, Betsy had retreated into her own world. He'd have to find a way to get her mind off her predicament, help her become aware of the danger she was in without completely destroying her sense of safety or her tenuous self-confidence.

Being stalked had a way of putting a damper on a person's enthusiasm for life.

After class, a few people lingered to speak to Abbott. Most of the eager students were women, anxious to have his full attention. He answered them each with charming alacrity, then turned his attention to Soldier . . . and Betsy.

As Abbott approached and extended his palm in greeting, Soldier rose to meet him. The two men shook hands and exchanged pleasantries.

"John, this is Betsy Tremaine." Out of spite, he'd leave it at that, letting John wonder if she was his girlfriend, coworker, mere acquaintance, lover, or country cousin.

Betsy remained seated in the folding chair. Smiling up into the tall detective's eyes, she said, "Hello. I enjoyed your class, Detective Abbott."

"John," he said, taking her hand between his two large palms.

"John, then," she replied, sliding her hand from his grasp.

Turning to Soldier, he said, "Heard you were back at it, Detective. Yeah?"

Soldier nodded in agreement. News traveled faster than lightning through the SPD. "Yeah."

Abbott nodded, his eyes serious for the first time. He reached for Soldier's hand again and shook it with a firm, sincere grip. "Welcome back, stranger. I'll see you around." Then he grinned and slid a look at Betsy. "Take care of the lady, champ. Looks like she's way out of my league."

As they were leaving the room, Betsy felt Soldier touch her elbow. "Time for dinner, then it'll be my turn to take the podium."

"Are you okay?" she asked.

"Sure." He smiled down into her eyes. "You know," he said in low tones, "you are a really nice person. I don't meet many nice people in my line of work, but you, you're special. Unique. Genuine. The real deal. I . . . well, I just wanted to say that."

He ushered her into the ballroom, converted once again for dining. At the far end, in front of the tall windows, a long buffet stretched from one side to the other, and was filled with a variety of Asian delights. The scent of spices and succulent meats permeated the air, making Betsy aware of just how hungry she was.

The room was filling up quickly, so Soldier guided her to a table near a wall and placed his jacket over one chair. Betsy put her note pad and pen on the other chair, to secure their places while they went through the buffet line.

"You like Chinese food?" he asked.

"Oh, sure. Gosh, who doesn't?" She was so hungry she was afraid she'd knock him down in her haste to get to the food line.

People chatted as the queue moved slowly forward. Standing near him as she was, Betsy was aware of Soldier's height and the warmth of his body. Even though she couldn't identify the scent, he smelled like a *man*, and she liked it. She let herself feel as though she were *with* him, they were together, a couple. It was a silly game, but it sure was nice to pretend that a man like Soldier could be interested in her.

All wrong, you're all wrong, Elizabeth. Lose weight, fix your hair, get some decent clothes, will you? No man in his right mind will give you a second glance, dear. Bless your heart, you have a certain healthy glow, but I'm afraid you're not what one would call pretty. And you're no spring chicken, either. Nearly thirty and no hope in sight? What am I going to do with you, Elizabeth?

Betsy shoved her mother's words into the darkest recesses of her mind where, sadly, they were only hidden, not gone. They hung about like tattered clothes in

her closet, waiting to be dragged back out and worn
again, because they were all she had.

From the corner of her eye, she could see women
glancing in Soldier's direction, smiling, even flirting.
He must get that all the time, she thought. The only
thing keeping him from taking one of them up on it
was his "duty" to her.

She gave herself a mental smack. *Snap out of it,
cupcake. Enjoy being with him now and quit bitch-
ing. So he won't be around forever, so what? You may
not be beautiful, but you're smart. Say something
smart!*

She looked up at Soldier. "E equals M C squared."

"What?"

She sighed. "Never mind."

Clever words suddenly made themselves as scarce as
iced tea in hell, so she contented herself with watching
as Soldier heaped his plate with almond duck and
sweet-and-sour ribs, pot stickers, egg rolls, and whatever else he could get on the plate without losing too
much over the sides. Betsy filled her own plate with
white rice and some vegetables and a little almond
chicken. Everything looked so delicious, she hardly
knew where to begin.

By the time they returned to their table, strangers
had filled the other six chairs. It was a companionable
group, and included Kristee Spangler, who still
couldn't keep her eyes off Soldier. The busy waiters
had obviously been around, because there was a large
pot of tea in the center of the table. Her teacup had
been filled, as had her water glass, and a fortune
cookie had been placed on her napkin.

She moved the cookie and napkin out of the way in order to set down her plate. Soldier's arm brushed against her shoulder as he took his seat, and the same thrill zapped her as when he'd kissed her.

Yes, he *had* kissed her, there was that. And the heat of that moment, the feel of his mouth on hers, would carry her forward for a long, long time. She mused that someday, when she was old and gray and they took her away to the Home, she'd look back on that kiss, and her ancient toes would curl and her congested heart would palpitate. Oh, that *kiss*.

Problem now was, she wanted more. Much more.

"So, Betsy," Soldier said, leaning toward her to be heard above the din. "What's your sign?"

She burst out laughing and almost choked on her almond chicken. "Wow, just how old is that line, anyway?"

"Hey, it worked for my dad."

"You're kidding."

"Nope. Dad had been discharged from the army. He'd flown from Da Nang to New York, then on to Chicago, then finally Seattle. He was bushed. But he perked right up when he saw my mother."

Soldier reached for his teacup, which appeared dwarfed in his large hand. The fragrant scent of the tea enveloped them both. He swallowed and Betsy watched, mesmerized, as his powerful throat worked. She was certain her palms began to sweat with the primitive urge to grab him and have her way with him. Her heart beat like a wild jungle drum every time she looked at him.

She gave herself a mental shake. "So, how exactly did your parents meet?"

Soldier picked up his chopsticks and began trying to stab an egg roll, without much luck. "My mom was in graduate school, a poli sci major. She was part of a picket line protesting the war. When my dad came out of SeaTac, he bumped straight into her. I've seen pictures. She was cute, and he fell, hard, even though she called him a baby killer."

"What? A ba— And he still wanted to go out with her?"

"Oh, yeah. Like I said, she was real cute, and he'd been at war a long, long time."

"Aha."

"Aha is right. The McKennitt men seem to have a soft spot in their heads for sassy, sexy women." He smiled into Betsy's eyes, and she nearly melted right off the chair. "So, he says to her, 'What's your sign? I'll bet you're a Leo,' and I'll be damned if he didn't guess it right. Turns out, it was the only sign he knew. But he asked her out to debate the pros and cons of the war. Eventually, he convinced her he'd never killed any babies and that she should really take a long hard look at the situation."

"And she agreed to go out with him simply to debate the war?"

"Oh, hell no." Soldier laughed. "He was the sexiest guy she'd ever laid eyes on, and she could hardly wait to get him alone. At least," he slid her a wry glance, "that's the way *he* tells it."

"So, is that where you got your name? Because your father was a soldier?"

"Yup. When I was a kid, everybody called me by my middle name, and it just stuck. My brother Taylor is about the only one who calls me Jack. It's sort of his reverse nickname for me."

"You have an odd family."

"Yup." He grinned down at her.

Betsy took a sip of her tea. Setting her cup down, she picked up the wrapped fortune cookie. Looking around the table, she said, "Well, I got mine. Where's everybody else's?"

Soldier glanced around the table. "I don't have one. How'd you get one? Are the Powers That Be telling us that you're the only one at this table with a future?" He laughed as he rose from his chair. A bowl of fortune cookies sat at the end of the buffet line. "I'll go get some for everybody. Be right back."

As Soldier made his way through the crowded dining room, Betsy turned the cookie over in her hand. Fortune cookies had always been kind to her. They had always delivered messages portending great wealth, a happy marriage, many children, success in business. Perhaps this particular cookie would promise a bright future with a tall, dark-haired detective.

The detective in question returned to the table and handed the other diners individually wrapped fortune cookies. As each person thanked him and opened their cookie, laughter and giggles went around the table.

Kristee Spangler was proud to announce that hers promised great wealth, according to Confucius, anyway. Another woman discovered she would soon inherit something of great value from a mysterious source.

Soldier tore open the little package and snapped open his cookie. Giving Betsy a suggestive smile, he said, "Good news."

She swallowed. "What's it say?"

Unfurling the small banner, he read, "Woman who reviews books will be drawn and quartered by furious fans of literary detective."

Betsy arched a brow. "Wow, that was great," she drawled. "And so specific, too. Usually they're sort of vague, you know, something like, '*Confucius say a wise detective knows when to shut the hell up and leave well enough alone.*'" She batted her eyelashes at him and gave him a fake innocent grin.

He crumpled the small paper in his fingers and thrust it in his pants pocket. "Yeah, well, Confucius also say, '*Sexy lady should watch how her own cookie crumbles.*'"

Betsy took a sip of her tea, then pressed her napkin to the corners of her mouth. "Confucius also say, '*Time flies like arrow. Fruit flies like bananas.*'"

Soldier bit back a laugh, but he did allow her a big grin. He nodded, then said, "Okay, I know a challenge when I hear one."

He cleared his throat, then narrowed his laser blue eyes on her. "Confucius say, '*War does not determine who's right. War determine who's left.*'" A round of applause broke out from the other guests at the table, and Betsy giggled in spite of herself.

Kristee Spangler straightened her spine and blurted out, "Confucius say, '*Man who pees through screen door only straining himself!*'"

Laughter erupted from the table as Betsy slid a glance to Soldier. When he laughed, his face was transformed. He looked boyish and young and happy. His eyes sparkled and his smile was brilliant. Deep dimples creased his lean cheeks, and the sound of his voice infused her muscles and bones with delight. Oh dear. She felt a little tug at her heart and realized it would be so easy, so very easy, to slide into love with J. Soldier McKennitt.

If she hadn't already.

The man sitting across from Betsy looked around the table, grinned and said, "Confucius say, '*Man who goes to bed with sex on his mind wake up with solution in hand.*'"

Before anybody could take a breath, Soldier counter-Confuciused. "Confucius say, '*Man who walk through airport turnstile sideways going to Bangkok.*'"

Smiling and laughing, he turned to Betsy. "You got anymore in that head of yours, or can we get on with seeing your fortune cookie now?"

Betsy held the cookie in her hands but didn't unwrap it. Nibbling on her lower lip she said, "Confucius say . . ."

Everyone smiled and leaned forward to catch her words. Delightful anticipation showed on their faces.

"Confucius say, '*Man with hand in pocket feeling cocky all day.*'" She felt the heat rising on her cheeks and covered her mouth with her fingertips and giggled.

Through the gales of laughter, Soldier said, "Okay, Miss Smarty Pants, you win."

Betsy smiled into his eyes, and when he smiled back, she felt another one of those tugs. Oh dear. He was going to break her heart. And she was just in love enough to let him.

"What's your cookie say, Betsy? Inquiring minds want to know."

She unwrapped it and cracked it open with her fingers. Unfolding the paper, she read the words, then dropped the broken cookie and paper onto the table as though they'd burned her hands. Abruptly, she shoved herself back and stood, moving as far away as she could before her back slammed up against the ballroom wall.

Soldier looked down at the small piece of paper that had evidently caused her such distress. With one of his chopsticks, he turned it over.

The message was hand printed in red ink. It was simple and to the point.

Confucius say, "Woman who betrays, dies slow and painful death."

Chapter 8

"I don't need to go to the hospital. I'm just fine." With a thermometer jutting out of her mouth like the stick on a sucker, Betsy looked flushed and nervous, which only added to Soldier's worries.

"Sure, you're fine now," he argued. "But what if there was something in the cookie, or in the food?" He glanced at the paramedic about to take her blood pressure. The young man said nothing, but wrapped her upper arm with the sleeve and began punching on the bulb.

Betsy glared up at Soldier and spoke through the side of her mouth. "I didn't eat the cookie. And the food was from the buffet. The same stuff everybody else had." She slipped a loose curl behind her ear. "Besides, you wouldn't even know what to check for. I don't have any symptoms. Wouldn't I have symptoms?" She looked to the paramedic as if for support in her cause.

He smiled. "Maybe, ma'am. Maybe not. You ought to listen to your husband."

She gasped and the thermometer fell out of her mouth and into the paramedic's quick hands. He looked at it. "Normal," he said.

"He's *not* my—"

"Blood pressure's a little elevated, but that could be due to the excitement. Pulse is up, too. But everything else checks out okay."

As the paramedic packed up his bags, Soldier thanked him and shifted his attention to Betsy's face. She seemed all right. Should he make her go to the hospital or not? True, she exhibited no symptoms except stress, but she was bound and determined to not make a big deal of this.

The lab guys had arrived and were checking for latents, taking food samples, doing whatever they could to accumulate even the smallest bit of evidence from the crime scene. Not that it really was a crime scene exactly, which made things that much more complicated.

Soldier had interviewed the other six people at the table. Nobody had seen who'd placed the cookie on the table. And none of them had received odd fortunes in their cookies. No, they hadn't seen anybody suspicious lingering or lurking or doing anything strange.

He smacked his note pad closed. Over the last hour, officers had gone from table to table asking if anyone had seen anything that might help them track this guy. No one had.

Soldier looked down at Betsy. She sat quietly, her hands clasped tightly in front of her on the white tablecloth. Her eyes were downcast, her shoulders slumped. He wanted nothing more than to take her into his arms, reassure her, protect her.

His heart gave that quick little jump he was getting used to feeling every time he looked at her. Or thought about her. Or heard mention of her name. How in the hell had she gotten to him so fast?

In confused frustration, he turned his attention to the matter at hand.

Whomever had slipped the cookie onto the table had vanished or blended into the crowd, which was even more worrisome. The cookie in question was being sent to the lab for analysis, and he hoped to hell it would show something.

It had been pretty easy to do. All it had taken was a pair of tweezers to pull the original fortune out of a cookie and replace it with the fake, then reseal the cellophane wrapper with a daub of glue. With the dining room a mass of chatting, hungry people, it would have been simple to walk by the table unnoticed and set the cookie where Betsy had left her notebook.

The ploy had worked, and now Betsy was a mass of nerves. She was being as brave as anybody could expect under the circumstances, but it bothered Soldier to see her tormented by this faceless, nameless bastard. It bothered him a lot.

He felt helpless. Watching her being victimized by a situation over which she had no control brought back all the insecurities he had felt after Marc's death.

Will life never be the same as it was? Will everything I see, everything I do, every move I make from now on remind me of Marc's murder? Will the guilt, remorse, frustration, gnaw at my guts fucking forever?

As Soldier blew out a harsh breath, Detective Atherton of the SPD approached him. "Aren't you teaching a seminar in a half hour?"

Soldier nodded, shoving his introspections aside for the moment. Atherton was a nice guy and a good cop, a bit on the arrogant side, though.

"Yeah," Soldier replied, "but what with all this—"

"Go on ahead," Atherton interjected with a sniff. "I can take it from here. I'll get the lab to move on the samples. If we find anything, I'll give you a call."

After the men parted, Soldier returned to Betsy. "I've got my class in a few minutes," he reminded her, "and you, dear lady, are going to be teacher's pet."

She stood and faced him. "If you don't mind, I'd rather go back to my room—"

"Sorry," he said, shaking his head. "I want you near me so I can check you for symptoms. The lab's going to call when they get the report on your blood draw. If anything shows up, I want to be able to get you to the hospital ASAP."

"If . . . if he'd put something into my food, wouldn't I be feeling some symptoms by now? I mean, I feel okay."

Soldier slipped his arm around her waist as she rose from the table. "Depends," he said softly. Barely giving it a thought, he curled his knuckles under her chin to raise her face to his. The look in her eyes was one of complete trust. He could tell her she'd just swallowed a lethal dose of strychnine but she would be okay, and she'd believe him.

He didn't deserve that kind of trust, but, godammit, it felt good.

Soldier smiled. "Don't worry. It's highly unlikely you've ingested anything. Most poisons taste terrible, and you didn't make any remarks about taste during dinner. It's been ninety minutes, and you're not convulsing or sweating. Most anything toxic would have begun to show up by now. But I'm going to watch you while Atherton rushes the tests through. Then we'll know for sure, and we can rest easy."

She looked up into his eyes and smiled. "Okay. Um, before your class starts, though, I need to use the rest room."

"Sure," he said. "They're just down the hall."

The carpeting in the hallway was thick, their footsteps muted as Betsy walked beside Soldier. At the door of the women's room, he knocked loudly. "Police," he said. "Anybody in there?"

Betsy's ears felt oddly sensitive, Soldier's pounding reverberating through her brain like a gong. She shook her head to clear it, and tightened her grip on his forearm as a slight wave of dizziness made her head spin a bit.

She had to admit her nerves were just about shot. As soon as Soldier's class was over, she was going to hit the hay and not get up until noon tomorrow.

When his call was met by silence, he pushed the door open and glanced around. Over his shoulder, Betsy could see there were only five stalls, all unoccupied.

"Okay," he said. "Go on in. I'll be right next door. If anybody comes in and tries anything, scream bloody murder and I'll be there in a flash, uh, so to speak."

Betsy giggled at the thought of Soldier's jeans in disarray as he tried to button up while grabbing for his gun. The more she thought about it, the more she giggled. Then she giggled some more.

"It wasn't that funny," he remarked dryly as he turned and entered the men's room.

Betsy sauntered into the bathroom and chose a stall. She closed and locked the door. Gosh, the stalls were so narrow. She suddenly felt very cramped, as though she'd just been locked inside a stand-up casket.

Hurrying to finish, she flushed the toilet then unlocked the stall door. Rushing forward, she gasped for air, the intense feeling of claustrophobia unnerving her, tilting her senses in abstract directions.

"Betsy Tremaine, isn't it?"

Her heart lurched as she turned to focus on the woman who had quietly entered the facilities. Her face was familiar, yet it was strangely distorted. The look in the woman's eyes was odd, almost challenging, definitely mocking.

"Oh, you're Kristee, aren't you? Kristee Spangler?" Betsy managed. Her mouth had gone dry and her lips seemed too thick to form words.

Kristee turned toward the line of sinks and proceeded to wash her hands. Betsy stared at her back, wondering why she felt so uncomfortable being alone in the bathroom with this woman. Should she scream bloody murder as instructed? Was Kristee going to assault her?

When Kristee reached for a paper towel, Betsy just about jumped out of her skin. She giggled at her own foolishness, but when she couldn't stop giggling, she realized she was both nervous and scared.

Kristee bent to pick up her briefcase. When she stood, she faced Betsy with a wry smile on her face. Blinking rapidly, Betsy tried to focus on the woman, but things kept moving. Kristee's eyes sort of slid around her face, and the wall behind her changed from a delicate almond color to bright orange, then back again.

"I h-have to leave," Betsy managed to say. She knew she should wash her hands, but if she didn't get past Kristee Spangler and out of the room immediately, she'd begin screaming.

As Betsy started to move, Kristee gave her a big smile. "Well, you go on now," she said. Her voice was soft, but held an undertone of menace that Betsy couldn't comprehend, yet couldn't ignore. "Oh, and by the way," she whispered, "have a nice . . . trip."

Betsy watched as Kristee turned on her heel and left the washroom. The door swung closed, creating a breeze that hurt her ears.

Turning toward the sinks, she slowly looked at her own image in the mirror, and let out a bloodcurdling scream.

Soldier had just exited the men's room when he saw a woman turn the far corner at the end of the hall. He only caught a glimpse of her back as she quickly left the corridor, either heading for her room or for the elevators.

From inside the women's room, Betsy began to scream hysterically.

"Shit!" he bit out as he plunged through the door, his hand thrust inside his jacket, his fingers feeling for the butt of his revolver.

She stood alone in the bathroom, staring in the mirror, screaming her head off.

"Betsy!" he yelled. He grabbed her shoulders and turned her to face him. "Betsy, calm down! What happened?"

She stopped screaming and looked up at him, huge tears sliding down her flushed cheeks. Flinging her arms around his neck, she pressed her body as close to his as she could get. He felt her breasts, her belly, her hips, and more, pressing snugly against him, and had to stifle a very serious groan.

Circling her waist with his arms, he pulled her closer and bent to her ear. "Shh, honey. It's okay. You're all right. There's nobody here."

She calmed a little, then shuddered. "I'm sorry. I . . . I overreacted. It's just that, well, she s-scared me—"

He pushed her to an arm's length. "Who scared you?"

"Um, that Kristee Spangler woman. She came in here and washed her hands!"

"Okay. She washed her hands. Like, what, aggressively or something? Did she splash you with water?"

"No."

"She do anything else?"

"No."

"Did she talk to you?"

"Yes. But that wasn't it. She was acting very strangely. Her eyes . . . they—they kept changing color. I think."

There was silence between them as Soldier weighed this information. "You've been under a lot of stress. Was that what made you scream? That her eyes changed color?"

"No," she said, shaking her head violently. "It was wh-when I looked into the mirror." She peeked over his shoulder to the large mirror behind him. Rising up on her toes, she pressed her soft mouth against his ear. Her breath was warm and little chills zipped down his spine.

"What did you see in the mirror that scared you, Betsy?"

She paused for a moment and seemed to gather her courage. Finally, "M-My face," she whispered. "It was m-melting."

"That's it," he snapped. "I'm taking you to the hospital. I'll cancel my class—"

"No!" Betsy insisted. "I've been waiting for this class, and so have many others. Don't you dare cancel. I'll be just fine." She blinked a few times then rubbed her eyes with her knuckles. "You're right, though. I am tired."

When she lifted her face to him, he thought she did look especially weary. Her lids were half closed and her cheeks were flushed.

"Your class is only an hour long," she urged, rubbing her nose with her index finger. "As soon as it's over, you can take me up to bed."

He *wished*.

Nodding, he slipped his arm through hers and they headed down the hall to the Glacier Room. The chairs were all filled with happy, chatting people, and Soldier was relieved to see that Kristee Spangler was not one of them. He didn't know what it was, but something had bothered him about her from the very beginning, and he couldn't help but wonder if her presence at their table and her sudden appearance in the women's room was a carefully constructed coincidence.

He would add her name to the list and send it off to Taylor tonight.

As he handed Betsy into the chair nearest the podium, she began giggling again.

"Something funny?" he asked.

She shook her head so enthusiastically, he thought she was going to fall off her chair. "Are you *sure* you're all right?"

Before she could answer, the moderator stepped to the podium and introduced Soldier. He was met with ardent applause.

Arching a brow, he sent her a "see? everybody loves my books but you" look, but she was busy examining a button on her sweater. All the buttons on her sweater. And her fingernails. And the toes of her shoes. What in the hell was she *doing*?

"Good evening, and welcome to class, everyone. As you know, tonight I'm going to be speaking to you about 'cold cases.' Who can tell me what a cold case is?"

"Twenty-four bottles of beer in my refrigerator."

Everybody laughed except Soldier, who glared at Betsy. "Well, yes. Thank you, Ms. Tremaine. That certainly qualifies, but that's not exactly it."

She grinned, but didn't look at him. She was busy inspecting for lint on the empty seat next to her.

He cleared his throat. "Cold cases are generally

homicides that have gone unsolved for a number of months, or years, sometimes even decades. Modern technology—DNA testing, for example—has enabled the police to clear many cases that might have gone unsolved even just months ago. As in the case of the Green River Strangler, after years of intense police work, within just a few weeks of—"

"Are you married, Detective McKennitt?"

Looking up from the podium, he scanned the members of the class, who were all staring at Betsy. She had a silly grin on her face, and her finger was busy twirling a silky lock of her beautiful hair.

"Excuse me?" he said. "Uh, no." Reaching into his jacket, he pulled a small stack of note cards out and placed them on the podium. Turning his attention to the notes, he said, "The first thing you should know about cold cases is—"

"You're really cute."

Betsy again. This time she was squirming in her seat, crossing and uncrossing the toes of her shoes as she lifted her face to him in a shy smile.

"Uh, thanks."

"Don't mention it."

"Cold ca—"

"Do you think I'm cute?"

Soldier coughed as several people in the class laughed, while others made quiet remarks about how "that woman" should shut the hell up and let the detective get on with it.

Leaning toward Betsy, he said softly, "I think you're absolutely adorable. Now, shut . . . *up!*"

She looked hurt. Damn it. The last thing in the

world he wanted to do was hurt her, but, Christ, what in the hell had come over her?

An icy worm of suspicion began inching its way through his brain. Leaning closer, he said, "Betsy, look at me. Look directly at me."

She did. And he knew.

Addressing the class, he said, "Sorry. Five minute break, everyone, while I make a quick phone call."

As he pulled his cell phone from his pocket, people got up from their seats and went to the back of the room, where coffee and other beverages had been set up.

He punched in the numbers, and while the phone was ringing, he said, "Betsy. Sit right where you are. Don't move a muscle. You hear me?"

She giggled again and rolled her eyes. Her lovely hazel eyes with the dilated pupils.

"Atherton? McKennitt. You got the results . . . Yeah? *Yeah?* Fuck. Yeah, she's out of it. How much? How long? Okay. Thanks."

Lifting his voice, he said, "Attention, everyone. Family emergency. Sorry. Class has been cancelled."

Snapping the phone closed, he shoved it back into his pocket. He moved in two strides to where Betsy sat, carefully counting the squares in the ceiling tiles.

"Four hundred seventy-five, four hundred seventy-six . . ."

"Betsy?"

"Four hun— Darn it, Soldier! You interrupted me. Now I'll have to start over." Heaving a weary sigh, she let her head loll back. "One . . . two . . . three . . ."

Taking her gently by the shoulders, he said, "Betsy.

Listen to me. Tell me exactly, and I mean *exactly*, what Kristee Spangler said to you in the bathroom."

" 'Zactly?" She seemed to try to focus on his eyes, but kept focusing on his nose. Her brow was furrowed in sincere concentration and her lips were parted. Oh, those lovely lips.

"Yes, exactly. Now!" he demanded.

"Um . . ." she closed her eyes and thought for a while. " *'Have a nice trip.'* That's what she said. Just, *'Have a nice trip.'* "

"Fuck!"

Her eyes flew open. "You said a really bad word."

"Yeah."

"What's wrong?"

"Kristee Spangler was probably the one who slipped the LSD into your water glass at dinner, and I didn't even get a chance to . . . Oh, fuck her!"

"Did you want to? Is that an Irish saying?"

"Did I want to what? What in the hell are you talking about?"

"Did you want to o'fuck her? You just said, 'I didn't even get the chance to o'fuck her' and I thought it was maybe an Irish sort of saying that meant—"

"No, honey." He gently shook her shoulders. "Listen. Don't be alarmed. You have LSD in your system. That's why you thought your face was melting. It's been coming on gradually since dinner. It's only a small amount, which is why you're not in worse shape than you are right now, but it's enough to make you hallucinate. Do you understand what I'm telling you?"

She shook her head in obvious confusion, and big tears appeared in her eyes. "I thought you liked me," she whispered. "But you really liked her better? And you wanted to sleep with her?" A huge tear trickled down her cheek, and Soldier had no idea what to do about it. "I know you could probably have any girl you wanted, but you've been so nice to me and everything. I just thought, well . . . never mind."

Betsy lowered her head and looked like somebody had just shot her puppy. Soldier blew out a heavy sigh. "C'mon, sweetheart. Let's get you out of here."

"Am I really on drugs?"

"Yes."

Her eyes grew wide, fearful. She curled her fingers into the fabric of his jacket and stared deeply into his eyes.

"Am I going to die, Soldier?" she asked softly, her voice tinged with regret. "I don't want to die. I'm not ready. I haven't done so many things, you know, like . . . like travel, and . . . and . . ." She slid her hands up to grip the lapels of his jacket as she seemed to search his face for the truth.

"I want to read all the classics," she whispered. "And get really good at playing chess. I was hoping to learn to tap-dance, but my mother says I have two left feet. I've never been on a cruise or kissed a man in the moonlight, or . . . Oh, wow," she interrupted herself. "God, your eyes are so blue. So very intensely hyper-electric blue! You should see them, I swear—"

"Betsy, calm down, honey. You're not going to die. And I can teach you to play ch—"

"And babies!" she squeaked, ignoring him as though he hadn't spoken at all. "I want babies. Beautiful babies with blue, blue eyes. And I've never been in love and I wanted so much to find somebody who loves me. I think my mother's wrong. I think men *do* like hourglass figures, don't you? I mean, just because she's so beautiful and I'm so not, you don't think I'm going to live alone and be lonely and single all my life, do you?"

She was crying full out now and her hands were trembling and all he could think of was how sweet she was, and how utterly defenseless under the influence of the drugs.

Soldier watched her intently. He teetered on the edge of a place he had never been before, and he tried hard not to think of how easy it would be to slide right over that precipice.

Removing a fresh handkerchief from his pocket, he dabbed the tears trickling down her flushed cheeks. "Betsy," he whispered. "You have the sweetest heart I've ever known. And you're beautiful, honey. Don't ever let anybody tell you you're not."

Lowering his head, he placed a kiss on her damp, salty lips. She blinked and smiled up at him, and he felt himself edge even closer to that precipice. What the hell, he was enjoying the view so much, he might even throw caution to the wind and jump.

Wrapping his arm around her waist, he began moving her toward the door. "You're not going to die. In a few hours, you'll be fine. I promise."

Babies with blue, blue eyes. He turned that image over and over in his head as he escorted her up to his room. Babies with blue, blue eyes. Yeah, he could go for that. Of course, a little girl with big hazel eyes might be nice, too.

By the time they arrived, Betsy had calmed down quite a bit, and in fact had begun focusing her attention on something else entirely.

As he keyed open the door, he said, "I'll bet you're hungry."

She shook her head and leered up at him. Soldier gave the suddenly clinging, giggling, squirming Betsy a gentle shove toward the bed. He watched as she moved slowly, her heavy-lidded gaze never leaving him.

She licked her lips, sat on the edge of the mattress and began unbuttoning her sweater.

He closed the door and slid the lock.

Blowing out a breath, he considered his predicament. He'd been out of a real relationship for nearly two years. His last ships-passing-in-the-night encounter was three months back. Truth be told, he wanted, needed, a woman. Now, he was all alone in his hotel room, with a cute, curvy, sexy blonde who was high on LSD and who had suddenly discovered her inner tart.

It was going to be a long night.

"Betsy? Are you hungry?"

She shook her head again.

"Thirsty?"

She nodded her head.

As he walked to the small bathroom where the water glasses sat resting on a clean towel, he said, "Do you want me to have Mrs. Fionorello bring Piddle up?"

Betsy giggled. "Pah-pah-pah-diddle," she snickered. "Leave it to Loretta to name a dog after a waste product."

He returned and handed the glass of water to Betsy.

As she reached for it, her gaze met his. "Thank you." She blinked sleepily and gave him a soft grin. Did she have *any* idea how utterly desirable she was? He slammed his hands into his pockets to keep from pushing her down on the bed and tearing off her clothes like it was Christmas morning and she was a gift wrapped up just for him.

"Look, Betsy, it's going to be a tough night. You don't have a lot of LSD in your system, but you are definitely under the influence. Have you ever done drugs?"

She drank the water all the way to the bottom. Tipping the glass in the air, she smiled. "Ah' gone! May I have more, please?" She tried to wink at him, but her eyes crossed a little and she lost her balance, falling over backward onto the bed.

Taking the glass from her hand, he refilled it and brought it back to her. She sat up, took it and drained it. "Yes," she said into the hollow of the empty glass, her words sounding like the echo from a well. "Are you going to arrest me?"

"No. You don't seem the type, though, to do drugs."

"Oh, I didn't do them on purpose!" Her eyes were huge as she put her fingertips over her mouth. "My cousin," she whispered through her fence of fingers, "my cousin slipped some pot into my brownies. He thought it would be funny. I didn't know until after I'd eaten some. I got mad at him. But that was a long time ago. I haven't seen him since."

Her eyes misted over and she lowered her lashes. Soldier thought she might cry again, but instead she surprised him. Patting the bed next to where she sat, she purred, "C'mere."

"I don't think that would be a good idea. Why don't I turn on the TV, or we can play cards or something."

"Don't wanna watch TV." Her full lower lip pouted a bit. "Don't wanna play cards. Wanna play with you, manly man."

Soldier swallowed past the Rock of Gibraltar lodged in his throat. "Betsy, it's going to be hard enough—"

"I'm sure it's hard enough."

"No, that isn't what I mean. The LSD is affecting your sense of reason, and I can't allow myself to take advantage of that."

Betsy stared intently into the empty water glass as though it held the answer to her most profound questions. Looking up at him, she said only, "Wow. That was incredible. Water molecules. You know?" Looking around, she said, "Where's Piddle?"

Jesus Christ. Running his fingers through his hair, he walked to the phone. His blood was hot, his John Thomas was hard, his brain was fried, he was dead tired, and now he would have to deal with a nervous bug-eyed rat-dog. Well, why the hell not?

Dialing Betsy's room, he said, "*Sì, Signora* Fionorelli? Would you please bring the dog, uh, the *piccolo cane*, up to my room? *Sì*, sure, room 437. And his blankie, too. Uh, blank-ee. It's purple. Soft, you know, to wrap him in. *Sì, coperta, coperta*. Blankie. Yes, and his squeaky toy, too. Uh, *squeak! squeak! Sì. Sì, squittio giocattolo*. Oh, of course, his food, *ali-*

mento di cane, sì. Okay, yeah, what else? Sure, why the f— uh, I mean, *sì, sì,* why not. Bring it all."

He slammed the phone down and blew out a breath. He needed a good night's sleep, but what he was going to get was a giggling mass of sexuality and a hyperactive Chihuahua with a squeaky toy.

Well, hell, this was the best Saturday night he'd had since Louie the Pimp had gotten his ding-dong stuck in the phone booth down on Third and he'd had to pry him loose or risk losing his best snitch.

While Soldier went to open the door for Mrs. Fionorelli, Betsy got up and turned on the TV. When the maid placed the dog on the floor, he made a beeline for Betsy. Squeals and kisses and hugs filled the air behind him as Soldier gave the gracious maid a tip and a smile, and thanked her for her kindness in watching the mini-Rin Tin Tin.

As he locked the door behind Mrs. Fionorelli, he stood for a moment, simply watching the woman he was to spend a platonic night with.

Betsy set the dog on the floor and raised her eyes to Soldier's. Slowly, and with great deliberation, she began to remove her sweater.

Chapter 9

Soldier froze. His eyes watered. His heart thundered. Betsy lowered her lashes as she squirmed out of the soft knit, letting it fall onto the bed behind her.

He swallowed, telling himself to look away, to stop her somehow, but he knew that if he touched her, he'd be lost.

His gazed lowered to her breasts. They were round and firm, her skin flawless. The thin lace of her bra skimmed the tops of each breast. Without hardly trying at all, he could make out the pink tips of her nipples.

Soldier's groin tightened as desire tugged at every nerve in his body.

Ah, hell . . .

In three strides he was across the room, lifting her into his arms, gathering her to his chest. She slid her hands to the nape of his neck and let her fingers play with his hair. Stroking the tight cords of his neck, her feathery touch nearly drove him insane. His erection pressed against his jeans, making him yearn to rub himself against her.

Betsy wriggled closer, so close he could feel the points of her nipples pushing against his chest through the fabric of his shirt. She raised her face to him, her lips slightly parted. He took them.

His kiss was hard, desperate, carnal. Her tongue flicked against his, sparking his desire for her into a wildfire of lust. He slid his hands up her naked waist. Her breasts filled his palms with their warmth and weight. He rubbed his thumbs over her lace-covered nipples until she moaned and rolled her hips against his groin.

God, but he loved touching a woman. And this woman, this particular woman, had curves so tantalizing, he'd wanted to touch her like this from the first moment he'd seen her.

Betsy pushed back from him a little, breaking the kiss. With dreamy eyes, she smiled up at him. "Will you please make love to me?"

She was so sweet, even in her present condition, her question had been tentative, uncertain, shy. Never a siren, but a seductress all the same.

He'd never wanted to make love to a woman so badly in his entire life. But he couldn't do it.

Tilting her chin up with the tip of his finger, he placed a soft kiss on her lips. "No, honey."

Her eyes widened. Her lips trembled. "I see." She lowered her head as her cheeks flushed in obvious embarrassment.

"No, Betsy, you don't see. I can't take advantage of

you like this. I couldn't live with myself if I did, and, tomorrow, when you're sober again, you'd hate me for doing it."

His assurances didn't matter. He'd rejected her, and that was all she'd heard. Talk about damned if you do and damned if you don't.

He left her for a moment to pull the bedcovers down. "Why don't you put your nightgown on and try to get some sleep. You're already working the drugs out of your system. Sleep's the best thing for you. You may feel a little cranky tomorrow."

Turning to him, she smiled again, her eyes moist, her lips still trembling. "Thank you," she whispered, and he felt his heart swell in response.

She could get to a man. Son of a bitch. If he weren't very, very careful, she could get to him, and he was *not* the marrying kind. He would not be the one to give her babies with blue, blue eyes.

As she picked up her nightgown from the bed, Piddle trotted stiffly along at her heels. Entering the bathroom, she closed the door behind her.

For a few minutes there was the rush of tap water, followed by silence. Quietly, then, came the crying. Gentle sobs, soft sniffs, the sounds of a woman coping with hurt.

Soldier fought going to her, pushing open the door, lifting her against him and taking her to bed. He wanted her so damned much, he ached from it. But he didn't move a muscle.

He didn't dare.

* * *

Betsy didn't dare move. Her head pounded, her eyes were swollen shut. Her nose was stuffed. She'd been crying, but she couldn't quite remember why.

All night long she'd had hot, erotic dreams of Soldier, naked and twisted together with her amidst tumbled sheets.

She tried to sit up, but groaned and flopped back down again on the disordered bedding. Her nightgown clung to her damp body and her hair fell into her eyes. Her breasts ached, and she didn't even want to think about what she was feeling between her legs.

Lust. Flaming, insane, pulse-pounding lust, that's what it was, and there was no denying it.

"Good morning, sleepyhead."

Betsy's eyes flew open. She turned her head. Soldier. Next to her, grinning at her, his arms sliding around her body. She searched her memory. Did they? Had she? Had he?

In a terrible rush, the evening came back to her. She'd tried to seduce him!

Oh, yes, and he had turned her down, flat.

Dear God. What had she done? How could she ever look him in the eye again? He must think her a pathetic, lonely, homely . . . slut.

"Um," she murmured. "I have to go to the bathroom." *Where I'm going to lock the door and stay all day long.*

"Betsy." Her name on his lips sounded so perfect. They were in bed together. He was holding her in his arms. He spoke her name softly. But it was not real. It was all a cruel joke. The tears she'd shed last night were nothing compared to the deluge she planned on shedding today. As soon as she could get into the god-damned bathroom!

"Betsy. Look at me."

"No. Bathroom," she mumbled against her pillow.

His fingers slid under her chin. Lifting her face out of the depths of the pillow, he said, "Nothing happened last night, but not because I didn't want it to. I did. You cannot begin to imagine how much I did. I couldn't do that to you, not under the circumstances."

"Okay," she said, her eyes still pinched tightly closed. "Now may I please go?"

He released her and she scurried off the bed, gathering her underwear and clothing as she shuffled across the room, Piddle dancing at her heels.

She looked in the mirror. She groaned. Her face after a crying jag was not a glamorous thing to behold. Her cheeks were red and her eyes swollen nearly shut. Her nose felt like it had cement in it, no air going in, no air going out. Her lips were chapped.

She'd had sex with exactly one guy in her whole life, and it just hadn't been all that great. She knew it could be so much better. She also knew that Solider McKennitt could prove her theory to within an inch of her life.

But he'd turned her down. Oh, he had been a gentleman about it, but still . . .

After she'd brushed her teeth, showered, and washed her hair, she felt a bit cheerier. When she made a window in the fog on the mirror, her hazy reflection told her she looked better, but her eyes were still swollen. Damn. Why couldn't she have been born beautiful, vivacious, stunning under any circumstances, gorgeous and hot and desirable. . . .

Why couldn't she be more like her mother?

After pulling on jeans and a white sweater with a lace collar, she combed her hair. When she exited the bathroom, Soldier was on the phone.

Something was very wrong.

His jaw was set against the grind of his teeth. He was scowling, his features tight. His gaze slid to her, and he gestured for her to sit down.

"Yeah, okay," he said. "No, that's probably not a good idea. I'm on my way."

When he hung up, he ran splayed fingers through his hair and hissed out a breath through clenched teeth. "Shit."

"What?" Betsy held her breath.

Soldier's voice was rough, angry. "I have bad news, honey." He searched her eyes as though to see if she was prepared. She said nothing, but waited in grim anticipation.

"They found Kristee Spangler this morning in the park across the street. Dead. Single blow to the head."

Betsy gasped; she couldn't help it. Kristee Spangler had been murdered? Somebody she had spoken to only hours before had been *murdered?* She was too stunned to speak.

"I have to leave," he continued, "but before I do, why don't I make you some coffee?"

"N-No," she muttered, her voice a thin, dry wisp of a sound. "No, I'll make the coffee. You're a cop. You probably make lousy coffee."

He tried for a grin, but she could tell it was half-hearted. "Guilty on both counts," he said. "You'll be okay while I'm gone. Just keep the door locked and don't go anywhere. I'll let Lemsky know you're here alone so he can keep an eye out."

From his suitcase, he pulled a shoulder holster, complete with weapon, and strapped it on over his black T-shirt. Betsy swallowed. He looked . . . sexy. Sexy, and terrifying.

Slipping on a black bomber jacket, he moved past her toward the door. With a quick smile, he left the room, shutting the door behind him.

Betsy looked around. The small space seemed so big all of a sudden, so quiet. In the short time she'd known Soldier, she'd gotten used to his presence, his energy, his being a man in her manless world.

She moved toward the sink and began absently fiddling with the coffeepot, trying not to think about where he'd gone, but found everything else had been shoved out of her brain.

Murder. Kristee Spangler had been murdered. Somehow, her mind just couldn't accept that reality.

She recalled the distant feeling of familiarity she'd had the first time she saw Kristee with her reddish hair and brown eyes. Her smile had not been a kind one, yet Betsy had felt as though they must have met before. Perhaps at other conferences?

Betsy shook her head. And now the poor woman was dead, and it was all a part of the stalking thing. God, what a nightmare.

As she went through the motions of making coffee, she tried to push down the panic that kept trying to burst to the surface. It was there, deep inside her, urging her to run, to hide, to get as far away as fast as possible.

But where could she go? Without knowing who was responsible for all this, she could turn and run the wrong way, right smack into danger.

"That's her all right." Soldier shoved his hands in his pockets and took a deep breath.

The late Kristee Spangler lay facedown in a small pool of thick, black blood. So little bleeding; the blow to her head must have killed her almost instantly.

He addressed Detective Ben Stewart, a short, bald man with bright blue eyes and a keen curiosity. "Any sign of the murder weapon, Ben?"

Stewart shook his head, rubbed his chin. "Medical examiner just got here. We won't know much until she takes a look. Uniforms are beating the bushes now. Could have been a rock, could have been a baseball bat. Could have been a Vaughan & Bushnell heavy-hitter, double-face sledgehammer with fiberglass handle."

"Been reading the Sears catalog again?"

"Yeah, we're remodeling. Guess I've got sledgehammers on the brain, no pun intended."

Soldier gestured in the direction of the dead woman. "How'd you ID her? And how'd you know to call me?"

Ben rubbed his chin again. "No ID. No purse, no nothing. Atherton arrived on scene same time as me, said he recognized her from an incident at the Crowne Plaza last night. Said to call you." He shrugged. "His wife went into labor, so he had to go. They're hoping for a boy this time."

Soldier pulled his coat a little closer around him,

hunching his shoulders against a chill blast of wind coming up off the sound. Above him towering trees bent and shivered, their branches swaying against invisible fists of wind.

Several SPD squad cars lined Sixth Avenue, their blue and red lights flashing brightly against the leaden sky. A small crowd of onlookers had gathered near the curb, and uniformed officers were taking statements.

Moving toward the body, he stood over the woman who had sat at his table just last night. She was wearing the same outfit.

The photographer had finished shooting the scene, so Soldier moved closer and crouched beside the body. She was lying prone on the cement walkway as though she'd been struck, flung her arms out in surprise, and fallen in exactly that position to the ground. No muss, no fuss. No footprints around her that he could see. It hadn't rained so there was no mud. Just a dead woman in a public park in the middle of a huge metropolitan area. Well, he thought on a heavy sigh, maybe the M.E. could find something during autopsy.

He scratched his chin. Why was she killed here? Why not in her room? Perhaps the killer had thought it would make too much noise. Yelling, maybe. People would notice, call Security. He'd be cornered in the room, maybe trapped inside the hotel. And if there was blood on his clothing, people would see it. But in the park, he could make the hit then run in any number of directions. Balanced against the possibility of somebody coming upon them in a public place, Soldier figured there was some logic to that.

Standing, he turned to the uniformed officer nearest him and asked, "Who discovered the body?"

The officer indicated an attractive woman, mid-thirties, slicked-back brown hair, wearing a bright blue jogging outfit and blindingly white designer running shoes. She was chattering to a uniform who was attempting to take her statement.

Soldier walked over, flashed his badge, and introduced himself. With a nod, the young officer excused himself, gave him a look of relief and nearly fled the area.

"I understand you found the body, Ms. . . ."

"Tate. Simone Tate."

"Ms. Tate," he repeated. Simone Tate had that hard, fit, competitive look about her that he had occasionally found interesting. She was more than attractive, had sharp brown eyes, and an air of unmistakable confidence that said she usually got what she went after. As he took his note pad from his jacket pocket, she blatantly checked him out, lifted her chin and shifted her weight from her right leg to her left, tilting her slim hips a bit.

"What do you do, Ms. Tate?"

"Real estate. Condos, preconstructs, properties, houses." She grinned. Nice smile. Strong teeth. "I bet I have just the thing for you and your family. A little three-bedroom in the U-district."

"I'm not married, ma'am, and I live in an apartment."

Her eyes glistened. "Well then, Detective, perhaps you're looking for a new place to hang your hat?"

He scribbled into his note pad. "Not just at the moment, Ms. Tate."

She was trolling, and he would be crazy not to take the bait. She was good-looking, built, smart, and it was beyond obvious that she was interested. He must be nuts to reject her offer out of hand, he told himself. There had been a time, not too long ago . . .

But something had happened over the last couple of days that had dramatically altered his taste in women. He knew what that something was, or rather who, but he didn't want Betsy's lush image in his brain while he was trying to do his job.

"Tell me what happened this morning, Ms. Tate." He flipped to a new page in his note pad.

Simone Tate crossed her arms under her nicely shaped breasts and pursed her full lips. "I was taking my morning run through the park before work. It was a few minutes after six."

"Dark?"

She nodded. "Yes, but the park is well lit, plus I have a can of mace, a flashlight, and a cell phone in my fanny pack."

Soldier studiously avoided looking at the fanny in question.

"Go on."

"Not much to tell," she said with a shrug. "I was heading up this path toward Sixth when I saw the body. Well, the foot. At first I thought it was a bag lady or somebody crashed out like they do, you know?"

"Homeless person."

"Right. Well, I got closer, and realized what I was seeing, so I called 911."

"Did you go near the body? Touch it?"

She gave him a look of disgust. "Why would I do that? It seemed pretty clear she was dead."

Simone Tate was definitely not the nurturing type. Betsy not only would have gone near the body, she would have tried to stop the bleeding with every item of clothing available to her. Of course, she would have contaminated the hell out of the crime scene, but that was beside the point.

"Did you see anybody else? Anybody running away, maybe getting into a car?"

She shook her head. "No. No one."

He asked her a few more questions, then closed his note pad and smiled. "You've been a big help. Thank you. We'll be in touch."

"Anytime at all, Detective." She slid him a catlike glance. "You have my number?"

"Yes ma'am," he said. "I believe I do."

By the time Soldier returned, it was nearly three o'clock. He came in and headed directly for the bathroom.

Betsy had paced the hotel room the entire time he'd been gone, waiting, wondering. The look on his face when he'd come back had been grim. What did it take to be a cop, to see on a daily basis the worst humanity had to offer?

Perhaps she should have made a break for it while he was gone. She could have gotten a taxi and had it take her all the way to Port Henry no matter how much it cost. At least she'd be home. Home, where she could lock her doors and not come out until all this was over.

Soldier was still in the bathroom when the phone rang.

Sitting on the side of the bed, she quickly picked up the receiver. "Hello?"

A muted laugh, barely audible, emanated through the line.

"Mr. Lemsky? Is that you?"

Breathing. No words. Betsy's blood turned so cold, she shivered. Her stomach felt hollow. Her fingers went numb and she nearly dropped the phone. She wanted to call out to Soldier, but didn't want the caller to know how terrified she was. The best defense was a good offense, she'd heard it said.

"Speak up, you coward!" she blurted. "Come on out and fight like a—"

"Did he fuck you last night, Betsy? Did you like it, Betsy? I'll bet you didn't. Just laid there like a slug. How very like you."

The words were electronically altered, but Betsy tried desperately to memorize every intonation she could. "Who is this? What do you want from me?" Her voice was more breath than words as she fought to stay calm.

"I'm somebody who's going to play you for a while, like you played me. Then, *wham!* Bye-bye, Betsy."

At the caller's words, Betsy felt her spine straighten. Her breathing steadied as anger and fear thickened her blood. No anonymous creep was going to threaten her and get away with it.

"Oh, yeah?" she cracked. "Well go for it, you son of a b-bitch! M-Make my day!"

Silence, then a snicker. "Ooh, look who grew a backbone all of a sudden. Too late, Betsy," the voice jeered.

What could she say next? How could she make the caller betray himself and give her a clue as to his identity? She fought down the panic in her brain and tried to come up with something, but failed. "I'm not going to play your game," she said quietly. "You don't scare me. You're going to get caught, and when you do . . ."

At the other end of the line, the caller began to cackle like a witch. When he spoke again, the words were raspy and threatening, made all the more bizarre for their electronic buzz. *"Ah, ha-ha-ha-ha. Oh, I'll get you, my pretty, and your little dog, too!"*

The phone line went dead. Silent. No static, no hum, just dead.

Her heart racing, her breathing accelerated into rapid pants. She gulped down a glass of water to soothe her parched throat and lips.

Soldier opened the bathroom door. "I heard the phone. Was it Lem—" Taking in her appearance, he snatched his cell phone from his pocket.

As he punched in the last number, he crouched before her, taking her shaking hand in his.

"He just called. Did you get it?" He spoke into the phone, but his eyes never left hers. "Shit. No, never mind."

She felt like an idiot. A scared, mindless, brainless idiot. Why hadn't she kept her senses about her and tried harder to find out who was on the phone? Instead, she had yelled the usual hysterical female stuff

in his ear. *Who is this, what do you want with me?*
Oh, sure. Like a stalker murderer was going to tell her.

Soldier sat next to her on the bed. "We didn't get
the trace, but we can check the phone records. It's
slower, but at least we'll come up with a number and a
location." He paused, giving her time to calm down a
bit. Then, "Tell me exactly what he said."

She shook her head.

"Pretty bad?"

She nodded.

*Did he fuck you last night, Betsy? Did you like it,
Betsy? I'll bet you didn't. Just laid there like a slug.
How very like you.*

She remained silent while Soldier sat there, obviously trying to figure out how to coax her into revealing the caller's remarks. But it was too embarrassing.
How could she possibly repeat those words to Soldier,
the man who had rejected her last night?

Betsy felt his warm knuckles under her chin, nudging her face toward his. He smiled reassuringly at her.

"Take it slow," he said softly. "Close your eyes.
Forget I'm here. Just say the words and trust me. They
were only words. They can't hurt you. I'm going to get
this guy, honey. Help me get this guy."

She nodded, lowered her head and closed her eyes.
When the words came, so did the humiliation.

Chapter 10

Soldier stood motionless as he watched Betsy turn away from him. Padding softly across the carpet, she entered the small bathroom. The slight sound of the door clicking shut behind her stirred to motion the small dog curled up at the foot of the bed.

Repeating what the caller had said had unnerved Betsy, and with good reason. Soldier was more convinced than ever that she knew the stalker, and knew him well. His words had been calculated and cruel. He'd struck at her most vulnerable spot, and the blows had done some damage.

He felt his anger rise not only at what the caller had said, but at the fact Betsy was exposed enough in the first place to let the words affect her.

Self-esteem had never been an issue with him, but it obviously was with Betsy, and somebody knew that big-time.

At the foot of the bed, Piddle stretched his tooth-pick legs, yawned and blinked his dark marble eyes.

He focused on Soldier for a second, then his long lashes swept down and he returned to Slumberland.

Soldier shook his head and nudged the mutt with his fingers. "Hey, sombrero butt, shake a leg." The dog growled but made no move to shake anything. Blowing out a heavy sigh, Soldier came to a decision.

There was a ferry out of Seattle in two hours. If they hurried, they could make it. Sitting on the edge of the bed, he ran his fingers through his hair while he concentrated on planning their escape and how he could keep Betsy safe.

Betsy.

God, what that woman did to his insides. If women only knew how they stirred a man, how they made a man get hard just thinking about them. Betsy had no idea how close he'd been to throwing his ethics out the window just for the chance to make love to her last night. It would have been good—hell, it would have been great. It would also have been dead wrong.

He was doing everything he could to concentrate on her predicament, but all he could think about was sleeping with her. She'd gotten to him. With her glowing skin, her plush lips, her intelligence, her sweet-natured innocence, her feistiness, she'd gotten to him like no other woman he'd ever known.

Gotta watch out for dem cute ones, pal. Lemsky's words elbowed Soldier's conscience. *Twenty years, three kids. Life's good.*

Soldier shrugged. Yeah, sure. It had worked for the tough Chicago cop, but it wouldn't work for him. He was too set in his ways, too independent. Besides, look what had happened to Marc. A beautiful wife, couple of great kids. Alone now, thanks to him.

That alone proved his point, didn't it? What if he did go ahead and get married someday? And what if he had a couple of great kids? And what if he, like Marc, someday walked into an ambush that took his life? Or what if he wasn't killed outright, but only disabled? He'd have to be taken care of for the rest of his goddamned life.

It turned his stomach to think of himself helpless as a baby with his family tending him. Of him not being able to work, to provide, to protect. Of not being able to make love to his wife.

Solider shoved the sickening images from his head. No, his original decision had been a good one. He was a loner, and he'd stay that way.

All this maudlin thinking had to stop, he told himself. What he really needed was to get laid. Damn. It'd just been too long since he'd had sex; that was it. A couple of nights of clean-out-the-barrels, head-banging sex, and he'd be just fine.

An image of Simone Tate slipped uninvited into his brain. No. Not Simone Tate, nor any of the Simone Tates out there. Only that little blond bombshell would do, and until that issue was settled, he'd just have to find a way to cope.

Opening his suitcase, he began tossing his stuff inside. He crammed his dirty socks and underwear in a plastic bag, and forced his mind to the case at hand.

Betsy was in big trouble. She'd had a series of hang-up calls over the last couple of months that she'd thought meant nothing. And there had been some rumors at work that didn't make sense. Maybe they were about her, maybe not. Not being suspicious by nature, she'd ignored them. But the note in her dog's collar, the break-in of her room, and that last phone call . . .

Nope, this guy was no stranger to Betsy. Somebody she *knew* was stalking her, and last night had committed murder; Soldier would bet his last Historic Americana Series Colorized Washington State quarter on it.

Kristee Spangler's skull had been crushed. No witnesses, no murder weapon, and a contaminated crime scene. Obviously, the killer was finished with Kristee's services. Any connection between the two of them had been severed last night at two in the morning.

As he snapped the suitcase closed, it occurred to him that the stalker-turned-killer wasn't new at this game. If the guy fit the profile, he'd stalked before, but had he murdered?

His instincts popped up with the answer. Yes. The perp had stalked before and had killed before. The Spangler murder was too clean, too neatly planned, and too soon after Kristee had done her job. She could not be tailed or questioned, and the crime scene was a blank. As for Kristee's past, she had not been staying at the hotel, so they had no room or personal effects to examine.

With no evidence and no leads, all roads pointed to Port Henry. That was where it had started, and that was where it would end.

It was nearing five o'clock when Soldier, Betsy, and Piddle, asleep in his dog carrier, boarded the passengers-only ferry, bound for the upper reaches of the Olympic Peninsula.

Quietly flashing his badge and explaining the situation, Soldier obtained permission to board first. He settled Betsy next to the window in a seat that had a clear view of all the passengers who came through the gates and climbed the stairway to the observation deck.

"When they start boarding the other passengers," he instructed, "take a long hard look at each person. Let me know if you even vaguely recognize anybody. It doesn't matter how long ago or how briefly you may have met them. They needn't look the way you're used to seeing them, either. Check out the way people walk, the shape of their heads, their hand movements. Those are things that aren't easily disguised. Even if you only get a sense of familiarity, point them out."

Betsy's pretty mouth was set in a determined line. "Okay," she said. "I know what to do."

Reaching over, he raised her chin with his forefinger until he could make eye contact. Her green-hazel eyes were huge with anxiety, but she hadn't complained or argued with him when he told her they were going to have to sneak out of the hotel. She'd simply nodded, packed her things, gathered her dog and settled him in his carrier, then followed him out the door.

She trusted him. Soldier didn't think Betsy trusted all that easily, so it made him more determined than ever to protect her, to not let her down, to be worthy of that trust.

Looking now into her troubled eyes, he renewed his vow. Betsy would get hurt only over his dead body.

The observation deck was as wide as the ferry itself, its low ceiling only a foot or so above Soldier's standing height. Even with the aid of fluorescent lamps, the interior seemed dim, thanks to the graphite clouds scudding across the dull surface of the water, thwarting the sun and heralding the approach of another autumn storm.

The entire deck was encased by huge, rain-splattered windows, outside of which hung squawking white gulls, their wings outstretched, greedy eyes searching for a tossed crust of bread or abandoned Frito. The center of the cabin held straight-back benches painted in nautical orange, decorated with the occasional forgotten newspaper, area map, or crumpled paper cup. Built-in tables and seats clung to the inside perimeter, enabling passengers to eat, play cards, chat, or simply sit back and watch as camel-backed islands dense with evergreens floated by.

As people reached the top of the stairs, they dispersed, taking seats, grabbing a cup of coffee from the snack bar, sitting with an open book, or talking on a cell phone. None glanced at Soldier or Betsy, none made any overt actions that would draw attention to them.

"Complete strangers," Betsy said to Soldier after everyone had boarded.

"That's okay, actually. Now we can relax."

"I feel too tense to relax."

Visions of how he would help Betsy relax if they had the time and space flitted through Soldier's mind, making him set his teeth against a lustful grin. "Want some coffee?"

"Yes, please."

"Sugar? Cream?"

"Mm, let's see. I'd like a sixteen ounce, single-shot orange latte. Oh, no, wait, make that a twenty ounce, double-shot raspberry mocha, nonfat. . . . No, make that one percent, no-whip, extra sugar, extra hot, with a single straw. Please." She smiled up at him as if what she had just said made some kind of sense.

He stared at her.

"I asked you if you wanted coffee," he groused. "*Coff . . . ee.* What you want is . . . ludicrous, is what it is. It's not even in the same league as coffee. If you wanted all that other crap, why in the hell don't you just have a candy bar with a cup of coffee on the side?"

"Ha, ha, and ha. What are you going to have?"

He straightened his spine, put his fists on his hips and spread his stance. Tucking in his chin, in his best, deepest John Wayne voice, he said, "Well, pilgrim, I'm havin' coffee. A cuppa Joe. Coffee, the way a *man* drinks it. Plain. Black. Hot. It'll put hair on your chest, ma'am."

"Well, pard, I don't want hair on my chest. I'm sure you have enough for both of us."

When Soldier returned with the coffees, he settled across from her, but remained turned in the direction of the doorway. "Here's your so-called *coffee*," he said as he handed her the tall paper cup. Moving next to her, he asked, "Are you anxious about going home?"

Instead of answering, Betsy lowered her lashes and took a sip of her drink. The scent of sweet raspberries and chocolate reached his nose and he fought against asking her for a sample.

She ran her fingers through the soft curls that framed her face. With a tired sigh, she let her head fall back against the padded vinyl seat. Somehow, with her head on it, it looked like a plump silk pillow.

"Yes," she breathed. "Anxious, and apprehensive. I don't know what will happen once I get there."

"We'll catch a murderer, Betsy. That's what will happen." He took a swallow of his very hot, very black, very plain coffee.

"Explain something to me," she said. "I mean, how can you just stop your life and take off for Port Henry like this? Don't you have a girlfriend or a family or a cat or some plants that need watering?"

He took another swig of coffee. "I live alone in a small apartment in north Seattle. I don't have a cat. I do have a black thumb, so my plants died a long time ago." He sent her an intense gaze. "I'm working on the girlfriend part."

A soft blush tinted Betsy's cheeks. "So, what do you do for fun?"

Soldier watched as a gull dipped in front of the window, then lifted away again. "You mean besides writing Pulitzer prize–winning quasi-fiction?"

She stiffened, then relaxed a bit and gave him an overly sympathetic smile.

"Oh, that can't possibly be what you do for fun, you poor dear," she crooned, feigning compassion. "I mean, your prose is so twisted and tormented, it's as though you were in terrible pain when you wrote it. Or was it that somebody was holding a gun to your head, forcing you to crank out overwrought, inflated hyperbolic epistles?" Betsy blinked at him with wide, fake innocent eyes.

"Well," he drawled, "I suppose you're the expert, having written so many best-sellers yourself." He arched a brow and took another gulp of coffee.

She glared at him as she nibbled on her straw. "Okay. Tell me, O Wise One, when was the last time you actually heard anybody use the word '*empyrean*' in casual conversation, let alone in a crime drama?"

"Is that what's bothering you about my books? You don't like my choice of nouns?"

She shrugged. "Among other things."

"I'm sorry," he said, placing his knuckles against his mouth in a theatrical gesture of distress. "I obviously didn't take your reading level into account. I promise, my next book won't be any problem for you." He sat back and crossed his arms over his chest.

Betsy looked bored, but Soldier wouldn't give it up.

"All right," he grumbled. "This ought to work for you." He stopped and cleared his throat. "See Spot run."

She clicked her tongue. "Oh, puh-leeze," she said, and looked away.

He sat up. "See Spot run into the convenience store, grab the cash and shoot the owner. Oh, oh, oh. See Spot run away. See the Detective chase Spot. Run, Detective. Run fast. Run after Spot."

Betsy rolled her eyes and took a big sip of coffee.

Soldier put his hands on his knees and widened his eyes. "See Sally walking down the street with her groceries. See Spot take Sally hostage. 'Beat it or I do the bitch!' growls Spot. The Detective is worried."

Betsy's mouth flattened. "You can be such a jerk."

"Oh no! Look, look, look. See Spot shoot Sally. See the blood. It is red! Spot is a very bad dog."

"You can stop now."

"See the Detective break down the door. It is loud. *Crash!* See Spot take aim at the Detective. The Detective has called for backup, but it is late in arriving. See the Detective sweat."

"All right. I get the *point.*"

"Poor Sally. Sally is an innocent bystander. She is bleeding. Spot is laughing. Laugh, Spot, laugh. The Detective points his thirty-eight Detective Special at Spot. 'Drop the gun, asshole!' orders the Detective."

Soldier clamped his jaw shut, sat back against the seat and finished off his coffee. Next to him, Betsy blew out an exaggerated breath. A few seconds ticked by. Finally, she turned and glared at him.

"Well?" she huffed impatiently.

"Well what?"

"What happened? Did you collar Spot?" She groaned. "I can't believe I just said that. But was Sally all right? I mean, you just can't leave me . . ." She twisted her mouth into a grimace. "Oh, I get it. You are too, too funny."

Soldier sent her a triumphant look. "The Detective is good. The Detective is smart. See the Detective rush Spot and tackle him. Look, look, look. The Detective arrests Spot and takes him away in a big car."

"What about Sally?"

"See Sally recover," he said, as though he were talking to a five-year-old. "Sally thinks the Detective is wonderful. See Sally tell the Detective he is *empyrean*. And he is."

"We are *so* not amused."

He sent her a toothy grin. "See Soldier smile in triumph. The end."

Betsy shrugged nonchalantly. "Well, if that's all it takes, I could write a book. If I wanted to."

"All right. If you wrote a book, what would it be about?"

"About four hundred pages."

He pursed his lips. "Four hundred *pages*? Medieval or Congressional?"

"You're being deliberately obtuse."

"I've been told I'm acute."

"Oh, ho . . . working a new angle?"

Soldier chuckled. "You're quick, I'll give you that."

Betsy scoffed and turned to look out the huge window. They had pushed off from the dock and were heading into the main corridor of the sound. In the distance, past the curve of Betsy's cheek, Soldier could see the deeply green water sparkling here and there in spite of the clouds that pressed heavily on its surface.

For a few more hours, he would have this feisty woman all to himself. After that, well, if they didn't kill each other first, he'd just have to see how it went.

"So," he said, nudging her with his elbow. "Where has that nimble mind of yours gone off to now?"

"I was thinking about my father."

Her father. Hmm. "Betsy, is it possible, I mean, do you think he could be the one who—"

"No," she declared. "Not Daddy. No matter how

strange he might be these days, he would never hurt me. He would never kill. Besides, he's still institutionalized."

"Where is he?"

"He's in Steilacoom, at Western." Her words were clipped, as though she was giving him the information grudgingly. "I was eighteen when my parents divorced and Daddy got hurt. He went to live with his brother for a while, but after a few months it got to be too much and Uncle Terry had him committed. I try to visit him as often as I can, but it's so far away. I wish he could live with me."

"It's not your fault, Betsy. You can only do so much."

"But he's my *father* and I love him. Loretta said—"

"Who's Loretta?" he interrupted.

"My mother."

"You call your mother Loretta?"

"It's her name."

"So I gathered. But why don't you call her Mom or Mother or Mumsy or something?"

"You'd really have to know Loretta to understand," she said through a wry smile. "At any rate, Loretta said Daddy won't get any better and it's best he stays where he is. I think she's wrong. I think she just doesn't want to deal with her own sense of guilt over what happened."

"Betsy, taking care of a mentally ill person can be an awesome burden. If he really isn't suited to living outside the hospital, then he, and you, are truly better off this way."

"And you know this because?" She clamped her jaw shut and sent him a decidedly pissed look.

Sliding closer to her, he took the paper cup from her hands and set it next to his on the table. "Let's talk about this some other time. Put your head on my shoulder," he coaxed. "Get some sleep. I'll wake you when we get to Port Henry." *I want you close to me. I want to feel your body next to mine.*

She looked up at him with wary eyes. "I know what you're really after, Soldier," she accused, and his heart gave a guilty lurch. "It has nothing to do with me getting any sleep, or the stalking, or the murder."

Her eyes glinted with mischief. "What you really want is for me to fall asleep so you can have my twenty ounce raspberry mocha. Coffee, plain, black. Right. You're dying for a taste, but you're too proud to admit it."

Oh, Christ. She'd done it again. Lifting his hand, he brushed her silky hair away from her cheek. He lowered his head and touched his mouth to hers and felt a raw heat flash through his body. The intensity of it shocked him. Just the slightest contact with her made him dizzy to the point of distraction and hungry to the point of desperation.

He tried to pull back, but her lips clung to his for a second too long. Cursing himself, he went back for seconds, kissing her deeply. She tasted like chocolate and raspberries and cream and he wanted to devour her.

When he finally ended the kiss, they were both out of breath. Betsy's mouth was swollen and damp. With her tousled hair and flushed cheeks, she looked like she had just tumbled from bed all warm and satisfied from his lovemaking.

He licked his lips. "You're right," he confessed.

"That was all I wanted, but it tasted much, much better this way."

It had been dark for a good three hours when the ferry finally slipped into its dock. Soldier had visited Port Henry many times and had always liked how the town was set on a series of low hills that rolled gently down into the Strait of Juan de Fuca.

The wharf area was a popular part of town, and it featured seaside businesses such as gift shops, seafood restaurants, and chandleries, all painted in muted blues and greens, colors of the sea. Despite the late hour, gulls circled and squawked overhead, filling the cold, salty air with their familiar squabbling.

The small landing was a confusion of people carrying briefcases or pushing strollers, all waiting to take the return ferry down the sound and into Seattle. Soldier looked for Taylor, and spotted his tall brother wearing blue jeans and a heavy corduroy jacket, leaning against the ticketing stand, his arms crossed over his chest.

Soldier turned his attention to the blond head resting against his shoulder.

She'd slept most of the way, giving him time to think, feel her soft body nestled against his, enjoy her scent . . . and polish off her coffee.

As passengers prepared to leave, Soldier wiggled his shoulder a little. "Wake up, Ms. Tremaine. We're home."

Betsy blinked and shifted her position, pushing away from him and sitting up on her own.

Ignoring her sexily sleepy eyes and flushed cheeks,

he said, "Taylor's here to drive us to your house. Once we're there, I want to go over the reports that he got from Winslow, especially the analysis done on the note. Taylor's already done some checking on the names you gave me, and I want to see what he's turned up on those. By the way," he said, "are there any good motels in Port Henry?"

Betsy arched her brows. "Sure, the place is full of them, but, if you don't mind the mess, you can stay at my house. It's huge. It's a Victorian my parents bought when they were first married. Daddy fixed it up."

"Well, that would be okay for me, but there's Taylor—"

"There's room for him, too. In fact, I'm sure I could fit the entire SPD in my house." Betsy furrowed her brow. "But you can't stay with me forever. You can't protect me every minute of every day. I have a life. I have a job, and a mother, and friends—"

"And," he interrupted, "you have a stalker-turned-killer who needs to be dealt with. Ready or not, here we go."

When the man approached them at the ferry terminal, Betsy thought she was seeing double. Taylor McKennitt was as tall as Soldier, as broad-shouldered, and as fit. He was also as devastatingly attractive. Although he appeared to be a couple of years younger than Soldier, he seemed tired somehow, like he never had any fun or didn't know how to relax. Earlier, Soldier had mentioned that Taylor had just gone through an especially bad divorce, and Betsy could see it had taken its toll.

The brothers grinned at each other and embraced, pounding each other on the back with their open palms. Betsy had rarely seen men engage in gestures of affection. In her own family, open displays of affection were rare, if they existed at all. But these two seemed to genuinely like each other. She didn't know why, but that gave her a good feeling inside.

Taking Betsy's hand, Taylor lifted a brow. "Gosh," he said, "you don't look anything like your picture."

"You've seen my—"

"Um," Soldier interjected. "Get the dog carrier, would you, bro?"

Taylor reached for the dog carrier in her hand. "Ah," he said as he took it from her and looked down at the shivering little dog. *"Deh Urinator."*

Piddle growled.

"Go ahead," Taylor said to the snarling pooch. "Make my day."

"I think you're getting your action heroes mixed up, pal." Soldier laughed, then returned his attention to the activity on the dock.

As Soldier and Taylor scanned the crowd, Betsy felt like a visiting dignitary with full security on alert.

She got in the backseat of Taylor's Forester and buckled up. Setting Piddle's carrier next to her, she spoke softly to the trembling dog until they were under way. The drone of the motor and the gentle movement over a smooth roadway never failed to put Piddle right to sleep.

But Betsy was far from sleepy. She was a nervous wreck. Even though she'd had nothing to do with the murder, she felt responsible somehow. She couldn't help but feel that if she'd been smarter or more clever, she could have figured out who was behind all this, and poor Kristee Spangler might still be alive.

Soldier liked the house the minute he saw it. Even though it was getting close to nine o'clock and the street was dark, he admired the two-story Victorian painted in muted blues and contrasting peach tones. It was a pretty house that suited her personality perfectly. Disgusting male that he was, he wondered which was her bedroom, and how far away from it his would be.

Given the late hour and the fact she had been out of town, he had expected the house to be dark, but the downstairs lights were on. Soldier shot a look of surprise at Betsy, who sat behind him staring out the car window, apparently distressed by what she was seeing.

Her eyes were wide with alarm and her cheeks were flushed. Sinking back into the seat cushion, she pinched the bridge of her nose between her fingers like she had a terrible headache.

"Do you always leave all your lights blazing when you go away for the weekend?"

In the relative darkness of the backseat she shook her head and sighed. "I never should have called Paris. I should have left well enough alone. I am simply too stupid to live. Dumb . . . dumb . . . dumb . . ."

Soldier reached for his weapon.

"No!" she gasped. Lifting her lashes, she looked sadly into his eyes. "No weapon," she murmured. "It's no big deal, really. It's just . . . my mother. God, I hope she didn't bring that Parisian, Dick, with her."

Soldier and Taylor slowly turned their heads to look at each other. They stared across the seat for a moment.

"Did she say Parisian *duck*?" Taylor asked.

"I heard *dick*," Soldier replied.

"What's a Parisian dick?"

"I don't think I want to know."

As Taylor parked the car in the long, shrubbery-lined drive, the front door of the house flew open. Soldier stepped out of the car and had turned to open Betsy's door when a man and a woman exited the house, hurried down the porch steps, and came running across the lawn toward the car.

Soldier heard Betsy, still in the backseat, talking to the mutt. "There there, Pids. I'm letting you out of your carrier. There's your mommy."

As Soldier pulled the door open, Betsy set the dog on the cement driveway. "Fly, little Chihuahua. Fly!"

Piddle took off like a geriatric marathoner and leaped a good two inches into the air, just in time to be caught in the woman's lowered arms. Soldier watched as female and dog screeched and whined and kissed and slobbered all over each other. Her male companion halted a few feet behind her, looking at a loss as to how to behave in the face of such unfettered devotion.

Soldier stole a glance at Betsy as she moved forward to approach her mother. In a flash of awareness, he saw what Betsy had probably seen all her life, and why she felt she could never measure up.

What young woman could possibly compare to the likes of Loretta Tremaine?

Betsy's mother was tall and lithe, with flaming red

hair that billowed around her head like an atomic cloud. Her makeup was minimal and she was tastefully dressed in a dark silk suit with a low-cut neckline. Her jewelry was fashionable but not overdone. Her features were stunning. She was an incredibly beautiful woman, full of verve and passion, and was the least motherly looking female Soldier had ever seen.

The man behind her was also tall, had dark hair, appeared somewhat younger than Mrs. Tremaine, and was very slim. He had a European look to him, which was confirmed when he spoke.

"*Loretta!*" he shouted above the din. "*Est-il ce Peedle? Oui?*"

"*Oui, Richard, c'est Piddle, mon petit chien!*" The woman hugged the rat-dog to her bosom and continued kissing its head.

"Hello, Loretta." Betsy stood still, apparently waiting for the nauseating reunion between lady and dog to end. Finally, her mother lifted her head to notice her daughter. Shoving the little dog into Richard's hands, she wrapped her arms around Betsy and pulled her close.

"I wasn't ignoring you, sweet," she said. "At least, I didn't mean to."

Soldier watched as Loretta Tremaine held her daughter at arm's length. Blatantly running her gaze up and down her daughter, the woman said, "Are you all right, Elizabeth? You've gained a little weight, haven't you? And that hair. You should really let me take you to my stylist. A little lipstick wouldn't hurt, either. I know you prefer the natural look, but really, darling."

Betsy's spine stiffened almost imperceptibly. Her pretty mouth was a grim line across her face, her eyes were downcast.

Fuck, why didn't the woman just take out a goddamned gun and shoot her? Did she treat Betsy like this all the time?

"And you look tired," Loretta blathered on. "Are you warm enough? You should be wearing a sweater. It's a chilly night and you don't want to catch cold, now do you? Why don't you come inside and take a hot bath and put your nightgown on. I can do something motherly, you know, like make hot chocolate or whatever. Like I used to do when you were little."

"You never made hot chocolate for me, Loretta. I made it for you, remember?"

Betsy put her hands on her mother's shoulders and looked up into the woman's elegant features. "I'm fine, Loretta," she said. "You've only been gone for three weeks, for heaven's sake. I've not been harmed, and these detectives are working on the case. You can stop worrying and go home."

Betsy turned toward Soldier. Although she seemed to be avoiding his eyes, he could see a bewildered softness in them. She loved her mother, but obviously found the woman exasperating. Big surprise there, he thought.

"Loretta, I'd like you to meet Soldier and Taylor McKennitt—"

"Call me Loretta," she interrupted stridently. "Soldier and Taylor? What, Beggerman and Thief couldn't make it?" She laughed riotously at her own joke while her traveling companion simply stared at her, a confused smile tilting his too thick lips.

Soldier pasted a grin on his face as he took the woman's hand. "Gosh, *Loretta*," he chided, "we've never heard that one before, have we, Taylor?"

"Aha! I remember!" proclaimed Loretta. "*'Tinker, Tailor, Soldier, Sailor, Rich man, Poor man, Beggar man, Thief!'* Then doesn't it go, *'Something, something, Doctor, Lawyer, Indian chief'?*"

As Taylor shook her hand, he said, "Yes, but we don't have any of those in the family. Only cops."

The woman's mirth abruptly vanished. "Cops? Oh, yes. I forgot." She spoke in rapid French over her shoulder to her companion, who shoved the dog under his left arm while he extended his right hand to both Soldier and Taylor.

"Richard du Par," he stated as he shook their hands in turn. Smiling hugely, he pointed to the Chihuahua nestled under his arm. "Peedle."

They all stared at him for a moment while he gazed directly into the dog's luminous marble eyes. Piddle had stopped yapping and lifted his muzzle to meet Richard's reverent stare. Apparently, it was love at first sight, and it was mutual.

Betsy addressed her mother. "There's been a new development in the case, Loretta. Let's go in the house, where it's warm, and I'll tell you all about it."

As she turned to lift her suitcase from the back of the truck, Soldier immediately stepped in and took it from her hand. "You three go on ahead. Taylor and I can handle the luggage."

Betsy gave him a smile that said she'd rather be dealing with the luggage than with her mother. Nonetheless, she took Loretta's elbow and proceeded to steer her across the damp lawn toward the front porch.

As Soldier dragged his own suitcase and laptop from the back, he became aware of a slow-moving car making its way up the street. All his instincts went on alert.

Closing the door, he took a long hard look at the approaching car, but the headlights were too bright for him to make out the driver. Just as the car was nearly close enough to see inside, the driver threw it into reverse and began backing away.

Soldier dropped his suitcase and ran up the street, pulling his weapon as he jumped a small boxwood hedge. Within seconds he heard Taylor's rapid footfalls behind him.

Reaching the intersection, the car continued its backward motion. Then, tires screeching, the engine gunned loudly as the driver whipped the car around and took off up the cross street.

By the time Soldier and Taylor got to the intersection, the street was silent, and empty.

Barely winded, Taylor said, "Did you get a look?"

"Goddammit," Soldier spat. "It was too damn dark. Did you make the plates?"

Taylor shook his head as he replaced his gun in his shoulder holster. "The license plate light was conveniently out. But at least we got a description of the car."

Soldier holstered his weapon and reached for the small note pad inside his jacket pocket. "Late model

Ford. Dark green sedan." He cussed again. "That's not very much to go on."

As they made their way up the drive, Soldier saw Betsy standing on the front porch, watching him approach. Her eyes were huge, her arms wrapped around her middle. She looked shell-shocked.

Without a word, Taylor picked up Soldier's suitcase and proceeded across the lawn up the steps to the wide, elegant porch.

Cupping Betsy's shoulders in his palms, Soldier let out a heavy breath. "Did you see?"

She nodded, her gaze firmly locked on the distant corner.

"Did you recognize the car?"

She shook her head.

"It could have been nothing, Betsy. A coincidence."

She shifted her weight from one foot to the other and looked up into his eyes. "I thought you said you didn't believe in coincidences."

Shaking his head, he confessed, "You're right. I don't."

Chapter 11

It was nearing midnight by the time everybody had been fed and fresh linens were distributed. As Betsy placed clean towels on the sink in the bathroom she and Soldier would share, she considered calling Claire. She needed to talk to another woman, somebody she trusted. She had so many emotions crashing together inside her heart and her head, she needed a reality check, and her oldest and dearest friend was certainly someone she could count on.

Betsy knew Claire wouldn't mind talking to her, no matter the time of night, but the problem was, she was so damned tired, she wasn't sure she'd even be able to carry on a decent conversation. First thing tomorrow, she decided, she'd give Claire a call.

She looked up to see her mother standing in the doorway.

"Hello, Loretta. You look lovely, as always." She meant it, but Betsy knew she herself looked as though she'd just been dragged through a knothole backward.

Glancing at her reflection in the oval bathroom mirror, she saw a very tired version of herself, not clean, not fresh, not happy. A shower would repair the clean and fresh part; as for the happy part, well, that might take some time yet.

"Your young detectives are quite breathtaking, Elizabeth," Loretta said, a flirty grin tilting her smooth lips. Her blue eyes snapped with interest. "Do me a favor, won't you darling, and throw back the one you don't want, hmm? In case I decide to go fishing?"

As blandly as she could, Betsy said, "They're both nice looking, Loretta. However, neither of them is mine."

"Well, in that case, did you notice that Soldier couldn't keep his eyes off me? Such a manly man. You were right. The younger one, Tyler—"

"Taylor."

"*Oui.* You and he look good together. He may be one of those men who actually likes the plumper type. Snag him while you have the chance, Elizabeth. You *are* pushing thirty, you know, dear, and I was already married and you were three years old when I was your age."

As her mother babbled on, Betsy let her thoughts flicker to the brothers McKennitt. Taylor seemed very nice, but he didn't make her heart do a back flip. His eyes, she'd noticed, were similar in color to Soldier's, but seemed faded by comparison. She got light-headed and nervous when Soldier walked toward her, smiled at her. Sure, Taylor was nice and all, but it was Soldier who had captured her heart.

Betsy's insides twisted. She was thoroughly and desperately attracted to him, and she couldn't deny it. Didn't want to. She felt like she had in junior high school when she'd had a crush on Jason Howard, but this was much worse. Jason had asked her to dance, and she had been engulfed in a fog of girlish infatuation. But Jason never kissed her or looked at her with eyes that short-circuited her nervous system. Only Soldier had ever done that.

". . . lumberjack types and possibly ex-convicts. Why, when I was your age, I—"

"*Loretta,*" Betsy interjected, cutting off her mother's insensitive tirade. "A woman has been murdered, most likely by the man who's stalking me! I'm a nervous wreck, in case you haven't noticed, but I'm trying to carry on here. I haven't had the time or the energy to even think about which of the McKennitt brothers would give me the time of day, even if one of them did like the plumper types, as you say. Yes, I'm nearing thirty. Yes, I'm no raving beauty. Yes, I've been dateless for—well, let's not go there. But there's too much going on now for me to worry about catching a *man*. Besides," she sighed irritably, "I'm not very good at relationships. I don't have your way with men. I don't know how to do dating and romance, and I'm not looking for an affair."

Loretta did stop talking, but stood still as though in shock, her mouth slightly open, her eyes wide.

"If I were to let him," Betsy murmured as she concentrated on folding the baby blue washcloth in her hands, "if I were to let him, he'd break my heart, Loretta. I could fall in love with him so easily."

Betsy lifted her gaze to make eye contact. *Please act*

*like a mother, just once? Please, please comfort me
and reassure me, just this once . . . Mother?* "I don't
want to get my heart broken," she continued softly,
"and then have nothing left after he goes."

"You do like Tyler!" Loretta nearly bellowed. "A
mother always knows. So you're saying that Soldier is
available?"

For three full heartbeats Betsy stared at Loretta, uncertain if the woman who bore her had one giving,
selfless, nurturing, motherly cell in her entire body.

Beaten down by exhaustion, fear, and frustration,
Betsy capitulated. "Sure, Loretta. Tyler." What was
the use? The woman had never listened to her in the
past, why should she begin now?

Loretta moved to Betsy and surrounded her with
her arms. Kissing her daughter's hair, she said, "Don't
be silly, Elizabeth. What makes you think Tyler will
leave? What makes you think he'll break your heart?"

Betsy expelled a soft laugh. They were speaking of
two different men, but it didn't really matter. "What
makes you think he won't? Aren't you always telling
me what a loser I am? I haven't had a long-term relationship in four years. Hey, I'm going for the record,
here."

"Tsk-tsk. It sounds to me like you're feeling sorry
for yourself. And I never said you were a loser. You
need to do something to make yourself a little more attractive, that's all. This . . ." Loretta reached up and
fluffed Betsy's hair. "This country girl look has got to
go. He's a sophisticated city man. Drop a few pounds,
get yourself some new clothes, seduce him, let him get
you pregnant, then make him marry you."

Betsy lost her train of thought completely and simply gaped at her mother. Loretta's brows were arched and the look in her eyes spoke of complete sincerity.

"*Loretta*. You can't . . . you don't . . . Am I adopted? I'm adopted, aren't I? You're not really my mother. It's all some horrible, twisted—"

Loretta's head fell back as she let loose a laugh that nearly rattled the windows.

She removed herself from her mother's embrace, sat on the closed lid of the commode and waited for Loretta to catch her breath. She wished the two of them had the kind of relationship where she could bare her feelings about Soldier. She wanted to talk about what it was like to fall in love, not to mention how afraid she was—of being stalked, of being hurt, of possibly being murdered.

But Loretta would just shrug it off as a peripheral thing, as something Betsy's overactive imagination had churned up in spite of any physical evidence to the contrary.

Loretta was . . . well, *Loretta,* and as cold and distant as the polar ice caps when it came to matters of the heart, the soul.

"Loretta," Betsy ventured. "Just exactly who is this Richard?"

"Ah, *mon dieu*. It's not pronounced that way. So American. You say it as the French do, *Ree-shar*."

"I don't care how you pronounce it, Loretta, he still looks like a Dick to me."

Loretta scowled and crossed her arms, leaning back against the doorjamb. "*Ree-shar* is my latest protégé, Elizabeth."

Betsy felt her eyes widen in astonishment. "Protégé? Exactly what kind of protégé?"

Loretta waved her elegant hand in the air in a gesture of dismissal. "Oh, he's just a man I met in Paris. He comes from an old French aristocratic family. No money or land, of course, but the titles, *oui!* He wants to learn English, American English, so I invited him home with me."

Betsy's head spun. Was her mother crazy? "Are you crazy? The French don't want to learn English. They want everybody on earth to learn *French*! He's using you, Loretta! Free room and board and God knows what else!" At least her mother had her own house across town so Betsy wouldn't have to watch that little drama unfold.

Loretta smiled, but seemed unmoved by her daughter's reasoning. Betsy sputtered on.

"You were only in Paris for a few weeks. You can't possibly know this guy, but you invited him to Port Henry to stay with you so he can *learn English*?" She shook her head in disbelief that her own mother was capable of such flamboyant stupidity.

Leaning forward, Loretta gave Betsy a kiss on the cheek. "Good night, lovie. I'm going home now. See you in the morning."

Without hesitation, Soldier chose the bedroom on the second floor next to Betsy's. Only a connecting bathroom would come between them tonight. Taylor took what had once been the maid's quarters just off the kitchen on the first floor. It had its own bathroom, and he could keep a watch on the downstairs and back door more easily.

Even though the house was a Victorian, Betsy's father had updated the kitchen and the plumbing, making the place modern and serviceable while still retaining its elegant nineteenth century charm.

Soldier's room was fairly spacious for a house of the period, and must have once been considered the master bedroom. The room faced east and would receive the first light of day, which probably gave the interior a cheerful appearance. Lace curtains adorned the windows, adding to the turn-of-the-century feel. Beside the double bed, there were two cherry nightstands with lamps and a bookcase filled with volumes on travel destinations and gardening. A cherry writing desk stood in the corner.

Sitting on the edge of the mattress, he rubbed his tired eyes. Damn, it had been a long day. He was beat. He knew he'd sleep like a rock, but he didn't want to. He wanted to be awake, with Betsy, in her arms, in her bed, in her body.

He nearly groaned out loud at the thought of making love to Betsy, comfortable between her rounded thighs while he kissed her mouth. She would moan softly and rise to his touch, seeking her own pleasure as she lifted her hips to take him in.

Shaking his head to erase the image, Soldier turned down the covers, readying himself for bed. Stretching out his long body on the soft quilt, he tried to relax. No dice.

He should go check on her, he thought, just to make

sure she was settled. She had been so nervous and anxious earlier, she really needed to have someone calm
her. Checking on her would be the right thing to do.
For her own good.

Carefully opening the bathroom door, he peered
across to the opposite door, which was tightly closed.
No light showed at the bottom of the threshold. As
late as it was, she was most certainly asleep.

Well, he'd just have to wake her up. To check on
her. To make sure she was okay. For her own sake.

And then he would kiss her back to sleep.

Betsy was just drifting off when she heard her bedroom door squeak open. She'd lain awake for hours, it
seemed, listening to Soldier pace his room. He was
working, she knew that. The walls in a Victorian were
paper thin, so she'd heard him talking on the phone,
making arrangements with the Homicide chief regard-
ing his duty time. She'd even heard him setting up his
laptop on the little desk in what used to be her parents'
bedroom.

He wasn't being noisy or insensitive, it was just that
she was alert to everything about him—his looks, his
scent, his sheer masculinity. All of those things got to
her, made her keenly aware of him, made her want his
body. His intelligent eyes, sense of humor, integrity,
kindness, those things got to her, too. They made her
want his heart.

When the door opened to the adjoining bathroom,
her body went on immediate alert.

She was curled into herself under the blankets, her
head resting deeply in her pillow. Squinting her eyes

open, she saw Soldier's broad, bare shoulders silhouetted in the bathroom doorway as he moved through it and into her room. Holding her breath, she stayed perfectly still as he sat on the edge of her bed. Her mattress dipped in response to his weight and she felt the heat from his body, so near her own.

"Betsy?" His whisper was soft in the darkness.

"Um, is there something you need?" she squeaked into her pillow. "A washcloth? Toothpaste? An extra blanket?" *Sex?*

In the shadows of the night, Soldier leaned down and brushed her hair with his lips. "I just wanted to make sure you were all right." His warm breath touched her cheek, stirring her senses.

She caught his scent; clean, male, unique to him. It roused something deep within her, a need so elemental her entire body responded as desire rushed through her. He kissed her hair again, this time closer to her temple. She felt his mouth on her skin and a tingle of excitement shimmied through her blood.

"I'm fine," she breathed. Every muscle in her body tightened and she thought the only way she could ease the tension was to stretch them. Uncurling herself, she faced Soldier and placed her palms against his firm, bare chest. His skin was soft, his muscles like iron. She fought the desire to run her hands all over his body.

"Tell me you're not naked," she whispered.

"I'm not naked. I'm wearing bottoms," he said against her skin as he slid his mouth to her cheek. "Are you wearing anything under those covers?"

"My nightgown."

"Is it one of those flimsy lacy things?"

Oh God. "Yes."

"Mm. Good," he murmured. He covered her mouth with his own and kissed her deeply. She made a soft, high-pitched little sound, and Soldier groaned and kissed her more thoroughly. Shoving her covers out of the way, he slipped the straps of her negligee down, exposing her breasts to the cool night air, and his hot mouth. Placing tiny kisses across her collarbone, he moved down, slowly, letting his tongue slide along her flesh until she wanted to scream with pleasure.

He hovered over one taut nipple, tracing circles around it with his tongue. She arched her back, trying to move so he would catch it in his mouth, but he shifted, refusing it, teasing her, making her crazy with desire.

Between her legs, she felt tense and urgent, and knew that if he stroked her there, it would feel so very, very good. Her insides went all tingly and achy and she could think of nothing but Soldier's hard body and how it would feel if she let him make love to her.

Just as she'd decided it would probably be best to push him away, his tongue flicked across her nipple and her breath caught. He suckled, first one, then the other, as she squirmed in his embrace.

He slid his hand down her stomach and found that place between her legs capable of driving her over the edge. She was so close to climaxing, she wanted to weep. She moved against his thick finger, increasing her pleasure. With his tongue teasing her nipple and his hand working its silken magic between her parted thighs, she felt as though she were ready to fly to heaven.

But it was not to be.

An irritating noise began to emanate from his room. His cell phone. His *cell phone* was bleeping!

Abruptly, he pulled his hand away, and his mouth.

"God damned son of a bitch," he bit out, each word a sentence of its own. "I have to take that, Betsy. Stay right where you are. Don't . . . move."

As if. She was paralyzed with pleasure. She could barely take a deep breath, let alone move.

Through the open doors between them, she heard him answer, grind out a reply, then snap the phone closed. A moment later he appeared in the bathroom doorway.

"I have to go," he said rapidly. "Can I take your car?"

" 'Kay," she squeaked, wound too tightly to utter a complete word.

He began backing away. "I'm sorry. I'm really, really sorry. I'll see you in the morning, okay?"

" 'Kay."

"Where are your keys?"

" 'Kay."

"Where?"

"Um, purse . . . table . . . kitchen." It was the best she could do under the circumstances.

Was it her imagination, or had he also been having trouble speaking? He closed the bathroom door behind him, leaving her totally hot and thoroughly bothered.

Betsy lay on her bed, naked from the waist up, the hem of her nightgown hiked up to her hips. Her mouth was wet from his kisses and her nipples ached. She was still swollen where he'd grazed her with his fingers.

Oh, man. How in the world was she ever going to get to sleep now? Damn him for leaving her in this condition!

Well, she mused as she envisioned Soldier's handsome face inches above her own. She could always take matters into her own hands. . . .

Across the breakfast table, Loretta Tremaine grinned at Soldier. If he didn't know better, he'd swear she was flirting with him. Nah. Betsy's *mother*? Flirting? With *him*?

Her bright red hair had been teased and sprayed into a sort of flaming match concoction, and she'd sprinkled glitter on it. With every movement, her hair flashed and winked at him.

She wore a tasteful emerald green ensemble, but again, the bodice was cut way too low for his comfort.

He'd been surprised to see Loretta at Betsy's house so early on a Sunday morning. He would have pegged her for a late riser, but she'd surprised him with coffee as soon as he'd sat down at the large oak table.

Piddle lay curled up under a chair, deep in slumber, as usual.

After taking a few sips of coffee, Soldier rose from the table and began rummaging around, looking for something to eat.

"I see her cupboards are practically bare," Loretta remarked as she sipped at her own coffee. "Elizabeth needs to go shopping. Oh, that girl. You'll just have to make do with odds and ends, I suppose."

"No problem," Soldier said. "When Taylor wakes up, we can go to the store."

He poured himself a hearty bowl of Fruit Loops and added evaporated milk and brown sugar, sliced off a large hunk of Velveeta, poured a glass of pulpy grapefruit juice, and grabbed a handful of chocolate chip cookies. "Just like home," he said.

Loretta winced as he tore into the eclectic assortment before him, but she said nothing about it. "How long are you planning on staying?" she asked. "That is to say, how long will Elizabeth need protection?"

Did the woman have something in her eye, or was she batting her lashes at him? Dear God, with a mother like Loretta, no wonder Betsy was among the walking wounded.

Soldier gulped down the grapefruit juice, then wiped his mouth on a cloth napkin that had tiny roosters printed on it.

"Well," he said, "I don't know. Hopefully, we can catch this guy soon and have done with it. Crime doesn't hold to any timetable, unfortunately."

Reaching for the carafe on the table, Soldier poured himself more coffee, then lifted his brows in inquiry as he tilted the container toward Loretta.

"No more for me," she said as she pushed her cup away.

Soldier leaned forward and looked Loretta in the eye. "I spoke to Betsy about the possibility that her father is behind this. She doesn't think so. You were married to the man. What do you think?"

The elegant line of the woman's body shifted and

tensed. She pursed her lips. Taking a deep breath, she let it trickle out slowly while she seemed to consider her words.

"I haven't seen Douglas for years. He was diagnosed as a paranoid schizophrenic after he'd sustained a head injury in a disgusting brawl."

"As opposed to a classy brawl?"

She ignored his obvious sarcasm.

"Did he ever indicate to you that he might be angry with Betsy? That he felt she may have betrayed him in some way?"

Loretta rose from the table and took her cup to the sink, where she proceeded to wash it, dry it, and put it away in the cupboard. All with an air of nobility that would have put the Royal Family to shame. "Yes. Elizabeth was just eighteen when I called a halt to that travesty of a marriage. Douglas asked her to come live with him, but she refused."

"Why?"

"You'll have to ask her. I only know that it hurt him very much."

"Was she afraid of him?"

The woman looked honestly taken aback. "Oh, no. Heavens no. She had nothing to fear from her father. He treated her like a princess."

"So her refusal to live with him might have hurt him deeply. Hurt him enough to make him want to hurt her back?"

"You assume too much, Detective. Douglas has been in the hospital for the last nine years."

She gathered her purse and her dog and walked to the door. "Douglas was a research scientist. He was very focused on his work, but he was ever the gentle man. And he adored Betsy. They were very close. Before his injuries, I would have said no, that he was not capable of hurting anybody. After he was afflicted, well, I can't speak to that."

"So you're saying that after his injuries, he might have developed a capacity for violence?"

"As I said, it's all rather moot, since he's still in the hospital."

"Are you certain? When was the last time you checked on him?"

Loretta sighed as though he'd been brow-beating her for hours and she had finally decided to yield. "All right," she snapped. "It's been six years since I've seen him. So I'm a shade self-involved. That's not a crime. Douglas and I were divorced. He wasn't my problem anymore. Lots of people get divorced. What happened to him that night was his own fault and none of my doing. I have nothing to feel guilty over. Nothing! He's his brother's responsibility now, not mine."

Soldier watched Loretta stalk out the door. The more he saw of the mother, the more he understood the daughter. How in the hell had Betsy turned out so sweet and giving with a mother like that?

He didn't want to hurt Betsy any more than necessary, but the fact of the matter was, Douglas Tremaine was most definitely a suspect.

As a result of one of his phone calls last night, he'd discovered something that Betsy and her mother were apparently unaware of, something that could mean nothing, or everything.

Three months ago, Douglas Tremaine had been declared well enough to be released from the hospital into his brother's care. According to Betsy's uncle Terry, her father was on his way to Port Henry, determined to see his daughter.

Chapter 12

Rinsing out his coffee mug, Soldier looked out the kitchen window in time to see his brother finish up an early morning run through the town. Ever since the divorce, Taylor seemed bent on burning off his anger—not to mention a storehouse of pent-up sexual frustration—with arduous physical workouts. As a result, his body was in top shape while his love life was stuck facedown on the bunny slopes.

Bursting through the back door in sweatpants and a damp white T-shirt, Taylor greeted him. "Hey, Jackson. Port Henry's a nifty little place."

"I know. I took a run before you got up," Soldier replied.

Wiping his face on a towel he'd left by the back door, Taylor said, "Where'd you go last night?"

He dried the coffee mug and replaced it on the shelf. "I got a call around midnight from Officer Winslow at the PHPD. There was a B and E at a dry cleaner's downtown and he wanted me to come and check it out."

Taylor leaned against the back door. "Why you?"

"He knew I was in the area, and they're short-staffed right now. It was an odd kind of break-in and he just wanted another pair of eyes."

"Much money taken?"

Soldier shook his head. "I don't think they were after money. The place was a total wreck, the interior vandalized, clothing cut to pieces and some even burned. Really weird. Until people come in to pick up their stuff, the owner's not sure he'll know what's missing. Anyway," he said, blowing out a tired sigh, "I've been up most of the night."

"Yeah, I thought you looked a little beat," Taylor said. "Sorry, Jackson. I'll get showered, then we can go over my reports."

"Show me yours and I'll show you mine." Soldier grinned.

His brother barked out a laugh. "Not much to see these days. You know how things tend to atrophy from lack of use."

"Quit complaining," Soldier chided. "Sounds like you just need to get a grip."

"Yuk-yuk. You're so funny, I forgot to laugh."

Taylor laughed anyway and left the kitchen through one door as Betsy entered through the other.

She looked beautiful, all soft and feminine. Her hair was still damp from her morning shower and she was dressed casually in a rose-colored sweater and faded jeans. On her feet, she wore pink socks with little white hearts on them.

She busied herself with coffee, getting a bowl of cereal, pouring some juice. All in all, she spent a good ten minutes trying to avoid him, and confronting what had nearly happened between them last night.

When Betsy finally caved in and glanced in his direction, her cheeks flushed. She turned away and opened a cupboard, reaching for the sugar. As she did, he came up behind her. Slipping his hands around her rib cage, he pulled her against him.

Before he could apologize for leaving her in the lurch last night, she lowered her head and snarled, "Let me put this in terms you can understand, Detective."

"Uh-oh."

"See Betsy?" she said lightly, with a dash of menace. "Betsy is angry. Betsy is angry at the Detective. 'Keep your hands to yourself,' snaps Betsy."

Soldier bent his head and placed a warm kiss at the nape of her neck. "The Detective is very sorry about last night. Detectives work strange hours sometimes. See the Detective lust after Betsy. He will make it up to Betsy, given half a chance."

She squirmed. "Look, look, look. Look at Betsy, embarrassed and humiliated. See Betsy knee the Detective in his groin."

" 'Oh, no!' groans the Detective. The Detective likes his groin just the way it is."

"See Betsy ignore the stupid Detective?"

"The Detective senses Betsy has a cold and unforgiving heart." He slid his hands up to cup her breasts. Her spine stiffened, but she didn't shove him away.

"Stop that," she protested, trying to wiggle out of

his embrace. "You're a jerk. A big fat jerk. Besides, someone could walk in—"

"Taylor's in the shower. Your mother was here, but she went home." He rubbed his thumbs across her nipples. She gasped and lay her head back against his shoulder.

"Men live to do this," he whispered almost inaudibly against the side of her neck. "There's nothing sexier than coming up behind a woman and settling her butt into your crotch while you fondle her breasts. Mmm. Doggie Heaven."

"Soldier—"

"Uh, woof." The deep baritone came from somewhere behind them.

Both Soldier and Betsy jumped nearly a foot, two kids caught with their fingers in the cookie jar. Betsy's trembling hands flew to cover her burning cheeks.

Without turning around, Soldier ground out, "Taylor, you are such a *dickhead*."

He glanced over his shoulder to see his freshly showered brother clad in only jeans, his soggy towel tossed over one shoulder.

He grinned. "Sorry. Didn't mean to interrupt."

As the door to Taylor's room closed, Soldier said, "I'm sorry, Betsy. I had no idea—"

"Mpf cnn nvrr fcc hm ngn."

"What was that? What did you say? Take your hands away from your face, Betsy."

She did. "I said, I can never face him again!" Her whole body shook, and when Soldier turned her around, he realized she was laughing so hard, she could barely contain herself.

"You're not . . . mad?" He viewed her with skepticism.

"Mad? Mad? Gosh, why would I be mad! I'm laughing, Detective Doggie-man," she gasped, "because I don't know what else to do! You rejected me when I got loaded and tried, clumsily no doubt, to seduce you. *That* was just great. Then, you humiliated me last night, leaving me just when— Oh, forget it. But this morning, you grab me in front of your brother! Some lunatic is stalking me and that same lunatic probably murdered a woman. And to top it all off, my charming mother and her *Dick* show up unexpectedly from Paris, and, and, and . . . well, if I don't laugh, I'll probably go friggin' nuts!"

She wiped the tears from her eyes. "Do you realize that ever since I met you I've done nothing but cry?"

"I often have that effect on women."

"Very funny," she snapped. "I've never been a crier. Sad movies, hurt animals, stuff like that make me cry. But for some reason, I just can't seem to get control of my emotions! I hate this! I want to tear this town apart. Go from door to door and say, 'Oh, hello. Are you the one stalking me? Yeah? Well cut it out, and by the way, you're under arrest!' "

"Hey, that's my line."

"Tough! Vengeance is mine, sayeth the stalked!"

"Betsy," he said, hiding a grin, "you're under a lot of stress—"

"Oh! You think? Is that how you got to be a detective? From brilliant deductions like that?"

"It's a gift."

"Can't you two keep your hands off each other for

five minutes?" It was Taylor, emerging from his bedroom, fully dressed in jeans and a sweater, briefcase in hand.

Soldier looked into Betsy's red-rimmed eyes. "Better now? Shall we get to work?"

She shrugged, then nodded. "Sorry I was sarcastic a minute ago. I know you're a good detective."

He smiled down at her and guided her toward the kitchen table where Taylor had tossed several manila file folders.

"Okay, I ran all the names you gave me," Taylor began, opening the first file. "Nothing out of the ordinary on Ryan Finlay, your boss," he said to Betsy. She seemed to sigh with relief. "I couldn't get much on Carla Denato, except that she moved to Port Henry about a year ago from the Midwest. Nothing popped since her arrival, but I'm still doing some checking.

"As far as Linda Mattson, the woman who got married and moved to, where'd you say, Minnesota?" Betsy nodded. "Couldn't get a line on her at all. She might be in Minnesota, but she might not. I'm still checking on that, too."

Soldier flipped through the pages of the file nearest him. "I sent you some more names. People Betsy works with. Anything on those?"

Taylor pulled another folder from his briefcase. "Yeah, but not much. Upstanding citizens for the most part. Pretty boring. Chet Grover, one of the guys in the print shop, has been in and out of rehab. Drinking mostly, some drugs a while back. Nothing recent."

"I don't know Chet very well, but he seems like a

really nice guy," Betsy interjected. "I can't see him doing anything like this."

Soldier and Taylor both gave Betsy a nod but said nothing. As the brothers knew, looks could be deceiving.

"Betsy," Soldier ventured, "we're just checking possibilities, that's all. We're not accusing anybody."

"Well, you hadn't better be," she admonished. "I know all these people. None of them are stalkers and none of them are capable of murder, and I'm sure of it." She paused and softened her tone. "I'm almost certainly positively sure of it. What else have you got?"

Taylor leaned back in his chair. "Holly Miller, Rita Barton, and the rest of the staff—Morgan, Neal, and Martin—are all longtime residents of Port Henry. I'm still checking, but other than one messy divorce, one speeding ticket, and a couple of parking violations, these people all seem to be clean. But who knows? If I keep digging, something may pop yet."

Soldier turned to Betsy. "We still haven't talked about neighbors, professional acquaintances, service people such as hair dressers, the mailman, grocery store clerks. The list is virtually endless."

"It just can't be one of them. They're all normal-looking, normal-behaving people who—"

"Betsy," Soldier interrupted, running his fingers through his hair in frustration at her refusal to accept the truth. "I'm sure the guy who's doing this is a seven-foot-tall, one-eyed drooling hunchback with a limp, with a tangle of greasy white hair, who holds a bloody butcher knife in one fist while the knuckles of his other hand drag along the ground."

Taylor looked up. "You didn't tell me we were looking for my ex-wife's boyfriend."

"But," Soldier continued, ignoring his brother's acerbic wit, "until there's a full moon and he emerges from his bone-strewn Dumpster to drag his decaying carcass up the street to accost you again, we've got to go with other possibilities."

Betsy sat back in her chair and crossed her arms under her breasts. "Well, you don't have to get all sarcastic about it." She shrugged and tilted her head. "It really could be anybody. I know that. I've known that all along. I just didn't want to believe it."

"I know," Soldier said softly.

Taylor left the table to pour a cup of coffee. When he'd settled himself again, he said, "Okay, the note on the dog's collar was a blank. No prints except for Betsy's." He took a sip from his mug. "Something did come up on someone else, though. It could be important, or it could be nothing."

Both Soldier and Betsy turned their attention to Taylor. His eyes scanned the sheet he held in front of him. Handing the paper to Soldier, he waited while his brother read it.

When Soldier had finished, the brothers exchanged glances. "Yeah," Soldier said. "I know. I talked to them late last night."

"Hey, cut it out," Betsy groused. "Enough with the meaningful looks. What's going on?"

Soldier slid the paper toward Betsy. With shaking hands, she lifted the report and read it. When she finished, she slid it back toward Soldier, then sat staring at the tips of her fingers.

"So, he's out. Daddy."

Soldier nodded.

"And they don't know where he is except he'd said he wanted to see me."

Soldier nodded again.

Betsy's eyes clouded with worry, bringing out Soldier's every protective instinct. She was a mass of nerves, and this new development had just made things worse. Pushing herself away from the table, she said, "He wouldn't hurt me. He would never *hurt* me!"

The back door swung open then, and Loretta walked in, Piddle under one arm, a bag of groceries under the other.

Soldier rose from his chair and took the groceries from her.

"Oh, you're all up. How cozy," Loretta observed. "Darling, I thought you'd need some necessities, what with guests and all. Champagne, very dry; caviar, very expensive." She pushed a lock of flaming hair away from her forehead. At last looking directly at her daughter, she said, "Who wouldn't hurt you, Elizabeth?"

Betsy blew out a breath, obviously unsure of what her mother's reaction to the news would be.

"Prepare yourself, Loretta. It's Daddy. He's out. The hospital released him three months ago, and Uncle Terry has no idea where he is."

An hour had passed since Loretta heard the news, flung herself into a fit of hysterics, clutched that mongrel to her bosom and fled out the back door. Taylor had decided to walk the seven blocks over to a farmer's market and pick up some real groceries, leaving him to watch Betsy as she paced her living room. Her usually gentle eyes were filled with resolve.

"I refuse to be a prisoner in my own house," she said evenly. Her eyes sparkled with determination, but her body language spoke of her fears: arms crossed, head down, mouth tight. "I refuse to believe my father has had anything to do with any of this. I refuse to listen to one more word about your so-called suspicions."

"Gosh, Betsy, tell me what you really think," Soldier chided.

She sent him a withering look, then turned away, allowing him a thoroughly enticing view of her scrumptious butt. Cute enough to eat, he thought.

"Tell me, Betsy," he said casually. "What kind of a kid were you?"

"Human." She stared out the front window, her lips pressed together tightly.

"Well, duh," he drawled, "but what were you like?"

"Shorter." She sighed and faced him. "Say, did you hear about the race between the two silk worms?"

"No," he answered warily. "What happened?"

"It resulted in a tie."

"Oh yuk-yuk. Did you hear the one about the woman who resorted to humor whenever she didn't want to talk about herself?"

Rolling her eyes, she said, "See the Detective turn into *Herr Doktor*. Well, analyze this, *Freud*." She lifted her nose and turned away from him.

"Come here." He stood in front of the mantel and stretched his arms out to her.

She looked back over her shoulder, shrugged and moved toward him, but sat in the large wing chair, averting her gaze by staring into the empty fireplace.

For a moment Soldier looked past her to the windows. The panes were old and thick, presenting a distorted view of the world. The irony of that was not lost on him. How had Betsy coped, living here with a haughty beauty queen for a mother and Mr. Science Guy for a father?

"You may not want to be a prisoner in your own home," he said, "but the reality is, you are, for the time being, at least. We could put you in a safe house, but I thought you'd prefer to be here rather than surrounded by strangers."

She nodded, relaxing a little. "Yes. I'd rather be here. Thank you."

Soldier grinned. "How about a word game?"

"What kind of word game?" She eyed him suspiciously.

"The kind where I say a word and you say the first thing that comes into your head."

"Like psychiatrists do when they think you're nuts."

"C'mon," he urged. "It'll be fun."

She nibbled on her lower lip. "So, like, if you were to say the word *'mother'* and I responded *'self-involved, ego-maniacal, cold-hearted drama queen,'* then you'd suspect I had issues."

"You have issues?" He blinked at her like an innocent baby chick.

She gazed up at him and her lips curled in a flirty little smile that about drove him crazy. "Okay," she purred, "but then we get to switch."

"That won't work." He shook his head for emphasis.

Her brow furrowed. "Why not?"

"Because all my answers would be the same."

She looked at him askance. "That's impossible. Like, for instance, what if I said '*food*.'"

"Then I'd say '*sex*.'"

She made a face. "How totally predictable. What if I said '*kitchen table*.'"

"Oh, then I'd have to say '*sex*.'"

She blew out a breath. "Um, '*tour bus*'?"

"'*Sex*' again."

"'Insomnia.'"

"'*Sex*.' Are you sensing the trend here?"

"'*Waterfall*'?" Exasperation was clear to hear in her voice.

"'*Sex*.'"

"You . . . are . . . disgusting."

"Tell me about it," he drawled. "Sorry to disappoint, ma'am, but I'm a typical male of the species interested in only one thing. I carry with me the proud tradition of having been born with a single track mind. Now, your turn."

He paused a moment while she resettled herself in the chair and looked down her nose at him. She was not going to let him off easy.

Soldier cleared his throat. "Okay, '*sex*.'"

She rolled her eyes and crossed her arms under her breasts. "Don't you have any imagination at all?"

He nodded. "You'd be surprised. You heard me, '*sex*.'"

"Then my response would be '*no*.'"

"That's not an acceptable response. You have to say a thing."

"All right," she sighed. "'*A thing*.'"

"Betsy—"

"What lays on its back a hundred feet in the air?"

He groaned. "What?"

"A dead centipede."

"Betsy, we really need to talk about what happened last night. I realize now that I shouldn't have come to your room. I had the best of intentions. I just wanted to make sure you were all right. But when I got closer to you, saw you all curled up in bed, all warm and sexy, I . . . I . . . I got hard."

Her cheeks flushed and she looked down. "You think I'm sexy?" She focused her attention on her fingers, twisting around themselves in her lap.

"Betsy, I've never met—"

Whatever Soldier was about to confess was lost under the scream of an approaching siren.

They searched each other's eyes for a split second, then ran to the window in time to see an ambulance tear by, turning the corner at top speed. A second later the siren went mute.

Soldier's fingers bit into Betsy's shoulders. "Where's Taylor?" His voice had gone harsh as he forced out the words. "How long has he been gone?"

She shook her head. "Um, fifteen minutes? Twenty? Maybe he came in the back door and we didn't hear—"

"Taylor!" Soldier shouted his brother's name. "Taylor! Answer me!" Silence. "Shit!"

Soldier grabbed Betsy's hand and took off at a dead run, his long legs carrying him out the front door and halfway down the street. Terrified of letting her out of his sight, he kept her pulled tightly against him as they ran toward the red and blue flashing lights.

As they rounded the corner, he saw a small crowd of neighbors huddled together, shaking their heads. A few of the older ladies had their fingertips to their mouths in an expression of shock and dismay.

The paramedics were there, bent over somebody lying in the middle of the street.

Panic gripped him and he heard Betsy gasp in shock.

Slowly, he approached the medics and tried to get a better look at the victim. But an officer on the scene lifted his hands, palms out, ordering them back.

"McKennitt, SPD," Soldier growled as he reached into his back pocket and flipped open his ID. "I just want to know who it is. My brother went out for a walk and hasn't come back."

The officer glanced at Soldier's credentials and nodded. "Detective McKennitt. Describe your brother."

In a calm voice, Soldier said, "Caucasian, thirty-one years of age, six-foot-two, dark brown hair, blue eyes—"

A worried look passed over the cop's face. When he spoke again, his voice was softer, much more personal. "I'm very sorry, Detective. You'd better come with me. We're going to need you to identify your brother's body."

Chapter 13

He awoke to pain. His skull throbbed and his body was one giant bruise. He tried to open his eyes but his lids wouldn't cooperate. He felt like he'd stumbled off a whirly ride at the fair, leaving him disoriented and queasy.

What the hell had happened?

The last thing he remembered was crossing the street to get back to . . . to . . . somebody's house. He could see her face in his mind but couldn't recall her name. His wife? No, he was divorced. That, he *knew*.

A bright flash of memory shot into his head and he groaned. There had been movement under a tree just down the street. A car. He had ignored it. Stupid move for a cop.

A cop. Okay, that fit. He was a cop. A bad one, apparently.

The morning was dark, overcast, cold. He remembered hearing the low thrumming of an engine, seeing lights flash on, shining in his eyes, blinding him. Then pain. Then . . . nothing.

Through his confusion he heard someone calling to him. Who was *Taylor*? Was that his name? He just couldn't seem to remember.

He focused on that distant voice, but the words were elusive. The bees buzzing in his ears drowned out all other sounds. But that insistent voice grew louder, stronger. It was deep, urgent, demanding . . . panicked.

Even so, the voice was familiar, and that brought him relief and comfort. He wanted to hear it again, needed to. He rolled his head an inch and regretted it. Pain gripped his skull like a vice, but he had to let the voice know he was okay, that he was still in there, still fighting.

He moved his mouth and tried to speak, but only a gagging sound emerged. He feared he might vomit.

Then he felt something grip his hand, strong, warm fingers and a broad palm. *Jack* . . . his brother. He had a brother whose name was Jack.

He relaxed a little. Maybe he would remember everything after all. Thank God.

It took every ounce of strength he had, but he squeezed his fingers around his brother's hand, and was rewarded with a word, joyfully spoken, and then a rush of words he could barely comprehend. Thankful words, he could tell that much. He wanted to smile, but the small movement would be too painful.

As the darkness closed around him again, he heard the sound of crying. Not a woman's soft keening, but crying the way men did it. Deep and gasping. Trying not to cry, but unable to stop the tears when they came.

Ah, Jack, he thought. *I'm all right. I'm in here, and I'm all right. . . .*

When Taylor came to again, his room was silent. A dull light penetrated his closed lids and he realized he wanted to open his eyes. He did, then pinched them shut again. Somebody was shining a bright light into his pupils.

Though his throat was parched, he growled, "Get that goddamned light out of my eyes."

With a little click, the beam went dark.

"Welcome back, Taylor." The voice was decidedly feminine, but he didn't recognize it. "Why don't you open your eyes again? I promise not to bite."

Opening his eyes a little at a time, he realized he was in a hospital bed and a blurry female form was leaning over him. He blinked a few more times, letting his eyes get used to the low light in the room while he tried to focus on the woman. No dice.

It was like trying to look at somebody through an aquarium at night. Though her features were distorted, he could see that she was smiling at him. He was sure he'd never seen her before in his life.

"You a nurse?" he murmured.

"Ah, not nearly as good," she said. "I'm a doctor. *Your* doctor. Can you tell me your name?"

"Tell me yours first."

She laughed a little. He liked it. "Ooo-hoo. Aren't you the stubborn one? Okay, I'm Claire Hunter."

"Okay, Claire Hunter," he growled. "Where's my brother? He can tell you what my name is."

"I'll get him in a minute," she said. "He and Betsy were pretty beat, so I sent them to get some coffee and food. Your brother was afraid you'd awaken while he was gone, so I promised to stay with you until he returned."

"Hmm. He's the oldest, you know. Pushy. Likes to be in charge."

"Yes, I know," she said. Her voice was soft, soothing, comforting. "I'm an oldest myself. We're beastly." Though he'd closed his eyes again, Taylor was sure she was smiling.

"Now," she said. "Your name?"

She'd called him Taylor. He'd start with that. "T-Taylor . . . um, Mc . . . Kennitt. Taylor McKennitt." His head throbbed with the effort to remember. "Why was that so hard?"

"You have a concussion, Taylor. I'm going to ask you some questions. How you answer them will help tell me how severe a concussion you have. Ready?"

"Yeah."

"Where are we?"

"Hospital."

She laughed. "No, what town are we in?"

"Uh, let me think about that one."

"Okay, let's try something else. How about counting backward from a hundred?"

Taylor tried to visualize the numbers. "One hundred. Ninety-something, ninety . . . ninety . . ."

"That's good," Dr. Hunter lied.

She had a great bedside manner, he thought, but was lousy at math. Why the hell couldn't he remember how to count?

"Do you know your brother's name?"

Taylor blinked his eyes open and looked at the doctor. "It's Jack, and I know it's short for something, but I can't remember what. I mean, it's on the tip of my tongue, but I just—"

Dr. Hunter smiled again and made some notes on the clipboard she was holding. "Don't worry about it. That's what happens with a concussion." Her voice was soft and her eyes softer. She had really pretty brown eyes. "Your brain gets bruised and things get a little confusing," she continued. "You'll be fine in a couple of days."

Panic made Taylor's heart lurch. His distress must have shown on his face because Dr. Hunter leaned a little closer and took his hand in a detached and doctorly way. Her skin was warm, and he let himself enjoy the contact.

"Not to worry," she reassured him. "You're probably a bit dizzy, yes? Have a helluva headache, and maybe a bit sick to your stomach?"

He nodded. Nothing wrong with his nasal passages, though. Dr. Claire smelled damn good. Fresh and sweet, feminine.

"The symptoms will pass," she assured him. "We'll keep you here until they do. We did an MRI while you were unconscious. Everything looks good."

"So I'm going to live after all."

"It's looking that way. You'll be back to normal in no time. The worst of the damage is the concussion, which, while not good, could have been a whole lot worse. You must have a skull of iron."

"It's been said."

"You also have fairly severe abrasions on your legs and arms from skidding on the pavement. No broken bones, but you'll have lots of big bruises, contusions you received when your body hit the street. We'll keep those iced to try to reduce swelling. No internal injuries, which is amazing. You are one lucky man."

Muddled images flashed through his head. Light, noise, pain. "They catch the guy who did this?"

She shook her head. "Not as far as I know. The police are investigating."

"I am the police."

She shook her head again. "Not today you're not." She seemed to observe him for a while. "What are you thinking, Detective McKennitt?"

"I'm thinking you're the cutest doctor I've ever had."

"How well can you see me?"

He narrowed his questionable gaze on her. "You look like a blurry watercolor. Blobs of paint but no discernable shape."

"Hmm. And after all that exercise, too." She laughed, and he liked the sound of it.

He wasn't that dizzy and his vision was clearing quickly. Claire Hunter was beautiful. She had soft brown hair pulled into a loose bun held by one of those clippy thingies women wore. Small pearl teardrops dangled from her earlobes. She had delicately arched brows and her eyes were a fawn brown, bright with humor and intelligence. He dropped his focus to her lips. Full and rosy, as though she'd just been kissed.

"Do all your patients fall in love with you, Doc?" he ventured.

Her tone shifted from friendly to all business, just that quick. "I think we should concentrate on getting you well, and never mind about my other patients. I'm going to be checking on you every couple of hours until the end of my shift. Then the night staff will take over. If you remain stable tonight and don't develop any new symptoms, you can go home tomorrow afternoon. But that's not a promise, just a big maybe."

"How long before I can get back to work?"

"Depends. If you were a football player, I'd say three months. But if you're real good and promise not to get another concussion, you can go back in a couple of weeks."

"What? No way! A couple of—"

"Hey, Tayo." The deep voice came from the open doorway behind the doctor.

Taylor felt a grin split his face, and even though it hurt like hell, he couldn't help it. "Hey yourself," he said. "Dr. Claire, this is my brother, Detective Jackson Soldier McKennitt." He spoke the name without thinking. Thank God, he was starting to *remember*.

The doctor grinned at him. "I already knew his name. But I'm glad to see that you know it, too."

Soldier was so relieved to see Taylor's eyes open, he wanted to collapse in a heap on the floor. His brother was going to live. His injuries would heal. Taylor was going to be fine.

There had been a moment of panic at the scene when the paramedics had pronounced Taylor dead. They couldn't get a pulse and thought they'd lost him. But Tayo had fooled them all and come roaring back with a strong heartbeat and a stronger will to survive.

Since the accident, Soldier hadn't let Betsy out of his sight. He'd held her hand all the way to the hospital and only let her go so he could sit by Taylor's bedside. She stood on the other side of the hospital room, staring into space, her face a tortured mask of despair and fear and remorse.

This was not her doing, but she blamed herself nonetheless. Man, did he ever know *that* feeling.

Now, staring into his brother's eyes, Soldier growled, "I'm going to get the son of a bitch who did this. If I have to take Port Henry apar—"

"Listen, Jackson," Taylor choked. His voice sounded raw. Soldier reached for the water pitcher and poured some in a glass. As Taylor took it, he said, "If you think this was your fault, get over it."

"I should have—"

"You should have nothing," he rasped. "I'm all grown up. I'm a cop. I even have a gun. A really big one. I heard the engine and ignored the possibilities. I got hurt. You may think you own all the guilt in the world and that you're personally responsible for every bad thing that happens to people, but you're not. Stop being so egotistical."

Soldier felt as though he'd been kicked in the head. "Egotis— What the— How can you—"

He gave up. Blowing out a heavy sigh, he turned to

Betsy. "Why don't you make yourself comfortable while I interrogate Patient Zero over here."

Betsy gave Taylor a smile then nodded to Soldier. Quietly, she made her way to a chair near the window.

Dr. Hunter remained standing in the doorway, watching, but she had made no comment on the brothers' discourse. Addressing her now, Soldier said, "Is it okay to ask him some questions?"

Claire Hunter was a very pretty woman and had a sympathetic smile. It was apparent his brother thought so, too, because Taylor hadn't taken his eyes off her, except to yell at him.

"All I ask is that you don't tire him out," she said. "And don't stay too long. I've got to check on some other patients, then I'll be back." She looked over at Taylor, who was watching her intently. "Behave yourself." She gave him a smile, then left the room. Betsy excused herself and followed.

Soldier pulled a chair next to Taylor's bed. "Pretty lady."

Taylor's gaze stayed for a moment on the threshold through which Dr. Hunter had just disappeared. Shifting his attention to Soldier, he said, "I suppose you want to know what happened."

"You read my mind."

"Yeah, well, don't try reading mine. Things are a little fuzzy just now."

Soldier reached toward Taylor and the two men clasped hands. Taylor's palm was warm, physical evidence that blood flowed through his veins and the life force was strong in him. Looking into his brother's eyes, Soldier said, "I was pretty worried about you, pal. Thanks for hanging in there."

Taylor gave him a tired grin. "Happy to oblige, Jackson."

For a moment, Soldier remembered back when they were kids, racing each other to see who could reach the schoolyard first. Panting and laughing and boasting that each was faster than the other. As though it were just yesterday, he heard Taylor's anguished gasps when he'd fallen from the big tree in the backyard and broken his wrist, and how he had reassured his younger brother that everything would be okay as he'd screamed at the top of his little boy lungs for their mom's help. He remembered the scent of hot cocoa that the two of them had shared around their first campfire, and how cocoa hadn't tasted nearly so good since.

Giving Taylor's hand one last squeeze, Soldier released it and settled back on the sturdy hospital chair. Clearing the emotion that threatened to choke his voice, he said, "What do you remember?"

Taylor let his head fall against his pillow, but the movement made him grimace. He closed his eyes and began to speak.

"I remember very clearly the few minutes before I was hit," he said. He took a swallow of water from the glass Soldier had given him, then relaxed against the pillow again. "I was crossing Rose Avenue between Third and Fourth, traveling in an east-west direction. Visibility was good. Before I began crossing, I glanced up and down the street to check for traffic. There was none, so I started across.

"When I got to the middle, I heard an engine

nearby, behind me, loud. I was surprised. I assumed it was a resident." He grinned at Soldier. "Guess you know what they say about assuming."

"Like, don't ever do it."

"Yeah. Well, the car seemed to shoot away from the curb. I turned, saw the headlights. Just before impact, I jumped out of the way. Front right bumper clipped my hip. I hit the ground and rolled. Next thing, I wake up in the hospital."

"You're certain you didn't see the driver? Try to concentrate, Taylor."

Taylor opened his eyes but kept his head steady. His brows furrowed and he closed his eyes again, as if to replay the scene in his mind. "The car was a blur, and I knew I was in deep shit if I didn't get out of the way. I *may* have seen the driver, but I don't remember. He was close enough by then, but I can't get a clear picture in my head. It just won't form. All I remember seeing was headlights."

"Was it the same car that drove by the night we got back from the conference?"

"I think so. Sorry. The next time I'm hit, I'll try to have my camera with me."

Betsy and Claire walked down the hospital corridor, the sound of their shoes making tapping sounds as they went along. When they reached the nurse's station, Claire put her hand on Betsy's arm. There was worry in her eyes when she said, "Why in the hell didn't you tell me you were being stalked? How long has it been going on? Why aren't the police protecting you better?"

"Hold on, sweetie." Betsy patted her friend's hand. "I'm okay, honest. To tell you the truth, I didn't believe I was being stalked, not until the conference this weekend. I almost called you the other night, but it was late and you've been so busy at the hospital and with your patients, I didn't want to disturb you."

Claire looked thoroughly pissed. "*Disturb* me. You're my dearest friend. Disturb me, already!"

Shoving her hands in her jacket pockets, Betsy said, "So, does Taylor really look okay? Will he be all right?"

"I have every confidence in his complete recovery. The man is built like a . . . well, never mind what he's built like. He's young and healthy and strong. His injuries will take time to heal, but he'll be fine."

Betsy felt relief ease the tension in every muscle she had. Thank God. She didn't know what she would have done if Taylor had been killed. Kristee Spangler's death was enough for her conscience to deal with, but the brother of the man she was falling in love with . . .

Claire must have picked up on her thoughts, because she smiled. "You want to tell me about it?"

"There's not much to tell."

"Right." She shoved her pen into the breast pocket of her toast-colored jacket. "You show up here with two of the hottest-looking men I have ever seen in my life, one of whom cannot keep his eyes or his hands off of you, both of whom are detectives and are sleeping in your house, you are being stalked, there's been a murder and an attempted murder, and you have the nerve to say to me there's not much to tell?" She rolled those pretty eyes of hers. "Well, I'd like to hear it when something interesting really does happen in your life!"

Betsy pursed her lips and said casually, "So, what did you think of Soldier?"

Claire's brow lifted and her lips twisted into a wry smile. "Have you slept with him yet?"

"Claire!"

"Well, what in the hell are you waiting for? I'm not one to advocate casual sex, but in his case, I think you should definitely make an exception. Besides, I think he really likes you."

"Yeah? Well, what about Taylor?"

"You want to sleep with them both? Wow, just thinking about that is getting me all hot."

"No," Betsy laughed. "For you. He liked you; I could tell."

Claire blushed and ran her fingers nervously through her hair. "I don't have time for a man in my life right now. Besides, I think I'm a couple of years older than he is."

Betsy began to protest, but Claire put her doctor face back on and said, "Taylor needs rest. Time for you and Soldier to beat it. I'll call you if his condition changes, okay?"

The Port Henry Community Hospital was only four stories tall. It was attractive, as hospitals went, made of red brick with natural stone trim. Offices, patient services, and the ER were on the first floor. The surgeries were on the top floor. In the middle were the wards and rooms.

Taylor McKennitt's room was on the second floor,

just down the hall from the nurses' station. The hospital had been told to keep a special eye on room 212, the patient might be in danger. A uniformed officer would stand guard outside to make sure nothing untoward happened to their precious cop patient.

In the dark, the watcher smirked. Counting the windows, room 212 would be right about . . . there. The light was on, but the blinds closed. Shadows moved around behind the square of yellow light like moths trapped inside a lamp shade. Soldier and Betsy, and her bosom pal, Claire. They were all in there right now.

The watcher was satisfied. Taylor McKennitt hadn't died after all, but things went that way sometimes. He was pretty banged up, and that would just have to do. The whole thing had been so spur of the moment, anyway. There hadn't been any plan to take Taylor out, but there he was, just a-walkin' down the street, just like in the song. The opportunity had presented itself, and it would have been foolish to pass it up.

The McKennitts were big boys; Taylor had left quite a dent in the fender. Kristee's car would have to be ditched.

Turning from the window, the watcher approached a white Accord and placed a note under its driver-side wiper blade. It wasn't much, just another nail in Betsy Tremaine's credibility coffin. Between the hints and gossip, the anonymous phone calls, the damned dog, and now Taylor McKennitt, things were beginning to come together. The disasters would all center around Betsy, as well they should.

If only there had been some way to use Kristee's death in all this, but the decision to finally eliminate her had been a long time coming. And she had, after all, brought it on herself. She could have given it all away with her stupid *Have a nice trip* comment in the bathroom at the hotel. Kristee never had been very bright, yet she'd been useful over the years, but now it was time to go solo.

The watcher glanced back up at Taylor's window. The light had gone out. Best get a move on before Soldier and La Tremaine showed up in the parking lot.

Around the corner, the damaged green sedan waited. The watcher slipped behind the wheel and pulled away from the curb. Yes, yes. Like dominoes, everything would begin to fall. Elizabeth Tremaine would lose her reputation, her job, her loved ones.

The final blow, her death, would be slow. Painful. A delightful agony. She would be made to understand that she alone was responsible for what was happening to her. That she had brought about her own ruin.

And then she would die.

Chapter 14

It was ten o'clock, Sunday night. Claire stood in the darkened hospital room and stared down at her patient. Taylor McKennitt was asleep. He was last on her rounds and now she could go home.

She glanced at his chart again just to make certain she hadn't missed anything. His vitals were good and the swelling on his legs where he'd skidded on the pavement looked a little better.

As she prepared to leave, she turned to take one last look. She was grateful he would be released tomorrow. He wouldn't be her patient anymore. Claire didn't like having Taylor McKennitt as her patient. He was too good-looking, too sexy, too tempting.

She'd treated attractive men before, but none of them had ever affected her the way this one did. There was something about his athletic body, his easy smile, those sharp eyes. He was the epitome of every girlish daydream she'd ever spun, and being near him made her feel feminine and warm.

Claire was attracted to him, and she knew she'd best be honest with herself about it or lose her professional detachment.

She had turned thirty-four her last birthday, nearly three years older than her hunky patient. But her age didn't stop her from remembering those silly stories she used to tell herself. Girlhood stories about when she would finally meet her one true love, what he would look like, how handsome he would be. No longer the idealist, long hours, hard work, constant competition, striving to be the best, all had turned her a little cynical about love and its place in her world.

The intense love she felt for medicine and for her career were deep and fulfilling, but the reality was, they didn't keep a lady's feet warm at night.

Returning her gaze to her patient, she watched as Taylor McKennitt slept deeply, his broad chest rising and falling rhythmically. One of the oddest things about being a female doctor was seeing men in situations she normally wouldn't unless she were intimately involved with them.

She pursed her lips. The words *intimate* and *Taylor McKennitt* would undoubtedly not appear in her vocabulary anytime soon.

Claire moved a bit closer and admired his hair. He had beautiful hair and she longed to touch it. It looked soft, and she hadn't touched a man's hair in forever. His long lashes were to be envied, dark and thick, emphasizing the bluest eyes she had ever seen. His brother's eyes were equally intense, but held no interest for her whatsoever.

It was his mouth, though, that really did her in.

Claire imagined kissing that wonderful mouth, and felt the heat rising in her chest.

Don't even get started, she thought as she headed for the door. He'd be released tomorrow and she'd never see him again. He didn't even live in Port Henry, for heaven's sake. After he was well enough to travel, he'd head home to Seattle and that would certainly be that.

Besides, this wasn't about her or Taylor or attraction . . . it was about Betsy and her safety. For a moment, Claire admonished herself for getting lost in thoughts about a man, when her friend was in real danger.

Claire exited the room, nodded a farewell to the night nurse, then went around the corner to her own office and began gathering the paperwork she wanted to take home with her.

A stiff breeze greeted her as the double-glass doors slid closed behind her. As she approached her car, covered with dew in the late night fog, she noticed a note shoved under her windshield.

The Port Henry Police Department was housed on the waterfront on the ground floor of a hundred-year-old building that had served at one time as a cannery. While the Victorian brick and mortar exterior exuded much of the charm the rest of the small town held, the interior had been designed for, and looked much the same as, any modern law enforcement office in the country.

The local joke was that there was always "something fishy" about the PHPD, since soap and water and paint had never been able to totally eradicate the odor of the building's original occupants.

Soldier sat next to Betsy at Officer Winslow's desk as they examined the note Claire had found on her car less than an hour ago.

> HEY DIDDLE-DIDDLE-DOC
> TIME WE HAD A LITTLE TALK
> BETSY IS TROUBLE AND TO BLAME
> FOR MAKING DET MCKENNITT LAME
> —A FRIEND

"Some *friend*," Betsy snarled as she gazed down at the accusatory poem encased in the evidence Baggie. Soldier watched as her emotions flitted across her face.

"I didn't feel guilty enough about what happened to Taylor," she choked as she crossed her arms. "And now this creep is practically charging *me* with being the one responsible?"

"It's all part of the stalker psychosis," Claire said quietly from her chair next to Betsy. "He wants you to feel responsible for everything he's doing."

Betsy looked over at her friend, giving Soldier a chance to take in the softness of her wind-ruffled hair, the curve of her pale cheek, the thickness of her downcast lashes. She sat at the desk in boots, blue jeans, and a jacket pulled tightly around her, as though she were trying to protect her most vulnerable side from attack.

Betsy turned back to Soldier and looked him squarely in the eye. "Well, then in that case, I refuse."

Soldier smiled down into her defiant face and

nudged her chin up with his knuckle. "Contrary as ever, hmm?"

"Damn straight," she growled.

Claire stood and bent over Betsy's shoulder. "I have to get home and get some sleep, honey. Big day tomorrow. But I can stay if you need me to."

Betsy patted her friend's hand. "No, you go on home, D.K. I'll be fine."

Soldier grinned. "D.K.?"

"As in Doctor Kildare," Betsy said. "It's been my pet name for Claire since we were kids and she told me she wanted to be a doctor when she grew up."

"And what's her pet name for you?"

As Claire reached the front door, she said over her shoulder, "I call her Bitsy. 'Night everybody."

Soldier felt his grin widen. "Why Bitsy?"

She shrugged. "When we were really little girls, I had trouble saying Elizabeth. It came out 'A-little-bit.' Eventually, it sort of boiled down to Bitsy."

Officer Winslow returned from the break room with a mug of herbal tea in one hand, an evidence bag in the other. Placing the bag on his desk, he said to Betsy, "This is the first note, the one stuck under the mutt's collar. The guy must have used gloves because the only prints on them belong to you on the first note and Dr. Hunter on the second."

The handwriting on both notes was identical—each word was printed using all capital letters. Soldier gestured to the evidence bags. "We can assume the guy disguised his handwriting at least a little, but maybe he wasn't very good at it. Do you recognize the handwriting at all, Betsy? The paper? Anything?"

Betsy leaned forward and carefully examined both notes.

"You know, I do recognize the handwriting. I just don't know whose it is. There's something about the D and the B and the C that seem familiar, like I've seen them written."

"Problem is," Soldier said, "nobody handwrites anything anymore except their signatures. Everything's voice mail or e-mail or typed on a computer."

Winslow took a sip of tea and laughed. "Yeah, I even write my grocery list on the computer. My handwriting's gone to hell ever since I learned how to type."

Soldier glanced at his watch. It was nearly midnight. He was exhausted, and he knew Betsy had to be on the verge of collapse after everything that had happened that day.

Pushing himself to his feet, he helped Betsy from her chair.

"Thanks, Sam," Soldier said.

"No problem," Winslow replied. "I don't like this guy. What do you say we catch him?"

Soldier sent the cop a wide grin. "I'm for that."

They said their good-nights and Soldier escorted Betsy to her car.

He drove her home in silence, both of them too tired to speak. When they got to her house, he checked the place out thoroughly before letting her go inside.

As Betsy started for her room, she paused on the staircase. "I'm truly sorry about your brother. Claire said he's going to be fine."

"Thanks. It seems he's every bit as hard-headed as I am."

She smiled at that and looked like she might say something else, but instead turned and walked up the staircase to her room. He heard her door close firmly behind her, and he couldn't help but grin.

The man stood across the street, gazing up at the Victorian. Such a pretty house. Beauty enough to make a fellow wax poetic just by standing and admiring.

Three seventy-three Rose Avenue. The perfect address for such a lovely house. The lines, the elegance, the charm of an age gone by, preserved in cedar and glass, brick and paint.

The era to which the house belonged had ticked away, minute by minute, hour by hour, until the heart of the house, its families, its many sons and daughters, were no more. All gone off to the city, to come back to build stiff, shapeless boxes in which to live. Now, only the cost mattered and none of the grace.

As he watched, the kitchen light went out. Mere moments later, two lights came on upstairs. He knew they were bedroom lights.

She was home again, but she wasn't alone.

He continued gazing at the old house, the panes in the windows staring back at him like square, hollow eyes. So many eyes, watching, watching.

Pushing down on his nerves, he ignored them. They could not hurt him; they were not real. Only windows. Her windows.

Patting his jacket pocket, he smiled. He could get in

anytime he wanted. She must have forgotten about the hiding place where the spare key was kept. But he hadn't forgotten.

He had it now, and it gave him comfort. But since she wasn't alone, it would have to wait for another day. He could wait. He had all the time in the world.

A car turned the corner, its headlights reaching out to try to touch him, grab him, reveal him. With a few steps, he receded back into the shadows, to see, but not be seen.

Oh yes. He could wait. After all, he'd waited this long.

Chapter 15

"It's Monday morning, and I *am* going to work."
Betsy crossed her arms under her bosom and
glared at Soldier, who stared at her bosom. He didn't
even have the courtesy to blush.

"Yes, it's Monday morning," he said, "and we're
both going to work. While you're busy ripping the
heart out of some other poor author, I'm going to be
talking to your coworkers. It's one of them, Betsy. I
can feel it in my bones." He put his arms around her.
"Hell, I can feel it in *your* bones."

"Yeah, well, maybe it's just old age you're feeling in
your bones, buster, because nobody I work with is a
stalker, let alone a murderer."

"*Denial* is a river in Egypt, or haven't you heard?"

"Like, that is such an old joke."

"Well, I'm fresh out of new material." He released
her and they went out through the kitchen door. He secured it behind them as Betsy went to unlock her car.

Last night's rainfall had emptied the clouds, leaving

the morning clear and crisp and rosy. In the driveway, Betsy's silver Saturn LS glittered with raindrops as though it had been strewn with tiny pink diamonds.

"Ah, sunshine!" Betsy said as she opened her door. "I can sure use some of that today." Though her world felt pretty heavy just now, a sunny day lightened the load a bit.

The *Ledger* was located in the downtown area of Port Henry, and was large enough to take up a two-floor natural brick warehouse. The offices were located on the upper floor, while the paper was actually printed and distributed at street level.

From Betsy's desk by the front window, she had a nice view of the strait, Port Henry's busy waterfront, and the ferry dock that signaled the end of Madison Street. Trees dressed in red, gold, and yellow leaves lined the avenues, celebrating autumn.

The first person Betsy saw when she walked in was her boss, Ryan Finlay. His kind smile greeted her, and Betsy was certain it was genuine. *Not a stalker*, she thought.

"Ryan, this is Detective McKennitt from the Seattle Police Department. He needs to speak with you."

As the two men shook hands, Ryan's forehead furrowed in obvious confusion. "What brings you to Port Henry, Detective?"

Glancing around at the desks piled high with papers, reference manuals, photographs, and the like, Soldier said, "Can we go in your office?"

Betsy had always thought Ryan's brown eyes were warm and he had nice crinkles at the corners. His hair was gray and thin, and he had a jagged little scar on his cheek that he'd gotten in his youth, a reminder of the two years he'd spent in Vietnam. "Sure, sure. Right this way," he said congenially.

As Soldier followed Ryan into the inner office, Betsy moved toward her desk. It was just as she had left it—in its normal disorderly, disorganized state. She pulled out her chair and glanced around the room. Six desks, all with computers, phones, the usual office paraphernalia. Nobody was in yet, but they should be arriving shortly. It was always tough getting in right at eight on a cold Monday morning.

Through the window that served as the enclosure to Ryan's office, she watched Soldier, his face animated and earnest. As he spoke, Ryan's brows shot up, his eyes widened, and his jaw dropped. He flashed a glance through the glass at Betsy, then returned his attention to the detective, who was obviously not leaving out a thing.

"So, how was the seminar?"

The voice behind her made Betsy jump half out of her chair. Turning, she recognized Carla Denato, her assistant. About Betsy's age, Carla had short, light brown hair, styled in a similar way to Betsy's. She considered Carla a friend and confidante, since they shared the same taste in clothing, books, and movies.

"Hi, Carla," she said. "Sorry, I didn't hear you come in."

"Apparently," Carla said through a laugh. "Anything interesting happen at the conference? Meet any tall, dark, handsome strangers?"

What in the hell was that supposed to mean? Betsy

wondered. Did she know about the stalker? Had she been there, seen Soldier? Was Carla a *murderer*?

Oh, no, what was she thinking? Just because a coworker asked about her weekend didn't mean she was a criminal.

Instantly, Betsy was filled with a deep sense of humiliation and regret. What was she going to do now, turn her every acquaintance into a stalker, or worse, just because they were making casual conversation?

"Um, it was great," she lied. Soldier had instructed her on how to behave today. She was to remain calm and observant. He would be interviewing her coworkers, but he didn't want her saying anything to any of them until he had a chance to speak with each one himself.

Smiling, Betsy continued, "I'm glad to be home, though. Kind of tired." That part sure was true enough. "So, what did you do this weekend?"

Carla dropped into the chair next to Betsy's desk. Wrapping her arms around the bundle of files she held, she said, "Boy, not much. Watched some TV. Read a book. Wished for a tall, dark, handsome stranger to come along and take me away from all this." She laughed, her pretty eyes sparkling with mirth.

No, Carla was not the stalker-murderer, Betsy mused. She was too nice. She just wasn't capable of putting a little dog in a refrigerator, or hitting somebody over the head, killing them.

No, it wasn't Carla.

Taking a breath, Betsy let it out and relaxed, having come to the conclusion that she could discount at least one person from her life as being an evildoer. Well, two, counting Ryan.

Glancing toward their boss's office, Carla's eyes widened and she leaned forward in the chair. "Say, who's that hunky guy who came in with you? Was he *with* you? God, he is so hot! Is he yours? What's he want with Ryan?"

Betsy was half inclined to confide in her assistant, but Soldier had expressly warned her to trust no one. He was wrong, of course, but she would do as he asked.

"You were here when we came in?" Betsy said, shifting the subject. "I didn't see you."

Just as Carla was about to reply, Ryan's office door opened and Soldier stepped out.

For the umpteenth time in five days, Betsy's heart gave a flip at the sight of him. She had a feeling it always would. His nearness affected her as though she had perpetual spring fever. Certain she was blushing, she tried to look away, but found she couldn't. It disgusted her to think that all women probably looked at him that way. He wasn't blind. When he saw her looking at him like every other woman on the planet, all he probably saw was just another silly conquest. Well, he hid his arrogance well, she'd give him that.

From the door of Ryan's office, Soldier locked gazes with her, his eyes startling in their clarity and intelligence. He had the height and build of an athlete, and it stirred her senses just to think about his body without clothing, without constraints of any kind, and how that body would move against hers when she was lying in his arms. The night he'd come to her room, the feel of his warm skin under her fingertips, the things he'd done to her . . .

As he walked toward her now, she felt her pulse speed up and her palms grow damp. She was falling in love, and there wasn't a damn thing she could do about it.

He stopped in front of her desk and placed his large hands palms down on the edge. Leaning forward a bit, he said, "Ryan wants to have a word with you."

Next to her, Carla stood up and smiled at Soldier.

"Hi," she said through a beaming smile. She looked chipper and eager and alert.

Pert, damn her, Betsy thought. She looked pert. *God help me, did I look that goofy the first time I saw him?* She cringed when she realized she probably had.

Betsy stood and gestured toward Carla. "Oh, uh, my manners. Sorry. Carla Denato, this is Detective McKennitt from Seattle."

Carla shot a glance at Betsy. *Detective?* her eyes seemed to say.

"Is there a room, someplace we can talk privately?" he said to Carla.

"A room? You and me? Privately?" she squeaked.

"Yes, sir. Right this way."

She took him by the arm and led him quickly down the hall to the small conference room where Ryan usually held his staff meetings.

Without giving Betsy so much as a parting glance, Soldier closed the door behind them. She fiddled with her pen for a moment, trying to pretend she hadn't seen the light in Soldier's eyes when he'd looked at Carla, and her obvious response to him.

Carla was cute and Carla was thin and Carla wasn't

shy. Betsy had the sinking feeling she may have just lost Soldier, although, truth be told, she'd never actually had him.

Taking a fortifying breath, she turned and walked toward Ryan's office. She would put Soldier and Carla out of her mind and get on with the business at hand. That would be the mature thing to do. Then she'd go buy a Carla doll at lunchtime and stick pins in it. That would be the satisfying thing to do.

Tapping on the partially open door to Ryan's office, she smiled and said, "Knock-knock."

"Yeah, come on in, Betsy. Close the door, would you?"

Well, that was ominous enough. She placed her hand on her stomach to try to quell the sick feeling that had begun churning her insides. *Stop it*, she warned herself. *Ryan is* not *a stalker,* not *a murderer.*

As she took a chair, Ryan leaned forward, placing his elbows on his desk.

"Betsy. I'm so sorry. I had no idea you were being stalked. And . . . and the murder. Jesus Christ. I don't know what to say. If there's anything I can do, anything you need, you just say the word. Okay?"

"Thanks, Ryan. I'm sure Detective McKennitt will get this all straightened out and things will return to normal."

Ryan nodded, but he seemed distracted. Well, murder was certain to do that. Finally, he caught her gaze and held it. "On another topic," he said. "I'm sorry to have to ask you about this today, after all you've been through, but it's something that needs to be cleared up right away."

Alarm bells clanged inside Betsy's head. Geez, now what? This wasn't going to be good. Ryan never spoke to her this way.

"Um, okay, Ryan. I'm listening."

He cleared his throat. "I don't know how to say this, so I'm just going to say it. Okay?"

"Okay." *Out with it man! I'm stressed enough!*

"There's a rumor going around," he began.

She swallowed. "A rumor?"

Ryan crossed his arms over his chest and leaned back in his chair. It squeaked a little in protest. "The rumor goes that you are, uh, having an affair with a member of the *Ledger* staff."

Shock slapped her in the face. She just sat there staring at him, unable to speak or even form a coherent thought.

"Me. And who, Ryan? Who am I having this so-called affair with?"

"Dave Hannigan."

Betsy burst out laughing. Oh, it was a joke! A sick joke, but a joke nonetheless.

"An affair? Dave Hannigan? You mean the kid from the copy room? *That* Dave Hannigen?" She relaxed in her chair and laughed some more.

Ryan's brow furrowed. "Well, are you or aren't you?" His face was red and the veins in his neck were prominent as his eyes probed hers, as if he could find his answer there.

Betsy's laughter died in her throat. "You're serious?" she said, gaping at him. "No!" she snapped. "*Hell* no! For one thing, Davey's just a kid, for another, he's a coworker. I wouldn't . . . I couldn't . . ."

She knew she was sputtering, but the more she thought about it, the angrier she got. An affair with Davey Hannigan? What a bizarre—and cruel—accusation!

Ryan sat back in his worn leather chair and closed his eyes. "I'm sorry, Betsy. But you do understand that I had to ask."

"Why? Why did you have to ask? In the five years you've known me, have I ever been anything other than completely professional? Have I ever done anything, said anything, that would lead you to believe I'd hit on a high school kid? Geez, Ryan, do I look that desperate?"

The truth struck at her heart. Is that what Ryan thought of her? That she was so lonely and pathetic she'd seduce a seventeen-year-old kid? Her throat hurt and she felt like she wanted to cry. Not from embarrassment, but from anger.

Ryan shook his head. "I believe you, Betsy. I never thought you'd do something like that, but I had to ask. I'm sorry for putting you through this. But it, um, came up, and I had to make sure."

"What do you mean, 'it came up'? Has somebody said something? Directly accused me? Davey wouldn't concoct such a story—"

"No, it wasn't Dave." Ryan reached for his coffee mug as though it held the miracle drug that would cure all his problems. "Never mind. Forget I said anything. I'll check into this. Just, uh, never mind, okay?"

His tired eyes beseeched her to leave well enough alone, but she couldn't. Not with everything that had happened over the past few days.

"Ryan, I am being stalked. A woman has been murdered. Detective McKennitt questioned you about it, didn't he?"

"Yes."

Ryan suddenly looked much older than his years. Tired and concerned. As though he carried the weight of the world on his shoulders.

"Did you tell Detective McKennitt about the rumored affair?"

"Look. I'm sure this affair thing doesn't have anything to do with what happened to you this weekend. It's just some kind of misunderstanding. I'll take care of it right away."

He closed his mouth and set his jaw, something Ryan did when he had reached a decision and was refusing any further discourse on the matter.

Betsy's insides were all churned up. Ryan didn't think there was a connection, and maybe there wasn't. But maybe there was.

"Ryan. If somebody here at work has been spreading rumors about me, that person could be the same person—"

"No." He shook his head. "The incidents can't possibly be related. This person . . . no. That can't be. It's just a big misunderstanding."

"Who is it, Ryan? Who made these accusations? I have the right to confront them directly, don't you think?"

Ryan shook his head again. "No. This is a work scenario, and it's my responsibility to take care of it. Don't give it another thought."

"But how can I—"

"I'll take care of it. End of story."

Betsy stood. Stepping toward the door, she turned back to her boss. "Judging from the guilty look on your face, the accusations against me must have been pretty bad. I'm sorry you believed them."

Ryan shot out of his chair and moved around his desk to take her arm. "No, no, Betsy. I didn't believe them. But I had to ask. Now I'll know how to proceed. In all fairness, I have to give this other person the benefit of the doubt; hear their side of the story. Believe me, this has nothing to do with stalking and murder." He gave a small laugh, as though the mere thought of a connection was ludicrous.

Betsy gave her boss a resigned smile. "First chance I get, Ryan," she said softly, "I'm going to talk to Detective McKennitt about this. I'm sure he'll be able to persuade you to divulge your source, even if I can't. In the meantime," she added, pausing to touch his shirt-sleeve, "promise me you'll be very careful."

Soldier sat across from Betsy's assistant in the conference room. Carla Denato was twenty-nine, neatly attired in a style that reminded him of the way Betsy dressed: feminine, flattering, pretty. Her light brown hair was styled a little like Betsy's, too: short, a bit curly, very flattering. He was glad so many professional women had stopped trying to dress like men. He liked to see a woman in soft fabrics and colors.

Soldier asked straightforward questions, and Carla gave straightforward answers. The young woman seemed pleased to be able to help out any way she could.

"Okay, Ms. Denato—"

"Please call me Carla," she said, and gave him a friendly smile.

"Carla, then. If you were to sum up your relationship with Ms. Tremaine, what would you say?"

Without hesitating, Carla responded. "Betsy is smart and very good at her job. I have admired her ever since I came to work here. Sure, there have been rumors, but I didn't believe any of them. In a small working environment like this, there are always rumors, it seems. But anybody who knows Betsy knows they're just not true."

"What kinds of rumors?"

"Gosh, Detective McKennitt, Betsy's my friend, not just my boss. I wouldn't be comfortable repeating those stupid lies."

"Do you know who started them?"

"I wish I did! I'd have a thing or two to say to the guy, that's for sure!"

Soldier sat back in the chair and considered Carla. "You're very devoted to Ms. Tremaine. That's nice."

Carla smiled back at him. "Well, Betsy's the greatest."

"Can you think of why anybody would want to hurt her?"

"Nope," she said, shaking her head. "Not one single reason." She blinked, bit her lip, avoided eye contact with him.

Was she nervous, or was it something else?

"Did you have anything you'd like to add?"

She gave him a blinding smile. "Not a thing."

By the time Soldier finished with Carla, it was nearly nine o'clock. He replenished his coffee mug, then called for Holly Miller.

Holly Miller was a college student working on the *Ledger* as part of an apprenticeship program to help her get her degree in journalism. As she settled into the chair across from Soldier, she smiled at him through shiny, fire-engine-red lips. Her long black hair seemed to shoot from her scalp in corkscrew curls that fanned out in all directions. She wore faded jeans and a fisherman's sweater that hung all the way to her knees. As she spoke to him, Solider realized all her sentences seemed to end up as questions.

"Oh, I just love Betsy?" she gushed. "She's smart and works hard, and those book reviews, like, what a hoot?"

Soldier grunted and decided not to mention his up close and personal experience with Betsy's book reviews.

To counter Holly's irritating speaking style, Soldier made his questions into statements.

"Holly, have you ever heard any gossip about Betsy? You know, the typical office kind of stuff."

She blinked her large, gray eyes and looked out the window as she suckled her lower lip. Soldier was amazed that he could watch that sexy, and obviously well-rehearsed, little maneuver with complete and utter detachment.

Now, if it had been *Betsy* . . .

"Well?" she finally said in a slow, deliberate drawl. "I did hear she was having an affair, like?"

"With . . ."

"Like, with Dave Hannigan? The copy clerk? But, like, he's even younger than me?"

Younger than *me*? This was a journalism major? "So, you didn't believe the rumor."

"Well, yah, I suppose I did, like?" She giggled. "I mean, why would anybody say something like that if it wasn't, you know, like, true?"

"Do you know who might have been spreading those rumors?"

Holly pursed her lips and rolled her eyes up and to the right, obviously thinking very hard about his question. Finally, she must have reached some kind of conclusion because she said, "Well, like, you know, like, see, no, um, hmm, you know?" She blinked her eyes and smiled as though he wouldn't actually need the Rosetta stone to decipher her answer.

He took a wild-assed guess. "That was a no."

"Yah, like, yah? Like, no?"

Soldier talked through the frozen smile he set on his face. "Thanks for your time, Ms. Miller. Please call me if you can think of anything else."

He dismissed Holly and resisted the urge to shake his head violently to try to dislodge the verbal litter her interview had deposited in his brain.

Soldier made some notes in her file, then rose from the chair he'd been glued to. He stretched his muscles and meandered over to the window. Below him lay downtown Port Henry, a neat little community with an old-fashioned sense of style.

The place was homey, and if he'd been looking for a

new place to settle, the little waterfront town might have appealed to him.

An image of his apartment popped into his head. It was functional, neat, nicely decorated, and once in a while he'd brought a woman there to share his bed. But most nights, when he turned the key in the lock and pushed open the door, the coldness and emptiness of the place made him wish he hadn't not come home at all. Yeah, it was the place he went when nothing else was going on, but by no stretch of the imagination could it be called a home.

He thought again of Betsy, her pretty face and compassionate eyes. A man could do a lot worse than come home to a woman like her every night. That is, if a man didn't have guilt eating away at him, assuring him that marriage and a family were things he did not deserve and should never even hope to have.

A knock at the door made Soldier turn from his thoughts and greet his next interviewee. Rita Barton was a middle-age woman, her appearance neat, her graying hair pulled back in a tight bun. She wore round-rimmed glasses that had lenses so thick, her brown eyes seemed to be floating in two little fishbowls.

"Mind my own business, thank you very much," she snapped when Solider asked her about rumors concerning Betsy and Dave Hannigan. "Don't give much thought to rumors. Don't know who started them, don't care, either."

"Can you think of anybody who might want to harm Ms. Tremaine?"

Rita shook her head. For a split second Soldier thought the woman looked on the verge of speaking, then thought better of it. It was those thoughts Soldier was most interested in hearing.

"Were you about to say something, Ms. Barton?"

Silence. Rita Barton pursed her unpainted lips and investigated the tips of her fingers.

"Ms. Barton. A woman has been murdered. Ms. Tremaine's life may be in danger. If you have heard or seen something, no matter how insignificant it may seem to you, please tell me."

Rita raised her thin lashes and stared into Soldier's eyes. She heaved a labored sigh. "Well . . ."

In the wake of Rita Barton's departure, a young man peeked around the jamb. He had serious brown eyes and a round face cursed with runaway acne. His light red hair had been cut in a short, military style, which exposed much of his pale scalp. When he entered the room fully, Soldier felt a pang of chagrin for the poor kid.

He stood taller than Soldier and was badly dressed in a wrinkled shirt and baggy jeans that were belted below his soft belly.

"Hi," the boy said, extending his hand to Soldier, who rose to greet him. "I'm Dave Hannigan." For all his awkward appearance, Dave had a firm handshake.

"Dave. Have a seat."

The whole time Soldier spent explaining who he was and why he was there, all he could think of was that somebody had started a rumor Betsy was having an affair with this poor, geeky kid? Not only was the rumor an obvious lie, but it was a heartless thing to do to the boy.

"Tell me about your relationship with Ms. Tremaine, Dave."

Dave Hannigan shifted in the chair, making it protest against the weight it held. He lowered his red lashes and stared at the plump hands he'd folded neatly across his stomach.

"She's very nice," he said. "Um, everybody sort of, you know, ignores me, but not Miss Tremaine." He lifted his gaze to Soldier as a furious red blush covered his round face. "I like her."

"How old are you, Dave?"

"Almost eighteen."

"You in high school?"

"Yeah. I graduate this June. Miss Tremaine, she helps me sometimes with my homework. I want to go to college. Major in journalism or communications. She knows that, so she helps me."

"How are your grades?"

"I'm not dumb, you know. Just because I'm sort of fat doesn't mean I'm dumb. I'm pulling a 4.0, but people think that when you're fat, you're stupid." He bent his head. "But it's not true," he said softly.

Soldier chose his next words carefully. "Do you maybe have a little crush on her?"

Dave's blush intensified until he was so red, his soft cheeks looked blistered. "Sure," he said. "Who wouldn't?"

Indeed, Soldier thought.

"Dave, have you heard the rumor, that you and Miss Tremaine—"

Shaking his head violently, Dave pushed himself out of the chair. "No! Miss Tremaine would never! Whoever said that is mean and horrible!"

"I agree, Dave," Soldier soothed. "I'm sorry, but I had to ask. It's obvious to me that you're not the kind of man to take advantage of a lady. To hurt her reputation like that."

Dave Hannigan straightened his spine and, for the first time, looked Soldier squarely in the eye. "No, sir," he said. "I'm not."

For the rest of the day, Soldier conducted interviews, taking time only to hit the head, get a coffee refill, or call the hospital to check on Taylor.

He'd worked through lunch, so he hadn't had a chance to speak to Betsy for several hours, but now that the day was winding down, he let the thoughts of her he'd been avoiding drift into his mind.

Leaning back in the conference room chair, he closed and rubbed his tired eyes. Immediately, Betsy's face and form slipped into his awareness. He let himself imagine he was kissing those plush lips again, and he nearly groaned in frustration. The longer he was around her, the more he wanted her, and it was driving him crazy.

It was the nature of the male of the species to want sex—anytime, anywhere, occasionally any woman. But this was different. He wanted sex, all right, but he wanted it with Betsy and only Betsy, and he wanted it *now*. A lot of it. As much as he could handle. More.

Remembering the night he'd bared her breasts, he regretted he hadn't been able to make love to her, not been able to get lost in the softness of her luscious body.

Everybody at work liked her, and why not? She was sweet-natured, smart, funny, easy to love. Of all the interviews he'd conducted today, nobody had a word to say against her, and a few made it clear they wouldn't, even if given the chance.

Yet, he believed that one of them was a stalker. A murderer. He *knew* it. One of them was either a complete sociopath or a very talented actor.

He let out a long breath and opened his eyes. Pulling out his cell phone, he called the hospital and asked for his brother's room.

"McKennitt here," Taylor said when he answered.

"McKennitt here, too. How's your head?"

"Still attached to my shoulders. Hey, Jackson. Any progress?"

Soldier leaned forward, resting his elbow on the conference table. "I talked with everybody. Nobody knows anything. They all appear to have alibis for the weekend, but with Kristee Spangler doing most of the dirty work, they don't really need alibis. As for Spangler's murder, it was the middle of the night, when everybody claims to have been fast asleep." He made a clicking sound with his tongue. "But it's one of them, Taylor. It's one of them. I just can't get a line on a motive. If I knew why, I'd know who."

"Okay," Taylor sighed. "Motives. The biggies are greed, love, jealousy, fear—"

"Okay, greed. Betsy doesn't have a lot of money or a lavish lifestyle. Cross that one off. Love. Some guy has secretly loved her from afar and has gone over the edge? She rejected somebody and doesn't even know it? That doesn't fit, either."

"Okay. How about jealousy? Anybody at work jealous of her for any reason?"

"As a matter of fact, there may be. Since we can probably rule out fear, my money's on envy. Somebody she works with is so jealous of her, they've become obsessed. They've tried to ruin her reputation with rumors, they've tried to hurt her dog, and now they've killed the one person who linked them with the conference. They've escalated, which increases the threat to Betsy."

Taylor was quiet for a moment. "So, did she get a promotion somebody else thought they should have? A big fat raise? Her own parking space? Did she win a local beauty contest or free groceries, the Publisher's Clearinghouse Sweepstakes? I mean, we're talking Port Henry, not New York or L.A. Under the circumstances, all this seems pretty rash."

"You know as well as I do that stalkers *are* rash. And irrational. That's what scares me the most. This guy could do *anything* at this point."

Soldier fiddled with his note pad as he checked over the names on his list. "I don't see her boss, Ryan Finlay, as having any reason to be jealous, but there are four or five women in the office and a couple of men who might see Betsy as some kind of threat to their careers, especially if they were after her job."

Taylor made a humming sound in his throat. "Her job? Hey, Jackson. We're talking about the 'Podunk Press' here, not the *Washington Post*."

"Doesn't matter. Jealous is jealous, and to a warped mind, that's all it might take."

Flipping through his notes, Soldier placed a checkmark next to the first name. "This Carla Denato, Betsy's assistant. Could be her. She seems devoted to Betsy, but it could be an act. Holly Miller's a possibility, although she seems too flaky to get it together enough to murder somebody."

"What about older women? Maybe somebody who thinks they've been left in the dust."

"That would most likely be Rita Barton. She's sure got the nuts for it. She didn't really want to talk about it, but she finally broke down and told me some of the rumors about Betsy that were going around. But, hell, she might have started them, for all I know."

For the next few minutes the brothers discussed the pros and cons of each person Soldier had interviewed. Snapping his notebook closed, Soldier said, "This is probably all making your head hurt. I'll take it from here, little brother."

Taylor laughed. "Hey, that reminds me. The lovely Dr. Claire decided to release me tomorrow morning. Can you pick me up?"

"Well, if she's that lovely, maybe she'll give you a ride home."

"Naw," he snorted. "I want my big brother. Besides, she's one of those what you'd call cool and aloof beauties."

Soldier paused for a moment, honing in on his brother's tone of voice. Interesting, he thought. Very interesting. "So, Taylor. You gonna go for it?"

Silence. Then, "What do you mean?"

"I mean, you like her. I think you should do something about it. Hell, she's a *doctor*. Mom would be so proud."

Taylor made a rude sound with his lips. "Shut up," he chided. "I've sworn off women. You know that."

"Don't give me that bullshit. You like her, and I think she likes you. Not all females are like the former ex-Mrs. McKennitt."

Taylor grunted. "Yeah? Well what about you and the adorable Miss Betsy? You put the moves on her yet? Don't wait too long, big brother. One of these days she's going to get over all that shit her mother handed her, and she's going to realize she's cute, and some guy is going to luck out right about then. You want it to be you, or not?"

Leaning back in his chair, Solider ran his fingers through his hair. "Doesn't matter. You're the marrying kind and I'm not. Besides, Betsy is made to be a wife and mother. She's not the kind for casual affairs, and that's all I'm interested in."

"Now who's full of bull?"

Soldier had told Betsy that *Denial* was a river in Egypt. Yeah, well it still was. "What time are they springing you?"

Taylor didn't answer right away, and Soldier knew his brother was gauging whether to pursue their conversation. Finally, "Eleven."

"Okay, I'll be there. In the meantime, I'm going to do some checking on this Linda Mattson."

"Who?"

"She was the woman who left a few months back to get married. Betsy replaced her as managing editor."

"So, you're thinking somebody *else* wanted that job badly enough to become obsessed with it."

"Not bad, Mr. McKennitt. You ever thought of becoming a detective?"

Taylor laughed while Soldier stood and began stacking his papers with his free hand. "My gut tells me something was too convenient about Linda Mattson's sudden departure and the fact that she was never heard from again. I asked several people about her today—people who knew her well—and the picture I'm getting is not good. In fact, my instincts tell me her disappearance is very much connected with this whole thing."

"Like, maybe she's been in hiding and maybe she's behind this whole thing?"

"No. More like, maybe she's dead."

Chapter 16

Betsy locked her desk and covered her keyboard just as Soldier finished up his interviews in the conference room.

Walking to her desk, he stood near her. Very near her. So near, she could feel the heat from his body, and it excited her to the point where she knew she couldn't be relied upon to produce coherent speech. So she said nothing, just looked up at him and smiled. Like an idiot.

"Hungry?" he said.

Oh, baby, am I, she thought. Tucking her purse under her arm, she nodded.

"Where can we get a bite?"

Pick your spot and dig in. I'm all yours. "You want Italian? Mexican? Um, sushi? Port Henry's got them all."

He looked down at her, his eyes probing hers. "You tell me. What are you hungry for?"

You! "I can cook tonight. Let's stop by the store on our way home."

An hour later they were in Betsy's kitchen. The aroma of bubbling spaghetti sauce filled the room, mingling with the scent of freshly chopped basil, oregano, and Parmesan cheese. Soldier had changed into jeans and a sweater, while Betsy still wore her work clothes, over which she'd tied an apron printed with pumpkins and autumn leaves. They were both nursing glasses of burgundy.

Betsy tried not to think about how right this all felt, she cooking while Soldier sat at the table reading the paper. She tried to pretend she didn't wonder what the sound of children's laughter coming from the living room would be like, or how it would feel to have a chubby-cheeked toddler with blue, blue eyes smiling up at her. She tried not to imagine finishing up and heading for bed upstairs with Soldier, his long, lean, strong body ready for hers, warming her, filling her up with love and passion. She tried not to think of any of those things, and failed miserably.

After all, this whole mess would get cleared up eventually, and when it was, Soldier would get on his horse and ride on out of Dodge and back to his regular life. He hadn't said a word to her about the long term, seeing her again when this was done. Sure, he liked her well enough, probably, but he obviously wasn't looking for any kind of permanence. At least, not with her.

As she attended to the pasta, stirring the boiling water, she said, "Can you tell me about anything you found out today?"

He took a sip of wine, then studied the translucent

red liquid in his glass. "No, not really. I have some things I need to check on, plus a ton of paperwork, so I'll be working a few more hours after dinner. Also, Winslow e-mailed me the list of things thought to be missing on that breaking and entering the other night at the dry cleaner's, and I need to do a follow-up on that."

He took another sip of wine. "Just so you'll know, I need to touch base with Stewart. He's doing the leg-work on the Spangler murder, and I may have to go down to Seattle myself for a few days. You'll have to come with me."

"I can't. I have a job." She emptied the boiled pasta into a strainer. Steam fogged the kitchen windows as she slid the noodles onto a platter and set it on the table next to the bowl of sauce. Soldier filled his plate as though he hadn't eaten in twenty years and added some sauce.

Without looking up, he said, "I have a job, too. It's called keeping you alive." Rolling some pasta onto his fork, he said, "This looks good. Where'd you learn how to cook?"

Betsy stood with her back against the sink and watched him virtually devour her dinner. *Fall in love with me and you can eat like this every night, pal. And the dessert . . . ooh-la-la.*

"I learned to cook by cooking," she said, taking a seat and filling her own plate. "My mother decided when I was nine or ten that cooking was a skill I should acquire and one she should relinquish, so she taught me the basics, and the rest I got from cookbooks."

Soldier looked up from his plate, a satisfied glint in his eyes. "You have learned well, young Jedi."

Betsy poured herself more wine just as Soldier said, "Tell me everything you remember about Linda Mattson."

"Linda? You're not thinking—"

He raised his hand in a hold-it-right-there gesture. "Don't draw any conclusions from my questions. Just tell me."

"I've already told you everything I know. She was a nice woman, she worked hard, she got married and moved to Minnesota, and I miss her."

"How close were you?"

"We were friends."

"Friends enough for her to e-mail you or write to you from Minnesota?"

"Well, I thought so, but she never did."

Lifting his glass to his lips, he said, "Didn't that bother you? Make you wonder a little, how she could be your friend then just vanish like that, with hardly a word?"

Betsy folded her arms across her stomach. "I told you days ago, yes, it seemed odd, but there was nothing we could do about it."

"Okay. So, tell me about Carla."

"Carla? But you don't think . . . Carla?" Betsy scoffed. "What, like Carla is clawing her way to the top of the *Port Henry Ledger* publishing empire, circulation twenty thousand? That she would stalk and murder all the way to my job? Or is it Ryan's job she's after?" Betsy giggled. "That's too silly to even think about. It doesn't make any sense at all."

"Maybe not," he said. "But crazy people do crazy things for crazy reasons. It doesn't make sense to us, as long as it makes sense to her."

Betsy took a few bites of dinner, letting Soldier's words simmer inside her head. She was coming to grips with the fact that her stalker probably was somebody she knew, and the idea scared the hell out of her.

Somebody she knew, but didn't know well at all. Who could that possibly be? One of the faces she saw every day was false, a lie. How could she ever trust her own judgment again if she wasn't with it enough to spot a stalker-murderer among her acquaintances?

Soldier polished off his dinner and was spooning the last of the sauce over the remaining spaghetti.

Betsy dear, the way to a man's heart is through his stomach. Betsy sighed. *Oh, Loretta, if only.*

Soldier looked up at her. Gosh, his eyes were blue. Betsy felt the pull of his attraction more powerfully each time she was near him. She didn't think she could take much more of being around him and keeping her hands off him, or of him keeping his off her.

"Port Henry's a nice place," he said, oblivious to her lustful thoughts. "I like the small town feel of it, and yet it's close to the city."

"When I was a little girl, on Saturdays, Daddy would take me down to the ice cream place. He would always have a hot fudge sundae and I would always have a banana split."

"Never varied?"

"Nope."

"Creatures of habit?"

"Yep. When I find something I like, I stick with it. Forever."

He sat back, shoving his empty plate away. "Are we still talking about banana splits?"

Betsy lifted a shoulder. "Is it safer that way, Mr. Isolationist Policy?"

"Yep."

"How old are you?"

"Thirty-three."

"Ever been married?"

He stuck out his lower lip and shook his head. "It has always been my plan to stay single."

Betsy clasped her hands in front of her and smiled knowingly. "That's probably a good plan, considering how arrogant and dictatorial you are. But you make it sound as though it's always been *your* choice. Maybe the women you've known have taken one look and run for the hills."

He smirked at her. "Hey, I'm very easy to live with. Just ask my horse."

"You live in a stable environment, do you?"

He leaned forward and looked into her eyes. She leaned forward and looked into his.

"You like me, don't you?" he said.

"What?" she laughed. "You're not going to trot out any horse puns? Not going to saddle me with any more of your bad humor? Just say neigh?"

"You do like me, don't you?"

"No," she replied softly. "I think you are a self-involved, self-centered, self-absorbed know-it-all, and I'm sick of your trying to run my life under the guise of police protection."

He grinned that killer grin. "I knew you liked me."

She pulled back. Yes, she liked him. She liked him way too much.

"So what if I do like you?" she challenged quietly. "What does that even mean? Am I supposed to allow myself to get involved with you for a brief affair, then smile as you walk out the door when you've decided you don't like me anymore, or that you like me too much and it's time to hit the road before Betsy starts hearing wedding bells?"

"Betsy—"

"Don't you Betsy me, Inspector Clouseau." She pushed herself away from the table and began clearing it. With plates in hand, she moved to the sink and kept her back to him.

"I know all about men like you," she said to the dinner plates. "You love 'em and leave 'em. Oh sure, I'm good enough to sleep with, to have around for a while, share a few home-cooked meals, laugh a little, do a bit of shopping, maybe pick out new drapes for the living room, go away for the weekend and maybe do some antiquing, find something adorable that would look great in the bedroom so that every time I looked at it, I'd think of you. We'd share moonlight strolls or walks in the rain or take long hot bubble baths together, look at other people's babies and think they're cute, but no thanks, catch a blockbuster movie and go out for a late dinner afterward where we'd have a bottle of wine and some long, hot kisses before we'd come back and you'd peel my clothes off me and touch me everywhere and make passionate love to me for hours."

"Betsy, wait, you—"

"Oh, sure," she interrupted. "And then one day you'd say, 'I'll call you,' but you'd never call me because men who say 'I'll call you' never call you, but women never, ever know why, but we sit by the stupid phone and look out the stupid window and wait and hope, but the bastard never calls and never shows up, and then you see him months later walking down Main Street with a bag from a trendy boutique and you know it's got a lace teddy in it, but it's not for you, and when he sees you, he ducks into a shop really fast but you walk right on by like you didn't even notice because, well, why humiliate yourself further with some stupid confrontation with some stupid guy who—"

Soldier flew out of his chair, grabbed her by the shoulders and turned her to face him. "I am *not* like those other guys," he growled, then silenced her protests with his mouth.

Oh, his mouth. On hers. His tongue, sliding in, tangling with her own, tasting of wine. His teeth, nipping at her lips, down her neck, across her collarbone.

Oh, his hands. On her. Shoving up her sweater, exposing her to his intense gaze. His fingers, unfastening her bra, sliding under the lace, caressing her nipples.

Oh, his lips. On her. Everywhere. Devouring her flesh as his hands held her breasts to his mouth. His tongue licking, teasing, sending trills of heat all through her body.

Soldier pulled her hips to his groin and ran his open palms down to grasp her bottom, yanking her closer, and she felt how hard he was and it excited her even more. Rubbing against her, he panted against her open mouth, "I . . . want to . . . make love to you. I have to. God, I can't . . . stand it. Do you know what you do to me?"

"M-Make your heart pound?"

"Yes, oh yes," he mumbled as he lowered his head and took one moist nipple into his mouth.

"Wow, your heart is pounding really loud," she whispered. "Or . . . or is that my front door?"

Soldier stopped and lifted his head. They heard it again, pounding, doubled fists on wood.

"No!" he choked. "Not now for chrissakes . . ."

At that moment they both realized that the walls of Betsy's kitchen were bathed with flashing red and blue lights.

Cursing under his breath, Soldier helped Betsy fasten her bra. He pulled her sweater down and gave her one last, hot, wet, thorough kiss. "I'm sorry," he rasped. "I'll make this up to you, I swear it."

"This had better not be some Girl Scout selling cookies," Betsy murmured, frustration nearly choking her. "Because I won't buy any if it is. Well, maybe the mint ones."

Grabbing her hand, Soldier moved with Betsy swiftly through the kitchen to the living room. When he opened the front door, a Port Henry police officer stood there, looking very, very grim.

Ryan Finlay had been killed at his desk. An aid unit with its red lights spinning was parked just outside the *Ledger*'s office where Soldier had spent most of the day interviewing the staff.

One of them had done this. *Which one, which one, which one?* he goaded himself. *Could I have protected Finlay? Why didn't I see this coming? Was there something I missed today, something that should have warned me?*

He had failed again. *Failed.* He'd failed to protect Ryan Finlay because he'd missed something. *What in the hell did I miss?*

And here he'd been fool enough to think he and Betsy might have a chance. He'd almost made love to her less than an hour ago. He was an idiot. He didn't deserve someone like her.

He'd let Marc down, and then Taylor, and now Ryan Finlay. Fuck.

What in the hell had he missed?

He had to clear his head of the anger, the frustration, the doubts, or he wouldn't be able to carry on. Impelling thoughts of his failures into the darkest recesses of his soul, he took Betsy's arm and walked her into the building. She was trembling, but didn't falter once.

When they entered, the officer at the scene had already secured the area. Sam Winslow was there, along with a couple of others from the PHPD.

"Sit here, Betsy," Soldier said, indicating a chair near the door that was far enough from Finlay's office so she wouldn't be able to see anything. Gunshot wounds were either very neat or very messy, and he wasn't sure which it would be until he got a closer look.

She was pale and quiet. Her gaze moved slowly

around the office as though she'd never seen the place before.

Winslow motioned him over.

"I'll be right back, Betsy. If you need anything, have one of these officers come and get me. Whatever you do, stay away from Finlay's office."

She looked up at him with trusting puppy eyes. She had placed a faith in him he didn't deserve. When she nodded, he was suddenly filled with renewed resolve. He'd find the bastard who did this, because if he didn't, this was all leading to a place he didn't want to go, where he didn't want Betsy to go.

As always, Winslow was strapping, handsome, spit-and-polish, a brand new Ken doll, right out of the box. Gesturing toward Finlay's office, he said, "Nothing's been touched. Coroner's on his way."

"Good. Thanks. Who called it in?"

"Got the call from his wife. She was hysterical. Said she'd been talking on the phone with him when she heard three shots. She screamed his name, no response. Called 911. Aid car arrived on scene within seven minutes, but he was dead. Forensics is already in there."

Soldier narrowed his gaze. "He didn't happen to shout the killer's name into the receiver when he was talking to his wife, did he?"

Winslow's grin was bleak. "Sorry."

"You find the weapon?"

"Yeah. Thirty-eight. Looks like it's been wiped clean. Registered owner, one Ryan Finlay."

Soldier's head snapped up. "He was shot with his own gun?"

"Kept it in his desk—"

"Ryan? Ryan! Let me see him. I want to see him now!" The woman's shrill pleas filled the air. Soldier turned to see Betsy holding an older woman's arms, trying to keep her from coming into the office.

Winslow sighed. "Damn. That would be the wife. How in the hell did she get in here?"

As Soldier and Winslow moved quickly to the two women, Betsy gently pulled Mrs. Finlay into her arms.

"Shh, Amy," she coaxed. "Why don't you come sit here with me." The sobbing woman collapsed against Betsy's shoulder and let herself be led to a chair where she cried uncontrollably into a fistful of tissues.

Winslow bent over Amy Finlay. "Ma'am? I'm Officer Winslow and this is Detective McKennitt from the Seattle PD. He needs to ask you some questions, okay?"

She shook her head and continued to cry. Betsy put her arms around Amy Finlay, who dabbed at her tears with more tissue.

"Amy, listen," Betsy said. "This is the worst possible time for you, I know. But the sooner you can answer the detective's questions, the sooner they can find whoever did this. Can you do that, Amy? For Ryan?"

Mrs. Finlay straightened a little and blew her nose. Lifting her chin, she looked at Soldier, her eyes red and swollen and vacant. He'd seen that look so many times before, and he hated it. Grief and loss and empty eyes. It twisted his guts into knots every time.

"Ma'am," he said as he crouched before her. "I'm profoundly sorry for your loss. But I do need to ask you some questions."

Amy Finlay nodded.

"Tell me exactly what your husband said to you on the phone. I need to know what he said, and what you heard in the background. Words, a voice, a door swinging open. Whatever you can remember."

She swallowed. "I . . . I called him so I'd know when to put the roast in the oven. I like to have dinner ready for Ryan right when he gets home."

"What time did you call him?"

"Um, a little before six. He . . . we were talking, then his voice changed. He seemed agitated all of a sudden."

"What did you hear?"

She sniffed, then blew her nose again. "His door has a glass window in it that always rattles. I heard the glass door rattle. Somebody must have opened it. But whether it was to enter or exit, I couldn't tell."

Soldier glanced at Ryan Finlay's door. "What did your husband say then?"

"He told me to wait a minute, that he had some unfinished business. He set the phone down. I heard it make that little thump kind of sound when it touched the desk, you know?"

"Go on."

"He must have gotten up from his desk because I heard his chair make a squeak and his voice sounded farther away. He was yelling, but I couldn't make out what he was saying. It was like he was calling after someone. Then I heard footsteps, running kind of, back to the desk. And breathing. Panting like. At first I thought it was Ryan, but now I'm not so sure."

"Why do you say that, Mrs. Finlay?"

"Well, because Ryan stomps and this was more like a skitter."

"You're doing fine. You're doing great. What else?" Soldier prompted.

Amy Finlay sighed and relaxed against the back of the chair. Soldier exchanged glances with Betsy. Her worried eyes were filled with compassion . . . and fear.

"I heard a sort of tussle," Amy continued. "Then Ryan picked up the phone again. He started to say something to me, but in the middle he yelled, *'No! Give me that!'* That's when I heard the shots. I didn't hear anything after that, because I was screaming. I'm sorry," she cried. "I should have stayed calm and listened, shouldn't I? If I'd stayed calm and listened, maybe I would have heard something. I did it all wrong, didn't I? If only—"

"Oh, Amy." Betsy put her arm around the sobbing woman. "You did fine, you did fine. You did everything you could."

With her arm still around the older woman's shoulders, Betsy looked up and stared into Soldier's eyes. Those lovely hazel eyes, so expressive, locked with his. He could see the compassion there, and something else, something deeper, something he didn't dare put a name to.

Her soft lips curved into a sympathetic smile and she said, "It all right, Amy. You did everything you could. You could not know this would happen. Nobody could have anticipated this. Nobody. You must not blame yourself. It is not your fault." She shook her head, her gaze still locked with his. "It's not your fault."

She continued staring intently into Soldier's eyes, but said nothing else, and never looked away. His emotions were frayed, his heart ravaged by guilt, and here was Betsy, throwing him a lifeline. Absolving him, freeing him.

Here he'd thought all along he was saving her, and it was she who was saving him.

Chapter 17

Betsy lay her throbbing skull against the headrest on the passenger side of her car while Soldier drove her home. The streets were empty, quiet, the air outside damp from the fog that had settled on the town. Soldier had turned the heater on full blast, yet Betsy could not find warmth.

Was Ryan really dead? Really and truly? Her exhausted brain felt chock full of conflicting thoughts and emotions. She was sad for Amy Finlay, now a widow, parted forever from the man she had loved and lived with for over twenty years. How would Amy cope? How would she move on with her life after such a tragedy?

But it wasn't just Amy's pain that affected her. Betsy hurt for herself, for the loss of a man she had known and liked for five years.

Yes, she had felt fear when Kristee Spangler had been murdered. And she'd felt guilty when Taylor had been hurt. But with Ryan it was different. She wasn't frightened and she felt no guilt. She was angry. Totally, thoroughly, magnificently pissed. Her blood boiled just beneath the surface. It wouldn't take much to push her over the edge to unbridled fury.

Sometime during the many hours it took to process the crime scene, Winslow had dispatched an officer to watch Betsy's house. Now, as Soldier walked her to her back door, he waved off the police car parked at the curb. At least there wouldn't be any surprises waiting inside for them tonight.

"Do you have your house keys?" Soldier said, his tired voice a soft rasp.

She nodded, then dug around in her purse. Handing them over, he cupped her tangle of keys in his palm. Closing his fingers over them, he enclosed her hand as well.

"Be careful," she said with a smirk. "One of those is the key to my heart."

By the light of the street lamp brushing against her back door, she watched Soldier arch a brow. His mouth tilted in a half smile. Dangling the key chain in front of his eyes, he said, "Which one is it? I don't see one with little lambies or unicorns or cupids on it."

"No." She moved toward him, wanting his heat, imploring his touch, craving whatever he would allow her to take from him this night. "I stopped believing in myths and fairy tales a long time ago."

He inched closer until she felt the warmth from his body envelop her own. Lowering his head, he brushed her lips with his open mouth. "I don't believe you," he whispered. His eyes glittered in the dark; his lids seemed heavy. "It's been a rough night, and maybe the fairy tales are on the back shelf at the moment." He licked her bottom lip. "But you're not the kind of woman who gives up on fairy tales. Ever." He licked her upper lip, nipped it with his teeth.

"You're not a fairy-tale kind of guy at all," she breathed. "So what does it for you?"

He kissed her. Against her mouth, he said, "Fires in the fireplace on snowy nights, hot jazz and cold beer, classic movies and classic moves." He kissed her again, turning her and pushing her against the back door.

Immediately, his hands were inside her jacket and under her sweater. She felt his fingers sliding up her rib cage, brushing the bottoms of her breasts. He hesitated.

"Yes . . ." She softly hissed the word against his lips. "Don't stop don't stop don't stop . . ."

Instantly, his warm hands moved higher, rubbing the tips of her nipples with his thumbs. His kisses became more urgent, deeper. He slid his hands around to her back and unfastened her bra.

Pushing it up and out of the way, his palms came around to cup her naked flesh, stroking, softly pinching, driving her crazy.

She slipped her arms around his shoulders, pressing herself as close to him as she could get. Lifting up on her toes, she rolled her hips against his groin until they both pulled away, panting.

"Where are the damn keys?" he choked.

"I thought you had them."

"Lost 'em. Maybe they're here," he said quietly, sliding his open palm down her stomach, and down and down. She stopped breathing.

"Nope, not there," he said. "Maybe here?" He reached around to cup her bottom. She moaned.

Placing her open palm against his zipper, her fingers measured his length and she murmured, "I thought I saw you drop them in here." She heard his sharp intake of breath. "Well, *something's* in there," she teased. "But I don't think it'll open this door."

"You'd be surprised," he growled.

He quickly produced the chain from his pocket, jammed the key in the lock and shoved the door open. Pulling Betsy inside, he slammed the door, locked it, and yanked off his jacket, letting it fall to the kitchen floor.

Reaching for her, Soldier pulled Betsy close, wrapping his arms around her. He was breathing hard. She could feel his heartbeat slamming against her chest as she snuggled into him.

"I need to know now," he panted, "if you want to do this. I don't want to hurt you, but you should know, I can't make you any promises." He reached under her chin, lifting her face to his, and searched her eyes.

"I want you, Betsy. I want to make love to you all night. But I can't offer you—"

She placed her fingertips against his mouth. "I know," she whispered. "I need this. I need you. Now. Tonight. No promises. No strings. Just us."

He lowered his head and kissed her again. The time for talking was over. Carefully, he helped her remove her jacket, then lifted her into his arms.

They made it as far as the living room, where it was

warm and comfortable. He kissed her again, touching her in places she never knew she liked being touched.

Layer by layer, their clothes slipped off their heated bodies and onto the carpet. When at last they were both naked, he pushed her gently down on the sofa and raised her arms over her head. Her breasts were lifted, exposed, bare. The nipples were taut and incredibly sensitive. He lowered his mouth and took full advantage, and she thought she would die from the sheer pleasure of it.

"Oh, yes," she breathed. She arched her back and whimpered, and when he slid his wet finger between her legs, she almost came right then and there.

Nibbling, suckling, kissing each tender inch of her flesh, he drove her passion on and on, and she fell all the way in love, down to her toes in love, down to the marrow of her bones in love with Soldier McKennitt.

His skin was smooth, his muscles tight and strong, and she adored the feel of her fingers and palms sliding over him.

She lay back on the velvety fabric of the sofa and lifted one leg over the back. She heard him tear open a packet and a few seconds later felt him settle between her thighs.

It had been a very long time, but when he slid inside her, it was glorious. He kissed her mouth and moved his hips against her, nudging that one special spot again and again. Building the tension, the need.

"*Soldier,*" she whispered, her voice soft and high and distant. "Oh, my . . ."

He kissed her deeply as he moved, angling his body

to make sure he rubbed against her with each long thrust.

She couldn't breathe, had to pull away from his kiss. Lifting her hips from the sofa in rhythm with his, she felt her pleasure mount until she was ready to beg him for release.

He arched over her, licked her nipples, biting them, sending shards of electric heat directly to where his flesh thrust into hers. Nothing else mattered, nothing else touched her. Just him. Just Soldier, the man she loved.

Her muscles tightened and she stilled. He slid against her, shoving her over the brink. She climaxed, softly gasping as her hips squirmed and wiggled against him, prolonging the intensity, the pleasure, the absolute delight.

"Oh, God . . ." she breathed. "Oh, Soldier . . ."

He smiled down at her, his lids heavy, his forehead damp with perspiration.

"All right," he said with hushed enthusiasm while she lay panting beneath him. With a grin, he murmured, "My turn."

He moved again, shoving himself harder, deeper. He bent his body to hers, gently taking the side of her neck in his mouth. His body stiffened for a second, his shaft poised just at her opening. His lungs bellowing, he waited. When he could wait no longer, he groaned, shoved into her, and completely lost control. His climax seemed to shake him, and he panted in rhythm with the wild thrust of his hips.

His sweat-slicked body stilled over hers as they both

recovered. They touched, belly to belly, and she felt the heavy intake of his breathing as it slowly returned to normal.

"You make very sexy sounds when you come," he panted softly against her neck. "I like it. Goddamn, I really, really like it."

"Th-Thank you," she choked. Her throat constricted and her eyes burned. "Th-Thank you," she repeated, her voice thick with tears. "I . . . I . . . you . . ."

Soldier lifted his head and stared worriedly into her eyes. Cupping her cheek in his palm, he whispered, "Betsy? Oh, Betsy, honey. It's okay. Go ahead. Let it all go."

Just as he pulled her closer, the dam burst. She began to sob, her body wracked by uncontrollable spasms. The tears on her cheeks felt hot, but she couldn't do anything to stop them.

There in Soldier's arms, she wept as though her heart were breaking.

He pulled a quilt from the back of the sofa and wrapped it around them both, snug and tight. She burrowed into his embrace and let the desolation she had been trying to deny for days and days, and maybe even years and years, spill out of her heart, out of her very soul, and into his safekeeping.

Soldier held Betsy in his arms, watching as pearly moonlight brushed softly across her cheek, the tip of her nose, her siren's mouth.

She was the sweetest woman he'd ever known. Her

tender heart, sharp wit, honesty, the very essence of her had gotten to him despite his best efforts to keep her at arm's length. It was getting more and more difficult to keep his feelings from pushing to the surface.

He told himself he could not allow himself to fall in love. He didn't need it, didn't want it, and sure as shit didn't deserve it.

She made a little mewling sound in her sleep and burrowed closer to him, skin-to-skin, heart-to-heart.

Ah, Betsy. What in the hell are you doing to me?

Her golden hair lay shimmering softly against the curve of her cheek. Twisting a silken strand around his finger, he idly let it fall into his palm. Somehow, her sweetness made her even more desirable, sexier than he could have imagined.

But she was so much more. Tonight, as she had comforted Amy Finlay, she had understood without him having said anything that he'd felt responsible for Finlay's death. And she'd absolved him.

When this was all over, and he had the son of a bitch responsible for this whole mess, how on earth was he ever going to let Betsy go? How could he let such a woman just walk out of his life?

She stirred in his arms, and he felt her leg slide over his as she moved closer. Man, he was in heaven.

Without opening her eyes, she whispered, "See Betsy. Betsy is satisfied. The Detective is good."

Soldier lowered his head and nibbled on her ear. "Look, look, look." He laughed softly. "Look at the Detective. He is ready to go again."

Against his chest, Betsy giggled. "Oh, oh, oh. Betsy is—"

Soldier slid his fingers between her legs and rubbed her in a languid rhythm.

"Oh, oh, oh," she said on an intake of breath. "Oh, oh . . . my. Oh yes, oh yes . . ."

Soldier pushed the quilt away and settled between her parted legs while still stroking, building the heat in her once more.

Her back arched and her breasts jiggled a bit as he put himself to her. He bent his head to take the very tip of one nipple in his teeth.

She gasped his name. Her hips rolled against his. Mindless of everything except the feel of her flesh tight around his penis, he pushed into her.

"Betsy," he breathed. "You're so beautiful. God, you're so damned beautiful."

Soldier lifted her arms above her head and intertwined his fingers with hers. He lay stretched on top of her, wanting to feel as much of her against him as he could. Her body was soft, the points of her nipples against his chest hard. He took her mouth just as she came, and he came with her, and it was a glory and a revelation.

A tap at the front door woke Soldier from a heavy sleep. In the predawn light, he could make out the hands on the grandfather clock standing sentry across the room. Five-thirty.

The tapping became louder, more urgent, rousing Betsy from sleep as well.

Pulling the quilt tightly around her, she whispered, "Somebody's at the door? Now?"

"You stay here. I'll check it out."

Rising from the sofa, he pulled on his jeans as Betsy quickly dressed. Glancing about, he located his shoulder holster laying in a heap by the coffee table.

He pulled his weapon and moved silently across the room. The tapping turned into a definite knocking. Edging aside the lace curtain that covered the oval glass on the front door, he simultaneously flipped on the porch light.

The man flinched and covered his eyes for a second then tried to peer through the glass. "B-Betsy?"

From behind him, Soldier heard Betsy's quick intake of breath. "Oh my God!"

"Betsy? H-Hurry and open the door before they s-see me!"

Soldier looked down at the woman beside him. Her eyes were huge with dismay . . . and joy?

Reaching for the lock, she turned it and yanked open the front door.

The man was Soldier's height, had graying hair and worried gray eyes. Though the night was cold, he wore no hat, but had on a rumpled wool coat. His arms dangled at his sides as he smiled and looked down at Betsy with weary and loving eyes.

"H-Hi, honey, I . . . I'm home."

"Daddy? Oh, Daddy, where have you been?"

Chapter 18

"Daddy," Betsy breathed, her throat tight with emotion. "You're here, and you're safe. Oh, thank God!"

Douglas Tremaine's trembling arms came around her and he rested his cheek on top of her head. They stood that way for a long while, not speaking, just being together. With her arms around her father, she could feel his bones beneath his coat and clothing. How had such a robust man gotten so thin?

Soldier gently tugged them both inside the threshold and closed the front door.

In the shadows of the foyer, the man she loved stood by watching as she comforted the other man she loved.

Betsy pushed her father to arm's length and examined him closely. Douglas Tremaine's brown wool overcoat was ragged and torn. His graying hair needed cutting and his unshaven beard was nearly an inch long.

"Daddy," she choked. "Where on earth have you been? You look half starved."

He made no response, but lifted his hands to his face to wipe away the tears that ran down his lean cheeks.

Betsy took his hands in hers and led him to the big chair in front of the fire while Soldier added more wood to the ruby embers. With a little encouragement from the brass poker, the small fire snapped to life.

Douglas had aged. Seeing him again in what had once been his own home, Betsy realized what the last decade had done to him.

He was still tall and good-looking, but the light that once shone so brightly in his eyes had dimmed. Ten years older and ten years more weary than when he had been her full-time father, he was greatly altered from the man who used to give her piggyback rides and read her stories of adventure and assure her she was his beautiful princess.

Soldier had slipped into his shirt, but left it unbuttoned. In one hand, he carried a small glass of brandy. In the other, a gun. Handing the brandy to her father, he said, "Take this, Mr. Tremaine. It should warm you up a bit."

Douglas nodded and accepted the snifter into his palms. Taking a close look at the sparkling goblet, he smiled.

"I remember this crystal." His tone was one of awe and enthusiasm. "Your mother and I . . . it was a wedding present." He admired the golden liquid in the glass but he didn't take a drink.

"Daddy. Where have you been? I only found out yesterday that you'd been released from the hospital, and that was months ago. Why didn't you call me? I would have come to get you. Are you hungry? Can I fix you something to eat?"

She crouched at his feet, looking up at him. He set the brandy on the small table adjacent to his chair. Reaching toward her, he cupped her cheek in his large hand.

"I'm all right, punkin. I . . . I have some medicine." Reaching into his pocket, he pulled out a small brown bottle and the tattered prescription he'd obviously been carrying around since his release. "I h-have two pills left. Better get some soon, or I'll go crazy again." He giggled softly as he looked into Betsy's eyes.

"Daddy—"

"Shh, sweet punkin. I don't need to s-stay in the hospital anymore. Good as I'm gonna get, they said. I c-can work a little, as long as I have the pills."

Soldier had gone into the kitchen and returned with a small bowl filled with cheese, crackers, and slices of fruit. Handing it to her father, he said, "Looks like you've missed a few meals. Eat this. You'll feel better."

Douglas gave Soldier a smile, then turned to Betsy. "Your husband is v-very thoughtful."

Betsy felt her heart leap about twenty feet then come crashing down again.

"Oh, no, Daddy, this is Soldier McKennitt. He's a Seattle policeman, a detective." *And my lover, and possibly the father of your grandchildren, but we're not going there just now.*

Douglas nodded as he took the bowl Soldier offered, then picked up a piece of cheese. For a few minutes he did nothing but nibble at the food. Then, "Bad things are happening to you, aren't they, punkin?"

Betsy nodded. Sliding a glance to Soldier, who had moved to stand a few feet away at the window, she said, "Tell me about the bad things, Daddy. What do you know about them?"

Her father's eyes closed and he shook his head, as though denying what he was seeing. "I thought it was you. Sh-She looked so much like you."

"Who did, Daddy? Who looked like me?"

"The woman. She watches you sometimes, and I w-watch her." He leaned forward as though to impart confidential information. "They told me at the hospital that I might still see the people," he whispered. "You know, the people who aren't there. But she *was* there. I'm . . . pretty sure of it."

Her father's head injury had been so severe, much of his normal brain function had been affected. As a result, he saw people who weren't there. At first he believed he was being conspired against by both friends and strangers alike. He lived in terror of being overpowered by some imaginary enemy, except Betsy knew that her father didn't have an enemy in the world. They were all in his head. Paranoid schizophrenia, they called it. Comparatively mild, they said, but debilitating just the same.

Moving up behind her, Soldier crouched and addressed her father. "Did you recognize the woman? Could you identify her from a photograph?"

With a bewildered look on his face, Douglas said, "You're a detective. That's good. You can p-protect her better than I can." He smiled and sat back in the chair, blowing out a breath as he did so. "*That's* a relief. B-Been watching the house, you know. My punkin needs protection. But I don't have a gun."

"Why do you need a gun, Mr. Tremaine?"

"She saw me once, t-talked to me once, said she knew who I w-was, said she knew all about Betsy and that Betsy was bad. I hid after that."

"Daddy." She placed her palm over his large hand. "Exactly what did she look like? What color was her hair? Were her eyes green or hazel like mine? Were they brown or blue? Can you remember?"

"It was night, but her eyes were d-darker, I think. And sort of . . . mean. And she's not beautiful, not like you."

Soldier said, "When was the last time you saw her? Did she tell you her name?"

Douglas shook his head in obvious bewilderment. "All the nights are the s-same to me. They sort of get mixed up in my head. But I do remember her name because I thought of fireworks a-and the Fourth of July." He grinned at Betsy and Soldier, his milky gray eyes fierce with pride that he had remembered. "Spangles."

"Span . . . Spangler?" Soldier said. "Kristee Spangler?"

"Yes, that's it. Just like the Fourth of July!"

"My father isn't stalking me and he didn't murder anyone. He's sweet and harmless, and he—"

"Absolutely adores you." Soldier slipped his arm around Betsy's waist and pulled her against his chest. "That man couldn't kill a gnat. There, feel better?"

Lowering his head, he kissed her. He'd meant it to

be a friendly sort of thing, but as soon as his mouth met hers, all that changed.

Heat swirled through him, speeding up his heart, making him dizzy. Their lovemaking had been good. Christ, it had been the *best*. He wanted to do it again, very, very soon.

Softly breaking the kiss, he said, "Things got off to an odd start this morning, what with your father showing up out of the blue. I never got a chance to thank you." He returned to kissing her, deeply. "So, thank you," he murmured against her parted lips.

They stood in front of the sink in the kitchen and watched the sky outside the window turn from a heavy, soggy indigo to a heavy, soggy lavender.

Betsy had called the office first thing, but there was a voice-mail announcement stating that the *Ledger* offices would be closed while the staff dealt with bereavement and the owners decided what to do next.

It had been a little after seven-thirty in the morning when they'd finished talking with Betsy's father and she helped him upstairs and put him to bed in the room across the hall from Soldier's. Now, the aroma of brewing coffee filled the air. The bright little rooster clock on the kitchen wall said it was nearly eight, and Soldier felt that if he didn't get some coffee soon, he'd collapse at 8:01.

Yesterday had been hell, and last night, heaven. But now it was back to hell. He had a murderer to catch.

Smiling down into Betsy's eyes, he said, "I doubt the woman your father talked to was Kristee Spangler. She didn't look a thing like you, and I'm pretty sure she wasn't dumb enough to have given your father her real name."

"So what happens now?"

"I'm going to arrange for him to take a look at a couple of your coworkers."

Betsy took a deep breath and seemed to consider her next words. "Which ones?"

"I think you know."

Betsy swallowed. "Carla. I think Carla."

He studied her for a moment. "I don't want to make this any tougher on you than it already has been. But I think we have to consider Carla and maybe even Holly persons of interest, and Linda Mattson, too. If your father can ID the woman who spoke to him, that would give us the break we've been looking for."

She nodded.

"I've got to pick up Taylor at the hospital. I'm going to bring him here, if that's okay with you, of course."

"Sure," she said. "The more the merrier."

"Stay in the house. Don't go anywhere and don't let anybody in, especially anybody from work."

"Here," she said, handing him her father's prescription. "Since I can't leave, would you please have the hospital fill this while you're at it? I'll pay you back."

Shoving the limp scrap of paper into his pocket, he said, "I'm sorry, ma'am. But we don't accept cash, traveler's checks, or any major credit cards."

She blinked up at him and put her fingertips over her mouth. "Oh, my! Whatever shall I do? Why, I have nothing to offer you, kind sir, except my naked body. Will that suffice?"

Soldier growled as he took her mouth in a ravaging kiss. They were both breathless when he finally lifted his head. "All I'm going to think about all day today is your naked body, you conniving little wench."

"Oh," she gasped theatrically, "but it'll be worth it, sir. All my gentlemen callers say so." She giggled.

With his arms still around her, Soldier said, "Despite all that's been going on, are you happy?"

The smile emanating from her glittering eyes told the whole story, but she confirmed it when she said, "My father is home, safe and sound, Taylor is well enough to be released from the hospital, my physical needs have been attended to beyond my wildest expectations, and I'm in l—uh, lust. I'm in lust with the most beautiful detective on the force." She gave him a toothy grin and her cheeks pinked brightly, but Soldier chose not to pursue what he was certain she had almost said, because the thought of Betsy being in love with him frightened—and also pleased—the hell out of him.

That being the case, he had a decision to make. And he needed to make it soon.

"Yoo-hoo! *Elizabeth,* open this door. I *know* you're in there!"

The last thing Soldier had said before he left to pick up Taylor was, *Don't let anybody in, and if you see or hear from Carla, let me know immediately!*

But he didn't understand her mother. If Betsy didn't let Loretta in, her mother would probably drive her car through the front door.

Slipping the lock, Betsy squeaked the door open.

"Get in here fast!" She reached out and grabbed her mother's arms, dragging the woman across the threshold. Richard and Piddle fell in right behind her. Slamming the door closed, Betsy slid the lock in place.

"Okay, you wanted in, now you're in. And you can't leave again until Soldier gets back."

Loretta tossed her hair like it was a feathered headdress. "Always so dramatic, Elizabeth." Giving Betsy the once-over, she said, "I've come to comfort and support you in your hour of need. I heard on the news about poor Ryan Finland . . ."

"Finlay."

". . . and knew you'd be upset, poor darling."

Taking a breath, Loretta looked around for the first time since she'd entered the house. "You say that magnificent creature isn't here?"

"Soldier? No. He went to pick up his brother from the hospital."

"Ah yes, the equally beautiful Tyler. My future son-in-law."

Betsy rolled her eyes. "It's *Taylor*, Loretta. *Taylor*. And he's not your future anything."

"Well, you needn't snap at me as though I were an insensitive cretin."

"Loretta, you *are* an insensitive cretin, and furthermore you—"

"Insensitive cretin!" The words came from behind the two women.

Both Betsy and Loretta turned to see Richard holding Piddle in one arm while shaking his index finger at the little dog, who seemed to be staring up at him in pained astonishment.

"You see?" Richard said, smiling at Betsy. "The English I am learning very well." He turned again to Piddle. "Insensitive cretin!"

Piddle blinked his large eyes and looked as though he might break down and cry.

"Wh-Who's an insensitive cretin?"

Betsy's heart skipped and she whirled to see her father standing at the foot of the stairs. He looked sleepy and rumpled wearing a pair of Soldier's sweats and a T-shirt. Staring into her eyes, he smiled, and her heart swelled with love for the father she had missed for so long.

Next to her, Loretta gasped as she gaped in astonishment at her ex-husband. "Douglas?"

Douglas's eyes widened.

Betsy stepped between them. "Daddy . . ."

Her father looked confused. "Betsy . . ."

Loretta caught her breath. "Douglas!"

Realization struck him. "L-Loretta!"

Richard scowled at Piddle. "Insensitive cretin!"

Except for a slight limp and a bandage around his head, Taylor felt pretty damn good. He was alive. That was enough to make any man who'd escaped death feel a little giddy.

As he waited for his brother to come and spring him from the hospital, Dr. Claire entered his room. White coat, chart and pen, efficient bedside manner, she looked lovelier than ever.

"So, all set to go home?" she asked.

"I guess so. I enjoyed my stay, though."

"Really."

"Yeah. Great food. I had no idea Jell-O came in so many flavors. And the room service is tops. Hot and cold running nurses at the snap of my fingers."

"We try."

"I guess I need to spend more time at home in the afternoons, though. Did you know that soap operas are now broadcast in English, Spanish, *and* Japanese? Gosh, I'm *really* going to miss this place."

"We hear that all the time." She laughed. "How's your head?"

He touched the bandage encircling his skull. "Okay. Tell me, Doc. Will I be able to play the trombone?"

She nodded. "Sure."

"Cool. I never could before."

She laughed, and he was once again entranced by the musical sound of her voice. "You're pretty funny for a cop."

"We cops are a funny group," he said. "Without a sense of humor, this job could bring you down real fast."

Slipping a lock of her silky looking shoulder-length hair behind her ear, she gave him a little shrug. "Well. You're all signed out, Detective. You can leave any time. You've got your meds and—"

"So you're not my doctor anymore?"

"Nope."

"And I'm not your patient?"

"Nope."

"So if I asked you out for dinner, it wouldn't be a violation of doctor-patient fooling-aroundishment?"

She blushed and laughed again. "Detective McKennitt, I—"

"It's Taylor."

He watched her intently as she lowered her lashes and nibbled on her bottom lip. "Look, I . . . it's not that I don't find you attractive. I really do."

"Really? *Really* really, or just really?"

She sighed. "You're not making this easy."

"Nope," he said.

Hugging the clipboard more tightly to her bosom, she looked up at him. "I'm a doctor and you're a detective. I get calls at all hours of the day and night, and I'll bet you do, too. I don't have time for a social life, let alone a relationship."

He moved toward her until he stood only inches away. "Is that what we'd have?" he said softly. "A relationship?"

"I hope you realize I'm not the casual affair type, Detective."

Slipping his knuckles under her chin, he raised her face to his. "Must be pretty hard on your sex life."

She arched a brow. "What sex life?"

He lowered his gaze to her lips. Man, what lips she had. Full, pink, and begging to be kissed. So he did.

She gave a small gasp when his mouth touched hers, but she didn't pull away. He ended the kiss with a brush of his tongue against hers and a nibble of her bottom lip.

Her eyes were closed, and when she opened them, she looked a little dazed.

"I was married," he said. "My ex-wife was a bitch on wheels. Faithless as they come, conniving, manipulative. But she was beautiful, and I was an idiot and didn't see her for what she was until too late."

"I'm sorry, Taylor. Truly."

"I'd sort of sworn off women . . . until I met you. I'm not interested in getting married again, but I am interested in you. Just have dinner with me. A meal. Food. Conversation. That's it. Nothing fancy, not if you don't want it."

"I'm older than you."

"I'm taller. Say yes."

"I hate it when men do that."

"That's why we do it. Say yes and hate me over dinner tomorrow night."

He lowered his head and kissed her again.

When she recovered, she gave him a defeated grin. "Yes, damn you. Yes."

Chapter 19

*S*oldier glanced at his watch. He had just over an hour to finish up at the PHPD and get over to the hospital in time to pick up his brother by eleven o'clock.

Slapping the file folder closed, he reached for his laptop and logged off. From the other side of the desk, Sam Winslow said, "You look like a man who just solved a crime."

Soldier smiled, giving Winslow a quick, "*damned right*" nod.

A few more hours and this would all be wrapped up. A few more hours, hopefully, and no more twenty-hour days to suck the energy right out of him. Since this case began, it had been one thing after another and barely any time to take a deep breath.

Getting to bed well after midnight several nights in a row sure didn't help, but that was the way it worked sometimes when a crime was fresh.

Of course, he could have slept last night but had

chosen instead to make love to Betsy for hours. And hours.

Betsy. This was almost over, and she was and would continue to be safe. Betsy. Christ, what that woman did to his insides. Was it possible to fall in love with someone in so short a time?

Did he love her? The mere thought should have sent him into panic, but it didn't. She hadn't quite said the words, but she'd come close. Even if she never said them, he could see it in her eyes. She was such a lousy poker player.

He looked at the file on the desk in front of him.

Turning to Winslow, Soldier pointed to the name on the file and said, "I'm heading over to her place now with a search warrant, but I want to put out an APB in case she's already on the run."

Winslow nodded. "You think she's the woman Ms. Tremaine's father saw?"

"Yep. I think she wanted Linda Mattson's job, then when it went to Betsy instead, her plans were screwed and she blamed Betsy. I'm hoping a search of her place will turn up some evidence we can use to make an arrest."

"So, what happened to the Mattson woman?"

Soldier stood, walked over to the window and gazed out over peaceable Port Henry. Almost peaceable, soon to be again.

"I had Seattle run a dental check on a Jane Doe found off I-90 about three months ago." He faced Sam Winslow and crossed his arms over his chest. "I got the results this morning. It was Linda Mattson.

No runaway marriage, no Minnesota. Skull was crushed."

"Sounds just like the Spangler thing."

Soldier shrugged. "Hey, if it worked once, it would work twice, right? Our killer swings a wicked tire iron, especially when the vic is somebody who trusts her and hasn't got a clue as to what's coming."

As Winslow shrugged into his regulation forest green jacket, he said, "Do you really think she's just going to be sitting in her apartment, watching TV or reading a magazine after having killed three people?"

"If she doesn't suspect we're on to her, she might," Soldier replied. "But I think she's gone into hiding. Nobody's seen her since the day Finlay was murdered, so she's found a little niche somewhere to hide until she's ready to make another move. My goal now is to find her before she makes that move."

Carla Denato stood across the street from her apartment building, watching her carefully planned life literally go up in smoke.

She'd packed everything she needed into her car, having ditched Kristee's green sedan days ago. As she watched, black plumes began to curl out the open window as tiny flames flitted along the eaves.

Fire had gotten her out of a jam once before, and it would again.

Even so, she was pissed. *Damn* Ryan Finlay for forcing her to kill him before she was ready. But he'd caught her off guard last night, and now she had to move quickly.

Everything was falling to pieces, she thought, and it was all *Betsy's* fault. And if she wasn't extremely careful, she'd miss the opportunity to deal the death blow to her nemesis, and have to hightail it to Canada before she was damn good and ready.

The shriek of sirens broke her angry reverie, and she stepped behind some low-growing evergreens. Neighbors were beginning to assemble on the sidewalk, their coats or robes pulled tightly around them to ward off the autumn chill as they stood in awe of the apartment house fire. The fire she had set.

Fire had such power, just like she herself did. Flames and smoke were quiet as they crept up on the unsuspecting, doing their deadly work before anybody realized exactly how much trouble they were in.

A fire engine screamed onto the scene to ostensibly save the day, and was soon followed by two police cars and another fire truck. More people gathered on the street and sidewalks, all gaping, all enraptured by the blaze.

Well, would you look at that? Detective Hunky McKennitt emerged from the squad car to stare at the fire, fury plain to see on his handsome face.

He stood with his back to her, his hands on his excellently lean hips as he surveyed the situation. She watched as he spoke to the fire captain.

What a bonus! Soldier McKennitt was here at her apartment! She had to admit that under other circumstances, she would have gone for him in a big way, but once he'd met little Betsy-wetsy, he'd stopped looking around. Even Kristee hadn't been able to snare his interest, and she had *certainly* tried.

McKennitt turned to scan the crowd. Right. She'd almost forgotten. The cops knew how much arsonists loved to watch a fire, so he figured he could spot her among the onlookers. Time to take off.

As she backed away, immersing herself in a thick stand of rhododendrons, Carla considered what to do next. She'd liked it in Port Henry and had hoped to stay on for a while. But thanks to Betsy, that little bubble had burst.

Betsy had taken everything she'd wanted, worked for, killed for.

The more she thought about it, the angrier she became. Her fingers twitched in anticipation of getting her hands on Betsy and ripping her hair out, and then her heart.

Betsy Tremaine was as good as dead, but first she needed to suffer a little more. As she herself had suffered. She'd assumed the rumors and insinuations would ruin Betsy, but they hadn't. Nobody had believed them! She'd even sent those stupid book reviews to McKennitt in the hope that he would write an angry letter to the *Ledger*, castigating Betsy, but he hadn't. Instead, he'd fallen for the little bitch! Was life too damn funny or what!

Carla pushed those thoughts out of her head and instead tried to focus on the days to come.

Dead leaves crunched beneath her feet as she scurried to her car, her steps lightening as she went.

Oh, goody, she thought. *It's time to take out another player.*

When Soldier knocked on Betsy's door, the last thing he expected was for her to fling herself into his arms.

Not that he didn't like it a whole hell of a lot.

"Save me," she whispered against his ear as she slid her arms around his neck.

Soldier let himself enjoy the feel of her body pushed tightly against his. Wrapping his arms around her, he bent his head and kissed her on the cheek. She lifted her face, and he kissed her on the mouth. "Save you from what?" he said roughly.

She gestured in the direction of the living room. "Them," she whispered. "They're all in there. It's horrible. Do you have your gun? Put me out of my misery, please?"

"I thought I told you not to let anybody in," he admonished through a scowl.

"It's just my mother and her Dick," she said, still wrapped in his arms. "They arrived just after you left. They've been here all day. With my father here, it's been . . . tense. I'm ready to go nuts."

"Here," he said, handing her the bouquet clenched tightly in his fist. "Maybe these will help."

Her eyes widened, and she inhaled deeply as her lips formed a delicate O. "Flowers? For me?" she breathed out.

Soldier had given women flowers before, but this was the first time in years he'd felt like blushing and digging his toe into the dirt like some lovestruck kid. "Yeah," he said. "They're just daisies. Nothing special."

Her face said they were very special. In fact, she looked as though he had just given her the Hope diamond.

"Thank you," she said, wrapping the huge bouquet

in her arms. "They're lovely. I'll go put them in some water. I have *just* the vase for these."

"Well," he offered, feeling more composed, "you know, they're just daisies, and a few little pink roses. And the woman put some of that white stuff in there, too."

"Baby's breath."

"Yeah. Baby's breath. My mom likes those, too."

"They're so lovely," she said through the sweetest smile he had ever seen, "they totally make up for my rotten day. Thank you."

Betsy placed her open palm on his chest, rose on her tiptoes and settled a soft kiss on his mouth. She might just as well have jabbed him with a cattle prod, because every nerve in his body zinged to life.

He cleared his throat. "Taylor's in the car. I need to get some food in him, then he needs rest."

"Dinner's on the stove."

"Thanks. After we eat, I need to fill you in on all that's happened today. The next twenty-four hours are going to be eventful."

"Well, that sounds pretty ominous."

"I'll tell you about it when we're alone."

A moment later Taylor hobbled up behind him and moved through the open door and into the foyer.

"Hi," he said to Betsy.

"Oh, Taylor, how are you feeling? Is there anything I can get you?"

"Food and sleep ought to do the trick."

Ignoring the trio of voices coming from the living room, Soldier closed and latched the front door, then followed Betsy and Taylor into the kitchen.

The savory fragrance of a home-cooked meal teased his senses and poked at his stomach. A man could get used to this really fast, he thought as he surveyed the goodies Betsy had prepared. Pot roast with carrots and potatoes, homemade biscuits, a freshly baked apple pie. For a man, that was about as close to heaven on earth as it got. Throw in some good sex, and there you had it.

For the first time, Soldier took a good look around the kitchen. It was cute. It was . . . Betsy. Lace curtains on the windows, herb pots on the sill, white wallpaper strewn with wildflowers. A cookie jar in the shape of a cow wearing a straw bonnet stood on the counter next to large, old-fashioned jars filled with flour and sugar.

He slid a look at Taylor, who had settled himself into a chair at the big table, only to find that Taylor was sending him a look in return. And Taylor's message was coming across loud and clear.

Pretty nice, hm? So, what are you waiting for, you idiot?

As Betsy wiped her hands on the pretty, forties-style apron she wore, the cacophony that had been sequestered in the living room burst into the quiet of the kitchen.

Loretta was dressed in royal purple. The omnipresent Piddle rested securely in her arms. Chattering in French, she led the hapless *Ree-shar*, who followed obediently behind, nodding and gesturing.

Bringing up the rear, Douglas Tremaine shuffled in and sat at the table next to Taylor. Betsy introduced them and they shook hands, but Douglas's sad gray eyes rarely left his ex-wife, except when he looked at Betsy and smiled.

Turning to the crowd, Betsy said, "I'm leaving the food on the stove. You may get a plate and help yourself. Except for Taylor. Taylor," she ordered, "you stay put. I'll serve you."

"I'll get a plate for Taylor," Soldier said. "He's my brother. I know how to feed him." He stood and began heaping food onto one of the dishes stacked next to the stove.

Betsy came up beside him and said, "Let me know if you need anything else."

He stared down into her eyes and lust hit him like a freight train. Behind him, Taylor, Douglas, Loretta, and Richard, not to mention Piddle, were all chattering away, unaware of the sexual tension strung tightly between himself and Betsy.

If he shot them all and shoved the plates and silverware off the table, he could take her right now on her barnyard print tablecloth, chickies and duckies be damned. Blood surged through him, stalling at his groin, sending him spinning into need.

In Loretta's arms, Piddle suddenly began to yelp, or squeak, or whatever a Chihuahua did to make that irritating sound.

"Shh," Loretta scolded. "Does Mommy's Pids need to go outside?" Nothing the woman could say calmed the nasty little beast, who kept growling and barking viciously.

Soldier shot a look at Taylor, who made as if to stand. "Taylor, don't move! Betsy," he snapped, "get the lights."

Turning to the light switch, she slammed her hand against the wall and the room went dark. Loretta squealed, *Ree-shar* gasped, Piddle yelped, and Douglas rose from the table.

"Wh-What can I do?" he said shakily. "T-Tell me what to do."

"Stay just where you are. Everybody down," Soldier ordered, and they all hit the floor. "Tayo, you're not supposed to do anything, so don't—"

But Taylor was halfway to his feet before Soldier could stop him. In the dim light of the kitchen, Soldier pulled his weapon and began moving cautiously toward the living room, while Taylor limped around to a side door that led to the garage. The house was shadowy and silent except for the popping of the small fire in the living room fireplace.

With his weapon pointing straight down, Soldier hurried to the front window, edged the drapes aside and peered out. The street lamps had come on, casting circles of light up and down the pavement. A movement far up the road caught his eye. Rushing to the door, he pulled the lock and ran down the walkway just as Taylor emerged from the back of the house.

In the distance, a car door slammed. An engine that had been idling roared violently to life. With a squeal of tires, it tore up the street and out of sight.

"Did you make the car?" huffed Taylor, who looked pale and near collapse even in the evening shadows.

"You idiot," Soldier growled as he grabbed his brother's arm and steered him toward the house. "Too dark to see. But it doesn't matter. There's already a warrant out for her arrest."

A soft voice behind Soldier made him turn. "It's Carla, isn't it?" Betsy's features were tense, her shoulders rigid. Her father stood next to her, tall and straight, with a feral gleam in his eye as he looked off up the road where the car disappeared around the corner.

Betsy shook her head. "I didn't want to believe it, but I wondered," she said as she followed her father's gaze. "When I thought about it, things only made sense if it was Carla."

Soldier nodded. "I'm sorry. I know she was your friend."

"Apparently not."

"Leave me!" Taylor interrupted. "Go after her!"

Soldier muttered something under his breath as he helped his brother into the house, settling him on the sofa. Pulling out his cell phone, he called Winslow.

The PHPD had the make and model of Carla Denato's car on file, and unless she hid the vehicle out of sight within the next few minutes, a patrol car was sure to spot her and pick her up. With his brother bleeding again, it was the best Soldier could do for the moment despite Taylor's protests.

Betsy had disappeared into the kitchen, to reemerge holding a cold compress and a clean towel. She placed the compress on Taylor's sweating brow and used the thin linen cloth to help stop the bleeding from a cut on his shoulder that had opened during the pursuit.

Her words to Taylor were soothing, calming, and it

made Soldier almost wish it was he she was ministering to.

"Betsy?" Soldier said, and she raised her head to look at him.

"Yes?"

"Your father . . . he's an all right guy. Now I know where your get your courage."

She smiled at him, and it lit her face all the way up to her eyes. "Thank you," she whispered, then took the stained cloth and vanished through the kitchen door.

Furious that the Denato woman had shown up, even more furious at his dumbass brother for pushing himself too far, Soldier turned to Taylor.

"God damn it, Taylor, I told you to stay put! They let you go from the hospital too soon. They should have kept you chained to the fucking bed—"

"Sounds kinky," Taylor wheezed. "I think I like it."

"Shut up."

"Relax, big brother," Taylor panted. "I just got a little light-headed, that's all. I'll be fine after I get some of that home cooking in me."

As Taylor limped into the kitchen to finish eating, Soldier called the hospital and had Dr. Hunter paged. When she came on the line, he growled, "What kind of doctor are you anyway, releasing a man in his condition? Taylor was in no shape to—"

"What are you talking about?" she interrupted. "Tell me what happened."

After he explained, she said curtly, "He was released to go home to bed rest, not to chase down murder suspects, Detective. I'll stop by to see him on my way home. If it looks bad, I'll have him readmitted. In the meantime, keep him quiet and make sure he gets plenty of fluids. And no more funny business!"

Fuming behind the steering wheel of her car, now safely hidden inside an old garage about a mile from Betsy's house, Carla considered what to do next.

What the hell, had half of Port Henry moved in with Betsy? What was with all the people at her house? She'd gone there to kill Soldier, and what did she find? Not only Soldier and Betsy, but the brother, the mother, the father, that French guy, and that fucking little dog! She should have had Kristee kill the damn mutt instead of just shoving it in the deep freeze.

Carla's plans were rapidly unraveling and she didn't like it one bit. *Okay, okay*, she told herself. She was nothing if not flexible. She'd just have to be a little more creative.

She briefly considered leaving town, bagging the whole plan, but she had worked too hard for too long to back out now. Betsy deserved to be ruined, and ruined she would be.

Well, there was no use going back to Betsy's house tonight, not with all those damned people there. What was called for now was a little diversion. Cause a disruption at point A so you could do your business at point B.

She would be patient; it would come to her. She was, after all, a very patient woman. Had she not waited for years to kill her stupid lech of a father and suffered her controlling mother's ravings until she had locked them both in the house and burned it to the ground? And Kristee? Well, it was only a matter of time before she knew she'd be forced to rid herself of her flaky sister.

She was invincible and they were fools. Murder was so easy, and she'd always gotten away clean. This time would be no different.

Chapter 20

A search of the area had turned up nothing. Carla Denato must have vanished into thin air. Just to be on the safe side, a patrol car arrived shortly after dinner to serve as escort home for Loretta and her adoring entourage, just in case Carla had targeted anybody else for fun and games tonight. As usual, Betsy's mother flirted outrageously with the shy young officer until his cheeks reddened and he practically gushed.

As Betsy stood at the front window, watching the cars drive off, she heard her father's voice behind her.

"I'm g-going to bed now," he said quietly. "Good night, punkin."

Betsy moved to the bottom of the stairs, where her father stood and gave him a warm hug. He kissed her on the forehead. "I love you, s-sweetheart," he said.

"You know, Daddy," she whispered, "you seem perfectly normal to me. Just as normal and as darling as ever."

He laughed. "I'm not cr-crazy, you know. That

wasn't the problem. It was just that there were all those W-Watergate prosecutors. I kept seeing James Dean following me."

"That was John Dean, Daddy, and he wasn't following you. Besides, you're safe now here with me."

He grinned and nodded and gave her a wink, then climbed the stairs and closed his bedroom door.

"Betsy." Soldier's voice. Behind her. Soft, caressing, filled with understanding. "When your parents divorced, you chose to stay with your mother and not your father. Why?"

She shrugged. "As the saying goes, it seemed like a good idea at the time." Turning to him, she laughed and said, "I thought she needed me. Isn't that silly? I thought one day, she'd wake up and look at me and decide she loved me terrifically, and that she needed me to make her life complete." Rolling her eyes, she said, "I . . . was an idiot."

Soldier slid his arms around her, pulling her close, encouraging her to let him help dissipate her ages-old anguish.

"It's not your fault, you know," he murmured against her hair. "Only Loretta can change Loretta. And here's a news flash . . . it ain't gonna happen."

"I know that now," she confessed. "When I was little, I used to think it was me. I mean, she was so beautiful. She was the most beautiful of all the moms, and all the kids envied me. But they didn't know how distant she could be." She swallowed. "I didn't even realize it myself until I got older. I'd always thought it was just . . . me. That I'd done something wrong. Displeased her in some way." She swallowed again. "So, I never let anybody get very close. I couldn't risk the rejection. It just hurt too damn much."

"Honey, listen, I—"

"You don't let people close, either," she interrupted before he could confess the words that would stab her to the core. Searching his eyes, she said, "Tell me about Marc."

Soldier was sure she must have felt his heart trip over itself, but she only kept her steady gaze on him, waiting for his answer.

"I've already told you—"

"No you haven't," she interrupted again. "You told me what happened, but you didn't tell me about the man who was your friend, the man who died, or what it's done to your insides. That's what I want to hear."

He blinked and looked away. "I don't think I want to talk about this."

She tightened her arms around his neck. "I think you do. I think you need to."

Soldier pulled her a little closer, held on a little tighter, as though she was the only thing keeping him from sinking under the surface and never coming up again.

He'd never talked about his most deeply held feelings for his late partner, not even to Taylor.

"Marc," he began, surprised at the roughness of his voice. "I loved the guy. He was a good man. He was a good husband, a terrific father, a great cop. My blunder, my miscalculation, my misjudgment took all of that away."

"No. A bad guy took all that away and—"

"Marc died in my arms," he said in a rush. "He . . .

he was in a garbage dump, covered in newspapers and potato peels and all kinds of crap, bleeding. I was alone. It was hard to climb in and pull him out without hurting him any more than he already was."

Soldier had never confessed that aloud before. His throat hurt from the effort, but once he had begun, it seemed important to tell her everything.

"I hauled him over the side and onto the grass. It had rained and everything was damp, sticky. I sat in the mud and held him, like you'd hold a baby, you know? I could hear the sirens coming closer, but he was hurt so bad . . . I knew, I mean, I was so afraid that . . ."

"Being afraid doesn't come naturally to you, does it?"

He shook his head. "No. No. It doesn't."

"Maybe that's why it was so shocking. So many awful things must have been going through your head."

He nodded and tightened his embrace, letting her warmth seep through to his cold, cold bones. Without even trying, she filled in all the hollow spaces, lightened all the shadows, healed all the wounds.

"What happened then?" she whispered.

"I called his name and he opened his eyes, stared up at me. His fingers curled around my wrist, hard, so hard. For a long time I thought it was because he blamed me and he was angry, but now I'm not so sure."

"What do you think it really was?"

"I think it was Marc, trying to hang on to life. Like, if he held on tight enough, it wouldn't slip away, out of his grasp." The images in his head were painful to endure, but he watched the scene unfold again, watched his friend die, again.

"He died just as the paramedics pulled up. He was there, and then he was just gone. Thirty-eight years on the planet, a snap of the fingers, and he's gone."

Soldier was silent for a moment, gathering his composure, trying to save Betsy from knowing how deeply he felt his failure and how much it affected their relationship. But she had to know the truth, so she'd stop looking at him with such hope and love in her eyes.

"I swore I'd never get that close to anybody ever again," he bit out. "I'd never set anybody else up for failure, my failure. And I'd never leave a wife and kids behind like that."

He looked down into her eyes. *Get it? I'm talking to you, Betsy. I'm saving you. Saving you from me.*

If she saw the message in his eyes, she ignored it. How typical of her.

"Do you think if Marc had it to do over again, he'd never marry, never have kids?"

"He adored his family," Soldier rasped, his voice thick with emotion. "They made his life complete. He talked about them all the time."

"And his wife, would she have given up the years she had with him if she'd known it was going to end badly?"

"I can't answer that. Nobody can answer that."

"I can," she said, smiling up into his eyes. "Maybe someday you'll let me."

It was nearly eleven o'clock when Claire greeted Soldier with a wry, weary smile on her face, and a black bag clutched in her hand.

"Sorry I'm so late. Rough night. How's he doing?" she said as she stepped across the threshold. "Have you managed to keep him quiet, or has he gone running after more criminals?"

"Nope. I promised him that if he was a real good boy, you'd give him a sponge bath when you got here."

"Is he in bed?"

"No, he's sitting in the bathtub with a bar of soap in one hand and a bottle of champagne in the other."

When she laughed, Soldier said, "Listen, I'm sorry about earlier. I shouldn't have gotten so worked up on the phone. I was really worried and I let it get the best of me."

"Oh, gosh," she gushed, "I've heard much worse from women in labor, and men passing kidney stones. Don't give it another thought." She glanced about the room. "Has Betsy gone up to bed?"

"Yeah, but I can go get her."

"Heavens no. She needs rest. I won't be long anyway."

Soldier opened his brother's bedroom door, to find him lying on his back, deep in sleep.

"Tell you what," Claire said. "You go ahead and go to bed. You look just as tired as I feel. I'll check him over, and when I'm done, I'll let myself out."

"That's okay," he replied. "I should stay and make sure—"

"Get the hell to bed and leave me in peace." Taylor's voice was raspy, sleepy, as he raised himself up on his elbows. "The lady can stay. You," he jutted his unshaven chin at Soldier, "beat it."

"All right. You got it, half-wit." Soldier turned to her. "Call me if you need anything. There's a patrol car on the corner keeping a close watch on the house, so if—"

"Anything the lady needs," Taylor mumbled, "I can provide. Now get lost."

"Mind if I turn on the light?" Claire asked once Soldier was out of the room. "Moonlight may become you, but it's damned hard to diagnose by." She set her medical bag on the small table next to Taylor's bed, then snapped on the bedside lamp.

Even though she'd seen his body before, seeing it again in an intimate setting made her heart flutter. He was obviously naked under that blanket, so she focused her efforts on the task at hand, and not on his excellent male form.

"Deep breaths," she said as she pressed the stethoscope to his bare chest.

Instead of looking around the room like most patients did when being examined, he looked straight at her. "Will I live?" he said.

"I'm almost sure of it, Detective."

"I'm off duty. You should call me Taylor."

"Well, I'm on duty, *Detective.*"

Flicking on her penlight, she said, "Focus on the corner of the ceiling over there."

He did, and she examined his pupils.

"Any dizziness or nausea? Have you felt faint, other than when you were running down a criminal against your doctor's orders?"

He lay back down again, his broad shoulders

smooth and muscular in the muted light of the small lamp. Taylor McKennitt was a very sexy man.

"We still on for dinner tomorrow night, Doc?"

As she packed up her medical bag, she chewed on her bottom lip. "Yes. But we'll have to go someplace quiet, and you'll have to behave." Turning back to him, she said, "I'll pick you up tomorrow night at six and take you to the quietest place in Port Henry."

He grinned. "Oh yeah? Where's that?"

Snapping her bag closed, she said, "My house."

His eyes grew wide as interest flared to life in their depths. "You can cook?"

"I can cook."

"Wow," he said, arching a dark brow. "You're beautiful, you're single, you're a doctor, and you can cook? Will you marry me and make my mother the happiest woman on earth?"

She smiled and said, "I'll let myself out. Get some rest, hotshot. See you tomorrow at six."

Soldier went into his room and began getting ready for bed. Tugging off his shirt, he tossed it on the bed and unbuckled his belt.

Tomorrow, he would institute an area-wide search for Denato. She was still around, he could feel it in his bones. Her plans had been wrecked and she was sure to blame Betsy. While most perps would cut their losses and run, stalkers who had murdered and gotten away with it were an arrogant lot. He was sure that Carla Denato wouldn't leave until she tried to finish what she'd begun.

And it was his job, his vow, to make sure she didn't.

He was so deep in his thoughts, he was barely aware that the connecting bathroom door between his room and Betsy's had inched open.

"Hey, Soldier. New in town?"

He turned at the low, sexy little remark. "It's, 'Hey, sailor,' and I've heard it bef—"

Soldier's words backed up in his throat, his mouth went dry, and his eyes came very near to popping out of his head. He'd never come so close to puckering up for a wolf whistle in his life.

Betsy stood in the threshold, every sweet, plump, curvy inch of her, in a dress so hot his eyelashes felt singed.

"My mother brought this from Paris," she said, her cheeks flushing as she said the words. "Now be honest. Do you like it?"

Like it? Hell, he liked it so much, if he tried to speak, he'd bite off his tongue.

The dress was a simple black velvet number. It had no frills, nothing about it to test a man's will, but the way it clung to Betsy's body from creamy cleavage to mid-calf was a sin.

The off-the-shoulder bodice fitted over her breasts, leaving absolutely nothing to the imagination. Whatever she had, it showed—from soft cleavage, to tight nipples, to the undercurve of each breast, to her cinched-in waist and the sweet camber of her hips. It covered everything, but could in no way be considered demure.

She twirled and the skirt flared a bit, showing the backs of her knees and part of her creamy thighs. The back was laced together from her shoulder blades down to the curve of her spine just above her . . . oh God.

On her feet, she wore black strappy heels.

He stood and stared at her, too paralyzed with desire to even speak.

"I think it's kind of tight," she said with a scrunched-up nose. "What do you think?"

It would have been nice if he could actually have formed a coherent sentence, but a few dry, choppy letters were the best he could do.

"T-T . . . I . . . uh . . ."

"Yeah, that's what I thought," she said, apparently oblivious to his speech impediment. "Maybe I can let it out a little at the hips." She wriggled them for emphasis.

"H-H . . . I . . . uh . . ."

She giggled and her breasts jiggled a tiny bit. *Oh, Christ.*

"I know exactly what you mean," she said, as though he had actually made an intelligible comment. "And the neckline's scooped too low for me. I feel almost completely exposed." She leaned forward a little. "See? Just a couple more inches and I'd spill like Hoover Dam."

"Sp-Sp . . . Hoo . . . Hoo . . ."

"You sound like Woodsy Owl. That's cute." She smiled at him, her deep dimples capturing him once more, the sparkle in her eyes shining for him. Had he ever met a more ingenuous, intriguing, incredible woman in his life?

"Betsy," he choked. Moving toward her, he tried to find some words, any words, he could actually speak without stumbling over. "Betsy, I—"

"Oh, you're right," she sighed. "I never would have guessed you'd have such a great fashion sense. You're absolutely right. The dress is totally wrong for me. It's so tight, I can't even wear a bra or any undies—"

Was she naive or was this some kind of tantalizing little game she was playing? Soldier didn't care.

Lowering his head, he took her mouth. His own mouth open, he fed on her kisses, using his tongue to lap up the honey of her lips.

His fingers dug into the firm, bare flesh of her arms, and she stepped into his kiss, into his embrace, into his forevermore.

Soldier let his hands slide down her back. Cupping the globes of her bottom in his fingers, he pulled her up against his erection. Through the velvet nap of her dress, he felt her heat, and it sent his blood to boiling.

In his mind, he could see under her dress, see her naked breasts, her pink nipples. In his hands, her bottom wriggled, driving him totally nuts.

No panties. She was not wearing panties, only this little black dress that looked like it had been spray-painted on.

She moaned, her lips parted, he thrust in, rubbing his tongue against hers until they were both panting. She tasted sweet and tart and hot. His body was nothing but sensation, his fingers, his mouth, his skin.

He kissed her hard, wanting to devour her. Her neck arched back, and he broke the kiss to trail nibbles down her throat. His hands slipped around to cup her generous breasts, and she sighed, a lovely, soft, thoroughly sexy sound.

Soldier moved her back toward the bedroom wall.

When he felt her press against it, he reached for the hem of her dress and hiked it up to her knees, thighs, hips, waist, exposing her to him.

Quickly, he moved his hand to the softness between her legs, sliding one finger into the cleavage. She choked his name, wrapped her arms around his neck and her leg around his thigh.

He kissed her again, long, slow, deep, soul kisses as he unbuttoned his fly, freeing himself. He pressed into her, then plunged into her.

She squealed softly, murmuring his name until he took her mouth again.

Rolling his hips, he pushed in as far as he could go. Reaching behind her, he grabbed at the laces until they came undone and he could slide the dress down, revealing her breasts. He kissed her, slanted his thumb across one taut nipple, rolled his hips against her. Inside her tightness, he felt himself pulse in time with his thundering heartbeat.

Breaking the kiss, he groaned and lowered his damp brow to the curve of her bare shoulder.

"Betsy," he breathed. "God, what you do to me. You're so good . . . never so good before . . . not ever . . ."

"So," she teased softly, "you don't think my dress is too tight?"

"Tight," he moaned. "I love that word."

He withdrew as far as he could, then slowly slid back in. It felt so damned good, he did it again. And then again.

"Oh . . . my . . . S-Soldier . . ." Betsy was panting, her body trembled against his. She was close.

Her naked bottom in his palms, he lifted her and took one nipple into his mouth. He sucked hard, played with it with his tongue, gently scraped it with his teeth.

She gasped. "I'm going to . . . oh. Yes. I'm going to . . ."

Her neck arched back and she breathed out a long, slow, totally sexy sigh as she came.

The feel of her clenching around him drove Soldier over the brink and he stroked again, groaned as his own pleasure rocketed through him, lighting his skin on fire, taking his breath away.

Wrapped together, they both breathed hard until they'd recovered a little. Soldier held Betsy against his chest, her legs wrapped around his waist, his flesh still a part of her.

I love you. You are beautiful and you are kind and you are strong and smart and irreplaceable. I love you.

Betsy raised her head and looked into Soldier's eyes. "Did you say something?" she asked, her voice a tremulous murmur in the dark.

He shook his head. "No. It must have been the wind."

Claire slid into her car and locked the doors, then waved to the cop in the patrol car assigned to keep close watch on Betsy's house.

A weary sigh escaped her lips. Taylor McKennitt was going to be trouble, she thought as she started the engine.

The man was attractive and charming. Tomorrow night he would try to charm the pants off her, as the saying went, but there was no way a relationship between them would work, so it was no use even getting started.

As she turned the far corner, she noticed headlights come up behind her. Somebody else was up at one o'clock in the morning on a quiet street in Port Henry? Poor sap, she thought.

She had early rounds in the morning and couldn't wait to get home and slip into bed. Her house was only a few miles from Betsy's, less than a ten minute drive. A nervous rumbling began in her stomach when she realized the headlights behind her had made every turn she had and had not been more than a block behind her the whole way home.

The next corner was her street. Should she take it and see what happened? If the car turned and followed her, she would drive on by her own house and head straight for the police station. Flitting her gaze between her rearview mirror and the street ahead, her fingers tightened on the steering wheel.

Slowly, she made the left hand turn and watched in the mirror to see if the car followed.

It didn't. It kept going, straight ahead.

Claire blew out a breath of relief. Port Henry just wasn't that big, so it was possible somebody would take the same route home as she. Anyway, they hadn't turned on her street.

Pressing her garage door opener, she drove in and immediately closed the garage door behind her.

There. Safe at home; safe inside.

Deactivating her home alarm system, Claire entered the house through the garage, snapping on the kitchen light as she greeted her fat calico cat, Agatha. "Hey, sweetie. Hungry?"

The sloe-eyed feline offered up a loud meow. Claire stood before the sink opening a can of cat food while Agatha wound a fluffy figure eight through her legs.

"There," she said, setting the bowl on the floor next to the water dish.

As Claire turned off the kitchen light and headed for the bedroom, headlights pierced the sheer curtains that covered the window. A tingle of fear shimmied up her spine as she watched the car drive slowly by, not stopping, not speeding up, just creeping along the street and then disappearing around the corner at the end of the block.

Could it have been the same car? she wondered. She could call the cops, but what would she say? The car hadn't stopped and the driver hadn't done anything aggressive. She couldn't even give a good description of it.

All her doors and windows were locked. Reactivating the alarm, she decided she was safe against an intruder, nevertheless, she sat on the edge of her bed and picked up the phone.

"I want to report a possible prowler," she said when the police department picked up. "This is Dr. Claire Hunter and I live at 535 Windjammer Road. Could you please have a patrol car cruise the area tonight? I'd feel a lot better. Yes. Thanks."

She let go a huge breath. Now she could get some much needed sleep.

As she snuggled down into her covers, her tired mind drifted to Taylor McKennitt and how his big, strong body affected her. Maybe she should consider trading her alarm system in for a flesh and blood man. . . .

Abruptly, she sat straight up in bed. She had been asleep, but something awakened her. A noise? The phone wasn't ringing, so what—

Tapping. Something was tapping or scratching at the window. In her sleepiness, she wasn't sure exactly where it was coming from.

Pushing the covers back, she stood and walked toward the side window—

And the window exploded. Glass shards, sharp as razor blades, sliced the air around her as she tried to cover her face and bare arms.

She screamed as thousands of tiny needles pricked her flesh and tore at her hands and scalp. Another explosion, and the other window shattered into knives of glass, showering her with splinters. She screamed again as something flew past her ear. Then pain, sharp and bright.

She clutched her head as she fell on her knees to the carpet, now strewn with chunks of broken glass.

Lights came from somewhere, the illumination turning her bedroom into an obscene tableau of debris and destruction. Amidst the sparkling splinters, her blood was splattered about like so much red confetti.

Voices, pounding, sirens . . . none of it made sense as Claire collapsed, her world suddenly gone dark.

Chapter 21

After a decade in law enforcement, Taylor thought he'd pretty much seen it all. In his line of work, he'd encountered perverts who preyed on guileless children, witnessed the devastation left after innocent bystanders had been run down by cars turned into weapons of destruction in the hands of someone too drunk to drive. He had seen domestic violence at its worst, and heroism at its finest. He had seen birth and death, and everything in between. But this was a new one.

The lunatic stalker had followed Claire home and riddled the doctor's bedroom with bullets, nearly killing her. It was only through a miracle, and because she'd called the police earlier, that she didn't bleed to death on the floor of her own bedroom.

Taylor stood with his brother in the doorway of the ER, where the paramedics had brought Claire. She lay on the narrow bed as the nurse finished applying antiseptic ointment to the unstitched cuts on her arms and face. It was a miracle none of the bullets had found their mark.

"Taylor," Soldier said. "You're not well enough to do this. Let me—"

"Shove off, Jackson. The lady and I had a date tonight, and I'm keeping it. As soon as they're done with her, I'm taking her home."

When his brother began to protest, Taylor said, "I don't need anything but one working arm, one working trigger finger, and my trusty little Glock. I'm doing this. If that bitch takes another swipe at Claire, I'll *be* there."

"Taylor?" Claire's voice sounded dry and far away somehow.

Immediately, Taylor moved from the doorway to her side. The pain in his leg hurt like hell, but it was nothing compared to the sharp ache he felt seeing the damage done to Claire's lovely face and body.

The treatment room was small and brightly lit, unforgiving in its intensity. Claire's face and arms were covered with tiny cuts. She looked like she was recovering from the measles. A neat row of stitches now adorned her bare shoulder, and her hands were bandaged against the cuts she'd gotten when trying to protect her face and eyes from flying glass. They'd taken away her torn and bloody nightgown and replaced it with one of those ugly cotton hospital things, but to Taylor's mind, rather than detracting from her beauty, she looked prettier than ever.

Maybe it was some weird male psychological thing, he thought. She looked vulnerable, she'd been hurt, and her guard was down. Maybe enough to let a man watch over and protect her. Maybe.

Her big brown eyes searched his, and while he saw fear in them, he also saw defiant determination. Claire Hunter was no easy mark. She was afraid, but she was also totally pissed.

Clasping her bandaged hand, Taylor wrapped her fingers over his palm. "We make a fine pair, don't we?" He chuckled. "I may not be able to run anybody to ground right now, but I promise to protect you with my life."

"No," she whispered, her words slurred from the pain medication the nurse had administered. "Soldier's right. As your doctor, I order you to—"

"You're not my doctor anymore, remember? But I'm your detective. So shut up," he ordered gently, "and let me take you home."

She closed her eyes. "My house is a mess," she whispered. "The bedroom looks like hell." Her soft mouth curved into a smirk. "And I have a cat."

"I love cats," he said. "Especially with *cat*sup."

She attempted a smile, but even that small movement was obviously painful for her.

Taylor swallowed the most disgusting curse he knew. He could hardly wait to get his hands on Carla Denato. This case would break any minute, and when it did, he only hoped he'd have a front row seat when the bitch was taken down.

As Soldier left Claire's room, he saw Betsy hang up the courtesy phone opposite the nurses' station. Seeing him, she sent him a very weary smile.

Zing went the strings of his heart.

Everyone was tired and on edge, but for Soldier, the sight of her was like mainlining adrenaline.

Did you say something? No. It must have been the wind.

Christ, he was a jerk. When this was all over . . .

"Loretta's taking care of Daddy," Betsy said when she reached him. "And the officer watching the house has reported no unusual activity. Things should be okay, at least until morning. How's Claire? Can I see her now?"

"They're just finishing up," he replied. "Taylor's going with her to her house. Until Carla is apprehended, it's probably best if we don't all stay in one place."

When Taylor emerged from the examination room, Soldier motioned him over.

"Any news?" his brother asked.

Soldier nodded. "While you were in with Claire, I made some calls and got the results of a background check on Kristee Spangler. Turns out she has an outstanding warrant in Texas, under her real name."

"What name?" Taylor asked.

"Kristine Lee Denato."

"You are shitting me."

"Nope. Carla's little sister."

Betsy's cheeks turned pale as she absorbed the news. "Carla killed her own sister?"

"Not only that," Soldier continued, "looks like the two of them did their parents by torching the house. The sisters have moved around some since then. There's not a whole lot on Kristine, but we've got some very interesting items on Carla. Several outstanding warrants, too. She's been a busy girl."

"How busy?"

"Besides her parents, at least two possible homicides, maybe more. She goes into a town, gets a job, seems to settle down. Then she becomes obsessed with somebody and starts to stalk them. The people get wise, they get a court order against her, she either leaves the state or resorts to violence. She's so arrogant, she doesn't even bother to use an alias or try to get a false ID."

Betsy covered her mouth with her fingertips. "I never would have suspected Carla of such . . . violence. Such anger. Hatred. She fooled me completely."

She looked up at Soldier, her eyes clouded with bewilderment. "I *trusted* her. How can I ever trust anybody again? From now on, how will I be able to trust my own judgment to know who's good and who's bad? I thought she liked Ryan and Linda, but she killed them! I never even suspected she was capable of such . . ." She seemed to search for the right word. "Evil. She's evil. I've never known anybody like her." She closed her eyes and slowly shook her head.

"Anybody ever done a psych eval on her?" Taylor asked.

"Yeah, back in, let's see . . ." Soldier took out his notebook and flipped some pages. "Yeah. Back in high school she was pulling some shit, so they set her up for a mandatory."

"And the results were?"

"She's fucking nuts, of course. Or do you want the clinical term?"

Taylor scoffed. "Nuts'll do."

"They tried to dry her out, but she bolted," Soldier continued. "So. We've got a homicidal maniac who tries to kill—and sometimes succeeds in killing—anybody who thwarts her plans. She's had it with her sister, so she offs her, too. She's killed Linda Mattson and Ryan Finlay. She's thoroughly pissed at Betsy, whom she blames for all her troubles. What in the hell is she going to do now?"

Chapter 22

Soldier stood at the living room window, hands on his hips, a scowl on his face. A day had passed and it was night again. A day and a night, and no Carla Denato.

He wanted to believe she'd moved on, but the hairs on the back of his neck were still standing at attention, warning him he couldn't relax just yet.

Ryan Finlay's funeral was tomorrow morning. If Denato was smart, she'd stay the hell away. But Carla Denato wasn't smart, she was nuts, unpredictable, and an opportunist. Soldier knew he had to be ready for anything.

He tugged the curtain back into place across the window then closed his eyes for a moment, focusing on his thoughts, trying to find a way to sort them all out. This would all be over very soon and life would return to normal. He'd go home to Seattle, bury himself in work, and try like crazy to stop thinking about Betsy.

Shoving his hands in his pockets, he leaned against the doorjamb and sighed. He'd known her less than two weeks, but that had been enough for him to realize that she was the most real, down-to-earth, perfect life's partner for him he could ever hope to find.

It wasn't just the sex, either. Making love with Betsy was an explosive almost ethereal experience, the kind of intimacy he believed was the result of being with the *right* woman. Sex was sex, but making love with a woman who belonged with you on so many levels, that was special. Too special to let go.

Let Betsy go? Could he?

Okay. Let's say I do let her go. And she meets some guy. And they hit it off and he asks her to mar—

No. No, no, no. No other man. He didn't even want to think of Betsy sleeping with another man, living with him, bearing his children. No. That just didn't work.

He felt his heart do a happy little flip as he began to absorb just what this meant. Yeah. Love. As hard as he'd tried to avoid it, he'd fallen ass end over teakettle in love with the prickly, witty, charming, totally delightful Ms. Tremaine.

And if the soft look she got in her eyes whenever he came near her was any indication, she'd fallen for him, too.

"S-Soldier?"

He shifted his stance to see Betsy's father approaching him from the kitchen.

With a smile left over from his mini epiphany, Soldier said, "Douglas. What can I do for you?"

Douglas Tremaine shuffled over and sat in one of

the chairs in front of the fireplace. Soldier dropped into the other one.

Douglas was clean-shaven, his hair neatly combed. He wore a pair of jeans and a faded University of Washington sweatshirt. At nearly sixty, he was still a good-looking man. Soldier could see the resemblance to his daughter in the high cheekbones, the arch of a brow, the line of the jaw.

The older man's gaze shifted from the hands he held in his lap up to Soldier, then down again.

"Is there something I can do for you, sir?" Soldier asked.

He nodded. "Betsy's upstairs. I w-wanted to talk to you when, you know, when she couldn't hear."

Soldier leaned forward, making eye contact with him. "Okay."

Douglas let out a long breath then returned Soldier's steady gaze. "I'm Betsy's father," he began, sitting a little taller in the chair. Soldier waited a few seconds for the man to gather his thoughts and words. "I'm Betsy's f-father," he repeated, "so—so I needed to talk to you, you know, about your intentions."

"My intentions?" Soldier said tonelessly. "*Oh*. My *intentions*."

For a moment he was caught off guard. Did fathers do that anymore? he wondered, then swallowed a grin. Sure they did, when the father was the stalwart Douglas Tremaine and the daughter happened to be the tastiest morsel in town.

"Yes." Douglas's gray eyes narrowed. "Your intentions. Th-They are honorable, I trust?"

Honorable? Soldier had always thought himself an

honorable sort; not perfect, but aware of his flaws and fairly willing to work on them. Well, to a certain point anyway.

"Mr. Tremaine," he said, the unaccountable need for formality punctuating his discomfort. Why in the hell did he suddenly feel like some pimply-faced teenager, nervous and shy? Douglas Tremaine had to know that he and Betsy had been sleeping together, a fact that probably didn't set all that well with the man.

For a split second Soldier saw himself somewhere down the line, oldish, grayish, pressing some hormonal son of a bitch about his intentions toward his own daughter. He bit down on a rueful smile.

He coughed. "Well, Betsy and I haven't really discussed—"

"You know," Douglas interrupted, "I haven't been a very good fa-father." His words were slow in coming, as though he had to pull them up from a long way away. "I haven't really had much of a chance to be one, as you know. I w-want to fix that." He looked beseechingly into Soldier's eyes. "Fathers don't ask much about intentions anymore." He sighed. "I just w-want to make sure that she doesn't get hurt. I hurt her plenty when they sent me away. I don't want that to happen to h-her again."

Soldier let the guilt he felt slide through him, chill him to the bone like winter fog. He'd been sleeping with Betsy, enjoying her body, her nurturing nature, but he'd not made any kind of commitment to her. He had feelings for her, yet hadn't had the courage to speak them. *It must have been the wind.* Betsy was not the kind of woman an honorable man should string along.

"I know my daughter," Douglas Tremaine offered with an affectionate grin. "When she loves, it's as plain as the nose on your face. Sh-She loves you, Soldier."

He nodded. "I know."

"And she deserves to be l-loved in return. And honored. And treated with respect."

"I know that, too."

Soldier swallowed, then let his gaze rest on the spent embers in the fireplace. Betsy deserved the best a man had to offer. How could he tell her father that his own best might not be good enough?

Somewhere in the pit of his stomach something tightened and squeezed until he felt sick. The image of Marc Franco spun its way into his mind. He'd failed Marc and he'd let that failure affect everything. If he died today after having fucked up so badly, he thought, it would be his only legacy.

Or he could pick up his sorry ass and his remorse and put the past where it belonged.

Since his conversation with Betsy, since he'd emptied his fears and regrets into her hands, he'd had a clearer picture of things. He realized that Marc had forgiven him, if Marc had even blamed him, just as he would have forgiven Marc had the situation been reversed. Since his partner's death, he had wallowed in grief and self-pity, not really knowing what else to do or how to put it all behind him. Or why he even should.

Then this lovely woman had entered his life and

given him a reason to look to the future, to what he could accomplish instead of what he had lost.

Clearing his throat, Soldier looked the older man in the eye. "Mr. Tremaine, I have only known Betsy a couple of weeks, but with her, a couple of minutes is enough to get hooked. I have to confess, I'm hopelessly in love with your daughter."

Soldier made a snorting laugh and rubbed his jaw with his knuckles. "It's true," he said, more to himself than to Douglas. "I don't know why I didn't see it before."

Lowering his head, he blew out a nervous laugh.

My God, did I just say that out loud?

He laughed again, suddenly feeling ten tons lighter. "I'm not sure if that's what you were hoping to hear," he said. "But that's how it is."

The two men stood and clasped hands in a hearty handshake.

"You are a good man, sir," Douglas said through a beaming smile. "A v-very good man."

"You've checked everybody?"

The uniformed officer nodded in response to Soldier's question. "Yes, sir. No guns, no knives, not so much as a crochet hook. Everybody's clean."

"You've seen the sketch? You know what Denato looks like?"

"As well as I know my own face, sir."

The first part of Ryan Finlay's funeral service had gone off without a hitch. Now, the crowd of a hundred or so people mingled about the large room, wait-

ing for the limos to be brought up for the procession
to the cemetery.

Soldier scanned the area. Around the mourning
room, heavy drapes had been drawn across the tall
windows in deference to the bereaved and their tears.
Candelabra had been lit and set on occasional tables,
adding to the serene and stately atmosphere. Red and
white carnations, pink roses, and yellow chrysanthe-
mums in arrangements large and small added subtle
fragrance to the gathering, while in the background
organ music played in dulcet tones.

An array of deeply cushioned chairs and sofas offered mourners the chance to either chat quietly together or simply sit in tranquil contemplation. Men in
dark suits escorted women in dark suits. There were
some children, but not many. Mostly, people stood
about in hushed conversation, shocked that someone
they knew and cared for had been taken from them so
brutally.

"Lot of people," Soldier commented to the officer
at the door as he examined the sea of faces in the dimly
lit room.

"Yeah, I don't like it either, sir. Too easy for something bad to go down."

Go down? And what was with the green-tinted
shades? Winslow had sent a uniform who definitely
watched too much TV.

He thanked the officer, then moved to the small
cluster of people where Betsy stood talking to Taylor
and Claire and members of the newspaper's staff.

He recognized Holly Miller, her wild hair subdued

in a clip, her lips painted the color of chocolate pudding. Amazingly, she was dressed in a conservative skirt and sweater. Rita Barton stood with her arms crossed, as though without constant vigilance, an emotion might find its way to her stony face, giving the impression of caring. Young Dave Hannigan looked at a loss and out of place in his too small brown suit, which made his size even more noticeable. His eyes were red and swollen as he gripped Soldier's hand in sincere greeting.

Soldier didn't think Carla was dumb enough to try anything here, but just in case, in addition to the officer at the door, there was Taylor plus two others in uniform.

But his money was on the graveside service. Veteran's Memorial Park covered several acres, was landscaped with clusters of trees and shrubs, and abutted forest land. An easy place to hide, and to escape from. Soldier already had several men in position at the park, scanning the grounds and checking for intruders.

Now, as he perused the room, Betsy looked up and their eyes locked. She lifted her chin and sent him a brave smile.

Soldier and Douglas had agreed that until this whole thing was over, he would wait to ask Betsy to marry him. He wanted his proposal to be separate and special, something positive in contrast to the pain and sorrow she'd had to endure.

Besides, it might take a bit of convincing, since she really hadn't known him all that long. Even so, she wouldn't turn him down, would she? She would surely recognize they were meant to be together, wouldn't she?

Man, love was sure hard on the old nervous system.

Now that he'd reached his decision, it was all he could do to keep from tucking her into his embrace and telling her he loved her, then springing a marriage proposal on her. She'd probably give him some feisty, sarcastic remark in response, but he didn't care. As long as she said yes.

He scanned the room again. The service itself had been quick. Finlay's widow was pretty broken up afterward. She had already been escorted out to the limousine to spend some quiet time with her children before going on to the cemetery.

Even though things were going smoothly, the back of Soldier's neck was still prickling. Damn, he hated when that happened. Something was wrong; something felt out of place. He just couldn't put his finger on what it was. He looked up at the officer at the door. Something about . . .

Just then a dog began to bark and whine. Now, who in the hell would bring a dog to a fune—

Oh, he reminded himself. Of course.

He turned toward the door where Loretta and Piddle were just making their entrance. The mutt was going postal, barking, snarling, whining, trying to wiggle free of Loretta's arms.

The officer at the door had stiffened, apparently not knowing whether to shoot the dog or put a muzzle on it.

Loretta swept across the threshold and into the

room, the lunatic Chihuahua still going nuts in her arms.

"Pids! Shhh! Calm down! Mommy will make everything all right!" She was doing her damnedest to quiet the mutt, but to no avail.

Behind Loretta a commotion arose; a woman screamed, and the officer at the door fired a shot. All hell broke loose.

Through the crowd, Soldier saw the officer whirl and run outside. A second explosion sounded as the cop fired again.

People continued to scream as they ran for cover. Soldier glanced frantically around for Betsy. She and Claire were huddled in a corner with Dave Hannigan standing protectively over them. Taylor was already in motion, his gun drawn as he limped toward the door.

Soldier pulled his weapon and followed where the cop had gone, Taylor close on his heels.

"Which way?" Soldier yelled to Taylor.

"There! Between those two cars and down that alley!"

While sirens blared and people screamed, Soldier and the three uniforms took off down the street.

When they reached the alley, they were greeted with overflowing trash bins, a rusty Ford station wagon with only three wheels, and brown autumn leaves blowing in the wind. But no Carla Denato.

"Fuck!" Soldier choked out. "We *couldn't* have lost her." Turning to a winded Taylor, he said, "You see anything?"

His brother shook his head and looked up and

down the street. The two uniforms looked just as stumped.

They hadn't lost any time getting out the door, and Carla Denato was certainly no athlete. There were no doors she could have ducked into and no cars had left the scene.

Soldier huffed out a huge breath and looked around.

"Where's the other officer?" he barked. "The one who fired the shots? I thought she was right behind us!"

Taylor wiped his brow. "No. When we ran out, she turned back into the—" He stopped mid-sentence, his eyes registering understanding.

Panic ripped through Soldier's brain as realization hit him with the force of a shotgun blast to the gut. "It's her. Goddammit, it's her!"

On a dead run, they took off back up the street. By the time they reached the funeral home, sweat slicked Soldier's face and neck. His weapon was slippery in his hand. As he plunged through the doorway, mourners parted to let him pass.

"Betsy!" he yelled into the confused gathering. "Betsy!"

In the far corner, Dave Hannigan leaned against the wall holding his head in his hands while blood seeped through his stubby fingers. Claire urged him to sit down so she could examine him as Loretta tried valiantly to slow the bleeding with her lace handkerchief. In her other hand she held a limp Chihuahua.

"S-Sorry, Detective," Dave slurred. "Tried to stop her. Hit me with the gun. Carla. Fuckin' Carla, man. Didn't recognize her at all . . . s-sorry—"

Soldier felt his heart turn over in his chest. *Was he too late to save Betsy?*

"Out the back door!" Claire yelled above the din. "She only has a two minute head start!"

Two minutes. A gun could empty into somebody's head in less time than that. Soldier sucked in a huge breath and tried to quell the panic in his heart.

As he raced toward the back of the building, an image formed in his head of Betsy at Carla Denato's mercy, facing the woman's lunatic rage. Shoving it aside, he refused to let the scenario form. He sucked in another breath and plunged through the door.

He knew Betsy. She'd find a way to take care of herself until he got there. She was smart and tough and brave. She'd find an edge somehow. Goddammit, she *would* because the alternative was just too sickening to even consider.

Hang on, sweetheart. I'm on my way. God, Betsy, please, hang on. . . .

Chapter 23

A shot was fired. Then another!

Betsy watched, her heart in her throat, as Soldier ran out the door and down the steps.

The noise in the room became deafening. People were screaming as they shuffled around, not certain whether they should stay or leave. Next to her, Claire said, "Sorry, honey, but I need to sit down."

Claire appeared pale and tense. Her cuts were healing, but she was still very weak.

"There's a spot over there," Betsy said as she escorted her friend to a vacant chair. "Why don't you let me get you some water."

"Ma'am." She barely heard the woman's voice above the din. When she turned, the uniformed officer who had been stationed at the door was standing there, her mouth a grim line.

"Yes, Officer?"

The woman said something, but the noise level was

so high, it was nearly impossible to understand her words.

The officer raised her voice and appeared to be making an effort to control her temper. "Detective McKennitt would like me to take you to a safe place until this is over! Come with me, now!"

Betsy shook her head. "No," she yelled over the noise in the room. "I need to stay with my friend." Turning away from the officer, she began to speak to Claire when, a few feet away, the violently yapping Piddle leaped from Loretta's arms and attached his sharp little teeth to the police officer's ankle.

The woman shrieked, then backhanded the dog, sending him flying across the room and into a wall, where he slumped to the floor in a furless heap.

Loretta screamed, and Dave Hannigan's eyes nearly bugged out of his head as he took a long look at the police officer.

Betsy's head snapped around, coming face-to-face with the barrel of a gun. A sickening feeling chilled her blood to thick sludge. She became queasy. It was Carla.

Carla sneered and pushed the gun closer to her face just as Dave Hannigan made a lunge for it. Carla swung her arm out of the way, clipping him at the temple, sending him backward into a candelabrum.

Reaching out, Carla grabbed Betsy by the hair and began pulling her toward the back entrance.

Betsy balled her fists and flailed about, trying to connect with Carla's jaw, but Carla snarled, "Stop it now, or I shoot your friend!" Turning the weapon, she pointed it directly at Claire.

Raising her hands, Betsy breathed, "No . . . don't . . . I'll go with you. Please don't . . ."

People made way for them as Carla dragged her through the room and out the door. In the back parking lot, Betsy recognized Carla's black Chevy. "Get in!" Carla ordered. "You're driving."

Betsy slid into the driver's side and put her shaking hands on the wheel. When Carla jumped in on the passenger side, she pressed the gun to Betsy's temple and ordered her to pull out onto the street.

So, this is what it's all boiled down to. Betsy guided the car onto the busy street. *How soon will it be before Carla gets tired of the game and blows my brains out?*

"Where'd you get the uniform, Carla?" Betsy said, her voice surprisingly calm under the circumstances.

Carla grinned, pulled off her hat and tossed it in the backseat. "Knocked off a dry cleaners. I made such a mess, they never even knew it was missing."

Betsy swallowed. "I've got to hand it to you. Not a soul recognized you."

Houses, trees, nicely trimmed yards crept by as Betsy kept her speed low, hoping, praying, the cops would fall in behind her any second.

"Not a soul except for that frigging mutt," Carla snapped as she turned to look behind them and smile. Betsy glanced in the rearview mirror. Nothing. She was on her own.

Where's Soldier? Did Carla shoot him when they were outside? Is he wounded, dead? Betsy's mind choked on that thought.

In the uniform, Carla looked totally different. She

had dyed her light hair black and cut it short, then darkened her fair skin with liquid makeup. She'd painted her lips a muted orange and given her mouth a different shape. With lifts in her shoes, dark glasses to hide her eyes, and padding to add bulk to her chest and hips, they could have passed each other on the street and Betsy would never have recognized her.

As she drove down Eisenhower Avenue toward the center of town, Betsy reached down and fastened her seat belt.

Carla laughed. "That seat belt won't save you from a speeding bullet, you moron."

Ignoring the comment, Betsy shrugged and said, "Where are we going?"

"Just keep driving until I tell you to stop. *I'm* in charge now. *I* give the orders now. *You* have to do what *I* say. I like that, Miss Betsy, practically perfect in every way. I like that a *lot*."

Betsy's hands were slick from sweat. The wheel slithered through her fingers. Her heart raced and her mind raced faster.

Stay calm. You can get out of this. You can.

"I thought we were friends, Carla."

"We were *never* friends, you stupid bitch!" Carla laughed again and shifted in her seat to glance out the back window. "But I know how to be nice. It serves me well sometimes. But the simple fact of the matter is, I hate your guts. Pretty basic when you boil it all down."

"Did you kill Linda?"

"Sure I did. But then *you* got her job instead of me!"

Sliding a quick look in the sideview mirror, Betsy

watched as a dark sedan turned the corner a few blocks back. *Soldier?*

Keep her busy, keep her talking. What to say? What to say?

Carla saw the car, too. "Drive faster! Step on it!"

Focusing on the road, Betsy said, "The light's turning red. What should I—"

"Run it, stupid!"

Betsy closed her eyes and ran the red light, barely avoiding a pedestrian and a kid on a bike.

Sorry! I'm sorry! I'll come back and apologize later!

As Betsy proceeded down the busy avenue, she said, "You know how, in the movies, when the bad guy—that's you—has the good guy—that's me—cornered and he confesses everything?"

Next to her, Carla said nothing.

"Well . . ." Betsy swallowed. "Before you kill me, is there time for you to tell me why?"

"Why what?"

"Why you killed Linda. And Ryan. Why you're going to kill me." She laughed, a dry, high, nervous sound. "I mean, this can't all be because of a job, right? There has to be some bigger, grander thing going on, right?"

As Carla considered her response, a calm began to slowly wash over Betsy. Her breathing steadied and her eyes seemed to be able to take everything in at once. She grasped the steering wheel firmly, her fingers no longer trembling. The knots in her stomach untied. She was not going to die today. She knew it, felt it down to the marrow of her bones, sensed it in the secret chambers of her heart where she'd always kept her most precious dreams. She had a life to live. A man to love. A future. And then she thought: *No, I am going to come out of this very much alive.*

Carla must have sensed a change in her demeanor because she pressed the barrel of the gun hard into her temple.

"No grander thing," Carla snarled. "You messed everything up for me, that's all. Everything. I lost my job, was forced to kill my boss, had to destroy my apartment. All because of you." She said the words as though they made perfect sense. "I killed my sister, *my sister*, Betsy! Because of you! You'll pay for that. I loved my sister and you made me kill her. Yeah," she screamed, "you'll pay for that!"

Okay, Carla was nuts. It was now official, and Betsy was able to accept the true, up close and personal meaning of *crazed stalker*.

Even so, even with a loaded gun pressed tightly to her temple, she was still able to focus on Soldier, on the way his eyes sparkled when he looked at her, on the way he loved her. No. She was most definitely not going to die today.

She just hadn't quite figured out how to stop it from happening.

Chapter 24

Soldier's fingers gripped the dashboard. "As long as Betsy's driving, Carla won't shoot her. Even Carla's not that stupid."

Behind the wheel, Taylor grunted. "Where do you think they're headed?"

"That's what worries me," Soldier said. "With all exits out of town blocked, she's either going to use Betsy as a hostage and make some demands, or do something really, really dumb."

One block ahead of them the black Chevy moved at a steady speed down Eisenhower Avenue, smack into the center of town. Soldier had ordered patrol cars follow at a distance and do nothing to force Carla into any kind of position where she might take the life of her hostage.

Her hostage . . . his future.

"They're turning left, heading for the ferry," Taylor said. "What in the hell is she thinking?"

Soldier's heart and mind raced. Every moment

counted. Betsy was caught in the middle and he had to get her out. Alive.

"She's not thinking. Her plans are toast, she's been made, and she's got a hostage. No clean kill, no getaway. It's all up to Betsy now."

Without warning, Carla shoved the barrel of the gun against Betsy's cheek. She wanted to cry out, but bit her lip instead.

"What was that for?" Betsy said, keeping her voice as controlled as she could.

" 'Cause I felt like it, that's why," Carla teased. "How does that song go? *'I've got the power, oh yeah*!' "

Carla was beginning to unravel. Her eyes were glazed with desperation, her hands and forehead sweaty. Her breathing had turned ragged, harsh. She flicked her gaze between Betsy and the car that had been tailing them for the last two miles.

"Carla," Betsy said, hoping to distract her, hoping to keep her from taking a potshot at Soldier. "I can't drive with that gun pressed into my—"

"Tough! Now shut up!" she screamed. "Uh, uh, when we get to Madison, turn left, toward the water. Yeah. Toward the water."

Betsy swallowed past a thick lump in her throat. "Carla, there is no way you can get away with this. Listen to me. If you stop now, turn yourself in, the police—"

"Fuck the police!" she yelled as she ground the barrel of the gun harder into Betsy's tender cheek.

Betsy whimpered, the pain almost too fierce to bear.

A trickle of hot blood slid down her jaw and neck as she fought to keep from crying out.

They crested a hill, and it was a straight shot down to the docks. In the distance, Betsy could see the ferry pulling out, heading south into the sound. There wouldn't be another one for hours.

Next to her, Carla was mumbling to herself, but Betsy tried to stay focused on the task at hand. She'd never been brave. Would she wail like a baby when Carla pulled the trigger? Would she plead for her life?

No. She would *not*. Besides, she'd already decided she wasn't going to die today.

She slid a quick glance at Carla. *No. Not today, sister.* She hunkered down and held onto the wheel for all she was worth.

Traffic was sparse as they ambled down Madison. The ferry dock loomed larger in the distance. In a matter of minutes they'd be there.

Betsy's toe pushed on the accelerator. Still mumbling to herself and panting, Carla didn't seem to notice.

Glancing quickly to her right, Betsy checked to see whether Carla had fastened her seat belt, and she felt a surge of joy when she saw it dangling behind the door.

She pressed down on the accelerator a little more and the car lurched ahead. In the rearview mirror the car behind them kept pace.

Carla pulled the gun away from Betsy's cheekbone and waved the weapon in the air. "What the hell are you doing? Slow down!"

In response, Betsy slammed her foot to the floor and the car leaped ahead, nearly causing Carla to lose her balance and drop the gun.

"What the fuck are you *doing*? Slow down or I'll shoot you *right now*!"

Betsy didn't spare Carla a glance, but checked to see if the car behind them had sped up as well. It had.

Only four blocks now, only three . . .

Keeping her hands tightly on the wheel, Betsy aimed the car toward the docks. As the decline of the hill increased, so did the speed of the car.

Carla screamed and tried to unlock her door. But Betsy had pressed the lock button. They were in to stay.

"Stop!" Carla's voice was thick with panic. "I'll kill you, I swear I will!" She swung the gun toward Betsy. The barrel touched her temple.

Betsy swallowed hard and lowered her head. Again pressing the accelerator full to the floor, she closed her eyes and hung on.

I love you, Soldier. I love you. . . .

One block more and they were on the dock, careening over the planking, roaring toward the water.

The explosion near her head nearly caused her to lose control, but the shot aimed at her head had gone through the roof as the car lurched onto the dock.

Betsy's ears rang, her nostrils burned. She narrowed her eyes and kept her hands welded to the wheel.

The sound of sirens blasted Betsy's eardrums, and tears slid down her cheeks. Releasing one hand from the wheel, she doubled her fist and swung it hard until it connected with Carla's nose. Carla screamed and turned the gun back in Betsy's direction. She felt the cold metal against her temple again and sent one last prayer heavenward.

Take care of my father, and my mother. And send Soldier somebody to love . . .

Betsy jerked her arm up just as Carla pulled the trigger. The blast shattered the front windshield.

Then the car crashed through the guardrail and sailed off the end of the dock.

Carla screamed, losing her voice as she clawed at her door, trying desperately to get it open.

A split second before the car hit the water, Betsy managed to catch Carla's eye. "Have a nice trip," she whispered, "you bitch."

The car slammed into the water, flinging Carla forward and through the windshield. Betsy's body strained against the seat belts but she stayed firmly in place as the airbag exploded in her face, punching her chin, making her see stars.

The concussion slammed her skull against the head rest and she was afraid she'd lose consciousness.

Immediately, the car began to sink. Icy water covered the floorboards up to her ankles, then her calves, her knees.

Her fingers were numb and shook uncontrollably as she tried to release her seat belt. She was panting, her heart raced, and terror choked her throat until she could barely breathe. Her mind felt thick and unresponsive.

Finally, a grateful snap and she was free. Flipping the door locks, she grabbed the handle and tried to push open her door, but at that moment the car lurched forward, taking Betsy down.

Cold, black water inched up her neck, her chin, into her mouth. Raising her face, she took one last, deep breath just as the water reached her nose.

Ten seconds passed . . . fifteen . . . twenty. How long could she hold her breath? A minute? More? Less?

She felt the weight of the car dragging her down and down into the cold. She couldn't see anything and her lungs were near bursting. She gulped for air but got none. Her throat hurt, her head spun. She gulped again.

Darkness closed in as she gave one last push against the door.

It opened.

Then she felt him. His hands on her. His fingers prying hers from the door handle.

He grabbed her hair, her clothes, wrapped his arm around her waist and yanked her through the opening, shooting for the surface. Feeling his hands on her, knowing he had come, she thought her heart would shatter.

He shoved her ahead of him, and her face broke the surface. She gulped for fresh air and began to cough violently, choking on cold salty water and hot salty tears.

She took another deep breath and choked again. And cried again. She cried because life was just so damned good, and she wasn't through living it yet.

Beside her, Soldier coughed and stammered, and called her name. But her eyes were pinched tightly shut and she couldn't see him.

Voices shouted and sirens sang, competing with the shriek of anxious gulls. Hands were on her, pulling her up, covering her with warm blankets, carrying her from the water to the safety of the dock.

She tried to breathe. Beside her, she heard him panting, calling her name over and over. But she was too tired to answer, too sleepy. Cold ate away her flesh. Lack of oxygen left her muscles and bones like jelly.

She heard him speaking, but it was so far away, and fading. The sound of his voice was low, urgent, and thick with tears.

His hands clasped her shoulders. She felt his warm breath against her face. He pinched her nose and blew into her mouth, and suddenly water erupted up her throat. She choked. More water came, and she gagged and choked again.

"Wake up," he whispered harshly. "Betsy . . . I love you. Marry me and I'll give you a baby with blue, blue eyes. But you've got to breathe. *Please* . . . wake up!"

She wanted to, she really did, but her chest burned and she just couldn't get enough air. Turning her head, she coughed again and her lungs began to work, and she could breathe.

Around her, she heard a cheer go up. "That's it, sweetheart," he sobbed. "That's my girl!"

Betsy lay on the dock and smiled. She'd known she wasn't going to die today. She just hadn't realized how much effort it was going to take to stay alive.

Opening her eyes a squint at a time, she saw Soldier's face, wet, worried, gloriously alive. His hair hung over his forehead and she wanted to smooth it away.

"Hi," he said. "Welcome back."

"I'm going to hold you to it, you know," she rasped. Soldier laughed and tears filled his blue, blue eyes as he pushed a wet lock of hair off her face. "God, I hope so."

She smiled up into his eyes. "You love me?"

"I love you."

"I love you, too."

He lowered his head and kissed her. His mouth was warm and held every promise she'd ever dreamed of.

When he pulled back, she choked, "And you want to marry me?"

He nodded. "I do."

"Get me a hankie, I'm gonna cry," came the bored voice of the paramedic crouched next to Betsy. "Now, will you kindly get your ass out of the way, Detective, so we can get this lady to the ER?"

Soldier quickly kissed her again, and took her hand in his, clasping it tightly, as though he would never let it go.

As the paramedics lifted her onto the stretcher, Betsy breathed softly, "And they all lived happily ever after."

Then she sneezed.

Epilogue

Six months later

> Hold on while I get out my thesaurus; this re-
> view is going to require more words than my
> paltry vocabulary contains. Ah, here we go:
> marvelous, extraordinary, splendid, meritori-
> ous (oh, that's a good one), bravo, spectacular,
> superlative . . .
>
> To continue would require more space than
> this column allows, so let me simply conclude
> by saying that Four Men and a Corpse, J. Soldier
> McKennitt's latest crime drama, is well worth
> your time and money.
>
> Not!
>
> The plot is silly, the characters dumb, the
> writing so-so. What less could you ask for? This
> is the fourth installment in the Crimes of the
> Northwest series, and while each entry has de-

fied common sense and literary style, Four Men
and a Corpse *is the worst to date . . .*

"There's more. Wanna hear it?"

"Betsy, darling," Soldier said as he pulled his wife
into his arms. "Do you think you can wait to castrate
me until we've conceived at least one child?"

She giggled and tossed the newspaper aside. Slipping her arms around his waist, she said, "Not a problem. At least, not as of a few minutes ago when I
tinkled on the stick. *And* the stick turned blue."

He raised his brows. "Really? A baby? You and me?
All right! When?"

"The end of September." She gazed up into his eyes.
"I love you."

He bent his head and whispered wonderful things in
her ear while she ran her fingers through his soft hair
and smiled. Then he kissed her. Then he kissed her
again. And again. Soon, his light kisses turned urgent
and hot.

Guiding her to the bed, he murmured against her
mouth, "Take off your nightgown. I want to look at
your tummy."

"It's too early to see any difference."

"That's not why I want to see your tummy," he
growled.

"Wait," she said, touching her fingertips to his lips.
"I have more good news. Daddy got a job!"

Soldier peered down at her. "Well, that's great,
honey. He must be really thrilled. But, well, given his,
uh, condition and everything . . . I mean, he's brilliant, but he doesn't seem to have any fashion sense,

his social skills are pretty bad, he has trouble getting projects done on time, and when he does, sometimes they don't work." He shrugged. "What kind of job could he do where he would fit in? Who hired him?"

"Microsoft. He starts tomorrow."

She grinned up at him, and he got lost in her all over again. He just had to be the luckiest man alive.

As he held her close, he remembered for the thousandth time watching that car sail off the end of the dock and disappear under the surface of the water. The impact had killed Carla, and might have killed Betsy, too, if she hadn't made sure to strap herself in.

He'd been out of the car, running like hell toward the water, and was in mid-dive before the car even broke the surface. Kicking off his shoes and thrashing out of his jacket, he'd fought the waves to reach her door with a single-minded strength he didn't know he possessed. When the car's rooftop disappeared beneath the water, he was nearly certain she was lost.

That first breath of air she'd taken on the dock as he'd hovered over her was like his own first breath, and his life had begun all over again.

He loved her so damn much that sometimes, when she looked up at him with a gleam in her eye or a sexy little smirk on her lips, he just wanted to bust out laughing. He was a lucky son of a bitch to have found a woman like her.

And now she was pregnant with their first child. A baby, their baby. It was almost too wonderful to grasp.

As she slipped out of her nightgown and snuggled back down into their warm bed, she said, "We don't have a lot of time. Claire will be here at ten with my mother and Piddle the Valiant."

Soldier grunted. "Piddle, the Dog Who Lived."

"Oh, stop it!" she giggled. "I'm just glad he was only knocked unconscious and not killed." She snuggled closer. "And Taylor's coming by later, too, so we can all have dinner and celebrate!"

Betsy nudged her leg over Soldier's thigh and inched her body closer to his. "Mmm," she hummed. "You want to take that T-shirt off, get naked, and have our own little celebration?"

Reaching for the hem, he pulled the shirt up and off and tossed it in a corner of their bedroom, which had been just her room before they'd begun remodeling the Victorian.

"Does that answer your question?" he said as he pulled her on top of him and raised his head to kiss her.

"Well," she purred as she slid her hand down his belly, and down and down and, oh, baby. "Let me put this in terms you'll understand . . ."

You'll fall for these irresistible, sexy romances coming in September from Avon Books

A SCANDAL TO REMEMBER by Linda Needham
An Avon Romantic Treasure

Caroline is in London to find a suitable husband and the last thing she needs is a man like Andrew Chase, Earl of Wexford, underfoot, watching her with an intensity that sets her senses on fire. But as strange incidents escalate into violent episodes, Caro knows she'll need Drew's protection . . . and much, much, more.

SINCE YOU'RE LEAVING ANYWAY, TAKE OUT THE TRASH by Dixie Cash
An Avon Contemporary Romance

Debbie Sue Overstreet knows everything about Saltlick, Texas, thanks to her bustling hair salon and the gossips who patronize it. But when her sheriff ex, Buddy, needs her help to investigate a murder case, Debbie is stumped by a much trickier question than whodunnit: why on earth did she ever let Buddy get away?

TAMING TESSA by Brenda Hiatt
An Avon Romance

Lord Anthony Northrup is in no hurry to marry, as all four of his brothers have already obligingly done so. But when he meets the feisty Tessa Seaton, he begins to reevaluate his plans. He thinks she's in need of rescuing, and he can't help but play the hero. But Tessa is no damsel in distress, and it might just be Anthony's heart that's in danger . . .

THE RETURN OF THE EARL by Edith Layton
An Avon Romance

The Earl of Egremont has returned . . . or has he? It's been fifteen years since Christian left England, and his dear Julianne. But now a stranger arrives claiming his name—and his inheritance. There is *some* resemblance to the boy Julianne once adored, but can this ruggedly handsome man be the real earl? Or has she fallen in love with an impostor?

Avon Romantic Treasures

*Unforgettable, enthralling love stories,
sparkling with passion and adventure
from Romance's bestselling authors*

Discover Contemporary Romances at Their Sizzling Hot Best from Avon Books

SOMEONE LIKE HIM by Karen Kendall
0-06-000723-0$5.99 US/$7.99 Can

A THOROUGHLY MODERN PRINCESS
0-380-82054-4/$5.99 US/$7.99 Can by Wendy Corsi Staub

A GREEK GOD AT THE LADIES' CLUB by Jenna McKnight
0-06-054927-0/$5.99 US/$7.99 Can

DO NOT DISTURB by Christie Ridgway
0-06-009348-X/$5.99 US/$7.99 Can

WANTED: ONE PERFECT MAN by Judi McCoy
0-06-056079-7/$5.99 US/$7.99 Can

FACING FEAR by Gennita Low
0-06-052339-5/$5.99 US/$7.99 Can

HOT STUFF by Elaine Fox
0-06-051724-7/$5.99 US/$7.99 Can

WHAT MEMORIES REMAIN by Cait London
0-06-055588-2/$5.99 US/$7.99 Can

LOVE: UNDERCOVER by Hailey North
0-06-058230-8/$5.99 US/$7.99 Can

IN THE MOOD by Suzanne Macpherson
0-06-051768-9/$5.99 US/$7.99 Can

Have you ever dreamed of writing a romance?

*And have you ever wanted
to get a romance published?*

Perhaps you have always wondered how to
become an Avon romance writer?
We are now seeking the best and brightest undiscovered
voices. We invite you to send us your query letter to
avonromance@harpercollins.com

What do you need to do?

Please send no more than two pages telling us
about your book. We'd like to know its setting—is it
contemporary or historical—and a bit about the hero,
heroine, and what happens to them.

Then, if it is right for Avon we'll ask to see part of the
manuscript. Remember, it's important that you have
material to send, in case we want to see your story quickly.

Of course, there are no guarantees of publication,
but you never know unless you try!

*We know there is new talent just waiting
to be found! Don't hesitate . . . send us
your query letter today.*

*The Editors
Avon Romance*